Reviewers on *Nicholas:*

"A well-written story with enough variety in the sexual situations to satisfy just about any reader. The characters are complex and intriguing and the leading man is the sexiest one this reader has seen in a long time! The author has cleverly set the stage for at least two sequels in the Lords of Satyr series and based on this book, they will be something to look forward to."
—*Romantic Times Book Reviews*

"Elizabeth Amber has drawn a world that pulls you in and keeps hold of your heart and mind."
—*Joyfully Reviewed*, a Recommended Read

"[Ms. Amber] gives great depth to her characters and the dialogues are smooth and natural. Everything about this story and the elements within worked . . . a wonderful book that did not disappoint!"
—*Paranormal Romance Reviews*

"I really didn't want this book to end, and when I finished I knew that it would stay with me for a while. This is one you don't want to miss."
—*TwoLips Reviews*, 5 lips; Reviewer's Choice Recommended Read

"Both Nicholas and Jane are well-matched, though it took a delicious tension-filled while for them to figure it out. There is a villainess to surpass all villains, and more supporting villains that fit into the story neatly . . . It was well-paced—it's engrossing and easy to read in one sitting. While the romance is lovely, the sex is knock-out hot."
—*Just Erotic Romance Reviews*, "O", their highest rating for hotness

"*Nicholas, The Lords of Satyr* has taken a place on my top ten favorite erotic books list."
—*Night Owl Romance*, 5 stars

"I have to admit, *Nicholas* left me wanting—wanting the next book in this wonderful new series, that is!"
—*CK2S Kwips & Kritiques*, 4.5 Klovers; 5 stars on Amazon.com

". . . a strong storyline with a very nasty villainess—one of the worst that this reader has come upon . . . This is a page turner from start to finish! Turn on the air conditioner or fan and enjoy!"
—*Fallen Angel Reviews*

"Elizabeth Amber has created a steamy, hot tale that scorches the pages. Her imagination skyrockets in this energizing story. I am anxious to read Raine's and Lyon's tales."
—*Coffee Time Romance*

"An excellent debut . . . Very highly recommended."
—Deborah MacGillivray, author of *A Restless Knight*

"Amber's unique voice and obvious knowledge of her subject and setting lead to beautifully written stories with powerful, well-drawn characters in a fascinating symbiosis of mythology, history, romance and eroticism. Like the fine wines from the vineyards of Tuscany where the Lords of Satyr make their home, these are stories to be savored for a satisfying, hedonistic treat."
—Kate Douglas, author of *Wolf Tales*

Reviewers on *Raine*:

"One of the the strongest heroines I have ever read . . . great, erotic sex. "
—*TwoLips Reviews* (5 lips, Recommended Read—Julianne)

". . . without question the best historical paranormal erotic romance this reviewer has ever read . . . This is a must read book for 2008!"
—*Paranormal Romance Reviews* (Janalee)

"Two thumbs up for another sensual read that will be gracing my keeper shelf."
—*Night Owl Romance* (Top Pick—Tammie)

Also by Elizabeth Amber:

NICHOLAS: The Lords of Satyr

RAINE: The Lords of Satyr

COMING IN 2009:
DOMINIC: The Lords of Satyr

LYON:
THE LORDS OF SATYR

ELIZABETH AMBER

APHRODISIA

KENSINGTON PUBLISHING CORP.
http://www.kensingtonbooks.com

APHRODISIA BOOKS are published by

Kensington Publishing Corp.
850 Third Avenue
New York, NY 10022

ISBN-13: 978-0-7582-2041-7
ISBN-10: 0-7582-2041-3

First Trade Paperback Printing: August 2008

10 9 8 7 6 5 4 3 2 1

Printed in the United States of America

PROLOGUE

When a parchment letter laced with a hint of ElseWorld magic arrived at the Satyr estate in Tuscany last spring, Lyon was highly skeptical of its contents. Penned by King Feydon, it called on the three Lords of Satyr to wed his progeny . . .

> *Lords of Satyr, Sons of Bacchus,*
> *Be it known that I lie dying and naught may be done. As my time draws near, the weight of past indiscretions haunts me. I must tell of them.*
> *Nineteen summers ago, I fathered daughters upon three highborn Human females of EarthWorld. I sowed my childseed whilst these females slumbered, leaving each unaware of my nocturnal visit.*
> *My three grown daughters are now vulnerable and must be shielded from Forces that would harm them. 'Tis my dying wish you will find it your duty to husband them and bring them under your protection. You may search them out among the society of Rome, Venice, and Paris.*
> *Thus is my Will.*

The demise of King Feydon and the news that his three half-Faerie, half-Human daughters are in danger sends the three wealthy, charismatic Satyr lords in search of FaerieBlend brides. Forces that protect the gate between EarthWorld and ElseWorld are at a low ebb when one of the Satyr brothers is away from the estate, so they must go singly.

Elder brothers Nicholas and Raine have already located two of the sisters and brought them under Satyr protection. Only the third remains at large and now Lyon's search begins . . .

1

Lord Lyon Satyr prowled the twilight streets of Paris, hunting. He breathed deep, searching the air and finding it rife with the scents of chimney smoke, dank river, and likely feminine prey. The blood of his ancestors pumped in him tonight, priming his body toward a carnal lust that was vital to the survival of his kind.

Because King Feydon had sown his seed where he should not have, Lyon would soon find himself yoked with a bride not of his own choosing. One whose name and face were unknown to him, but whom he nevertheless had journeyed here from Tuscany to find.

According to Feydon, his three FaerieBlend daughters were each in some sort of danger and time was of the essence. Nicholas, his eldest brother, had found the first of the daughters on the outskirts of Rome in a matter of weeks and quickly wed her. Raine had recently located the second daughter in Venice and brought her under his protection.

Now Lyon was left with the task of finding the third daughter here in Paris. But tomorrow would be time enough for duty. Tonight was for something altogether different.

This–his first night in Paris—could well be his last night of freedom. He planned to enjoy it.

A shout drew his attention. There was some sort of revelry commencing ahead, atop the Pont Neuf, the Seine River's most famous bridge. The "new bridge" it was called, though it had seen complètion over two centuries earlier.

Lyon veered in its direction, abandoning the row of stately town homes along the Quai de Conti for the opposite sidewalk that edged the river. As the light waned, the black-clad booksellers who lined the walk had begun to pack away unsold books in their boxes. In the depths of the channel just beyond them, the river flowed like molasses, cutting a long serpentine swath through Paris.

His hotel was expecting him. He'd sent his bag ahead and could be there himself within thirty minutes. Which meant his cock could be buried deep inside a conjured Shimmerskin female within thirty-one. No doubt his brothers would have made their way there and done exactly that in his place. It would be the wise thing to do. The careful thing.

But unlike his brothers, he craved variation in both setting and partner in his liaisons. And an element of risk.

He was on the bridge now. Kiosks in the half-round bastions that protruded at intervals from the railings were being abandoned by the costumers, perfumers, and sellers of fans, trinkets, crêpes, and *fromage*. These were giving way to street performers, chestnut carts, and throngs of unusually high-spirited Parisians. Pickpockets seeking prey, and prostitutes vying for custom, had come as well to rub elbows with the finely dressed.

As Lyon threaded among them, women of every rank in society turned to gaze after him, analyzing his worth and weighing the outward signs of his sexual prowess all in the sweep of a well-trained feminine eye. Taller and more muscular than his brothers and blessed with a masculine face so remarkably handsome it had actually caused women to swoon, he was accustomed to such attention and hardly noticed.

A couple passed and the lady's skirt brushed him, wafting her natural feminine perfume to his nostrils. He took it in, closing his eyes briefly at the jolt of euphoria it afforded. It mingled with those of other nameless females, a jumble of waxy pomades, spicy fragrances spritzed from crystal bottles, and Human musk. A heady combination for a man who was already consumed with libidinous intentions.

Whispers reached his ears. Glancing over his shoulder, he was startled to note that at least a half dozen women trailed in his wake. And all were eyeing him as though he were a prime cut of meat at the local butcher shop.

Dismayed, he ground to a halt. His entourage took this as an invitation and swarmed. Prettily gloved hands petted his arm, his back, his hair.

"Bon soir, monsieur."

"Bienvenue, monsieur."

"Est-ce que je peux vous aider?"

A chill crawled its way between his shoulder blades and up the back of his neck. He'd never suffered from an inability to attract the opposite sex, but this level of overt attention was disconcertingly bizarre. The notion that something was very out of kilter tugged at him, but it lost out to other more overwhelming considerations. Whatever magic troubled Paris tonight would have to wait for his attention until after this soul-deep hunger within him was satisfied.

"Bon soir, mesdames," he greeted them, for it would have been insulting to presume that the situation of any unfamiliar French female was that of spinster. He stroked a cheek, a throat, a pulse.

Carefully powdered faces returned his smiles and touches.

Soft voices cajoled. Padded, shapely garments rustled and enticed. A covetous hand brushed his cock—*mano morte*. It could have been any one of them, pretending it was an accident.

All acted on him like aphrodisiacs sending blood coursing ever hotter through his system. The fabric of his trousers and shirt rasped the sensitized skin of his thighs, massive shoulders, and broad chest.

He needed a woman. Now.

With a brief dip of his head in her direction, he singled out a plump female in a pink dress, who stood just outside the circle of admirers. She'd been staring at him as had the others, but more shyly. His instincts told him she was a woman who'd known men. One who yearned for what he would offer. One whose body would accommodate his better than those of most Human women.

Unsure of his invitation, she touched her chest and raised her brows. At his nod, pin lights of delight brightened her mellow brown eyes and transformed a plain countenance into a pretty one. With a brusque word or two, she brushed off her young attendant before parting the crowd and moving toward him in tacit acceptance of his summons.

Though the rest of the besotted troupe must have realized he'd made a selection, they lingered, reluctant to accept it. He fanned his fingers, palm toward them, disbursing a hint of magic in the air.

"*Allez*," he murmured. "Go."

As one, they immediately dispersed to carry on with their business, seeming to forget why they'd gathered around him in the first place.

The silk gloving the hand of his chosen one slid across his work-toughened palm. She smiled shyly at him and his cock twitched, thirsting for a taste of her. He wrapped an arm around her and tucked her head to the hollow of his shoulder.

Eyes narrowed, he surveyed the bridge, quickly locating an

area of isolation and leading her toward it. She went unquestioningly and within a few steps, they'd quit the thick of the crowd for the shadows behind the equestrian statue that lorded over the center of the bridge. Other couples had already congregated there along the railing, their heads close. Surreptitious hands moved busily under clothing and covert encouragements warmed the air. Intent on their own gratification, the current residents paid the new arrivals no attention.

"*Madame?*"

Lyon's head whipped in the direction of the speaker and saw it was a servant, who took a nervous step back at his fierce expression. Apparently, his lady's maid had decided to trail after them, trying to dissuade her mistress from folly.

He reached out and touched the girl's cheek, sending a Calm over her. The concerned expression on her young face instantly eased and she returned to the place on the bridge where he'd first seen her, prepared to placidly await her employer.

Lyon looked down and found the woman's gaze on him. He ducked his head close. "*Bon soir, Madame.*"

"*Bon soir,*" she whispered.

He pressed her back against the base of the statue—against inscribed words which explained that it was a bronze King Henri IV who rode majestically above them—the very monarch who had seen this bridge finished.

"*Ici?* Here?" His lover's rapt attention had never once left his face, but now an uncertain frown puckered her brow and she glanced about them.

He touched the underside of her jaw with two fingertips, lifting her to his kiss. His hand slid into her hair, his palm so broad that it encompassed the back of her skull. "No one will see. Nor care," his husky voice promised against her parted lips. "Just enjoy."

His body crowded hers flush against the gritty stone and still he spoke to her—low reassuring words that warmed her ear and readied her for what was to come. Here, he would take his clandestine pleasure of her under sky and, later, star.

Her body was Human and would require considerable time to adjust to the size and strength of his. Even then she would be unable to take all of him in as well as the half-Faerie he'd come to Paris to find might have.

Annoyed that thoughts of that duty had intruded, he shook them off. Still, it was true that women in EarthWorld were frail and he could safely join himself to this one no more than a half dozen times here in this alcove. It would have to be enough.

With gentle lips, he brushed the tendon that ran from her ear to the hollow at the base of her throat. His pawlike hands roamed lower, gathering and lifting the front of her skirt and petticoat in great fistfuls, baring her to the cool air.

Her bosom rose on a sharp indrawn breath and her fingers fluttered to clutch the chiseled muscles of his shoulders. He leaned in, surrounding her with his body and scent.

Long, knowing fingers slipped under her skirts—first warming a thigh, then sliding between them and roving even higher to thread through soft, feminine bristle. A strangled moan escaped her as the first finger brushed her clit. At the second brush, she closed her eyes on a sigh.

He stroked her again and again, knowing all the while that it wasn't a kindness he would be doing her in this act. Far from it. For after this night, a remembrance of their joining would remain with this woman, a new constant in her physical makeup. Though he would wipe the specifics of the hours they spent here from her mind, a small part of her would hereafter always pine for him, not knowing why or for whom she longed. And though this was a hurt he was reluctant to give her, he needed her too badly to let her go. The least he could do was to make sure that any impression he left was an extremely pleasant one.

She was panting now, emitting a tiny whimper each time he caressed her. Her arms had gone lax, hanging on either side of her hips against the stone. Slender wrists were turned upward in a pose of vulnerability, a sign she'd placed herself at his mercy.

His desire to possess her ratcheted higher. Heat pooled in his scrotum, tightening his balls into fists and thickening knotted blue veins that corded the length of his cock. He drew one of her hands to his groin and taught her the shape of him. She groaned against his neck.

His middle finger pressed urgently at the brink of humid feminine folds that gated what he sought. She was wet. Ready. He pushed her hand aside and found the fastening of his trousers, releasing himself.

Gods! Relief could not come soon enough!

Abruptly, an eerie crooning broke the air around them, reaching him even through a haze of lust and the surrounding din. A breath away from his sweet goal, he faltered. His head lifted and cocked to better listen.

The song came again. Eyes narrowed, he tipped his face in the direction from which it had issued. The river.

It came yet again familiar and feminine.

Nymphs. From the sound of things, they, too, were out hunting tonight. And they'd scented his presence. Voracious lovers, their bodies would be well able to handle all he had to offer. And they were noted gossips as well, a fact that might prove beneficial to his purpose in coming to Paris. Perhaps they'd gotten wind of the whereabouts of a certain female with a mix of both Faerie and Human blood in her veins.

He glanced at the willing woman before him. Her soft, experienced fingers warmed his cock. His body urged him to take her, to finish what he'd scarcely begun. But some latent sense of compassion impelled him to let her go. Now, before they mated and he gained a lasting hold over her.

Biting off a curse, he tamped his need and lay a palm against her cheek to bespell her. Silently, he commanded her to go.

Willed her to forget her desire for the act they'd left unconsummated as best she could.

Tugging her hand away, he refastened his trousers. For long seconds, her brown eyes only blinked up at him, wounded and confused. He stepped back and her skirts swished into place again, covering thighs, dimpled knees, then ankles.

Her flushed face was a picture of reluctance, but she nevertheless straightened and turned away as he'd bid her. As she retraced her steps toward her waiting servant, her eyes followed him. Within hours, the particulars of their encounter would fade, but a vague yearning for him would remain with her for far longer, like a bruise on her heart.

Thoughts of her already fading, Lyon took the worn stone steps on the Pont Neuf's north side two at a time. Descending to the brick walkway on a level with the river, he then veered under a wide arch, passing the *clochards*—harmless beggars who huddled in the nooks and crannies of Paris.

Behind him stretched the bulk of the island called Île de la Cité. Ahead of him, at its western tip lay the Parc Vert Gallant, a triangular spit formed by centuries of sediment deposits. Jutting into the Seine from just below the bridge, it pointed downstream like the prow of a ship.

Stepping into the park, he quickly swept the banks with his eyes, but saw nothing move. Where were they?

The crooning reached him again, louder and more beguiling this time. He walked the perimeters of the park where land met water, searching more keenly.

Here, the fresh natural odors of loam and vegetation filled him, offering a welcome respite from less pleasant smells of brick and smoke above in the bustling city. Cities were entertaining in their own way and on occasion, but why anyone of means would choose to inhabit an urban area in preference to the vast expanses of rural terrain that lay outside its borders was beyond his reasoning. Something in his soul tied him to the land.

Suddenly, he whipped around. The crooning had come again, this time from the park's north bank. An unanticipated thrill engulfed him, prickling his skin, and hardening his cock to ever-greater dimensions.

For this time, the sound had brought with it something new. A precious fragrance. It entwined the call, separating itself from Human smells and marking itself as peculiar. It was an unmistakable scent. That of Faerie. Aroused Faerie.

Was it possible he'd so easily located the very female he'd come to Paris to find? He paced the length of the north shore again, more impatient than ever for a first glimpse of the river nymphs. Convinced now, that King Feydon's third daughter was among them.

Never mind that until this moment he'd been aggrieved at this duty and reluctant to meet her. Never mind that having *her* find *him* the very night of his arrival in Paris seemed an errand too easily accomplished. Never mind that it appeared she was inexplicably of the sea, rather than of the land.

One thought and one only rode him—that within minutes, in this very park, he would make her his. Reason could wait until after his cock had found a haven in her.

His eyes scanned the bank. Where was she, damn it all?

Something stirred the river just beyond a patch of grassy silt beneath a plane tree. A lithe form rose from the depths, water streaming from its dark hair and slicking over shoulders and full, tipped breasts. Silhouetted against the sunset's brilliant orange reflection on the Seine's surface, a nymph reached toward the park embankment. Bracing her arms there, she pulled herself higher and turned to sit onshore with her glistening back toward him.

Lyon devoured the distance between them. Earlier, he hadn't wanted to find her, but now that he had . . .

He came to stand just behind her, his legs warm on either side of her river-chilled spine. Twin opalescent dorsal fins at her shoulder blades twitched against him, like the gentle flutter of faerie wings.

Her body was sleek and curved, beautiful and mysterious. Her hair was a dark wet scarf, its length wrapped once around her neck and its ends draping forward to cling damply at her hips and lap. The tip of her tail remained hidden, still swallowed by the Seine.

His hands touched the sides of her face and caught her hair, smoothing it from her cheeks and unwinding it until its length hung free down her back, soaking the front of his trousers.

Beyond her he heard two more nymphs making their way to shore, but he ignored them. This one was Feydon's daughter. From the moment he'd drawn near to her, he'd been certain of it.

Slipping his hands under her armpits he gently lifted her dripping figure clear of the river. The sooner he got her on land, the sooner she'd dry enough to transform for him.

Over her shoulder, her head angled his way, but otherwise she didn't acknowledge him.

Other heads had swiveled toward him as well, for the crowds had spilled down the staircases on either side of the bridge and out into the park. Human voyeurs, eager to be shocked and entertained, craned their necks and whispered.

"You see nothing," he murmured in their direction. Eddies of air caught his words and carried them, spreading a mindspell throughout the atmosphere of the park and beyond.

One by one, the gawkers turned away and forgot what had captured their interest in the first place. No longer would they be able to detect him or the fey in any way. The more perceptive among them could still see had they chosen to do so, but now they would no longer be inclined to look.

Turning the nymph to face him, Lyon anchored her against him with a muscular forearm at her lower back. Of necessity, he supported her entire weight, for she would remain unable to stand on her own until the transformation occurred that would replace her tail with two limbs.

His gritted his teeth at the thought of the wait ahead. As a protection against rape, nymphs' mating cavities were sealed until their bodies had been sufficiently aroused by their partners. It would take at least a half an hour on land before her tail would bisect. Only then would she be available for mounting.

He pulled back to see her, but she kept her face averted. Her arms lay on his chest and gleamed with the phosphorescence of sea creatures that haunted only the deepest parts of the ocean. It would fade with her metamorphosis, disappearing completely if she remained on land. Which, if things worked out as he expected, she would.

The curtain of her hair streamed over shoulders made strong by many days of battling sea currents. It partially cloaked her like ropes of wet satin hanging almost to her knees.

Against him, her ice-blue breasts soaked his shirt in dual fat circles. A dozen or more strands of sumptuous jewels draped her neck. Frigid, pointed nipples peeked from among them, poking his chest as hard as two fingertips.

Having grown to its usual legendary proportions, his long-suffering cock nudged her through his trousers, beyond anxious for a taste. It occurred to him that wedding this half-Faerie might not be as bad as he'd feared.

"Look at me," he growled.

With the smooth elegance that typified water-dwellers, she lifted her gaze. His head jerked back as he got his first look at her face, for it bore telltale pearlescent V-shaped scales.

"Twelve hells! You're a Nereid?"

She cocked her head. "You expected something tamer?"

Damn! King Feydon had saddled him for life with a Nereid? A nymph who was equal parts sea-faerie and she-devil?

Her hands clutched the hard swells of his biceps as though she feared he'd withdraw from her. "I am the king's child—the one you seek," she assured him.

"Your name?" Lyon heard himself ask.

"Sibela, my love." Her voice was pleasing, her every utterance a lilting chant of the kind that had lured legions of males to their doom.

She tugged him closer and her lips found his jaw, nibbling delicately along it. Then she licked his cheek with a firm upward sweep of her abnormally long tongue. He'd forgotten that the Nereid liked to taste their men.

He heard a splash and used the excuse to turn his face from her. A distance behind her, two more of her kind had levered themselves up on the banks. Their covetous eyes ran over him as they began drying themselves with crisp ruby and gold maple leaves as big as his hands, anxious to hurry their own metamorphoses.

Sibela's eyes flashed seashell pink, then green again and her tailfin slapped the earth at his feet, its two sharp points ripping at his boots. Her melodious voice was the yowl of a harpy now as she scolded and warned them off, laying claim to him. The acolytes shrank back, but didn't go.

Lyon winced, envisioning his future with this creature.

"What are Nereids doing in the river?" he asked, silently cursing King Feydon. "Your kind normally frequent the Mediterranean or even the oceans, leaving the rivers to Naiads."

"I've come for *you*," she whispered, all smiles and sweetness again.

"How did you know to come searching for me here?" he asked, suspicious.

"News of your coming and the reasons behind it was brought to me by the currents. I know what you want of me tonight. And I am willing." Claws ripped at his shirt, opening it and pushing it off his shoulders. "Eager."

Her story was viable. It was no secret that he and his brothers had begun searching out brides of late. And he was well aware that EarthWorld's waterways circulated such gossip more rapidly than its land roads.

Cool hands slid lower around him to knead the cheeks of his buttocks through his trousers. Her sea-green eyes turned sly and knowing as she ground her groin against his and felt how much he wanted her.

Instinctively, he shifted aside, evading her overture. He stared down at her, shocked at himself. His body was well primed for a mating, so why the fuck had he done that?

She was glaring at him now, clearly wondering the same thing. "Lie with me," she coaxed.

Feeling that everything was wrong about this, Lyon nevertheless summoned a grim smile. "Yes. Of course."

He swung her into his arms and carried her farther onto shore, leaving a trail of liquid phosphorescence in their wake. She touched his cheek and something akin to panic filled him when he realized he felt no special attachment toward her.

Where was the instantaneous bonding Nicholas and Raine had felt toward King Feydon's first two daughters upon meeting them? Where was the craving to join his body to Sibela's to the exclusion of all others? The kind of impatient desire he'd witnessed in Nick, only when he was in Jane's presence? The intense, selective need even his remote brother Raine had been unable to hide when Jordan was near?

As he lay her upon a soft bed of reed grasses a distance away from shore, the realization that he felt nothing above ordinary lust toward the female in his arms shook him. Yet his body did clamor to claim hers, and he took heart from that.

So he stretched himself on the ground beside her, preparing to mount her here on the very spot where Jacques de Molay, Grand Master of the Knights Templar, had been burnt at the stake in medieval times. She was willing and her body would give his ease. More importantly, their joining would initiate the protection that a lengthier mating during Moonful tomorrow night would greatly extend and reinforce.

But he was certain now that she would not leave her stamp upon his heart. No woman ever had.

Lying with a forearm pillowing her head, he nudged her onto her back and ran his hands over the bones of ribs and hip, then lower. As her body dried, a shallow furrow was forming along the central length of her, from groin to tailfin. The flat of his fingers traced over it, slicking away the droplets of seawater that had pooled in the depression.

"How long?" he growled, as desire rose hotter in him.

Seawater eyes brimming with sexual promise caught his. "Soon, my sweet."

Sweet? It was obvious from her tone that she enjoyed the fact that he was suffering for want of her.

His finger found the tip of a luminous breast amid the tangle of rubies, pearls, and other less exotic stones encircling her neck. Hooking an inexpensive strand from amid the more costly necklaces, he lifted it for closer study.

"Where did you come by all this?" he asked, nodding toward the bounty.

She snatched it from him and carefully patted it back into place. "From here and there. My most recent finds were from the hold of a vessel. A sunken one littered with dead Spaniards who were so kind as to leave a trunk full of gems at my disposal. However grateful I was for their gifts, they proved quite a trial." Her eyes were cunning as she slid her hand lower between them. "For their flaccid organs provided little in the way of entertainment."

He caught her hand, thwarting it from finding him. "Do you think to make me jealous with your talk of other men?"

"No. Of course not." She shook off his restraint and he let

her. "It's only that your carnal exploits are the stuff of legend and I wish to assure you that as a woman of experience, I'm your match in such matters."

Her hand found his cock then, and her voice turned intimate. "And I find myself hungry tonight for a more lively joining with a far greater treasure than limp Spaniards."

Clawed fingertips pricked through his trousers, fondling his tumescent shaft.

Hissing inwardly between his teeth, Lyon gave her a warning squeeze. "If you want my 'treasure' so badly, I suggest you exercise care not to damage it before it can perform as you like."

She looked ready to speak, but then something beyond him caught her eye. Abruptly, she rose on an elbow to glower menacingly over his shoulder. Slithering on their bellies across the grass, the others of her kind had trailed them and had drawn too near to suit her.

Reminded of Sibela's wrath, they halted a distance away combing their hair with their fingers and eyeing him.

With mechanical expertise, his fingers continued to caress, deepening the trench along Sibela's tail. But his mind worked apart from his hands. "How is it that King Feydon's third daughter comes from the river instead of land?"

"My secrets are not yours to hear until we've grown closer," she crooned, all cloying again as her attention returned to him. Her bony, translucent fingers made quick work of the fastenings of his trousers. Freed, his cock surged from the gape of fabric and she reached for it.

"Careful," he reminded softly.

She nodded and stroked him once. Twice. "You seem sufficiently roused for the task ahead."

Then her hand covered his where it massaged the furrow forming directly along the center of her tail. What had been one long, solid form from hip to tip was beginning to remodel itself into two distinct limbs. A true separation had already begun at her groin and this was where she led his touch.

"So am I," she whispered. "I'm open for you! Feel me?"

Under their combined touch, the tender slit at her groin deepened. It would take some time for the separation to continue along thighs, knees, calves, and ankles. And longer still for it to form webbed-toed feet from angled fins. But he needn't wait any longer, and she wouldn't require him to.

Bracing his hands in the grass on either side of her, he slung himself over her and replaced their fingers with the crown of his cock. He flexed his hips, beginning his push.

"Are you ready for me?" His voice was gruff, trembling with need.

She flattened her palms against his chest, staying him. "You understand my price?"

Their eyes caught and his jaw hardened. "I'm more than willing to meet it—if you're truly King Feydon's daughter." He had little choice. The third fey child was destined to be his for all eternity whether he cared for her or not. It was what his brothers expected. Cleaving himself to her was his duty and would protect both her and the gate on Satyr land that stood as the only barrier between two disparate worlds.

"You will wed me in the Human way?" she asked, demanding a clearer agreement. "Take me to your lands where the Arno flows?"

Everything in him—except his cock—rebelled at the idea. "Yes," he told her.

She smiled slowly. Releasing him, she threw her arms wide on the grass to tangle in the hair that fanned around her.

"Then come into me, husband," she breathed.

His tip dipped farther into her, widening and stretching her small gap. Her milky readiness coated his crown and stirred every nerve ending he possessed.

"Gods, yes," he breathed.

"I know," she crooned. "I know you need me, darling. And I'm yours."

He drew back and pressed forward again. And again, in an erotic dance that teased her entrance wider and lodged him farther inside her each time. He lowered his head to her, nuzzling the hair along her temple. "Yesss."

Her crooning turned louder and more harmonious, becoming a vibrant hum. "Fuck me, fuck me!" she chanted.

With a vigorous shove of his hips, he penetrated her, tunneling hard and deep. Sheathed inside the newly formed gelatinous core of the woman he would marry, he shivered, recalling yet another reason he'd always shrunk from fornicating with Nereids. Sibela was cold—inside and out.

"Welcome home," she lilted at his ear. "I am meant for you."

Finding himself at a loss for a convincingly ardent reply, he kissed her instead. And to make up for his lack of affection, he then proceeded to rut her with all the considerable skill he'd acquired over the past decade. Gripping the soft-scaled rounds of her buttocks, he drove himself into her, then pulled away, reveling in the feel of her inner muscles sucking at him. He slammed home again and again, beginning to lose himself in the animal act.

Whap! Her tail swept upward to slap his rear, and the twin tips of her caudal fin pierced his skin.

"Gods!" Lyon jerked at the pain and shifted his leg so it weighted her tail. Shoving fingers tight in her hair, he spoke to her nose to nose. "There's something about me you'll want to remember. Rough, I like." At the beginning and finish of each sentence, he bucked her in emphatic slams. "Violent, I don't."

Her channel undulated, squeezing him in a way that urged him toward orgasm but let him know she intended to be the one who'd decide when he'd attain it.

A hoarse, carnal groan escaped him, and she smiled knowingly.

"You will grow used to my ways in time," she told him.

A part of him reveled in the frank coarseness of her. But something in him craved variety, and she would always demand that his lovemaking be an assault. The Nereid considered pain and aggression an inalienable part of this act. For them, every mating was a test of their partner's worthiness. It was not her fault, he reminded himself. She was who she was.

So he fucked her, rough and aggressive, ruthlessly taking what he needed and giving her what she wanted. She licked the strong column of his neck and then nipped him there and he let her. Her necklaces bit into his chest and her claws raked up and down his back and ripped at his clothing as she pelted his ears with raw pleas.

"Fuck! Ram it! Give it to me!"

To save his own skin as much as anything else, he wrenched her wrists above her head and secured them with one hand. Holding nothing back, he gave her what she begged for, sending shock waves through her body with each lusty hammer of his hips. He grunted like an animal as the force of each plow slammed his balls against her. The stubble on his jaw chafed her throat and his mouth bruised her, but she only pleaded for more.

"Yes!" she shouted, "Yes," over and over until his ears rung and he wondered if he should bespell himself into deafness. Her frigid, slushy core warmed, and she began to hum a soft siren's song deep in her chest, indicating her heightening pleasure. His balls tightened in response, presaging the monumental release that often came with the fucking of a creature with ElseWorld blood.

Yet all the while, he remained alert to his surroundings. Apart from the actions of his body, he tracked where every Human within a hundred feet stood and used his acute senses to filter the air for sounds or signs of danger.

Above him, the Pont Neuf still bustled with activity and the enthusiastic crowd pounded across the bridge like a herd of cattle. The acrid scent of smoke told him the *lampiste* was illuminating the lamps along the bridge. Some of the chestnuts in the vendor's cart had burned, a container of beer had just been broken at King Henri's feet, and another man had just spilled his cum inside the brown-eyed Human woman Lyon had earlier abandoned.

Then, without warning, something unfamiliar and . . . pleasing . . . reached him. It was a new, momentous fragrance unlike any he'd ever experienced. Riding on the air, it invaded his lungs, his mind. And sought to leave its mark on other organs no female had ever yet touched. On his heart—his very soul.

His head jerked back from Sibela's. His brows knit in concentration as he scrutinized her face. She was staring beyond him, toward something above him on the bridge.

"Your scent—" he gasped, never breaking the rhythm of his rut. Her eyes flicked guiltily to his.

"Ignore her," she urged, and he heard the fear in her voice. "She's nothing to us."

She wrenched her wrists from his hold in order to clutch him to her and kiss his throat with cloying desperation.

"Ignore who?"

And then, impossibly—despite Sibela's pleas and despite the din on the bridge—a single word reached him. A single word made of two sweet syllables, fallen from feminine lips. A word that in and of itself meant nothing to him. But which fell upon his ears with the subtle impact of a delicate leaf drifting to lie upon a still pond on a quiet autumn day.

It was a simple, quiet utterance. Yet one that wreaked havoc on his senses. He felt himself losing control. Felt his gut wrench. Felt himself being forcibly hurtled toward the fiercest ejaculation of his life. His cock swelled and hardened to stone as unyielding as the bridge supports. His teeth bared and every muscle in his body seized.

Bone-deep ecstasy shuddered over him, then he shot off, harder than he ever had before. Cum flooded from him, thick and hot and never-ending.

"Gods! Gods!" he gasped, barely registering the fact that his partner was coming as well. It was as though he were experiencing his orgasm with someone other than the woman under him.

His back arched and he looked upward, toward the place on the bridge from which the unexpected sound and scent had emanated.

Above him, a shadowy form watched from along the balustrade of the bridge. He had only a quick glimpse of a pale, rosy-cheeked feminine face within a crimson hood, before it ducked out of sight.

2

A crisp breeze wafted off the River Seine, rouging the pallor of Mademoiselle Juliette Rabelais' cheeks and loosening tendrils of her almond-colored hair as she paused at the entrance to the Pont Neuf. Beside her, young Fleur kept up a running commentary on everything and everyone they passed as she had all morning.

Juliette rarely came to this side of the river, but the Rive Droit—the right bank—was the location of Les Halles, the marketplace popularly known as the stomach of Paris. There was to be an entertainment in the salon at home tonight, so she'd gone shopping to replenish her supplies. Herbs and other cooking ingredients she'd gathered were now packed in the baskets she and Fleur carried.

But far more precious than the foodstuffs was the single sheet of rag paper rolled tightly and tucked in her basket among the figs, chives, spearmint, cinnamon, sage, and nutmeg. She'd paid Madame Elbe, the herbalist, a small fortune to have it stolen and delivered to her today and she'd been careful not to let Fleur see. Excitement fizzed inside her as it had since she'd scanned the paper and found her name. And another one that was familiar to her as well.

"*Allez*, Fleur," she said, waving her younger companion ahead and indicating that she should cross the bridge alone. "Continue on and tell them I'm coming."

"Of course, mademoiselle. But you are certain?" Fleur touched her gloved hand in concern.

With anyone else, Juliette might have been embarrassed to admit her own fears, but Fleur was too kindhearted to judge her. She swallowed a lump of affection for the girl and nodded. "*Oui.* Go and make yourself ready for tonight."

Fleur grinned, bobbed a curtsey, and departed. Juliette watched her cap until the throng on the Pont Neuf engulfed it.

She usually took care not to associate with the other girls, for past experience had schooled her that doing so only brought sadness when they departed or were dismissed. But Fleur was lively and genuine and it was difficult not to like her. She feared they were fast becoming friends.

Her eyes located the townhouse set in an unrelieved row of residences along the Rive Gauche, the left bank of the river on the far periphery of the bridge. It was the less fashionable district, but Monsieur Valmont and his activities would not have been welcome in the more desirable neighborhood on this side of the river. Though the house looked pleasant enough with its gray plaster, red door, and wrought iron rails, revulsion welled at the thought of returning there.

A *jongleur* clutching an assortment of brightly colored balls, clubs, and rings passed her on his way on to the bridge and tipped his hat, giving her a long, significant glance. Accustomed to such sidelong glances from men, she ignored him. A group of finely dressed ladies pulled their skirts from her path and whispered as they, too, passed. She ignored them as well. Over the past year since she'd returned to Paris with M. Valmont, she and the other girls had become infamous in this neighborhood, objects of curiosity to some, and of scorn and suspicion to others.

She saw the red door open and shut in the row of houses lining the Quai di Conti, indicating that Fleur had arrived safely. It should have been a simple matter for her to dash across the bridge too.

It should have been. Yet it was not. Though she knew the bridge to be over ninety-two feet wide and nine hundred feet long and supported by twelve arches, crossing it nevertheless seemed as dangerous to her as traversing the river via tightrope.

"Move. You have to go," she scolded herself under her breath. She'd lingered here far too long.

Determinedly she fixed her eyes on the equestrian statue of King Henri that stood at the center of the bridge. Reaching it would mean she was halfway home.

She adjusted the basket more securely in the crook of her arm. Straightening her spine, she took a hesitant step forward, then another. And then she was on the bridge.

"*Un, deux, trois . . . quinze, seize . . .*" As she counted her steps in a hushed voice, she combated her irrational fears by running tonight's menu through her mind.

. . . Should she add the figs to the cakes again? Valmont hadn't liked them done up in that manner, but Fleur and Gina had. Yes, she would add them . . . and she must remind Madame Gris to let the pear sauce cool before dousing the truffles, which must be checked for rot and the fromage as well . . .

With meticulous care, she trained her gaze on Henri, glancing neither right nor left, for in both directions lay the swirling waters of the Seine. Not overly fond of nature in general, she was particularly terrified of water. It was a fear that had come upon her suddenly three years ago at age sixteen and only grown worse in the years since.

Unfortunately for her, the Pont Neuf was an anomaly in that it had been constructed without buildings lining its sides.

It was the only bridge in all of Paris where there was nothing to obscure the river from view except a collection of vendors that set up temporary shop here and there selling everything from scarves to tobacco.

A *fleuriste* pushing a colorful flower cart, a *chef de pâtisserie*, and a groomer *des chiens*, who had all been neatly tucked in the half-round bastions along the bridge's railings by day, were now fleeing with the approach of nightfall. Entertainers—*jongleurs*, acrobats, fire-eaters, and slight-of-hand tricksters—were swiftly replacing them, and the air was filling with evening cold and the smells of fresh roasted chestnuts.

Some sort of impromptu festival seemed to be getting under-way, and it was making her journey homeward more hazardous than usual. In fact, the pont was swelling with a riot of human-ity this evening, she realized. Why, she didn't know.

A lively farandole had begun and dancers had formed a linked chain, some by means of joined hands and others by means of holding handkerchiefs stretched between them. The meandering line snaked through the crowd, increasing in length as more participants were drawn in. She pulled the hood of her crimson-colored wrap more closely around her and side-stepped, avoiding them.

"Something's odd here tonight," she murmured. Absently, she resettled the weighty basket to hang from her opposite arm, the knowledge of its tightly-rolled secret comforting her.

She jiggled her free hand in the pocket of her skirt finding the flakes of oatmeal and the crust of bread there with her finger-tips. Both were said to ward off ill magic. Or so her foster mother had claimed. The superstitious Madame Fouche had instilled a knowledge of such charms in Juliette and now she never left home without a talisman of some sort.

Suddenly, the chestnut cart cut between her and her goal, forcing her to veer around it and bump into a lady carrying a poodle.

"*Excusez-moi, madame!*" she tossed behind her not bothering to stop. She had to keep moving. She had to stay focused. If her mind wandered, there could be trouble. Tuning out the jubilance around her, she glued her eyes to the statue.

"Almost there, almost there," she chanted. Her breath came in shallow, quick puffs, visible in the raw autumn twilight.

Someone jostled her, nudging her off course and toward the western balustrade. More shoves—harder this time—knocked her to her knees. Her basket hit the ground, spilling half of its contents. Fast as frogs' tongues, two sets of hands shot out and rifled through the spillage, snatching items at random and leaving others to be trampled.

The familiar, pungent smell of grapemust mixed with something unearthly reached her and she gasped. A quick glance behind her told her it was exactly as she'd feared. Scant inches away were two imps, with pointed ears and grins too wide to be Human and skin that emitted an unattractive mottled glow of violet and puce.

It was them. The "bright-children." This was the nickname she'd given these creatures as a girl, but she hadn't seen any of them for three years. She'd begun to think—to hope—that they'd only been figments of her young imagination. So much for the talismans in her pocket. They warded off nothing.

Delighted with themselves, the hooligans giggled and tossed the objects they'd pilfered between one another, thinking it a merry game. One of their new toys was long and slender—a tube tied with a ribbon. The sheet of paper that she'd paid to have stolen had now been stolen from her!

"*Arrêtez!*" She lifted her skirts and lunged to snatch it back. Heads turned, but no one bothered to assist her. She hadn't expected them to. No one ever saw these beings, except her.

Grinning, the two pixies made off with their ill-gotten gains, having no idea what they'd done. Scraping the bulk of the foodstuffs back into her basket, Juliette found her feet and gave chase. Their unnatural light flickered ahead whenever the throng shifted just right. But each time she lost them from sight, she feared it was for good.

"Wait! Let's trade! I'll give you something else from my basket instead!" she promised, hoping they would hear. "Pears!"

Non! *They didn't care for food. What had she once used to bribe them? Think! Think! Ah, yes! Shiny things. Pins. Polished agates.*

Of course she had none of those with her now and the peak-eared creatures were getting away. "Come back!"

The cacophony of the dancers, musicians, and idlers along the bridge rose, drowning her out as the current of hundreds of revelers carried her along.

She found herself disgorged at the far end of the bridge at the Rive Droit, right back where she'd begun her crossing. Frustrated, she spun in a circle that swirled her skirts. She'd lost them—and her cherished parchment tube along with them!

At this rate, there would be no time to add the goods in her basket to tonight's menu. The culinary delicacies she'd already prepared would have to suffice.

What to do? In her agitated state it was becoming ever more difficult to make a coherent decision. She'd let herself become over-stimulated here in the outdoors, a dangerous thing to let happen.

Frantic, she dove back into the melee, determined to search the length of the Pont Neuf. The line of dancers had grown into a mob and it careened by, nearly squashing her. The bridge almost seemed to bounce under the thunderous pounding of boisterous footsteps. Could it take such abuse? Would it fall and topple her into the river? Dizzying fear flooded her.

She tried to focus; to shut out the crowds. Someone bumped her and the basket fell from her fingers, as she was herded into one of the semicircular bastions that projected outward from the northwest side of the bridge. Bent over the balustrade and pressed there by the surge of the crowd, she almost pitched over it into the garden twenty feet below. Her slippers left the ground and her feet dangled in midair.

Flinging her head back in an effort to right herself, she suddenly found her vision filled with a river of blood that stretched ahead as far as she could see. The Seine. The sunset had turned it into a winding slash of stunning scarlet. Like some sort of immense open vein, it pumped its sanguine waters, slicing through the heart of Paris.

"*Non!*" she wailed. Rearing back, she tried to regain her balance, only to be shoved forward again so vigorously that the railing squeezed the breath from her lungs and bruised her ribs. Averting her gaze from the river, she peered directly downward, into the comparatively placid Parc Vert Gallant. A smattering of couples dotted its walkways and benches, embracing to form clandestine shadows under the umbrella of foliage turned a seasonable ochre and cherry. Nowhere did she see the pesky thieves who'd taken her things.

Something moved on the ground below, drawing her gaze. An apparition, fading in and out of view. It was like some sort of erotic mirage, which at first appeared only as a series of undulating curves and valleys cast in high relief.

Narrowing her eyes, she tried to bring it into focus. With shocking abruptness, it solidified into reality. She gaped then, unable to believe what she was viewing.

Directly below in the park, was a gentleman. One who was surely as handsome and nearly as brazenly naked as any statue in the royal collection she'd seen at the Louvre. He was lying face down in the grass, his backside and hair painted a brilliant red-gold by the brush of sunset.

The muscles of his shoulders were carved rock, his arms strong and straining, and his weight rested on hands braced where his shadow darkened the grass. A light-colored band haphazardly bisected his ridged torso at the waist. It was his shirt, she realized, which had been thrown back off his shoulders and had caught at his elbows. Trousers sagged low on sleek narrow hips, baring the upper swells of buttocks that were moving in a powerful, rolling rhythm.

As she watched, a woman's delicate hands slipped under her lover's arms and around his ribs to stroke the concave curve of his lower back and the globes of his rear. His body was massive, completely obscuring every other part of her with the exception of her long hair spread out on the grass like some dark peacock's fan.

For the briefest of moments, he angled his head in such a way that her pale cheek peeked from below him. Then his head moved again and she disappeared from view.

Juliette's eyes rounded. Could they really be doing what it appeared they were doing? Right there in the open? And if so, why did no one object? Her gaze made a sweep of the park and of those nearby on the bridge who still pinned her. And a terrifying realization struck her.

No one objected because . . . no one but she could see them! Just as no one had seen the bright-children who'd stolen her page, and whose coming had portended this other strange sighting. Mischief and unearthly happenings had always followed in the wake of their intermittent appearances in her life.

Transfixed, she could only stare at the bodies copulating in the park. For without a doubt that's what the pair was doing. Fornicating, right there in the open as flagrantly as two jungle animals.

The man moved sensuously on his partner, grinding and rotating his hips. With the ardor of a salacious symphony, the slash of his spine arched and bowed as muscles bunched and slackened.

Juliette's teeth tugged at her lower lip and she put a hand to the erratic thrum at the base of her throat. How would it feel to find oneself the object of all that masculine energy, brute strength, and desire? To be covered and dominated by a man so overtaken by his lustful instincts that he'd heeded them with no care for his surroundings?

How would it feel to be wanted so desperately? She could only imagine.

Once, she'd longed for such things, but she'd been punished when she'd sought them. Or at least those who loved her had. And there would undoubtedly be repercussions were she ever again to act on her base urges.

She should look away.

Yet she didn't. Instead, she watched like one mesmerized, and an unexpected, forbidden yearning swept her chilled skin like a summer breeze infused with some exotic aphrodisiac. The folds gating her private channel pulsed gently, hinting at what that man could provide were she his.

She should look away.

Instead, she let desire swamp her, relishing its unfamiliar thrill. Her gloved hands fisted on the railing. Beneath layers of cloak, bodice, and chemise, her nipples tightened. And under her petticoats, high in her most secret place, she was a hollow void aching to be filled.

With each powerful thrust, the cheeks of the man's buttocks contracted. The well-defined muscles of his back, shoulders, and arms flexed and relaxed in fluid harmony. As she watched, his hips lifted slightly and his hand slipped between his body and the one under him.

She should look away. She should . . .

. . . Yet she didn't.

And slowly, so slowly, a touch came to her. As soft as a whisper, it caressed and comforted so tenderly that she hardly noticed it as something apart from her own body at first. It was as though a warm, knowing hand had worked its way high between her legs to gently cup her, offering to heal the hurt of her need. At first she ignored the sensation, thinking it only her unreliable imagination.

When the touch grew more tangible and masculine she wriggled and kicked out, thinking someone in the crowd was manhandling her. Whipping her head side to side, she could see that no one nearby seemed to be paying particular attention to her. Her slippers now rested on solid ground again, but she remained locked to the rail by the press of humanity behind her on the bridge.

The furtive hand molded itself to her unguarded flesh, its palm flattening against her feminine opening and its heel firm against her pubic mound. Still locked to the railing, she stood wide-eyed and perfectly motionless. Terrified and titillated at the same time.

Gently, the hand palpated her once, twice—sending waves of heat through her core. Its heel sawed at her clit as it pulled forward toward her belly, then shifted back again until its longest finger slipped just along her rear cleft, shocking her system more in this than all that had come before.

Lazily, it rocked back and forth and back and forth . . . back . . . and . . . forth.

Just when she thought she might be driven mad by the stimulation, it ceased and the hand folded in on itself. Its fingers brushed her intimate creases as it gathered itself into something resembling a fist.

At the very same moment, the man's hips drew back from his partner's.

She gulped as the fist aligned itself with her slit, its knuckles putting an upward, driving pressure on that vulnerable entrance to her channel.

The man in the park! Somehow, she'd become connected to him. To what he was doing to that other woman. A similar sort of transference had happened on occasion when she was a child, but certainly nothing so visceral as this!

Her fingers dug into the railing, fraying the tips of her gloves. She scarcely dared breathe as the fisted intruder insistently stormed her gate, wooing her with its erotic promise. Deep inside, her core began to melt for it, coating its nib with a natural feminine slickness meant to ease its way.

The crowds had ebbed around her enough to allow for breathing room, but she scarcely noticed for there was no question of departure now. Her body was weeping for this.

The muscles of the man's back and buttocks rippled with the effort of restraint as he slowly flexed his hips forward . . .

With a humid sigh, Juliette's nether lips succumbed, parting for him.

Her eyes fluttered closed and her lips drew inward over clenched teeth to keep from crying out as she felt herself give way to the masculine pressure. Her arms ached with tension and the grit of the stone rail grazed the soft skin of her wrists where sleeve and glove had slid apart. How it burned. And still the warm fist pressed on, languidly screwing itself into her.

Coiling need twisted and built, higher and higher until the innermost flesh hidden deep in her channel cried for want of the entirety of its hard heat. The sensation of it plumbing ever deeper was a completely foreign one. A wickedly delicious one. So this was what it felt like to have a man's member come inside one's body!

In this moment, she cared about nothing else—only that she wanted more of it. Would die if she didn't get it.

As if reacting to her need, the man bucked into the woman under him, so hard that she was shoved several inches across the grass. Shallows formed in the sides of his rear cheeks as muscles drove him deep.

Heat speared Juliette at the same precise moment, delving

farther inside her than she could have imagined her body might accept. Butting at the gate to her womb. The impact of it lifted her to her toes. She covered her mouth, trapping a cry in her palm.

In the park below, brawny sculpted haunches as sleek as those of a stallion relaxed then clenched, relaxed, clenched. Again and again and again.

She became his puppet, dancing to the tune of his slamming rut. It wasn't just her imagination. Her body was physically yielding—opening when he bucked forward and pursing when he relented. At the mercy of sensation, she had no desire other than to go where he led.

Her thighs trembled. The tissues of her core were wet, swollen, and invaded by the man who fucked another woman down in the park. She could almost smell his male musk and feel his fresh breath on her cheek.

Somewhere behind her, the chain of dancers had doubled back on itself, retracing its path to stir the crowds again. To her right, a businessman was telling a story involving oxen, and his companions were hooting with laughter. To her left, a horn player was tuning up and two ladies were engaged in an argument over a gentleman they both admired.

Yet through it all she heard the sounds of fevered coupling—of the man's velvet murmurs and harsh grunts and the woman's groans and demands. His words—words meant only for the ears of the woman he caressed—were rough and carnal. Words no man ever spoke to a lady. Words meant to urge them both toward release. They tickled Juliette's ear and sent her reaching desperately for . . . something.

The sensation gathered within her less quickly than she'd imagined it might, like a slow tightening of a screw that sent a wave of heat through her each time it turned. It was at the same time excruciating and exhilarating and she both feared and wanted what it promised. The other girls at Valmont's had described this to her—this hanging on a precipice of ecstasy. But until now, she'd never truly understood.

Every ounce of blood in her seemed to recede as she waited there, unfulfilled. A single tear fell, trickling down her cheek. Her white-knuckled fingers clenched between her breasts, gripping the crimson wool of her cloak as she bent at the railing, her entire body locked tight. A mere breath away from her first orgasm.

Then a hoarse, anguished shout split the air, and the man in the park climaxed. A simultaneous, feminine wail from his partner echoed his.

Oh, God!

The avid wave abruptly broke inside Juliette and blood went *whooshing* back through her system. Hurtling through every vein and artery, it all rushed toward one tempestuous goal. High between her legs, the shiny-pink, hidden heart of her swelled with it and gaped in a silent, passionate scream.

With a muffled cry, she came! In rolling, wracking spasms that pounded and tripped one upon the next, scarcely affording her time to breathe. Her nether mouth gulped and gasped and choked in an ecstatic, creamy rhythm. Her hand crept low and she cupped herself through her dress, trying to hold onto the rapture of it, and hoping no one would see.

This! This was what she'd yearned for.

Forgotten were the reasons she'd denied herself this for so long. Forgotten were the guilt and the pain of loss that had led her down a path of celibacy for the past three years.

The press of bodies behind her lessened intermittently, but she was unable to take advantage of any slack. She was frozen in place, helpless to escape, her inner thighs welded to one another, as her furious coming went on and on.

Below her the woman's face remained hidden and anonymous, but now the man had shifted so that her legs had become visible between his sprawled ones. There was something unnatural about the woman's body, Juliette realized. In disbelief, she watched her legs curve upward between his in an odd manner that bent them in the direction opposite that which knees normally went.

Her legs—they were conjoined! And they finished in a tail whose slender fins had curled themselves around the man's calf!

No! Don't look! She squeezed her eyes shut, fearing what might happen if she allowed her imagination to overtake her.

But it was too late.

Horrified, Juliette slapped both hands on her thighs, gripping their long muscles through her skirts. The flesh between them, from groin to knee, had begun to tingle and soften. To reshape. One limb had begun to kiss the other, longing to join in imitation of the creature lying under that man.

Pressing her palms together in a position of prayer, she wedged them, and by her action the fabric of her skirts as well, between her thighs. She dug and wiggled and poked. But in spite of her efforts, the inner seam was turning gelatinous. Fusing.

Her legs crumpled, refusing to support her. Quickly, she hooked both arms around the rail, gripping it for dear life.

She was transforming! It had been three years since anything like this had last happened! She'd assumed she'd outgrown the ability. The curse, as her foster mother had termed it.

Oh, why had she ventured out today? Why had she stayed out so late? Why had she let herself ogle this couple for so long?

The man in the park shifted again, suddenly revealing the face of the woman under him. A pair of feminine eyes the exact shape and sea-green color of her own met hers. The woman's hands froze on the sloping hollow of her lover's back as their shocked gazes tangled.

Recognition slid an icicle down Juliette's spine. Her throat worked. Then a single word escaped her.

"Elise?"

Her near-silent whisper was one no human could have heard in the midst of the uproar on the bridge. But even as the syllables still hovered on her lips, the masculine giant shuddered under their impact. Rising on his arms, he arched his back turning his face upward.

In his shadow the woman still regarded her in dismay. But Juliette saw only the man now.

Bathed in moonlight, he was a handsome pagan god. Amber eyes as bright as jewels that might have adorned the crown of Croesus were set in a face limned by the faint bluish-white glow of the skin of woman under him. His jaw was square cut, his nose aquiline, and his throat was thick and strong with a distinct Adam's apple. Framing his face, his hair was a tousled, gilded halo, washed in moonlight and damp at the temples from his exertion.

His gaze narrowed on Juliette as though he were trying to make out her features. Gasping, she fell back a step and hit the back of her head against someone's shoulder.

Once eye contact was broken, she was swiftly released from the strangers' spell and her body began trying to right itself. Swamped with dizziness and feeling like a well-loved rag doll, she drooped her head to lie upon her forearm along the rail. She took great gulps of air, filling her lungs and trying to regain a sense of normalcy. For the last few moments, she'd almost forgotten to breathe. No wonder she'd been lightheaded. And likely hallucinating.

"Madame, are you ill?" someone asked from nearby.

"Wh-what?"

She lifted her head to stare blankly at the gentleman's hand on her arm, then followed it to the face of an elderly, whiskered man with concerned eyes. Coming alive, she groped at the offer of assistance, clasping his sleeve in a death grip.

"*Oui,* I've twisted an ankle, monsieur." She had to shout in order to be heard above the din. "Can you assist me to my destination—the townhouse just across the quai there?"

"*Certainment!*" Her savior tucked her arm under his, giving it a comforting pat, then took the basket she nudged toward him with her foot.

Her legs quivered like wet pasta as she pushed off from the railing and she grasped him with both hands. They moved slowly at first as she tried to stave off any further transformation. Forcing her mind away from the scene she'd just witnessed would help, she was sure, so she counted her footsteps and ran mundane facts through her brain one after another trying to keep the memory at bay.

They passed King Henri and she informed her companion of every fact she'd learned about the statue over the past year. That he'd been cast from bronze obtained by the melting of two other effigies of France's former ruler, Napoleon. That official documents had been secreted within the statue's base. The man must've surely have thought her strange, but he only smiled and nodded, likely unable to catch every word anyway.

As her equilibrium returned, her legs firmed. They grew sturdy and dependable under her as they carried her away from the bridge and toward normalcy.

She had to get home. Once inside, the bizarre changes in her would reverse more quickly. Transformation was only possible to sustain under sky. Which was precisely why she preferred to spend her life indoors rather than out. Nothing suited her better than being neatly encased in a chamber constructed of brick and mortar topped by a slate roof.

Now they were moving along the Quai di Conti. Then she was up the steps, thanking her rescuer, and she was inside. Safe.

Or as close to it as she ever could be.

*   *   *

"Who the devil was that?" Lyon demanded. His incredulous eyes burned into Sibela's stunned ones.

"What?" she stuttered. "I don't know—"

He gave her a little shake. "That woman on the bridge. You recognized her. I saw it in your face."

Sibela's mouth opened and shut like a mackerel's as she obviously sought a convincing fabrication.

"Save your lies." He pulled from her channel with a lack of finesse he knew was appalling, but the sense of urgency that gripped him was so great that he did it anyway. In one lithe move, he was standing, straddling her with his feet planted on either side of her hips.

"I'll ask her myself," he said, yanking on his shirt.

Sibela drew herself up to kneel between his legs and grip his thighs, her expression beseeching. "She is nothing to us."

Lyon ruched up his trousers, wincing as he forced his still turgid cock inside and slid fastenings home. It had just achieved the most gratifying orgasm of its lecherous career, yet it was still angled high, at the ready.

Gods, what a night. "Stay here until I return," he grimly instructed his companion.

"Damnation!" Her angry fist aimed for his groin but was deflected and only hit his thigh when he jerked back in time. "I am your chosen one. Not her!"

He bent and lifted her so they stood eye to eye. "That remains to be seen."

"Bastard!" With her coming, her transformation had concluded and she tottered uncertainly before him on newly formed web-toed feet. Were she to remain on land now that the change was complete, all signs of her origins would soon fade. Her scales and luminescence would recede altogether until she appeared completely Human. Or near enough to pass.

Sibela wrapped desperate arms about his shoulders and lifted her lips to his ear. "If you must go, just first tell me this," she whispered. "Your seed. Was it potent?"

He wrested her claws from his neck and set her firmly away from him, giving her time to steady before he released her. "You know it wasn't. It couldn't be."

His eyes lifted to search the bridge rail. Nothing made him more eager to escape a scene such as this than a woman who clung. She had a right to be angry. Such post-coital behavior on his part was beyond ungentlemanly, but something was wrong here.

She was far too determined to keep him from the mysterious woman on the bridge, and he was conversely filled with an intense, inexplicable determination to find her.

"Do you forget that tomorrow night marks the conclusion of Bright Half?" she went on, referring to the two weeks of the monthly cycle in which the moon waxed. "You will need me then, when the full moon comes."

"Stay, Sibela. I'll return later." He flicked his fingers toward her in a gesture that bolstered the magic surrounding her. "Until then you'll remain undetectable by Human sight. But when next we speak, I'll want answers. Truthful ones."

"You dare speak to me as you would your dog? We have mated!" she shrieked. "You cannot leave me in this way. We are bound!"

Ignoring her, he turned and loped across the park. He'd already lost too much time and would not linger to untangle Sibela's lies now. Her claim to him was not as thorough as she might have wished and he suspected that, rather than any true feeling for him, was at the root of her shrewishness. For until they mated under the full Moon, any bond between them was not irrevocable.

By taking the southern staircase closest to the direction in which the woman on the bridge had gone, he avoided the crowds. But when he reached the Quai di Conti, her scent had already largely dissipated. He searched the air for the path she'd taken, for once wishing his olfactory abilities were as keen as those of his brothers.

Behind him, Sibela had commenced her screeching again. He grimaced. Bacchus, please let there be some mistake! Was he truly destined to be tied to such a female for a lifetime?

A door shut along the quai. He turned toward the sound and located the scent again. He tracked it past ten buildings and lost it just short of the stoop leading to a townhouse of plastered gray with a red door.

Had the pretty *voyeuse* he sought retreated here? Instinct had him taking the steps and rapping the knocker for admittance. If he was wrong, he was about to embarrass himself.

Almost immediately, the door was snatched open and a *majordome* appeared. When his gaze swept Lyon, his nose lifted and his lips curled into a sneer. He made to shut the door.

Lyon's palm smacked flat upon it, holding it wide. "I seek a word with the lady who just entered here . . ." Something beyond the man caught his attention. Just inside, a woman's wrap had been cast upon a hook. It was crimson red.

"Thee salon weel not beegin for one hour. At nine o'clock tonight," the man informed him with a supercilious sniff. He eyed Lyon up and down. "And eet eez by eenvitation onlee."

A rivulet of blood trickled down Lyon's neck and he mentally cringed, recalling his bedraggled state. His neck still stung from Sibela's claws and his shoulders were striped with welts where she'd gripped him as they'd mated. His shirt hung open and was sliced in ribbons, and his grass-stained trousers were damp with seawater.

He was probably not the sort of guest who normally called here.

The Human obstacle before him stepped back for greater leverage and again tried to close the door. Lyon's huge paw remained fast, preventing him. His other hand delved into his trouser pocket and whipped out an assortment of Tuscan *lire* and *soldi,* which he deposited inside the servant's vest without bothering to determine the amount of his offering. "I believe you'll find that to be adequate invitation," he informed him. "I'll expect to be allowed in when I return."

The *majordome* patted his bulging vest pocket, peeked inside it, and then favored him with a grudging nod. "Onlee eef you are suitablee attired. And do not bring your entourage."

Lyon straightened and looked over his shoulder, surprised to see that an assortment of women loitered there, some openly ogling him and others doing the same in a more circumspect manner. Behind him, the door shut with a haughty *snick.*

He took the steps and strode back into the lane, sighing when his admirers decided to trail him. He was weary of this inexplicable Human attention and he had no time for it. He was a mess, and he had but one hour to get himself to his hotel, clean himself up, and return.

"I'm not what you want," he murmured to the group at large. Sending a light mindspell over the women, he crossed the quai not waiting to see them disband.

At the park's edge, he glanced back toward the gray house. A curtain twitched at a window on the top floor. Someone watched him. Was it the woman from the bridge? Such an attic window would most likely open to servants' quarters. Was she a maid or a governess?

Was she the woman who'd just given him the hardest orgasm of his life?

He would find out at nine o'clock tonight.

3

Reaching her solitary bedchamber in the rafters at the front of the house she so despised, Juliette soundlessly shut her door behind her. Without lighting a candle, she hurried to the single window along the wall and, taking care to keep herself hidden, pulled back the curtain's edge to peer down toward the quai.

She gasped. There he was! That man she'd seen from the bridge was loitering on the front sidewalk, studying the house. Now that he stood upright, she could see he truly was a giant. A disheveled one.

His tattered shirt was misbuttoned and damp with dew and sweat. It faithfully molded shoulders nearly twice as broad as her own and a muscled torso that rivaled the mythical statues carved on the Palais de Justice. Thoughts of that place sent a shiver over her.

Her breath hitched as she watched him disappear up the front steps and heard the door open for him. His coming here was no accident. He'd seen her on the bridge and followed her. Why? What did he want? Was it simple curiosity? Or, even worse, was it possible he was one of her persecutors and she'd inadvertently led him here?

In semi-darkness, she groped along the wall until she reached the washstand. Her hand found the vial there and by ease of practice, she splashed wine into a glass and squeezed a small dose of the vial's tincture into it. Though she craved more, she limited herself, for she'd need her wits later tonight. She swallowed it in one gulp and returned to the window.

Long moments later, the man reappeared below her again on the sidewalk. The servants had rebuffed him!

Her gaze followed him as he crossed the quai and continued on. Her emotions were in such a tangle that she wasn't sure whether to be glad of his departure or not. Then he paused unexpectedly at the park's edge and turned to look up at her window.

Swiveling on the ball of one foot, she fell back against the wall and put a hand over her thumping heart. How long would he remain out there?

It didn't matter, she told herself. She rarely left the house and Monsieur Valmont's watchdogs were fierce. That stranger could watch this window for the next year for all she cared.

Ridiculous. As if he would. He'd affected her far more than she'd likely affected him. She was glad he'd gone, she decided.

Sliding down the wall, she crouched on her heels hugging her drawn-up knees. The drops were already beginning to warm her, dulling the sharp corners of reality. As usual, they had another effect—making her long for what she would not seek. A man's touch.

Remembered sensation still hummed deep inside her most private feminine crevice. The wanting was worst than usual.

Because of him.

What had happened out there? How had it come to pass that she—the only female in the house who'd never had a man between her legs—had been violated by one tonight?

A horrible thought struck her.

Oh, God! Had he taken her first blood?! She hadn't even considered that possibility. Stupid. Stupid!

Her knees hit the floor. She hunched her back as one hand dove under her skirts. Gingerly, she slipped a finger high between her legs, searching. The private folds gating her channel were slick. Juices, sticky and heady, coated her inner thighs.

He'd done this to her, made her body sob for him. Her forefinger dipped inside, a little deeper. Oh, please, please, where was it? Then her fingertip gently butted against what she sought. The delicate membrane. Her hymen. It still held.

She slumped in relief, more confused than ever. Withdrawing her hand, she wiped it on the linen that hung from her washstand. Had his shaft—or something of him—truly come inside her or not?

Pushing from the floor, she stood to peek out of the window again. The man was nowhere to be seen. She pressed her forehead to the cool windowpane, searching the quai more thoroughly. He was gone.

If only it had been possible to find out what he knew without a face-to-face conversation with him. But such a meeting would be impossible to arrange, even if he returned again.

She could just imagine asking Valmont's servants to question him: Pardonnez-moi, monsieur, *but could you tell me the identity of the woman you lay with tonight under the bridge? And also if you would be so kind, can you tell me if you are able to supply orgasms to women without touching them? Mademoiselle Juliette wishes to know.*

Absurd!

Looking east, her eyes located a familiar building—the Hospice des Enfants Trouvés—The Hospital of Found Children. Its spires pricked heavenward like great thorns, prodding her with painful memories. She let the thin curtain fall closed to obscure them and stood very still, almost afraid to breathe.

"*Je ne suis pas folle,*" she whispered unsteadily. "I am not insane. I am not."

It had been three years since most of the magic had left her.

Three years since she'd last transformed in the way her body had attempted to just moments ago.

Three years since she'd been accused of murder and lost the person most dear to her in this world.

Her gaze went to the second floorboard from the wall beside her bed. On legs that were still unsure, she went to kneel there. Darting a look at the door, she reassured herself it was shut. There was no privacy lock, so she turned her back toward it and listened for footsteps.

Pushing on one end of the wooden slat raised its other end revealing a leather pouch secreted below. She pulled it out, opened it, and lifted a strand of olive-shaped beads from among the coins within.

Raising one bent knee, she draped the necklace over it so its ends dangled on either side, then ran her fingers over each bone bead. There were precisely seventeen of them, strung on a long silken cord, which had looped her neck until she was sixteen years of age. When Valmont had bade her to put aside such things.

Her fingers found the thick pewter and iron medal tied at one end of the cord. A picture of Saint Vincent de Paul was engraved on one side and the flip side bore identifying information in the form of two numbers: 1804 and 8900.

In the year 1804, she'd been the 8,900th child abandoned at the Hospice des Enfants Trouvés. Though it was less than an hour's walking distance from here, she'd visited only once, during the first week she'd returned to Paris a year ago. It had been more painful than expected and she'd avoided it since. But every day it haunted her from where it stood in the distant shadow of the Cathédral Notre Dame.

That she was illegitimate was a virtual certainty. That her

mother had never planned to come back to the hospital for her was as well. She'd left no notes or identifying tokens as had been tucked in the blankets of some of the other abandoned children. She had no way of knowing if her mother had done the deed alone, but she'd always assumed her father had not accompanied her, since that was the usual story with orphans.

Upon her arrival at the foundling hospital, the only known facts of her origins had been faithfully entered into the large recording book, the Registre d'Admission. Sex: female. Age: one day. Name: Juliette. There were also notations that included a brief description of her clothing and blanket. And she'd learned the actual day of her birth, something she hadn't known. She would be nineteen next month.

It seemed that sometime in the wee hours of December 20, 1804, she'd been birthed, bathed, and wrapped in blankets of fine wool before being deposited upon the hospital's infamous "tour." This stone wheel lay flat on its side, serving as a rotating turntable set in an aperture in the building's exterior wall. A wooden box, which acted as a makeshift cradle, rested upon the half of the wheel that was exposed outside the wall. It would have been a simple matter for her mother to stealthily and anonymously place her there, inside the box.

Had her mother wept as she turned the wheel? Had she watched until the cradle—and her baby within it—had been entirely re-situated on the inside of the hospital? Before leaving, she would have rung a bell alerting the Sisters of Charity that yet another deposit of an unwanted, pink-faced infant had been made.

Juliette gathered the beads in her fist and held them tight. Her heart cried out for the loss of the page that had been stolen from her today. Not wanting anyone to question her about it, she had only quickly scanned it. Then she'd tucked it in her basket, planning to later scrutinize it at leisure, here in her private room.

It had been a silly, costly whim to have it stolen in the first place. But from the moment she'd learned of the book's existence, she'd longed to know whatever details of her beginnings it contained. Another orphan might've been allowed to view his or her personal information, but she dared not reveal her identity at the hospital and risk being turned over to authorities.

She had not expected to be surprised by anything she read on that page, but she had been.

For directly below her name, there had been another, familiar one.

Elise.

A sharp rapping came at her door, causing her to jump.

"*Mademoiselle?*"

"*Un moment!*" Juliette hastily replaced the necklace in its box and then the box in its hiding place. Her *domestique* had arrived to fuss over her. In less than one hour, she was expected downstairs. And then tonight's performance would begin.

"Sweet victory," Monsieur Valmont murmured from beside Juliette.

Her breath caught as she peered at the new arrival through the decorative punched-metal screen. It was he. The man from the bridge. The one who'd given her her first orgasm.

Wasn't it? She leaned closer to the grillwork trying to get a better look through the perforations.

From the privacy of this upstairs nook, she and Valmont observed the golden giant who'd entered the salon below them on the main floor of the townhouse. Only snatches of conversation, music from the harpist, and tinkling laughter reached them here so they didn't hear his introduction. Two dozen other gentlemen had already gathered in the salon before him, and a dozen more would likely come before the evening was done.

Agnes, Gina, Fleur, and the other girls circulated among them, all brightly gowned coquettes who knew how to flirt, flatter, and fornicate. M. Valmont always sent them down first to work the group and build anticipation in preparation for her entrance. They were the appetizers, he liked to say. And she, the main course.

In moments Juliette and Valmont would join the assemblage and she would hold court under his keen supervision. But for now, they lingered here to discuss the patrons with a frankness that would have been impossible in a more public venue.

"I'd hoped he might come. But I dared not expect him," Valmont continued as the new arrival made his way into the room.

"Who is he?" Juliette enquired, carefully concealing any sign of recognition. When her companion didn't reply, she glanced his way and saw he was so fixated on his surveillance of the man that he hadn't even heard her.

In the center of the room below, the giant paused to contemplate the bubbling of the marble absinthe fountain. Valmont had installed it when they'd arrived in Paris a year ago and it had become a popular feature of these gatherings. Since the blight had devastated vineyards throughout Europe over the last decade, wine was in short supply. As a result, its cost had risen and this had ignited great interest in the less expensive absinthe as a substitute.

When Fleur approached the new guest with an offer of refreshment, he allowed her to divert him toward the wine cart. Though she was but sixteen and was fairly new to the household, Valmont had recently decided to involve her in the business rather than keep her to the kitchen, much to Juliette's dismay. However, delighted with her new finery and increased income, Fleur had taken to the work of pleasuring men with surprising ease.

The man smiled indulgently down at Fleur as she filled his glass and chattered away. Grinning, she linked a hand through his arm and proceeded to flirt in her usual engaging manner, doing her best to attract him before one of the others did.

In profile, his features were strong—a granite jaw, straight brow, and prominent, well-shaped nose. These were only slightly tempered by sensual lips, cheekbones flushed with good health, and glorious disorderly hair of many shimmering golden shades that hung almost to the line of his jaw.

Juliette willed him to glance her way, so she might furtively study his face full on, but he didn't.

"Who is he?" she asked again.

Valmont twitched at the question and she realized he'd completely forgotten her presence until she'd spoken.

"Lord Lyon Satyr." He tapped the fingertips of both hands together under his chin in tiny soundless claps. He sounded almost giddy.

"Lyon." Turning back to the screen, Juliette tasted the name, exploring its shape and texture in her mouth and testing its flavor on her tongue. It suited him.

Valmont returned to his study as well. "Is the name familiar to you?"

He was testing her. The purpose for which they met here prior to these Thursday night soirées was to allow him to school her on the backgrounds of his guests. He made it his business to know every detail of their circumstances and fortunes. Operating on motives unknown to her, he was always ready with instruction regarding whom to flirt with and what information to elicit. It was usually left to her to determine the manner best calculated to achieve his goals.

Juliette's brow knit. "An Italian with his surname came to Paris several months ago, did he not? A vintner from Tuscany?"

Beside her, Valmont nodded, pleased she'd remembered. "A cold fish, that one—Raine Satyr, the middle son of three. Unfortunately he departed Paris before he could be reeled in." He gestured toward the room below. "This one tonight is the youngest of the brothers at twenty-six years. There is another in Tuscany—the eldest of them, who has recently wed. After years of fucking anything that moves, all three have recently confounded the gossips by commencing bride searches."

She soaked up this news of him and wanted more. "Are they attractive prospects?"

"Exceedingly. Among them, they own vast holdings—estates, an immense flourishing vineyard, and coffers overflowing with inherited riches."

"Their vineyards still flourish?" Juliette asked, glancing at him in surprise. "Untouched by the phylloxera?"

Valmont's expression twisted with bitterness. "*Oui.* Though it's beyond anyone's understanding why that should be so. And it's certainly beyond all fairness."

In the salon, Fleur had been supplanted on the newcomer's arm by the more aggressive Gina, who was giving him a tour of Valmont's art collection. The hoard of busts, statues, oils, and watercolors was but a small fraction of what his family had once owned. However, it and the rest of the items in the other rooms here were all he'd been able to abscond with before his Burgundy château had been recently claimed by taxmen.

Juliette had been there to watch his once-affluent father's vast winemaking enterprises in Burgundy felled by the phylloxera over the years. It had been among the first of the many to succumb to the ravages of the aphid-like pest, which had gone on to decimate many of Europe's vineyards.

His father had killed himself over the debacle. This townhouse, the smallest property of the many his family had once owned, was now all Valmont possessed of his father's legacy. And he'd filled it with prostitutes to provide his income.

She could almost pity him because of the reversal of fortune the pest had wrought in his family and in his life. Almost. But not quite.

As he escorted Gina, Satyr's panther gait was masculine, easy, and loose-limbed. It reminded her of how she'd seen him in the park, moving on that other woman. Of how she'd felt him moving inside her. Goosebumps rose on her arms.

If he was indeed the same man as the one she'd seen earlier tonight at Pont Neuf, he'd changed his clothing in the last hour. Wool trousers dyed the color of mustard seed faithfully molded his derriere with each shift of his hips or step of his booted feet. These were paired with a natural linen cambric shirt and a casual jacket of drab olive. It was an attractive look on him, but so profoundly *démodé* that it could never have been considered modish in the first place by anyone of society.

Nevertheless, she saw how Agnes and the others eyed him. Against a backdrop of dandified peacocks, he stood out as a brawny, earthy animal in his prime. One who chose his own path and was confident enough not to bow too deeply to the whims of style.

For a man so large, he moved with sleek grace. But even as she made this observation, he contradicted it. She gasped as his elbow caught on the outstretched bow of a statue, sending it rocking. It was a sculpture of Diana, Roman goddess of the hunt, a favorite subject of Valmont's.

Large pawlike hands caught at the wobbling goddess. An awkward juggling act ensued in which he fondled various portions of her anatomy before ultimately rescuing her from peril and returning her safely to her pedestal.

The attention of everyone in the room now on him, the giant rolled his shoulders and heaved a great sigh as though accustomed to causing such calamities in salons. His words didn't reach their hiding place, but whatever he said sent laughter rippling over the room.

"A man who can laugh at himself—a rare animal," murmured Juliette.

"Buffoon," Valmont muttered. "He'll pay for that if it's damaged. Among other things."

Juliette turned her head in time to surprise a vengeful expression on his face. "What do you mean?"

Avoiding a direct reply, he eyed her thoughtfully. "You will favor him tonight. All those years you lived on the fringes of my family's vineyard should be to your advantage in snaring his interest. Flatter him and draw him out regarding his work."

"What precisely do you wish me to glean from my conversation with him?" she asked guardedly.

"Any details about the inner workings of his estate. Any weaknesses in him or in his family. Ask the source of his vines' immunity to the phylloxera epidemic. If they've been infected and cured by some secret remedy, I want to know of it."

"And you think he'll simply tell me all this for the asking?"

"Dazzle him in your usual way," Valmont went on, flicking his fingers in the air as if to whisk away her incredulity. He turned to quit their hiding place, indicating it was time to descend to the salon. "Show him the rooms. Whatever it takes to keep him with you long enough to pump him for information."

"The rooms? But you never ask that of me! Usually only Agnes or Gina or one of the others . . ." Stunned by his request, she turned blindly back to her study of the salon below.

Abruptly a pair of jeweled amber eyes cut to the nook where she was hidden. A wave of erotic awareness prickled over her.

God! It was him! She stepped back, knocking against Valmont. Recoiling from the contact, she whipped around accidentally brushing against the screen. For an instant, the grillwork singed her shoulder blade in that confusing metallic way that made it impossible to determine if it was chilling or heating her skin.

Catching her arm, Valmont jerked her away from it to study her face. Obviously disliking what he read there, he pulled her close and lifted her chin, brushing a dangerously gentle thumb along the underside of her jaw. She hunched her shoulders to keep her breasts from grazing the front of his jacket.

"You find him attractive?"

She shrugged, erasing all expression from her face. "You know I never take particular interest in any gentleman."

"Your cheeks are flushed," he accused.

"Only because it's warm."

His face loomed closer. Absinthe-soaked breath soughed in and out of him. The heady licorice scent of anise reached her, unmistakable at close range.

She cringed inwardly, but was careful not to reveal her distaste as cold, moist lips touched hers. Once, as a girl, she'd thought him handsome and good and she'd wanted his kiss. How foolish she'd been.

Heedless of the roomful of guests that waited for them below, he brushed his mouth over hers, back and forth. "Such an attraction would be understandable," he murmured. "He *is* handsome. And rich, with an impeccable title. The names of Satyr scions have been inscribed in the registers at the *Libro d'Oro della Nobiltà Italiana* for centuries."

"If you don't trust my word on my feelings, how can you trust me to be alone with him?"

"You won't be alone. I hire many eyes to watch for me in this house and elsewhere. I'm well aware that women are wicked and untrustworthy by nature. You more than most."

"That's untrue. You know it is."

Fingers slid under her hair and gripped her nape to hold her and underscore her entrapment. A pale hand found her breast in a hard massage meant to hurt. She clutched at his hand, but his grip only tightened. His eyes smiled into hers, daring her to rebel.

"Your mother abandoned you—something only the lowest slut would do to her child. What's bred in the bone . . ."

"You're hurting," she gritted.

He ignored her. "You *will* take Satyr to the back rooms if he requests it. In fact, *you* will suggest such a move. You will elicit the information I desire. And no matter what pressure he applies, you will resist the temptation to whore for him."

His kissed her then, eagerly sampling her powerlessness. His tongue struck, filling her mouth and nearly choking her on her own revulsion. Her hands dropped, fisting at her sides.

Finally he seemed to remember their guests. He drew away.

"Gina, Fleur, and the others are not what our patrons come for, you know," he said, cupping her face. "It's you they want. Though beautiful women proliferate here in Paris, something about you draws men like bees to your honey pot. Little do they know it's dry and unused, eh? More fools they."

His reptilian tongue stroked over the seam of his lips, as though savoring a last taste of her. Pulling a square of linen from his pocket, he delicately dabbed his mouth and turned away to stare through the screen again.

"Go to your chamber and make yourself presentable."

She stared at his back, imagining herself striking a dagger into it. But instead she only scurried off, despising herself for a coward. She hadn't always been so.

"Don't take too long," he warned as she slipped through the door.

By the time she reached her room, she was breathing hard from her rush and from frustrated anger.

With trembling fingers, she splashed wine into a glass, then opened the vial on her washstand and extracted a measure of laudanum. It fell from the dropper's tip into the wine, like tears on blood. She stirred the tincture with the dropper and drank.

She didn't meet her eyes in the mirror as she scrubbed the rouge from her lips and refreshed it. She didn't like herself at the moment. Wouldn't like herself again until she left Valmont and this place far behind. With any luck, that day would come soon.

The pleasant floating feeling, which the tincture could be re-
lied upon to supply, slowly began to enfold her in its calming
caress. She rolled her neck in a languid circle.

Umm. It was pleasurable sensation not unlike a much gen-
tler version of the orgasm the golden giant had supplied earlier
today.

Sighing, she powdered her cheeks and straightened her hair
and gown, primping like an actress about to go on stage.

"First time here?" a heavily accented male voice enquired at
Lyon's elbow.

Lyon swirled the wine in his glass, studying its sparkle as
candlelight danced through its amber depths. Not a Satyr Vineyard label, he noted absently. Still, the *Clairette* his host had
served was adequate and no doubt meant to dull his wits and
lure him into bidding generously on tonight's prize.

And bid he would. For whatever the cost, he intended to
win the jewel on offer here—one Mademoiselle Juliette Rabelais, who it seemed was a courtesan.

Eyes that were the precise color of the wine he drank rose to
observe her where she perched on a tufted chaise across the
room. From beneath her dark lashes, a flash of sea green flickered, then darted away. She'd been watching him.

Her remarkable eye color was identical to Sibela's. The
shape of their faces and their features were strikingly similar as
well. So much so that it couldn't be coincidence. This one and
the Nereid had to be related.

Incredibly, it appeared that King Feydon had spawned four
daughters instead of the three his letter had indicated. Did this
woman know she had a sister? As he lay dying, had Feydon
known? It would have been typical of his tricks to take the secret to his grave.

Lyon nodded an assent in the general direction of the Cossack who'd spoken to him, responding to his question belatedly and without words. These flamboyant Russians in their fleece hats and wide trousers were rife in Paris these days, lingering long after they'd come to help the allies repel Napoleon.

After the one called Agnes had given up on him, Lyon had sensed the Russian's approach and had deduced a great deal about him without so much as a glance in his direction. His boots had been recently polished with bear grease, he wore a tonic on his mustache, and his body reeked of desire. This last made him no different than any other gentleman in this salon.

Though less acute than that of his brothers, Lyon's olfactory sense was far more finely honed than that of any Human. Which made it all the more bizarre that he could detect nothing of Mademoiselle Rabelais's scent.

Yet he'd detected a scent from the female voyeur on the bridge. Weren't the women one and the same? It was puzzling and he had no patience for more puzzles.

Perhaps if he made his way closer. No. It was that sort of rambling that had very nearly led to the demise of a statue earlier. Numerous other *objets d'art* were displayed along the path to her. Better to maintain his position and hope she approached him. He'd been here nearly an hour and she was the only female in the room who hadn't.

The Cossack spoke again, raising his glass in a caricature of a toast. "Good luck to you then. I've attended these salons every Thursday for the past three months and still haven't won a turn in that one's bed. My pockets are deep enough, so I can only assume it's my pedigree that Mademoiselle Rabelais's guardian finds objectionable."

Lyon's gaze narrowed on their host, Monsieur Valmont, the apparent owner of these apartments. A tall, slender man with preternaturally white hair, he was handsome, Lyon supposed. But so pale that he put him in mind of a portrait his eldest brother had in his vast collection. The one that depicted Vlad the Impaler, a Romanian prince with an infamous past and an appetite for blood.

He returned his gaze to the more pleasant perspective of Juliette Rabelais. One of ten women set amid nearly three dozen men, she was the obvious trophy. She was one of those women whose every gesture put him in mind of the soft slide of a velvet drape across warm flesh—soothing, lush, and full of sexual promise. Something about her was hypnotic. Watching her was a pleasure he could quickly grow accustomed to.

As if she were blithely unaware that every man in this luxurious salon panted after her, she serenely held court on her satin throne, like an orchid set among a besotted cast of dandified thistles, pigweed, and toadflax.

"Six months for me and still nothing," a Frenchman on the Cossack's other side commiserated. "Why I still come is *un mystère.*" He gazed into the depths of his glass, then back at the green-eyed object of his desire as though unable to prevent himself.

Lyon never understood this sort of talk from men. Like his brothers, he had a voracious appetite for the company of women, both in and out of bed. But though he had come to Paris specifically to locate his bride and had to his amazement found two candidates rather than one, he was under no illusion that Juliette Rabelais would fell his heart any more than Sibela had.

Conversation ebbed around him and her voice reached his ears. His hand tightened on his glass. Hearing an attractive, available woman speak in French was almost guaranteed to gift him with an erection. Particularly a woman with almond hair and a long white throat. Particularly one whose every deliciously accented syllable caused her lips to purse as though she were kissing the air. Particularly a woman he planned to bed.

That decision had been made for him the moment he'd

scented her on the bridge. Then, when she'd spoken, he'd felt something inside himself shift. Unlock. Open.

In that instant, even as he lay atop another woman, a need to protect this one had been born within him. A need to keep her from want. A need to bury his heated, straining cock so deep inside her that she would be forever branded as his.

Here was the intense, immediate attraction he'd not found with Sibela. But of course, it wasn't love.

"If you wish to visit Valmont's back rooms, approach one of the girls for hire," yet another Frenchman volunteered. "Negotiations for the favors of Mademoiselle Juliette are done in a different manner than for the others."

Lyon cocked his head. "How so?"

The first Frenchman eyed him, obviously beginning to worry all this coaching might lead Lyon to usurp his own chances with her. "Such arrangements are made through M. Valmont," he said with reluctance. "Ask about her culinary talents. You'll only waste your breath if you directly request that she visit your bed. If an agreement for her favors is made, it's understood she'll serve you at your table as well as in your boudoir."

"It's said that she sets a table comparable to some of the finest chefs in all of Paris," someone chimed in.

"It's likely true if these *éclairs* are anything to judge by," said the second Frenchman as he lifted one from his plate. He consumed the pastry with a single gulp of his greedy mouth. "And have you tried the cream-filled baguettes?"

"If I ever get Mademoiselle Rabelais to myself she is more than welcome to suck the cream from my baguette," the Cossack groused darkly into his glass.

This was met with a burst of randy, good-natured guffaws from his companions. Except for Lyon, who shifted all six and a half feet of his muscular form toward the man, sending a crystal, swan-shaped bowl on the pedestal between them tumbling to the floor in the process.

"I'm certain you must have business elsewhere that calls you away from this establishment. I suggest you attend to it." Amber glinted dangerously, coloring his words.

The Cossack's eyes widened and his drink sloshed as he sidled away. "Pardon me—I must . . . yes, I . . ." Without finishing, he strode off, his boots tripping in his haste to put distance between himself and Lyon's annoyance.

The others drifted off on various excuses as well, wary of him now. He stared into his wine, shocked at himself. And a little embarrassed. He'd never been jealous about a woman in his life.

If he was testy, it was likely due to the frustrations of the evening and anticipation of Moonful, he reassured himself. His blood was already quickening in preparation for tomorrow night's Calling, and he was more easily roused to lechery, anger— and jealousy, apparently.

He looked up, toward the woman across the room. Her eyes darted away. She'd been watching him again. Could she handle what he would become tomorrow? Would she, willingly?

With a curl of her delicate wrist, the tip of her painted Chinese fan traced her collarbone, then drifted lower toward the ripe curve of a porcelain breast. More than one male eye followed its downward path.

She was dressed to tempt, in a shimmering gown the color of her hair with silver edging along a neckline that barely concealed her nipples. A frown creased his brow. No doubt even those were on display to the man seated beside her, if the direction of his eyes were any indication. He and every other man in the room studied the shift of her breasts as she turned, evading his overly familiar hand.

He realized he'd begun staring at her in a manner he feared was as besotted as his previous companions and his fist tightened on the fragile stem of his glass. That she'd had other men before him mattered not a whit. Considering the inauspicious circumstances of their prior meeting, he could only hope she would be as generous toward him.

His gaze slid over her bodice and traveled boldly lower. In another venue, he'd have been more circumspect, but everyone here knew her body was on exhibition. He studied the drape of her skirts, looking forward to discovering the shape of her below them, for a woman's derriere held her greatest attraction for him.

Never mind a blushing cheek or pretty lips. Give him a nicely rounded ass and he was more than content with that asset alone.

Mademoiselle Rabelais chose that moment to rise to her feet and see to one of her duties as hostess. Leaving the men on the dais to their own conversation, she went to survey the food displayed on the side table.

Lyon saw his chance and took it.

4

Juliette stiffened, noting the golden giant's approach with her peripheral vision. Visiting the sideboard to determine if anything was amiss or needed replenishment offered an occasional respite from admirers.

However, coming this way had been an intentional maneuver, intended to draw him out. In the opening gambit of flirtation, it was her opinion that it was always wise to let men come to her rather than the opposite.

As she straightened a tray, she felt the warmth of him at her back and a charge of excitement zinged through her. Was he the man she'd watched under the bridge? If so, would he recognize her?

Hesitantly, she turned, fearing he would prove to be odious or boring. Or a complete stranger.

"*Mademoiselle,*" he greeted. "We meet again."

He didn't bow, but she didn't notice.

Time seemed to slow and the clink of crystal and rap of conversation to cease as cool green tangled with warm amber. Silently, curiously they weighed one another.

Though she'd only seen them once and for brief seconds in twilight, she'd have known those eyes anywhere. They were the eyes of the very man who'd supplied her first orgasm. Without touching her. Outside on the bridge. As she'd stood in the midst of hundreds of other people.

He'd recognized her. So it followed that he must also be aware that she'd seen him half-naked, fornicating with another woman. Even though he was the one who should be embarrassed, she was the one who blushed.

At close quarters, he was even more potently beautiful. A ruggedly masculine angel, all brawn and confidence and a full head taller than she with massive shoulders that blocked the rest of the room from view. His gaze was intelligent and warm and the curve of his mouth invited her—and likely every woman he chanced to meet, she cautioned herself—to join him in some secret carnal amusement.

With those muscles and big hands . . . and that appendage of his . . . he had likely pleased legions of females. Did he know what his body had done to hers? Would he dare attempt it again here and now? Her eyes dilated and she tingled with a dangerous desire to press against him and beg him to do exactly that.

The splash and gurgle of the fountain jolted her back to her surroundings. Flustered, she put a hand to her cheek—she'd taken too much of the tincture tonight.

How was she to speak to a man who had sexual knowledge of her, yet to whom she had never been introduced? Bon soir, monsieur. Merci beaucoup *for giving me my first orgasm a few hours ago. And by the by, how did you do it without laying a finger on me?*

It sounded insane, even to her own ears. She would avoid all mention of that subject, she decided, at least for the present. After all, Valmont's agenda dictated that she discuss other matters first. And his spies would be listening.

"*Pardonnez moi? Je ne comprends pas,*" she asked in pretended confusion.

"*Nous nous rencontrons encore,*" Lyon repeated, this time in French.

Not such a buffoon as Valmont seemed to believe, after all. Had he underestimated this one?

Cocking her head, she touched the tip of her painted fan to her chin, considering him.

"I'm afraid I don't recall a prior meeting. We've been here a year now and so many come to our Thursday gatherings. But naturally I'm pleased you've chosen to return to us." Knowing M. Valmont was undoubtedly observing them, she remembered to flash a flirtatious grin.

"You were on the bridge tonight," he announced without warning.

Stunned for a second, she emitted a guilty, "*Oui.*" Quickly, she rearranged her expression, widening her eyes and raising her brows in an attempt to appear guileless. "You were there? It was quite a tangle and I'm afraid I didn't notice you. Still, I'm pleased you've come, as I said. I hope we can tempt you. With a truffle perhaps?"

Setting a hand on his sleeve she turned his attention to the buffet. *Lord! His forearm was as thick as her calf!*

"Or a canapé? Or if you have a sweet tooth, a custard and raspberry tart? I prepared everything myself earlier today with the assistance of the cookstaff." Gesturing, she indicated the sideboards groaning with platters of refreshments she'd concocted. "I confess I'm a bit of an experimenter in the kitchen and never know if I've created a masterpiece or a disaster. You must sample a variety and tell me how successful I've been. You're a large man. I imagine your appetites for many things must be equally sizeable."

The corners of his lips tilted upward. *Were those dimples?*

"I assure you they are," he said.

She blinked in surprise, before realizing he hadn't read her thoughts but was only making a reply.

Feu d'enfer! She'd never seen a more angelic, devilish man. The dichotomy was lethal. No wonder the other girls had vied so diligently for him. Agnes, who was far more beautiful than she, was glowering at her even now for having snagged his attention.

Dragging her eyes from his seductive smile, she gave herself a mental scolding as she selected one of the silver trays etched with flourishes and an ornate V shaped monogram. Valmont had stationed her here for the sole purpose of interrogating this man. The quicker she accomplished that, the sooner she could retire to her room and leave him to Agnes and the other man-hungry sharks who enjoyed swimming in these waters far more than she.

As she lifted the tray by its olivewood handles and turned toward him, her breasts rested on its edge as though they, too, were on offer. Cut far too low for decency, her gown and others like it were an important part of her arsenal. While men were distracted by their survey of her bosom, she was quick to take their measure.

"Do try some, Monsieur Satyr," she said, gazing up at him through her lashes.

But as he lifted a delicacy at random from the salver, his eyes remained on hers, not taking the visual bait. It confounded her, shaking her confidence. Wasn't he attracted to her? Of course he was. For some reason, men had been all of her life. And why else would he have sought her out?

"You know who I am," he said.

"Your name was made known to me by another gentleman earlier tonight." She favored him with an engaging smile sure to please the ever-vigilant Valmont.

As Lyon bit into the truffle, surprised interest lit his eyes and he held the *hors d'oeuvre* away to examine the remainder of it before he finished it off. "You made this?"

Intense satisfaction rose in her. Pleasing a man with the sharing of her culinary efforts was as close as she ever allowed herself to come to pleasing him with the sharing of her body. Bridge encounters notwithstanding.

"*Oui.* With the assistance of the kitchen staff, as I mentioned." She leaned closer and confided, "The secret ingredient is a pinch of Chile pepper. The spicy with the sweet. I was fortunate to find some dried espelettes in *Les Halles* last week. And I thought—why not try them in the truffles?"

Lyon picked up another truffle and downed it as well, closing his eyes in ecstasy. "Delicious!" he proclaimed.

He didn't try to impress her with a volley of effusive compliments as most men did. She returned the tray to the sideboard and needlessly adjusted the already-perfect display there in order to hide how much his relish had delighted her. "I can copy the recipe for your wife if you wish."

"Alas, I'm unwed."

"Your chef then," she said, pleased that she would at least be able to confirm his marital status when she next spoke to Valmont.

"Actually, with our auction looming, I could very well use your advice . . ."

She missed the rest of his reply when a boisterous trio arrived to sample the offerings at the opposite end of the buffet. It was Fleur, with two besotted gentlemen in tow. The girl shot Juliette a mischievous grin. Hoping to eavesdrop no doubt. The minx.

One of her admirers was Monsieur Arlette, a particular friend of Valmont's. He no doubt planned to do the same. She stiffened as his gimlet eyes swept her. She would have to guard her words.

Beside her, Lyon took a sip of wine, seemingly oblivious to the intrigue swirling around them. She sensed he was about to quiz her further about subjects she'd rather avoid within Arlette's hearing. Valmont sought revelations and gossip from this man and she'd better set about obtaining them.

"Shall I replenish your wine?" she asked, hoping to segue into a discussion of his vineyard.

"No." His fingers covered the top of the glass. "Thank you."

She fluttered her fan in the direction the marble absinthe fountain in the center of the room. "Would you prefer *La Fée Verte*—The Green Fairy—then?" Daringly, she tucked a hand in the crook of his elbow, urging him into action. Anything to get him away from Fleur, whom she suspected was about to do something scandalous. And anything to hie him away from Arlette's big ears as well.

Lyon glanced toward the fountain, with its chilled water trickling merrily from its spigots into the shallow trough that encircled it. The Cossack had set a glass partly filled with absinthe below one of the spigots and now stood waiting as water diluted the liquor, rendering its strong taste more palatable.

Setting his drink on the buffet behind her, Lyon took her other arm and drew her close. "I would prefer to discuss what happened at the bridge earlier tonight."

Heat singed her cheeks and she shook her head. "Not here," she whispered.

His expression filled with the understanding that they were being observed. "Where then?"

Fleur let out a small shriek, drawing their eyes. To Juliette's dismay, the girl had allowed one of her beaus to lower the front of her bodice to expose a breast. He was now in the process of buttering its nipple with a silver knife dipped in pâté Juliette had made earlier that very day. Fleur braced both hands behind her, amid the platters on the buffet, and her head fell back, displaying a slender throat.

Juliette's eyes widened with reluctant fascination. This kind of flagrantly erotic activity was usually reserved for the rooms in the back, so she didn't often witness such things.

The knife swirled back and forth, hypnotizing her. What must it be like to have that cold silver burnishing one's nipple in such a manner? she wondered. She could almost feel its brand. Her hand lifted toward her own breast before she registered what she was doing and caught herself.

She looked up at Lyon. He'd been watching her observe the sexual byplay. Her fingers were now gripping his arm hard enough to leave marks. She withdrew them, letting her hands fall to her sides.

Lyon's eyes twinkled. "A friend of yours?" His face was an open and undeceitful one, she realized. Unlike hers. She wanted to warn him to run far from here before Valmont did him harm. Or she did.

"*Oui.* She's . . . Her name is Fleur," she told him somberly.

She glanced toward the threesome again and gasped. Now Arlette was setting a dollop of olive garnish upon Fleur's nipple, where it clung to the tacky *pâté*. At least the girl's coquettishness was having one good result. Arlette had forgotten to eavesdrop.

Fleur glanced her way and gave her a saucy wink. Juliette shook her head, silently scolding her. But she only grinned again and cradled Arlette's head as he bent closer. Juliette held her breath. He was going to nibble from her as though she were some sort of human . . .

"*Hors d'oeuvre?*"

Her eyes jerked to Lyon. He'd lifted a small dish of canapés and was proffering them to her.

"It's only fair that you sample your own wares," he teased knowingly.

Embarrassed at being caught acting the voyeur once again,

she opened her lips, automatically taking his offer. She even chewed several times before noting her mistake.

She darted a look across the room, meeting Valmont's condemning expression. Lyon's gaze followed hers and he frowned, instinctively moving closer to her as though to protect her from the other man's displeasure.

A distressed sound left her, then she then began to cough. Lyon tossed the dish on the table with little care for the other china and crystal serving platters. Several somethings fell to the floor, but she was too distraught to determine what.

A large, male hand branded her back, warming her even through layers of clothing. "Are you all right?"

"Yes," she croaked, grabbing a napkin from the sideboard. She pressed it to her mouth, spat the canapé into it, then discarded the napkin on a platter of soiled china and cutlery.

All the girls were forbidden to eat in Valmont's presence. He found the sight of a woman masticating to be highly disgusting. Fleur or the others might be forgiven their missteps, but she'd pay for her *gaffe* at some later time when he was in a mood for retribution.

"He watches you differently than he does the others," Lyon observed. "What's your relationship?"

Juliette cleared her throat and saw that Lyon, too, was contemplating Valmont. Finally, an opening.

"He's my guardian. Perhaps you've heard of him? His father owned a winemaking enterprise in Burgundy."

Lyon's eyes pierced her. "Owned?"

"The phylloxera destroyed it three years ago."

"Yes, of course. The Valmont family. They had over five hundred acres if I recall correctly?"

"*Oui.* Everyone in my family was employed there. If it still existed, we would be picking the vines today from sunup to sundown. I can't help but wonder how you find time to sojourn in Paris at such a busy time of year. Is the harvest completed earlier in Tuscany than in France?"

He shook his head at her quizzically, obviously wondering why she'd gone down this conversational path. "No," he answered slowly. "Though it will be finished by the time I return home. There'll be other tasks to see to in preparation for winter as I'm sure you're aware."

"Your vineyard . . ." She gazed up at him from beneath her lashes. ". . . how is it that it continues to thrive in the face of the scourge?"

An infinitesimal pause alerted her to the fact he'd recognized that there was an agenda behind her questioning. The effects of the tincture were making her interrogation clumsy.

"Did he tell you to ask?" He briefly jerked his jaw toward Valmont, his eyes never leaving her face.

Juliette opened her fan and collapsed it again in quick snaps. "Is it some secret? It's only natural that we all take an interest. You must know, of course, that the reason he fled to Paris is that his father's entire holdings were ruined by the infestation. Everything lost."

"The father—" Lyon's brow knit as he searched for some memory.

"You no doubt heard that he killed himself, leaving debts. This . . ." She spread her arms to indicate the salon. "It's all that's left of the Valmont fortune. The fields his ancestors worked for decades now lie fallow. This is the first year since antiquity that there'll be virtually no grape harvest anywhere in France."

Lyon nodded. "The story is the same for many vineyards throughout Europe. My family has contributed much in the way of study, experimentation, and financial support to those who've been devastated. But you may tell your keeper that, yes, our plots continue unscathed. And, no, we haven't found a cure. When we do, we'll share it."

"So confident? Shall I infer that you are close to finding one?" she pressed.

His gaze narrowed and he leaned a forearm on the wall, cornering her. His scent was fresh, masculine, and his breath teased the hair by her ear as he murmured, "Answer my original question and I'll answer your question in return."

"Please . . . it's not possible . . . here."

Fleur and one of her admirers passed them, heading for the green door set along the wall nearby. She lay hand on Juliette's arm in brief acknowledgement before disappearing through the door and down a hall, where she would no doubt pleasure her companion. Arlette gazed longingly after her, but he lingered to mill at the sideboard, listening.

Lyon watched them go. "What's back there?"

"Private rooms. For private amusements. M. Valmont had them lavishly decorated last year, and they're quite impressive. Would you like to visit them?"

"With little Fleur?"

She tried to pretend to herself that it wasn't jealousy that filled her at the idea of him bedding her friend. "Or with one of the others who's more available at the moment."

"You won't show them to me yourself? That's not part of your keeper's plans?"

She shrugged, affecting nonchalance. "He instructed me to show them to you if you wished to see them. However, I prefer to entertain only in the salon."

He pushed the green door wide and put a hand at her lower back urging her in its direction. "Make an exception."

Instinctively, her eyes searched out Valmont. Across the room, someone had engaged him at the card table in a game of *vingt-et-un*.

She couldn't count on Satyr to return here again. Many guests were regulars, but sometimes newcomers came only once. This might be her only chance to learn more of what Valmont wanted. His questions must come first, but then she had questions of her own.

So she tapped her fan to her companion's chest and shot him a warning glance. "Very well. But not for a dalliance. For private conversation only, and I'm not certain how private we will be, even there. *Comprenez-vous?*"

He nodded and she picked up a candle and turned to lead him from the salon, half-expecting at any moment to hear Valmont protest. Though he'd suggested it, she knew he wouldn't like seeing her leave with this man he so envied. But he didn't interrupt them and she soon found herself in the quiet of the hall, breathing easier as the door to the salon swung shut behind them.

A guard stood sentry there, his presence rendering it relatively safe to be alone with a gentleman. Juliette nodded to him. He would remain posted within earshot of the rooms until the wee hours.

Lyon had followed her into the dim corridor and she felt him behind her when she paused at a door on the left. "First," she announced, "we have the Moorish room."

But a sign on the door read *occupé*. Though the night was young, someone had already retired here.

The sound of leather stinging flesh came from within, sharp and shocking. The flogger. It wasn't difficult to guess who was entertaining a client inside. Only one of the girls enjoyed such things—Gina.

"It appears to be in use," Lyon noted. "Fleur?"

Juliette raised her chin, refusing to be embarrassed. "No— another girl. It doesn't matter," she said crisply. "There are numerous other rooms of interest along this way."

She rushed on to the next door, which bore no sign of occupation. Recalling its interior, she hesitated with her hand on the knob, belatedly thinking better of this choice. "Now that I consider it, there's yet another room farther on that you might prefer to view."

Backing away, she found herself inadvertently pressed against him. Though he hadn't moved, a hard length now prodded her lower spine. She drew herself up, stilling like a doe sensing the presence of a predator.

His erection. Even through layers of clothing, she could feel it—immense and scalding hot. And topped with a crown that felt as fat and unforgiving as the knob under her fingers.

A broad hand settled at the bone of her hip and tightened reflexively, sending an erotic charge through her. The air between them crackled with tension as volatile as that before a lightning storm. For infinitesimal seconds, they stood that way, locked in silence.

"I want you," he rumbled.

Juliette shook her head. "The guard."

Lyon reached around her and gently covered cold fingers with warm ones, helping her to turn the handle. At his nudge, the door swung open before them. She automatically stepped inside the room. Forfeiting the shelter of his body, she immediately felt a chill. A fire had been laid in each room earlier, but in this one, it had died down.

Behind her, the door swung shut. She eyed the bed and him warily, expecting that he would force himself or his questions on her now that they were alone, and not sure how she would respond. But he only went to the corner grate and stirred the fire higher.

Her gaze went to the carved mantel that he now stood beside. It was possible they weren't truly alone here. Each room had secret portals through which the goings-on within could be monitored, supposedly a measure that insured the safety of both the women and their patrons.

Lighting the candles in the wall sconces with the one she

held, she studied him, curious to gauge his reaction as he took in the decoration of the exotic room. Having already examined it in fascinated detail on her own, she knew precisely what it contained.

For instance, she knew that above the fireplace, in the frescoed eyes of a lecherous soldier, was a set of hidden peepholes. She lifted two carafes of wine from the cart and set them there on the mantel, adjusting them so their necks blocked the soldier's—and therefore any voyeur's—view of the room. As an extra measure, she opened her fan and propped it behind them.

"What is this chamber called?" Lyon asked at length, having finished stoking the fire. His voice was velvet, well suited to their sensual surroundings.

"The Pompeii Room. Its design is based on the excavations in the ancient Italian city of that name, near Naples."

"Tell me what is done here in this room," he prompted.

"I think you know."

"But I would enjoy hearing it from your lips."

She set her candle in an empty sconce and approached him. "Very well. Its design and the frescoes and statuary are meant to emulate the *Lupanare*, which are—"

"—the brothels of Pompeii."

"Have you been there?" she asked in surprise.

"No, only heard of it from my eldest brother. He—Nicholas—collects antiquities and delights in visiting ruins and the like. We rarely leave our estate simultaneously, so our pursuits are solitary. But, go on. You were describing the purposes of this room?"

"Well, like the brothels, its decoration is intended to inspire lust as you might imagine. To encourage illicit intercourse and such."

When his eyes shaded with amusement, she stiffened in affront. "You have a strange sense of humor, monsieur."

"*Tu me comprends mal.* I meant a more particular description. For instance, what is done with these?" He indicated a selection of wood and leather dildos set alongside a goatskin filled with olive oil lubricant. A riding crop, restraints, and other devices were hung on the wall above them.

She gazed unwaveringly into those jeweled eyes of his. Once, her eyes had smiled as his did, but life had turned serious and she now guarded her laughter.

"I suppose some might say they are instruments utilized in gratifying unnatural lusts."

"Unnatural?" His brows rose and his smile now seemed to mock her Catholic attitude. "But lust is one of the most natural instincts in Humankind is it not?"

She tried not to notice that he was standing before a wall fresco depicting Priapus, the ancient Greco-Roman god of sex and fertility. He lorded over a garden and sported an extremely elongated penis, which was meant as a threat to frighten off would-be thieves.

Lyon's gaze followed hers and he studied the scene. "According to my brother, the ruins at Pompeii have been found to be full of erotic art, frescoes, symbols, and inscriptions regarded by its excavators as pornographic. Even many recovered household items were decorated with prurient themes. The ubiquity of such objects would indicate that the sexual mores of the time were more liberal than ours of today."

The sound of the lash cut the quiet in several staccato slashes. Gina whimpered.

Juliette cleared her throat. "I suppose. Shall we visit another room now, monsieur?"

"I'm content to hear more of this one." He moved away from her along the wall, surveying the continuous fresco, which portrayed interconnected scenes of antiquity, each more debauched than the former. He paused before a painting of a low prostitute posing as if in wait for a customer. It was one of the oils from Valmont's ancestral home.

"A *prostibula*," he said, reading from the small gilt plate in the center of the frame's bottom edge.

"A *'morue'*, we call her in France. She who stands in front of her *stabulum*—a cell or stall—to be visited by men," Juliette clarified, coming to stand beside him. "She doesn't look particularly happy about it, does she?"

His gaze cut to hers. "Would you be happy, in her place?"

From the adjoining room, a rhythmic thumping began, accompanied by feminine moans and ribald masculine grunts.

What the *prostibula* did was a baser form of what went on here in Valmont's establishment. Surely this man realized that.

"*Non*," she replied.

Lyon turned back to study the expression of the woman in the painting. "You answer too quickly and without consideration. First, you must look at her. Really look. Imagine yourself in her situation. On a day that completely changes your life from what it was before."

He circled her, moving to stand at her back, so they both faced the painting. He set his hands at her shoulders and his disembodied voice came, low and mesmerizing. "Imagine you are she, waiting there for a man. Any man. Hoping one will walk by and notice you.

"You are fairly new at this work and shy. You've had two customers this morning, but you know that if no one else comes, you do not eat that day. So you hope for more.

"Men of every class walk by, weighing your worth in terms of the coins in their pockets. You preen and woo them with your smile. But no one stops . . . until . . . finally, one man passes . . . and slows. He stops."

Juliette shivered, in spite of the fire he'd roused in the corner grate. Behind her, his palms slid up and down her chilled arms, connecting her to him and warming her far more than did the fire.

Why didn't he ask his questions and get them over with? She opened her mouth to provoke him with questions of her own, but the words that came out were not those she intended.

"You should flee this place," she whispered.

His hands paused only briefly, then dropped, finding her waist. Gently they slid upwards along her sides, shaping over her ribs, and higher. Then back to her hip, then upward again, retracing the same path time and time again. And with each upward sweep, he brushed nearer to the underswells of her breasts, until she was nearly mad with the need to have him take their weight in his palms.

"But he wants you," Lyon murmured in that same hypnotic rumble. "You can see it in his eyes.

"You nod and turn to lead him inside the *lupanare* to your small cell. There are paintings along the hall, depicting various carnal positions he might enjoy engaging in with you. Various fetishes you might cater to. Some clients require such inspiration and instruction. You wonder if he gazes at them as you pass. You glance back and find his eyes are on you as though he wonders how you will look without your tunic. You wonder what he will do to you when you're alone with him . . ."

Next door, Gina's moans had turned husky and passionate. They entwined with the metered thumps of a bed hitting against the wall and were erratically punctuated by the crack of the lash. Tomorrow her skin would be welted where all could see, but she enjoyed showing off the marks almost as much as she enjoyed receiving them.

And, seeing them, Juliette would silently envy her.

The other girls assumed she was happy in her self-imposed celibacy. That she had no desire to experience the visceral entertainments all of them enjoyed. But she knew her own fleshly failings and knew she was on dangerous ground here. She would call a halt soon, but not yet. Not yet.

"At last you arrive in your windowless cell. You pull the worn fabric of the curtain aside. Your customer looms larger here and his body seems to fill up the room.

"You move toward your cot, leading him, as you have led other men before him. It's stone, covered with a pallet of straw you laid freshly after your last customer.

"While you're turned away from him, he comes behind you. And moves your hair aside. And puts his lips here, along your throat."

Something brushed the tendon behind Juliette's ear. Lush, masculine lips. She angled her neck inviting more and they followed the downward slope to kiss the ridge of her shoulder.

Yearning traveled in their wake, and she waited to hear what he would say next. Would die if she did not.

"He touches you and you feel his warmth through the lone garment you wear. Most customers merely lift up the front of your shift and push their way inside you. But this one. His touch is different. Slow."

Lyon's groan blended with her gasp as his hands went lower, bunching in the fabric at her hips to grasp and rock her against him. Caged in his trousers, his shaft was a thick, knotted bulge that nestled along her rear cleft and soared to sear her spine. Strong capable fingers teased and rustled and massaged, seeming intent on memorizing the rounded shape of her dèrriere.

Every sentence he spoke wound Juliette's emotions tighter and tighter in her chest. She clasped her hands at the front of her waist, nails biting into her skin.

"He waits for a sign that you're ready for him. That you want what he offers. He asks if he's your first that day and you lie, thinking he wants to be. But he hasn't a care for such matters. He enjoys an experienced woman . . ."

Juliette's lips parted, and she stared straight ahead, unable to look away from the painting that inspired him. For the first time in years, she was actually responding to the physical touch of a man. He'd come to her as a phantom earlier tonight, but now he was all too real.

Seeking relief, she shifted ever so slightly, igniting the slick, pleasurable drag of the nether lips high between her legs. They were swollen, puckered. Wet with her own gush. And gasping for want of what he could provide.

It was as though she were on the bridge again. The memory of his size and shape moving inside her channel was vivid. The real thing was hard at her back. He could lift her skirts and be inside her. So easily.

Her head lolled back on the strong shoulder behind her and she covered his hands with hers. And ever so gently, she squeezed.

A guttural bellow from the next room shattered the spell Lyon had woven around them. Gina's customer had found his release.

Juliette straightened in Lyon's hold, staring blindly at the wall. "Stop. Th-that's enough." She dropped his hands and fisted her own between her breasts, shielding her heart against her own emotions and from whatever he would say next.

What had she been thinking? Valmont would come and she had learned scant news in the vein of what he wanted. Nor had she voiced her own questions.

Lyon's breath stirred her hair. "It was you on the bridge tonight, was it not?" he demanded softly.

She spun within the circle of his arms and pulled him close.

"Answer me," he repeated, holding her away.

"You know it was," she gritted.

"You could see us," he stated, searching her eyes.

"*Oui*! For pity's sake!" Clasping a hand at his nape, she forced his lips down to hers. "Speak to me only in whispers," she scolded, nodding toward the mantel and its peepholes. "The walls have ears, even here."

Lyon adjusted his legs wider. His paws dropped to cup the

cheeks of her rear, lifting her to his heat. Hungry lips slanted over hers and it felt like a homecoming. Everything was at risk yet she had never felt safer and more protected. Except for the snap of the fire and the intermittent sound of their heated moans, quiet reigned.

"That creature with you. I saw how she was made," Juliette managed between kisses. Was that besotted voice really hers?

"Umm."

She cupped his strong jaw in both hands and drew away just enough to part their lips. Amber glinted at her from beneath half-closed lids. In the firelight, his lashes threw spiked shadows across his cheeks.

"What was she?" Juliette breathed.

His gaze fell to her mouth. ". . . a Nereid." His lips went back to their exploration.

Nereid. Juliette considered the word. *Not a mermaid.*

"Her name?" she insisted, turning her face aside.

"Sibela."

Disappointment shaded her features, but she only said, "What is she to you?"

"What is Valmont to you?" He kissed her once, too briefly, then leaned in until his hips pinned hers to the frescoed wall. Muscled forearms planted themselves on either side of her with a harsh thump. "A lover?"

From next door, they heard movement and voices as the neighboring occupants quit the Moorish room. Footsteps moved down the hall toward the salon leaving stark silence in their wake.

Would the guard switch his attention to them now? Who else might be listening?

She lowered her voice until he could barely hear it. "Nothing. He is nothing."

Lyon groaned and his lips slid down the side of her throat.

A slender, silk-encased leg rose to curl around the back of his thigh.

Through layers of clothing, his prick burned at the entrance to her channel. He shifted his weight and the hard ridge rubbed her. *Mmm.*

"What were his instructions to you concerning me?" he asked against her skin.

"I'm supposed to be courting you. More than the other patrons, at least tonight. I'm to learn more of your business." There would be hell to pay if she did not.

"Toward what end?"

"He's jealous. Of your success. It would not help matters if he knew I was with you . . ." Between them, his cock twitched and she moaned. "Like this."

Determination lit his face. "I'm lodging in the hotel at Quai d'Anjou. Do you know it?"

She caught his eyes and nodded curtly. Of course she knew it. Set along a tree-lined lane adjacent to the River Seine on the Île Saint-Louis, it was one of the most enduring and costly lodgings in all of Paris.

"Come with me there."

"Now?"

With his hand, he hooked her bent leg higher around him, bringing them indecently close. "So that we may speak freely." His voice lowered, sexy and beguiling. "And so that I can fuck you without an audience."

She gasped, pushing against his hold. "*Non!* Did you not hear what I just said?"

"If not tonight, then tomorrow night. Prepare one of your infamous dinners if it affords you a worthy excuse to visit me."

She shook her head. "I'm otherwise engaged. Forever. Go back to Tuscany. Tonight. Don't come back here."

He growled, kissing her long and deeply until she was ready

to agree to anything. She shouldn't want this, she berated herself. Whatever it was he made her feel just by being near, it was a mistake to want it. Had she learned nothing three years ago?

His lips pulled back slightly and hers followed, loath to let him go.

"Your monsieur comes," he grudgingly informed her.

She blinked up at him. "What?"

"Valmont."

Juliette let out a squeak of distress and jumped away from him, her heart skittering wildly. Somehow Valmont had slithered near without her being aware. She began straightening her clothing and repinning her hair.

Lyon leaned a shoulder against the wall, folding his arms over his chest and watching her.

A moment later, the sharp rap of knuckles came at the door. "Juliette? Are you within? Is Lord Satyr with you?"

The door opened.

5

With the arrival of M. Valmont, the stench of murder hit Lyon with the impact of a rifle blast. Anger roiled, slashing red high along his cheekbones. Though not as well developed as that of his brothers, his olfactory sense was far keener than theirs when it came to a few isolated scents. Such as blood.

His gaze fell to the man's clean, manicured hands. They'd been wet with it earlier today. Drenched with the lifeblood of hapless, innocent victims. Animals slaughtered more for the thrill of it than for the necessity of filling a stew pot.

Muttering under his breath, Valmont bypassed the two of them and pointedly strode to the mantel, where he moved the carafes and fan aside until they no longer blocked the peepholes. Then he joined them, all smiles and beneficence.

Up close, the man appeared even more cadaverous, Lyon decided, complete with sunken cheeks and blue lips. His black eyes sparkled with the sheen induced by the imbibing of drink. Absinthe, by the smell of him. He had probably once been considered handsome, but his addiction was taking a toll on his health.

"I see you are becoming acquainted with our Juliette, Monsieur Satyr," Valmont offered by way of opening conversation. He stroked a length of lustrous hair from where it lay on her breast, brushing it over her shoulder in a way that lay subtle claim to her. Her features grew still, carefully arranging themselves into an innocuous, doll-like expression.

"Attempting to," Lyon replied. His eyes narrowed on her. Had she lied? Was she fucking this corpse? It mattered not to him that she'd had men before. But none—and especially not this one—would ever find their way between her legs again. That pleasure, he would reserve for himself from now on.

Something else had changed about her as well. He inhaled carefully, searching the air. While he'd held her there toward the end, she'd begun to want him in spite of her contention that she shouldn't. And with the wanting, her scent had escaped its fetters and entered the air like an alluring incense fleeing some exotic genie's lamp.

Yet now, it had abruptly gone again. Was she able to rein it in at will? Such a feat would take an incredible amount of resolve. Of self-denial.

Lyon reached between her and her keeper, ostensibly to select a libation from the wine cart, but at the same time managing to part the pair. Lingering, he poured himself a drink he didn't want and offered them drinks they refused. And in the process, he managed to widen the gap between his companions until Valmont was completely nudged aside.

"Are you relations?" he enquired then, using his glass to gesture between the two and indicate a possible connection.

"Oh! *Pardonnez moi!* I must introduce myself." Valmont made a show of politeness, pressing that recently bloodied hand to his crisp white shirt and ducking his head in a half-bow. "I am Monsieur Pierre Valmont. I function as guardian to Juliette and have for the past—" He looked around Lyon's bulk toward her. "How long has it been, *chèrie*?"

"Three years," she supplied woodenly.

"*Oui,* but of course," said Valmont.

"That's about the time your family's fortunes soured, wasn't it?" Lyon asked, turning the screw.

"*Oui,*" Valmont said again, eyeing him. A look of intense hatred he couldn't quite conceal flitted over his face and then was gone.

His father's vines had been felled by the phylloxera, and it appeared he held Lyon and his family accountable for some reason. Or perhaps it was simple jealousy for another's good fortune. He was no good at untangling such things.

"Mademoiselle Rabelais and I were discussing that very circumstance earlier this evening," Lyon told him. "But our conversation had since moved on to other matters. In fact, when you joined us, I was attempting to coax her into preparing one of her dinners at my hotel tomorrow night. I've traveled over a week to reach Paris, and the thought of a well-prepared meal holds great appeal."

Beyond Valmont, Juliette was shaking her head and making furtive hand gestures in an attempt to dissuade him from pursuing his course. He ignored her. As smarmy as Valmont was, perhaps he would aid him in one thing—securing her consent.

"I have informed monsieur that my Friday nights are engaged for the foreseeable future," Juliette interrupted.

"Alas, and I must return to my estate soon," Lyon went on. "Though I have assured her I am willing to meet any price for the offer of dining in such excellent company as hers, I cannot seem to budge her from her position."

Valmont's eyes lit at the promise of a hefty payment. "Happily, Juliette is mistaken," he said, drawing her surprised glance. "Her calendar has an unexpected opening and she will be available to you after all. Tomorrow night, did you say?"

Her eyes flew to his face. "*Mais non—*"

M. Valmont maneuvered around Lyon to capture the fluttering bird of her hand in the cage of his. Lifting it, he stroked its back. "*Ma chère*, Monsieur Satyr sojourns in Paris only briefly. It is a great compliment to find him vying for the favor of your culinary talents."

Lyon studied her, expecting some debate on the issue. She obviously wanted to refuse. But she only stared at the pale hands caressing hers.

"I can assure you my ward will provide an unforgettable repast. I imagine you're already planning it in that lovely head of yours, are you not, Juliette?" Valmont straightened the lace along her neckline, touching her intimately in the process. She showed no indication she'd noticed.

"Of course," she replied tonelessly.

Eyeing that proprietary hand on her, Lyon imagined himself ripping it away and breaking its every bone. The instinct to claim and protect her rose in him.

His thoughts went to the door. He could shove Valmont through it and into the hallway. He could keep Juliette with him inside this room, lock the door with his mind, yank up her skirts, and have at her. His cock surged, heartily endorsing this plan.

On the other hand, getting himself arrested on his first night in Paris was undoubtedly the wrong way to go about things. He'd elicited Valmont's assurances that she would come to him tomorrow.

He should depart. Now, or he'd act on his plan, providing fodder for the Parisian gossips for years to come. It wouldn't matter to him personally, but it would adversely affect his family. Always his first consideration.

Slicing the undercurrents that swirled around him, Lyon spoke. "It's settled then. Juliette will visit me tomorrow at my hotel. No later than four in the afternoon."

Her eyes protested, letting him know she would not come to him willingly.

But once the arrangements were finalized, he left, feeling his gut wrench at the loss of her as he did so. Outside on the street, he glanced back toward the lights warming the windows of Valmont's apartments and shoved his hands into his pockets. Considering the fact that she was somehow subduing her scent, the pull of Juliette Rabelais's charms was surprisingly strong.

Having been within touching distance and yet not mated her, he was finding it physically painful to withdraw. The remembrance of her scent still lingered in his lungs, urging him to return to her and make her his.

Her skin would be cool against his heat, her lips soft yet not too sweet. He would drown his cock in her. Drown in her sea-green eyes . . .

. . . sea-green . . . eyes. Sibela. Twenty hells!

Lyon's head whipped around toward the park. For the past hours, he'd largely managed to forget there were *two* Faerie daughters in Paris. And that he had promised to meet with Sibela again tonight.

His long gait ate up the ground as he crossed the deserted street and took the steps down to the park. He wasn't looking forward to this assignation.

He was hurting for lack of sex, but for the first time in his life the need was specific to one woman. And it wasn't Sibela his body pined for.

One coupling with Feydon's sea-child might be excused, but if he were to make the mistake of mating with her again, his fate would be sealed with hers. Regardless, it would be impossible to lie with another after having found Juliette. He didn't delude himself that he was in love with her. But he was infatuated in a way he couldn't remember ever having been with anyone before her, and felt boyishly eager at the prospect of seeing her again.

Sibela wouldn't take kindly to the change in their relationship and would demand an explanation. He had a feeling that mentioning he'd spent the past half hour wrapped in her sister's arms would be unwise. But he needed to settle things with her and determine what she knew of Juliette, if anything.

He'd lain with Sibela only once and not during Moonful. A bond had been forged, but it was weak and could still be broken. That would be easier with her cooperation. Therein lay the rub.

Surely, she had no deep attachment to him, though he'd sensed she had some underlying motive for seeking him out. What would induce her to give up any claim to him? He ran his holdings through his mind, pondering which might suit her best. An offer of jewels? Land? He had a wealth of both. He would simply determine what it was she desired and give it, rather than himself, to her.

Of course, something must be done to keep her protected, but he was currently at a loss as to a solution. There were no more of his kind here on earth. No fourth half-Satyr brother to husband a superfluous fourth half-Faerie.

However, it seemed his questions and any rendezvous were to be postponed. Though he paced the riverbank on all sides of the park twice, neither Sibela nor her scent were anywhere to be found.

"Excellent," he muttered irritably. He threw himself onto one of the benches lining the park walk, choosing it because it afforded a view of the gray townhouse with the red door across the way.

He had no doubt that Sibela would return once she'd finished pouting, and it occurred to him that perhaps it would be best if their confrontation were delayed. Once Moonful passed, they would both be in a more reasonable frame of mind and body. Then he could calmly introduce Feydon's daughters to one another and take them both with him to Tuscany. There, he and his brothers could sort out their parentage and determine any obligations toward each of them.

He groaned inwardly at the prospect of Nick and Raine's reactions when he arrived with two females in tow, rather than one. They would no doubt take great delight in teasing him about his supposed magnetic qualities.

As though to punctuate his thoughts, a woman drifted over the grass toward him, seeming about to speak.

"I'm not here," he murmured, with a curt gesture of dismissal. She paused, gave her head a confused little shake, and then turned back toward the steps that would take her up to the bridge.

He glanced around. There was no one else in the park. She must've descended from the Pont Neuf specifically to visit him. Sighing, he erected a mild force-spell around himself, so no others would be drawn here.

What was enticing them to him in such droves? he wondered. Was it the fact that three creatures with ElseWorld blood had come together here in Paris? In a Human city unused to such things, they very well could have stirred up some latent magic. He didn't want to consider the other possibility—that ElseWorld itself was somehow seeping into this world.

There was movement at the high window of Valmont's apartments. As Lyon watched, Juliette came to the glass. So, that was her bedchamber, as he'd guessed earlier in the day.

Seeing her again sent a quick jolt of lust through him. Unfortunately, she didn't linger, but only twitched the curtains closed, leaving him humming with it.

Normally in this sort of situation, he would've conjured a Shimmerskin to fuck away the idle hours while he stood—or sat in this case—guard over Juliette. A Shimmerskin's iridescence was difficult to subdue even under a bespelling. Still, he'd taken such chances before in the open. He could've found a hiding place. Perhaps sequestered himself and a partner in the shadows of the bridge or gone to his hotel.

However, the urge to mate just any random female had quieted in him. His eyes went to the high window again.

Because of her.

Unfastening the front of his trousers, he slipped a hand inside. It dove deep, settling itself in the warm nest of bristle at his groin.

Experienced fingers that knew what he liked curled around the root of his shaft and he gripped himself. *Umm.*

He tipped his head back and luxuriated in the caress of moonlight on his face and throat. Tonight's moon waxed only one cycle shy of complete fullness. Less than twenty-four hours from now, the most sacred night of the month for the Satyr would occur, gripping him in its carnal thrall.

Under an uncut moon, he would be at his most potent. Able to impart childseed if he so chose. It was a serendipity that his kind had been designed so that they could fornicate where and with whom they chose on all other nights, without worry of siring children or contracting disease.

A woman of experience, Juliette would no doubt take precautions against conception, unaware that he could easily supercede them at his discretion. She would be angry if he did so. But it was tempting. A child would go a long way toward protecting her in the way King Feydon had commanded. Since a Satyr child required only one month's gestation, he could become a father with staggering swiftness.

The very thought of her growing round with their child and the manner of its begetting, had his cock twitching under his hand. His eyes narrowed on her darkened window as he began a long, slow, upward tug. He kept his cock close to his belly at first and forced himself not to rush. In the wake of his hand, a labyrinth of purpled veins sprouted along his length, heating him.

Finally, at the top of his stroke, the O of his fist met the jutted ridge that encircled the brim of his crown. His grip angled so the knuckle of his forefinger massaged the sensitive notch at its underside.

His eyelashes fluttered, drooping lower. Amber glinted from beneath them, searing that high black mirror she hid behind across the quai. A soft breeze brushed over his skin and he imagined it was her, lifting her skirts to kneel on the bench and straddle him.

Slouching back, he planted his feet wide in the grass in front of himself, uncaring that he'd turned exhibitionist. No one would see through the spell he'd woven and he was beyond caring if they did.

An opalescent dribble of pre-cum pumped from him and he smeared it over his crown with his thumb. And imagined himself pressing into her . . . stretching her tight lips wide with his knob . . . imagined her coating him with her slick, hot nether kiss. Another pump of semen came, inside her this time. Then she was slipping away, only to return for another all too brief taste of him, and another.

Umm.

When it became too much, he dragged his fist downward and imagined tunneling himself deeper, higher between her legs. Imagined the long, subtly curving hug of her taking more and more of him. And more.

The side of his hand depressed his scrotum at the finish of his downward push, and he imagined instead that she had sunk over him. That she was so completely open for him and he was so deep inside of her that the cleft of her ass coddled his sacs.

And then she was sliding away again until her rim massaged his plinth and she almost lost him. And then down over him, more urgently this time.

Flushed and ruddy now, his cock angled high and hard from him, glistening with the drench of moonlight and his own seepage. As he worked himself ever faster, his slitted eyes went to the railing of the bridge where he'd first seen her. He summoned the memory of her skin and lips and perfect scent.

His thrusts turned harsh and his breathing labored. His

belly tautened toward his impending release. His fist rammed itself down his shaft one . . . last . . . time . . .

A strangled, guttural cry escaped him. His cock jerked in his hand and a forceful spurt of cum shot from it, fountaining across the grass between his feet. More came, surging and spewing and dribbling over the back of his hand to smear his belly and balls and cling in his nest. His breath sawed in his lungs, as it seemed to go on forever.

Gods, would it never stop? Rarely had he come in such magnificent, wrenching pulses, especially by his own hand.

Eventually it did ease and his spill slowed. He squeezed gently, bringing a last well of it from the slit of his crown. *Ahh.*

For long moments afterward, he reveled in the contented balm of satiation. But the heated blood of his ancestors still sang through his arteries and his cock remained thick and turgid under his hand, ready for more. In time, it demanded that he begin again and he did.

There, in the shadows of cypress and maple, in the dewy autumn air, he fucked himself over and over far into the night. And each time he came in his own fist, he dreamed of her. Juliette. His chosen one.

The moon had traveled halfway across the sky before he ultimately tired. He rinsed off at the river, then returned to the bench and stationed himself more comfortably.

Raising his arms, he stretched, then folded them across his chest, prepared to watch over Mademoiselle Rabelais throughout what remained of the night.

Somewhere in the ether, King Feydon was probably laughing himself silly at having handed him this dilemma. Sisters—one a cranky water nymph and the other a wary *grande horizontale*.

Though all was in a tangle and he shouldn't have been happy, he was. The night ahead was to be Moonful. And Juliette would be coming. In more ways than one.

* * *

Just before sunrise, there was a knock on the door of the high attic room Lyon unwaveringly monitored.

Juliette stirred in her bed. The knock came again, then the door opened and Fleur poked her head inside.

"Are you awake?"

"*Oui.* Come in." Juliette sat up, tucking her knees high to her chest. She'd been unable to sleep and was glad of the company.

Fleur slipped inside smelling of sex and perfume and looking as fresh and innocent as someone who hadn't just passed the entire evening in the company of men.

Juliette moved aside, making room for her on the bed. With her usual easy manner, Fleur flopped onto her belly on the mattress and propped her chin on one elbow to contemplate her.

"Look! Monsieur Tremont has geeven me a geeft." Holding out her other wrist, the girl briskly rotated it, so the bracelet she wore sparkled in the moonlight filtering through the curtains.

"It's lovely," said Juliette, reaching out to examine it.

"*Oui.*" Fleur yawned behind her hand. "But I haven't come to talk of this. Tell me what happened with the beeg gentleman with the golden hair. The others are wild with jealousy that Monsieur Satyr chose you as his companion in the salon. Then, when you went together to the hall of rooms! O la la! I'm certain that Agnes turned as green as the absinthe when she told me of it. You have never taken a man to veezeet the rooms before. Did he veezeet your quim as well?"

"Fleur!" Juliette looked toward the heavens as if seeking help. "You're incorrigible. You may tell Agnes and the others that we only engaged in conversation. Nothing more. They are welcome to try their luck with him if he comes again."

Fleur tsked. "You should let the gentlemen veezeet! For geefts if nothing else." She shook her wrist, rattling her shiny bracelet as a reminder. "Weeth your beauty, you'd acquire a trunk full of finery in no time at all!"

"I think you overestimate my powers of attraction ever so slightly." Juliette held up a hand when the girl made to protest. "However, you'll be pleased to know I'm to cook for Monsieur Satyr. Valmont is sending me to his hotel tonight."

"*Alors*! But this eez wonderful." Fleur leaped to her knees and clasped her hands over her heart. "*La!* So handsome. So beeg. But with his sorry clothing I guess maybe he is not so rich for buying geefts." Her brow knit at this insurmountable problem.

. Juliette only shrugged, knowing his fiscal circumstances were lofty, but not bothering to contradict her.

Brightening, Fleur bounced on the mattress. Palms outward, she wiggled her fingers. "But he has such beeg hands." She raised and lowered her brows meaningfully.

"And?" prodded Juliette, not catching her meaning.

"Eet means he grows a beeg wanker between his legs. Perhaps that is geeft enough!" Fleur giggled merrily.

"Oh! Trust you to locate a happy side to every situation." Juliette couldn't help joining the girl in laughter, though she couldn't imagine why she found such a thing comical.

The door pushed open and suddenly Valmont stood there. In his grim shadow, they both fell silent.

"A word," he said to Juliette.

Mute for once, Fleur jumped up and made to depart. As she passed him, he tipped up her chin to study her face. "You're a plain little thing, aren't you? And recently from the kitchen help?"

"*Oui.*"

"Your name?"

"Fleur."

"Well, little Fleur, your sense of decorum leaves something to be desired." His hand cupped her cheek and Juliette tensed.

"*Monsieur?*" Fleur asked tilting her head.

"In the salon last night. You allowed liberties to Messieurs

Arlette and Tremont that were not permissible outside of the back rooms. We are not a common whorehouse."

Fleur nodded, looking chastised.

"Don't worry, ma petite. You may be forgiven one such lapse." His gaze slid over her. "You're a shapely little package. I'll invite you to my bed soon, eh? I'd like a sample to determine what draws the others your way. But maybe first we'll see about your hair." He lifted a dark lock of it and let it drift from his fingers, staring at it consideringly. "Something more flattering in the way of color. Perhaps blond, like our Juliette here."

Fleur darted a knowing look her way that was as expressive as a roll of the eyes. He will change me in order to pretend I'm you when he fucks me, it said, as loudly as if she'd spoken her thoughts.

"Her hair is beautiful as it is," Juliette protested.

Valmont ignored her and instead found Fleur's bracelet and lifted her arm to examine it. "You like the bangles?" he asked. "If you please me, I might just have a little reward for you myself."

"Jewels?"

"Perhaps," he said, dropping her hand. "See to your hair first. Now leave us. And shut the door behind you."

"*Oui*, monsieur."

Fleur turned to go. From the doorway, she made a face at Valmont's back, then winked at Juliette before slipping away down the hall.

"Why her?" Juliette demanded once she'd gone. "She's not your usual style."

"I take an interest in all your interests, *chèrie*. You know that."

It was a threat. Whatever or whomever she came to care for, he would besmirch or destroy. Concern for Fleur's wellbeing blossomed.

"She should be warned of your violent tendencies if nothing else," Valmont went on.

Juliette wrapped her arms tighter around her knees. "You wanted something?" she asked, refusing to argue.

His eyes went to the flask on her dressing table. "Did you take your drops?"

"*Oui.* Too many in fact."

"Yet you do not sleep? I wonder if lecherous thoughts of Monsieur Satyr are what keep you awake?"

"Fleur woke me. I assure you I was sleeping quite soundly before her arrival."

He didn't leave then as she expected, but instead came to sit beside her on the bed, his hip warming her thigh.

"Rest. You must be tired." He nudged her flat on her back and made a place for himself to lie on the mattress beside her. Joining her on her bed in this way was an unprecedented event and it scared her nearly out of her wits.

As she lay back, she pulled the covers to her chin. He curled close to her on his side, his head on the pillow beside hers.

He lay a hand on the cover, on her belly. "You're tense. Relax."

"I'm tired," she hinted, making to turn away.

But his hand snaked beneath the coverlet and around her waist, holding her still. Between them, his cock was rigid against her hip. Panic swept her.

"You were right earlier. I am jealous," he whispered at her ear. "I can tell Satyr interests you."

She stared at the ceiling, refusing to look at him. "No. He doesn't," she lied. Any other response would have been foolish. "You're the one who suggested I show him the rooms last night. You're the one who arranged a meeting between us tonight. Not I. I would gladly cancel it."

His voice and his grip on her tightened. "Then you were only acting on my behalf when you let him maul you?"

She glared at him, noting the changes in him that were even

more startling at close range. Absinthe had been slowly leaching the color from his skin since they'd come to Paris, turning him gaunt.

"What did you expect would happen if I took him to the rooms?" She sometimes thought he put her in the way of other men to test her. To see if she would succumb. It was all some insane game only he understood.

"However, I did gather some gossip before you interrupted us," she informed him, going on to relate the meager facts she'd learned, embellishing and inflating their importance as best she could.

"It's not much for all the time you spent with him," he groused when she finished.

"Since I haven't been particularly successful with him thus far, why are you sending me to him tonight? Why not send one of the others?"

"You know why." His eyes bore into hers and she looked away. Yes, she knew.

"It will be no more than what he deserves," he told her. "He and his brothers lord themselves over me, enjoying my father's failures and seeing me laid low. How he must be laughing at me to see me running women here." His hand fisted on her stomach. "All of Paris society currently scorns us, though many of them patronize us on the sly. The police will eventually be forced to expel us, despite my bribes. But rest assured that I have a plan to see myself reinstated among the *haut monde* and in a more respectable business enterprise."

"What is it?"

His eyes turned furtive. "I'll tell you only this for now. That it's likely Satyr and his brothers are Europe's best hope for combating the phylloxera. He has admitted they're putting all their resources to work toward finding a cure. However, they cannot be allowed to succeed."

"But why not?" she exclaimed.

"The time isn't right to talk of that. By coming here, I only meant to inform you that I'll be away today, but I'll expect all to be in readiness for your departure to Satyr's hotel this afternoon when I return to escort you there."

Worry spiraled through her as she searched his eyes. He expected her to do whatever she had to in order to aid his devious plans, whatever they might be. To become a Trojan horse when she went to Lyon's hotel, bringing him trouble.

She was jarred from her thoughts in an instant, when Valmont shifted, laying his head at her breast as though he were a child and she his mother. Her muscles quivered in rejection.

"My *maman* died in childbirth. Did you know?" he murmured.

"Everyone knew the circumstances of your family. You were our livelihood. That of the entire village," she answered brittlely.

He was quiet for a moment, then his hand moved, smoothing over her belly in flat circles. "Have you ever wanted children? A girl like young Fleur to suckle at your breast, or a son?"

His touch went higher over her figure, then gently curved around her breast. A forefinger found her nipple through her chemise.

She caught his hand, but not his eyes. "*Non,*" she whispered, staring at the far wall.

For a suspended moment, he did nothing. She sensed his frustration, felt its hard length at her hip, but at last he only gave her breast a quick squeeze and withdrew to stand beside the bed.

"Get some sleep. Tonight will be a busy one for you. I expect you to do your job well with Satyr. But not too well. I'm certain you know what I mean."

"*Oui*," she said in a small voice. She turned her back to him and heard him move away.

"You know I love you, *ma chèrie*," he said from the doorway. "You do, don't you?"

She had believed him once. Her mistake. "*Oui*," she said automatically.

The door opened and shut. After a moment, she peeked over her shoulder. He'd gone. The fact that he didn't see any need to lock her in was humiliating. He knew she was too much the coward to leave.

She stirred from the bed and went to the basin at her washstand. With trembling hands, she reached under her chemise and sponged his touch away.

If she hadn't let herself become such a mouse, she would take Fleur tonight and run. Leave Paris behind. But contemplations along those lines were ludicrous for one who could scarcely force herself to cross a bridge or gaze upon a river, much less flee across the countryside.

And once Valmont poisoned Fleur with his lies, would she be willing to run with her? Even if they fled, where would they be safe? Worries continued to chase around her mind with no finish line in sight as she slipped back into bed.

After a time, she rose again and took another weak dose from her vial. She'd spent the past three years in a living coma, calmly accepting and repenting. But tonight she felt herself beginning to hurtle toward some momentous, terrifying change the outside world was intent on thrusting upon her. She pulled the window shut, in an unconscious effort to keep it at bay. Eventually, she slept.

Sometime later, daybreak arrived outside her window. The masculine giant who—unknown to her—had guarded it from a distance throughout the night, stood from his bench. Stretching, he gazed toward the sunrise-pink river.

Then, he turned and loped his way through the winding streets of Île de la Cité, where he passed only the occasional straggler. Once on the adjoining island of Île Saint-Louis, he headed toward his lodgings, where he would sleep the day away.

And await Juliette.

6

The polished gilt knocker had tapped only once when the paneled door opened under Juliette's hand and Lyon appeared. His massive body stood blocking the late afternoon light from the windows behind him, casting his features in shadow. Though, actually, he lounged more than stood, with one muscular forearm braced high against the doorframe.

His gaze swept her approvingly as he took in her appearance. On her part, she was disappointed to see that he was every bit as handsome as she recalled. Same brawny, rugged body. Same devilish amber eyes. Same charming smile. However, she was in no mood to appreciate his physical attractions.

Less than one hour ago in her boudoir, her maid had seasoned and dressed her like a prize turkey. Now she was to serve herself up to this man along with a meal in hopes of wooing him into giving her what Valmont wanted of him. But she had arrived here with an agenda of her own as well.

"Welcome," he rumbled in a voice that stroked her nerve endings. "I'm glad you've come."

"You left me with little choice in the matter," she said tartly.

He stepped closer and she took an involuntary step back. But he only reached out to relieve her of her basket. "You could've refused me, but I had the distinct impression it was your guardian you were loath to refuse."

He was right, of course. Even now, M. Valmont and his coachman awaited her return, outside in a carriage. After dropping her off, they'd planned to station themselves close by at a vantage point that afforded a clear view of the hotel. Usually, Valmont remained at home when he sent her on these sporadic jaunts. That he had come along tonight and now twiddled his thumbs nearby said much about how important her work here was to him. Or about how little he trusted her with this man.

"Your kitchen and dining rooms?" she asked, ignoring Lyon's comment as her gaze searched the apartment beyond him.

Belatedly, he seemed to notice the trio of servants that had accompanied her.

"Through here," he directed, motioning for them all to follow him inside. His rooms included a small kitchen for residents of means, and that was where he led them.

Her entourage paraded behind them bearing cooking utensils, bowls, woven baskets, and one domed silver tray. They lingered to help her unwrap and unveil, taking all but a few of the dishes with them so that she would be able to carry what remained when she departed. With any luck, that would be within the hour.

She scarcely paid Lyon any attention while she issued instructions and arranged her things on the counters to her liking. Once their duties had been executed, the servants bustled off and left her to perform hers. No one commented on the impropriety of a young mademoiselle tarrying in a hotel in the company of a worldly gentleman. It was tacitly understood by all what the entirety of her performance tonight would include.

Deep inside the bag of toiletries she'd brought was a leather godemiche and a syringe, both wrapped in clean linen. A bottle containing a contraceptive douche of astringent alum, hemlock bark, and raspberry leaf was secreted there as well.

Only she knew the complete truth of what went on at these tête-à-tête dinners. And she'd never yet reached the point of having to employ either the leather or the syringe. But every time she prepared yet another meal for an unfamiliar gentleman, she also prepared the antidote and equipment to prevent a child, and brought them with her to his lodgings. Just in case.

Once the last of the minions had gone, Lyon closed the door on them and rejoined her in the kitchen. When he didn't speak, she turned to find him poking among the things she'd brought.

"How long will all this take?" he asked, giving the whisk in his hand a perplexed look.

"Is there some rush?" she asked, removing the cheesecloth covering the butter and egg so that she could complete the sauce Béarnaise.

He glanced toward the window and her eyes followed his. The sun was low, less than two hours from dipping itself in the Seine.

"I admit I'm surprised you actually brought the makings of a dinner," he said obliquely.

"It's what was promised," she said, pretending for the moment that she wasn't aware of what else he no doubt expected of her. "I know it's early, but the time was an arrangement you specifically made. I hope you're hungry?"

A corner of his mouth turned up in secret amusement, as he studied one of her more unusual basters. "Oh, I am."

"All will be ready within a half hour," she informed him, deciding to assume he referred to their meal. "Would you care to assist me?"

He surveyed the scatter of utensils and foodstuffs doubtfully. "What's left to be done? Everything already looks and smells delicious."

"I spent the day preparing things, and now it merely requires a last minute dousing of sauces and sprinkles. A bit of cutting, dicing. Here, tie this on, and I'll set you to chopping," she suggested.

He took the oversized square of white linen from her and secured it over his clothes. "I'll warn you I'm somewhat clumsy among delicate objects," he said, eyeing the herbs and vegetables that languished in fragile bowls.

"Nothing here is precious," she said, quickly instructing him on the handling of tarragon and chervil. As she worked nearby, she observed him begin the unaccustomed tasks she'd assigned, finding him charming in his determination to get it right. She began to relax slightly under the familiar routine of preparing a repast and the fact that he hadn't immediately pressured her into his bedroom.

In view of his reputed wealth, his manner of dress continued to surprise her. He hadn't made any attempt to impress her tonight with flamboyant satins, but instead was as informally attired as he'd been last night, with the exception of the addition of a fawn-colored coat. It was impeccable but plain and she wondered if it was, in fact, his small way of trying to impress her. From time to time he shifted his massive shoulders within its fabric as though a tailored jacket were too great a prison for his well-muscled form. For a moment she forgot herself and smiled at him, her eyes full of sympathy.

Noting her gaze, he grinned at her, eyes twinkling. "Does domesticity suit me?"

"*Oui.* You are quite possibly the most beautiful man I have ever laid eyes upon," she informed him.

He looked taken aback. "*Grazie.*"

He might doubt her sincerity, but she meant it. She had spoken compliments to many men at this juncture, but more often than not, they were lies. Not so, this time.

Besides, it mattered little what she said to him. He'd have forgotten her words and everything about their time together by morning. She would make sure of it.

He cleared his throat and turned to a collection of wine bottles on the sideboard. "I've procured some of my family's Sangiovese, vintage 1820, from the hotel's sommelier. A true Tuscan wine. Will you take some before dinner?"

"If you wish," she said, hearing the pride for his family's accomplishments that was evident in his voice. Watching him from under her lashes, she continued to put the finishing touches on the meal he'd paid an astounding sum to Valmont to enjoy. Such a price was nothing to this man, she'd been told.

"Tell me," she said once he'd poured and set the stemmed glass beside her. "What will you do upon your return home? I know your family makes wine, but what is your specific role in the operation?"

"Are these your questions or your guardian's?" he enquired.

"Mine, for now. But be warned I have brought his with me as well."

His smile flashed and he toasted her glass. "Warning noted. In answer to your question, I'm in charge of much of the work during the fallow season. Once the harvest finishes, old vine stock must be removed. We cover the remaining vines' feet with soil to protect against frost. Later, there's the dormant pruning. And the first racking of new wine is traditionally done in January on the last day of the moon's waxing."

"Why then?" she interrupted. "There's no such tradition in France."

"It's a family ritual," he said, a bit too casually. His gaze flicked briefly to the window, then back to her. "As is the planning for the winter and spring auctions. Another task that falls to me this year, only because my brothers and I alternate in the obligation."

"The Valmont family held an auction each spring. When I was a girl . . ." She faltered.

"When you were a girl?" he prompted.

"Nothing of consequence. I only . . . I helped in the kitchens during several of the auctions. A lavish dinner was prepared for buyers who came from all over Europe."

"It's the same for us. An elaborate dinner. Then we introduce the wine; there are tastings, social discourse. There is much talking around our true purpose, which is of course to sell our wine. A successful event is more crucial to the success of orders for it than you might imagine."

His eyes went to the window again. He was looking at the sky, she realized. It was turning pink with the beginnings of a sunset.

"Why do you keep glancing outside?" she was driven to enquire.

An odd, significant look came and went in his eyes. But he only tossed back a drink, then said, "Tonight is to be a full moon."

"And?"

"And I suppose I'm becoming . . . anxious . . . to get on with our evening." His voice had turned low and velvet. As it had been in the Pompeii room at Valmont's. As it had been when he'd caressed and kissed her skin. As it would be again if she only could allow herself to give him what he expected of her once dinner was complete.

She looked away, wishing it were possible. Knowing it wasn't.

"Then you'll be pleased to know I pronounce our dinner ready," she told him softly, lifting a platter and hoping he didn't notice how her hand trembled. "You may lead the way to your table, monsieur."

Together, they carried the plates and bowls to the table, and she began naming the various dishes she'd chosen to serve. "First we have the crostini and white bean soup with escargot." She lifted the covers from each as she spoke, and their mingled aromas began to infuse the air. "Then the poultry in Béarnaise, and fruit. And later, dessert."

"Ah! To dessert!" He toasted the concept, then seated her

and sat himself next to her at the head of the intimate table. Neither of them remarked on the fact that no dessert course was displayed.

As she watched him eat, relief began to fill her. He was taking her food. Food she'd prepared with her own hands. It was the first step in felling him.

However, his appetite for cuisine proved limited as was hers. He replenished their wine, and they quickly settled into a contemplation of one another and their drinks.

"You know much about the inner workings of my family, yet I know little of yours," he told her.

Juliette sat back, relaxed by the knowledge that, within minutes, he would begin to feel the effects of having eaten her meal. The food had contained no secret ingredient. And it would have no unusual impact upon her whatsoever. However, though she'd never known why, all that was pertinent in initiating its magic toward another individual was the fact that she in particular had been the one to prepare and serve it.

She gestured expansively with the hand that held her glass. "Ask me what you will. I'm an open book." It mattered not what questions he posed, for he would soon forget her replies.

He sat back, too, appearing somewhat suspicious at her willingness to talk. "Who were your parents?"

She smiled at him. "Madame Fouche. A plump, merry woman who taught me to cook and whose husband beat her when the whim took him."

"He wasn't your father?"

"*Non*, and the madame wasn't my birth mother. I was a foundling, born in this very city." With a nod of her chin, she indicated the spires of the Hospice des Enfants Trouvés, visible in the distance from his window. "But my family is a dismal subject. Introduce another."

His eyes were sharp on her for a moment as his fingers stroked the stem of his glass. Then he spoke again. "Very well. I wonder at this odd arrangement you have with your guardian. The taking of bids for the offer of a meal and your hire. Most of your lofty status have long-term lovers."

"Lovers." She set her glass aside and folded her forearms on the table to gaze at him through lowered lashes. "Are you hoping to be my lover, Monsieur Satyr?"

His eyes filled with masculine speculation, but he didn't rush matters and only leisurely swirled his wine, studying her. "That and perhaps more."

"More? What more do you imagine you might be to me?" she goaded sweetly.

"Your protector."

A stab of longing shot down her spine, swiftly replaced by a spurt of anger. She lifted her glass and analyzed his features over its rim. "In my experience, men don't protect women. They put them in jeopardy."

"Are we speaking of M. Valmont?"

She took a drink. "I don't necessarily speak of a physical jeopardy. I've heard the stories about you and your brothers."

"Oh?"

"The three of you leave a string of broken hearts wherever you go. Particularly you."

He looked uncomfortable. "Not intentionally." He took a grape from the bowl of fruit and the blinding white of his teeth gleamed for a moment as he bit into it. "What else have you heard?"

"That you hide secrets on those estates of yours."

His eyes narrowed. "And who was your informant?"

She shrugged. "Is it true?"

"We all have secrets, I suppose. Even you. And in that vein, it's now my turn again for questions."

"Ask away," she replied magnanimously.

"I'm curious regarding your plans for the future."

Her glass thumped to the table. "My future?! I have little

enough say in that, monsieur. What woman does? We find ourselves tossed about like brightly colored autumn leaves on the
capricious breezes of lecherous males." She fluttered a hand to
illustrate her words.

"You have a low opinion of my sex, considering we are your
primary occupation. Don't you wish to marry one day?"

"Why, Monsieur Satyr, are you proposing?" she enquired.

He reached across the table and took her wrist, his thumb
tracing its lacework of blue veins. "What if I am?"

Juliette stiffened at his unexpected response. "Then I accept,
by all means." Craning her neck, she made a pretense of scan-
ning the room. "In fact, if you have a member of the clergy secreted in a closet, perhaps we might proceed immediately with
a wedding?"

He leaned closer, earnest. "This is no jest. I wish to take you
to wife. On the morrow, or as soon as it can be arranged."

Sea-green eyes fell to his drink and were turbulent when
they rose to meet his again. "I've heard such words before.
Usually at night from amorous men with wine in their hands."

"You've not heard them from me." The foot of his glass hit
the table and he reached for her, all in one easy motion.

Because she was weak, she let him fold her close. His mind
was already malleable enough for her spells by now. She should
get on with it.

"Most gentlemen wish to marry virgins," she mumbled into
his chest.

Strong fingers tilted her chin up and amber glinted over her
face, finding her lips. His mouth brushed hers. "I prefer a more
experienced woman."

"Such as that woman in the park?" she said, suddenly anxious to wedge some distance between them. "You profess a desire to bind yourself to me, yet you were with another only last
night. It leads me to wonder if you might have proposed to her
as well?"

He hesitated. "Not exactly."

She raised her brows. "You *don't know* whether or not you asked her to wed you?"

"Do you have any siblings?" he countered, nailing her with his eyes. "A sister perhaps?"

Gasping, she flattened both hands on his chest, holding him away. "Why would you ask such a thing?"

"Why did you run last night, on the bridge?" he countered.

She shot him a confounded look. "I saw a man fornicating in the park! With a woman who sported a fishtail! Wouldn't you have run from such a sight?"

"I can explain that," he said, looking discomfited.

"Please do, monsieur," she offered, folding her arms between them.

"Do you know of the mythological satyrs?"

"Followers of the wine god, Dionysus? Urns and amphorae and all that?"

He nodded. "Or followers of Bacchus, in Italy. My brothers and I are descended from—"

Lyon opened his mouth as if to continue, but then his expression suddenly arrested and his jaw clenched. His hand fumbled behind him to grip the the nearest chair for support. Something frightening flared in his eyes and a peculiar, queasy look passed over his face. Grimacing, he glanced toward the window again as though seeking the source of his ailment.

"What's —?" Her gaze followed his. The sun was a sinking slice of orange now. Valmont would begin to wonder what kept her.

When she looked back at him, his features and bearing seemed to have altered somehow. His eyes were wilder, and his lips had taken on a more sensual, determined curve. His body loomed larger and closer and more threatening. It almost seemed that he was devolving into something less human. Into something more . . . animalistic.

"Come here." It was the growl of a dominant male intent on corralling female prey.

"W-what's happening to you?" she stuttered, recoiling from him.

His eyes stalked her and an arm lashed out, herding her into the warm, sculpted cave of his chest. Tucking her snug, he smoothed the flat of his hands down her, over the contours of shoulders, spine, waist, and hips, as if to accustom her to his possession. His cheek brushed hers as he drew back just enough to find her lips.

Her hands crept up his back, and with a sigh, she opened for him, letting him gentle her and wrap her in the strength of his desire. It felt like a haven. Like protection and naked wanting and she wished it could go on forever. She needed this. Him. If only for a moment or two.

He groaned against her mouth and those big hands roamed lower to mold the curves of her rear. Hefting her higher against him, he crowded her backward.

The clatter of dishes shattered the air as his hips shoved hers onto the edge of the lacquered tabletop. His heated grip tilted her until it seemed the most natural thing in the world for her to clasp her legs around his waist. Widening his stance, he scooped her impossibly close and his kiss deepened into a full-blown carnal assault on her senses. The thick knot of his erection taunted her through layers of clothing, plowing her furrow in long, hot drags until she wanted to scream for the relief of penetration.

"Gods! I need you," he husked, and his words reverberated through her marrow.

Her eyes opened in alarm. Clutching his shoulders, she wrenched her mouth from his. "Your boudoir," she gasped.

Hmm? His glazed eyes were fixed on her lips, and his head began to lower toward them again.

She twisted her face away. "Your bedchamber! Where is it?"

His mouth found her throat instead, and she felt the drag of teeth. "No," he rasped. "Here."

"Here?!" she echoed weakly. He wanted to do this here? No man had ever dared suggest such a thing to her and a prurient thrill shot through her at the prospect of abandoning herself to him on the dining table. But she had long ago established a routine in these matters and deviating was out of the question. This was not a night for taking chances.

Cool air brushed her ankles. A hand had begun lifting her skirts and was already sliding along a stockinged thigh.

"*Non!*" She struggled fiercely, until her slippers touched ground and she stumbled from his hold. "Upstairs!" she gasped.

With that, she took his hand in hers and headed up the carpeted stairway. On the landing, she let him go, and without instruction, tried a door and found it to be a bedchamber.

Entering, she glanced back at him. "Coming?"

He followed her. Just as men always did on these occasions.

Inside, she scanned the room as she headed straight for its bed, automatically noting all possible exits and items that might be used as weapons should one be needed. Kicking off her slippers, she scampered onto the mattress and strategically positioned herself amid its plush cushions. She'd seen the other girls at Valmont's work their wiles often enough and knew that a look of submission in a woman lying upon a bed was what men preferred.

Her fingers played with the curl of hair that had fallen over her breast. Her other hand patted the coverlet beside her. "Take off your jacket. Lie with me," she coaxed in a sultry voice.

Bending one knee, she surreptitiously tugged her skirt up to display an ankle, then reclined, laying the backs of both hands on the pillow alongside her head. It was her patented alluring pose and it had never yet failed her.

Advancing on her, Lyon surveyed the scene as though his instincts told him something was awry, but he couldn't determine precisely what.

She curved her lips into a provocative smile. He smiled back at her, easily entranced. Easily ensnared.

Yanking the jacket from his arms, he heedlessly flung it off, planting one knee on the mattress. Instantly, she leaped up to sit before him and flatten a staying hand on his chest.

"And your shirt as well," she insisted, beginning to unfetter his buttons. "I want to see you."

Tugging her to him with a hand at her spine, he propelled her backward, following her down to the bed. Straddling her with his legs, he braced his elbows on either side of her shoulders, so his chest hovered but a breath above hers, barely affording her room to work.

Hands delved into her hair, cupping her head. Lips parted hers. Between their bodies, her nimble fingers desperately ripped the last of his buttons free. Spreading his shirt wide, she pushed it off his shoulders. With a muffled curse, he helped her, shrugging it off with an aggressive twist of his torso.

He fell upon her again, his mouth rejoining hers in a voracious, carnal dance. Her restless hands roved his chiseled back, learning its inclines, planes, and valleys.

Outside, the weary crimson sun surrendered the battle to stay afloat and drowned itself in the river. In its wake, stealthy rays of young moonlight slipped through the windowpane. Oh so gently, they stole across the floor, then slanted high onto the bed to lovingly caress its occupants.

With an anguished cry, Lyon threw back his head and arced away from Juliette until the small of his back was bent at an acute angle. Hard hips anchored hers as his arms locked straight and his fingers bit the covers beside her.

Going up on one elbow, she lay a hand at his waist.

"Lyon!" she whispered. "What's wrong?"

But he either didn't hear or was simply in too much pain to respond. Caught in some invisible, torturous grip, his taut body quaked with intermittent shivers. Cool moonlight limned his golden skin, starkly rendering features drawn rigid. A muscle worked in his jaw and blood throbbed visibly in the hollow of his throat. Between them, his cock gave a single, violent jolt, and a low bestial snarl welled from somewhere deep within him.

Juliette's back hit the mattress again and she pressed her palms in the lee of his ribs, holding him off. "Lyon?" she whispered.

Above her, masculine eyes opened to slits and seared over her, making her aware of how she must look with her wild hair and her breasts plumped so high that her nipples peeked from her bodice. Foolishly embarrassed, she tried to tug her neckline higher.

His body began to lower over her, so slowly that she felt the seam between their flesh unite, inch by inch. Belly met belly, then rib met rib, and then the soft tissue of her breasts gave against his chest and his fingers threaded her hair.

Covetous amber glinted, locking with green as they stared at one another, separated only by centimeters of air fraught with mutual need.

"I'm going to fuck you," he growled softly.

The raw words shocked her, excited her, as he'd meant them to. Big hands framed her skull and those beautiful lips descended to scald hers. His thighs forced hers wide and he began to rock his strangled rod against her vulnerable notch in long, lustful thrusts. The fabric of her skirts and his trousers molded the bulge that was his cock, and with each shove, muslin dipped just inside her to blot at tissue that was slick with her own juices.

Her knees rose at his sides and the tips of her fingers tucked themselves in the back of his trousers. Pressing her core against the unyielding shape of him, she intensified the sharp, sweet bite of desire.

Strong arms lifted her shoulders, hugging her to him, and his mouth turned to deeply kiss her throat. With a will of its own, her hand rose to curve at his nape and she lifted her lips to his ear. At that moment, she came so close. So, so close to giving in.

"Yes, I *want* you to fuck me," she whispered. He wouldn't remember, and she needed to say it aloud to him. Just once.

"Gods, yes!" Levering himself away, he got to his knees, beginning to unfasten his trousers.

Her eyes widened. What was she doing! If he were to find his way inside her skirts with that thing of his, she was done for. Seeking to regain control of the situation, she wriggled violently away from him.

"No! Juliette!" he protested, instinctively reaching to restrain her. When he saw she only meant to reverse their positions, his grip loosened and slid to her thighs, helping her to saddle him.

His cock felt even more impossibly huge in this new position and she squirmed, sitting atop him with both palms braced on his chest. His hands curved around her rear and he began helping her to ride him. "Like this, just for another moment . . . then . . . I . . . must . . ."

Her slit pulsed and a surprised sob escaped her, drawing his gaze. But she only smiled at him and told herself not to yearn for that which she couldn't have. Firmly stowing any wayward emotions away, she reached deep within her essence, tapping that facet of herself that made her unique in the world.

Her head fell back and she closed her eyes, rising to her knees. Warm hands slipped around the backs of her thighs to wrap themselves just below the rounds of her bottom. Fingertips leisurely stroked the sensitive depressions high along her inner thighs.

"Juliette," he growled.

At the sound of his voice, she swayed slightly over him like a willow wishing to bend his way. Combing her fingers from her temples to the back of her scalp and beyond, she ripped out the pins binding her hair, then shook it loose to fall in waves of almond, wheat, and flax around her.

Then she brought both her hands to her breastbone, cupping them together as if they held a crystal ball between them. A snapping, sparkling sphere of wintry radiance formed where the ball might have been.

Her eyes opened and found his.

"I have something for you," she whispered.

He was ready. The food he'd eaten had prepared him to receive what was to come. Slowly and with great care, she spread her hands apart, letting her gift spill forth.

Glitter burst from among her fingers like a bevy of frenzied fireflies freed from captivity. Because it must normally be kept leashed, these rare scatterings of magic were a joy and she breathed deep, for she loved the scent of her own glamour.

Mesmerized, Lyon watched the jewel-like mist hover in the air above him. His hands lifted and she thought he would try to touch it. But instead he curved them at her bodice, taking the weight of her breasts. Beneath his palms her skin heated and tingled as though the magic had somehow discovered them as well. She drew a quick, uncertain breath.

Then her finely woven tapestry of deceit drifted lower to drape itself over him. Twinkling lights sparked on his skin here and there for brief seconds. One by one, they began to wink and fizzle out.

His expression turned oddly satisfied, as if she had just confirmed some privately held suspicion of his.

"Faerie," he murmured. "I knew it."

She froze, arms still widespread. "What did you say?"

But he only yawned once, displaying perfect, white teeth.

Then his eyes turned witless. Lashes fluttered lower, spiking shadows on his cheeks.

His hands released her breasts and slinked down her sides. Settling on her upper thighs, they squeezed gently. Once. Then they fell limp upon the bed linens on either side of him, palms upward.

As always, the unleashing of her magic left her exhilarated, but this time an unsettling hum entwined the feeling. Why? Everything seemed to have gone as planned.

And then she looked down, seeing what those hands of his had done to her.

7

Juliette clasped her bodice tight to keep it from gaping, hiding her breasts in her open palms as she scuttled off his supine form. Leaping from the bed, she tripped, tumbling to the floor in her haste.

Scrambling across the rug, she felt the skin of her knees chafe and burn. Halfway across the room, she managed to pull herself upright, then stumbled backward a few steps to lean against the wall.

Breath heaved in and out of her lungs and her heart attempted to thump its way out of her chest as she lifted her fingers away from her skin. Under them, she no longer saw anything extra-ordinary. But a mere moment ago, her rose-colored nipples had been suffused with a strange luminescence. One induced by *his* touch. God, what was he that could do such a thing to her?

Turning her back on him, she monitored him warily over her shoulder as she refastened hooks and ties she hadn't even realized he'd opened.

His jaw clenched and unclenched and his head rocked back and forth on the pillow, mussing his shimmery tresses. He was fighting her spell harder than most. Would he remain caught in its snare?

"Sleep. Sleep!" She whispered the mantra over and over, willing her magic to do its work.

His dark, gold-tipped lashes batted rapidly at first, then more feebly . . . then one last time before they stilled. He'd lost the battle to remain awake.

She straightened from the half-crouch she'd assumed. If he'd wakened and expressed a desire to carry on, things might've taken an ugly turn, and she'd wanted to be ready to take flight.

Even from a distance, she could see that the bulge at his groin was every bit as tremendous as it had felt against her. She'd previously run across men who'd stuffed the crotches of their trousers to accentuate their masculinity, and that had to be the case here. No one was this well endowed, except perhaps a horse. He hadn't seemed the type who needed to prove himself in such a superficial way, but one never knew what drove men.

Though she wanted to move closer and give his assets a more thorough study, she made herself turn away and leave the room. Heading downstairs, she began mentally checking off the duties on her list.

First, she poured an inch or so of Sangiovese into each of the two goblets they'd earlier discarded in the dining room. Taking the bottle, she then opened a window, and leaned over the iron-work banister with her arm extended outward. Upending the wine, she emptied the remainder of it, watching its ruby contents drain away into the garden far below. However, the fact that she was wasting the money of yet another wealthy man who'd sought to buy her proved less gratifying than usual. The man upstairs was different than the others. Less deserving of what she would do to him next.

Setting the empty bottle on the table, where it could not be overlooked by him tomorrow, she hurriedly gathered all of the dishes and utensils she'd brought and took them to the kitchen.

120 / Elizabeth Amber

After packing them haphazardly in her baskets, she selected a sharp knife from the sideboard. Carrying that and the two partially filled goblets, she returned to his bedchamber.

Pausing just outside the door, she peeked inside. He lay as before, with one leg slightly bent and his arms at his sides. It appeared Lord Satyr still slept, but she would take nothing for granted.

Keeping a close eye on him, she ventured into the room and set one goblet on his dressing table. Setting the other on the floor near the bed, she then nudged it with her foot so it tipped and sloshed a few drops on the carpet.

Her hand clenched reflexively on the knife as she approached the end of his bed. Watching his face for the slightest indication he might be stirring, she pricked the point of the blade along the tender sole of his left foot. He didn't flinch. She poked him with it again. Twice. Nary a twitch.

Satisfied that he remained under her spell, she went around to the side of the bed. Stepping close, she lay the flat of the blade on his skin just below his ribs, so it pointed toward his feet. Its tip slid easily under the waistband of his trousers. It was sharp, ready for the purpose she intended.

Eyeing his crotch, she shook her head in amazement. Surely it had to be padding.

With a brisk jerk of the knife, she rent the fabric, slicing neatly along the outside of his trouser leg, from waist to ankle. The front of his pants burst open with the force his erection applied. The bulge at his groin unfolded, pushing the lap of the fabric away.

Her knife clattered to the floor.

"*Mon Dieu!*" she whispered, covering her mouth with a hand. His *service trois pièces* was a *service quatre pièces*!

She squeezed her eyes shut, then reopened them. Nothing had changed. He possessed the usual two balls like other men, but, amazingly, instead of a single cock—there were two!

One extended high from the dark golden thatch at his groin,

where it should be. But an inch or so directly above it, another identical cock angled from his pelvis! Both were ruddy and hard and begging. And both were, by far, the largest specimens she'd ever seen.

Eyes glued to this alarming display, she retrieved the knife and circled the end of the bed. At its opposite side, she hesitated for a moment, suddenly reluctant to go near him. What did he do with two? she wondered. Ruminating on various possibilities cost her precious time and confidence.

Eventually she made herself move closer and slip the knife just inside the waist of his other pants leg. Her hands were shaking so badly by this time that she nicked him, drawing a beaded line of blood. Ripping the blade in one long slash through the fine wool, she cut the second trouser leg full length.

Then she tossed the knife away, aiming it in the general direction of the door, to be reclaimed later upon her departure. Tugging and shifting, she managed with great difficulty to completely remove the trousers from him. She stood at the bed's foot then, clutching them to her chest as she realized she'd uncovered yet another oddity.

He was furred! A dusting of sepia down lightly covered both of his legs! It looked soft, like the pelt of a young deer and was thicker on his haunches and calves than on his ankles where it lessened, then disappeared. It grew sparser toward his hipbones as well, meshing and disappearing in the thicket of a somewhat darker color at his groin.

"What are you?" she breathed, shaking her head in bemusement.

She tossed the ruined trousers toward the door as well, not bothering to watch where they landed. Drawing another pair from his armoire, she crumpled them in her hands until they were creased enough to appear he'd worn them this evening, then she dropped them on the floor beside the shirt she'd earlier helped him remove.

Finding his jacket, she considered giving it a similar treatment, but in the end only folded it over the back of a chair. The thought that he might have worn it especially for her was one she would cherish, and she couldn't bear to ruin it.

With an efficiency born of practice, she untucked the bed linen at one corner and stirred the bedcovers into a bedraggled heap on either side of him. Afterward, she stood back and gazed at the scene, weighing the effect she'd created.

Returning to the bed, she flung one of its pillows to the floor. It was a nice touch, she decided, definitely adding credence to the portrayal of debauched disarray. With any luck, her efforts would convince him he'd fully succeeded in his intentions with her. She inhaled a fortifying breath, and allowed her gaze to locate him where he slumbered amid the disheveled linens. She was almost done here, but the most difficult task still lay ahead.

Unable to help herself, she drew closer to the bed and studied the penis *á deux* that sprang from him. One was slightly longer and of greater girth than the other, she realized—the lower one that was rooted in the thatch at the apex of his thighs, where a male rod usually grew.

She'd seen the bodies of more men than she'd cared to. But she'd never seen a man built in this way. He was made like some sort of beast.

Why didn't it terrify her? Why didn't it repel her? Why, oh, why, did it only tempt her instead?

Of its own volition, her hand reached out toward the lesser shaft of the two to determine whether it was a figment of her imagination. Mesmerized, she ran her fingers up its bumpy-smooth column and around the circumference of its blushing cap. At her touch, a pearly bead of fluid pumped, welling in the small slit at its tip.

She snatched her hand back, her guilty eyes flying to his. His lips parted and a sigh soughed from between them. But he slept on.

Her gaze swung back to its fascinated study of his privates.

She should stop this and return to her work. *In a minute*, she promised herself.

Daringly, she pressed the pad of her thumb on his tip, widening the squishy mouth and smearing the pearl over him. He was huge, but this was nature's method of helping him to ease his way inside a woman without damaging her.

Some prurient compulsion had her lifting her wet thumb to her lips, and suckling it.

Oh! In startled reaction, the feminine slit high between her legs clenched. A single time, like a hand contracting to form a tight erotic fist. With an appalled glance at his face, she crumpled forward in a half-bow, wrapping a forearm at her waist. The taste of him had acted on her like some bizarre kind of aphrodisiac!

Slowly, the fist released. A residual buzz of sensation continued to tickle at her nether lips for long seconds, then it faded away. Stunned, she uncurled, her avid eyes riveted to his groin. Would the other one taste the same? Would it have a similarly glorious effect on her?

No! It was time to concern herself with other matters.

But like a helpless addict, she found herself drawn back to him. Just one more taste, then she would get on with things.

She watched her hand reach out again. As if it belonged to someone other than she, she saw it wrap snugly around the girth of his lengthier shaft. In long, gentle squeezes, it worked its way upward along his prick and still higher, forcing the tiny mouth at its crest to open. Another bubble of seed pooled.

She darted a look at Lyon's still face. He was oblivious. Vulnerable. She could do as she wished to him.

This was wrong. So wrong of her to want this. Though carnal longing was her constant companion, she'd never even considered doing such things with the others she'd duped.

Her tongue slipped out, wetting her lips. Waves of almond

hair drifted over his belly and snagged in the fur of his thighs as she leaned forward . . .

. . . and gently kissed him.

Ohhh, Dieu! Orgasm swelled—fierce and so overwhelming this time that it buckled her to the bed. Her cheek fell to nest in his masculine thatch and her white-knuckled fingers knit themselves in the linens between her chest and the mattress. Under her skirts, her ankles crossed and her knees pressed together. So tightly that knobbed bones bruised flesh as she tried to capture the all-too-brief series of magnificent, lovely convulsions.

Though she desperately clung to it, the intoxicating pleasure ebbed away all too soon. The room grew quiet except for the sound of her breathing and his. Pushing herself to stand, she nudged her hair back over her shoulders to gaze down at his handsome face.

Last night, she had wanted him. But now she ached for him, desperately and in private places no man had ever ventured. She'd been foolish tonight, and because of that, she knew this yearning for him would remain with her for a very long time.

However, he would forget. She would help him to. She gazed at him, sad. But it was past time to begin.

The mattress gave slightly under her weight as she sat beside him and began to caress his face, feeling the slight bristle of his evening beard. Valmont had given her an assignment. She must steal now, and steal wisely so her victim wouldn't suspect.

Palm and cheek began to warm to each other and then heat, and Juliette imagined herself transforming into something more fluid. Something that slipped easily from her own flesh and into his. Something that moved effortlessly inside him, becoming one with the frothy rhythmic spurts of blood that traveled along a maze of fibers and synapses whirling in his brain.

Moving deeper through minute passages and microscopic caverns, she soon located the archives she sought.

His memories.

With unfocused eyes, she stared into space, listening. Observing.

The first vision that came to her was that of an extensive, flourishing vineyard. Scenes of it in every season strobed like illustrations on a deck of playing cards that was being fanned.

She saw the patchworked rows covering hillsides and valleys, and the workers toiling among them. And estates—three of them. And a curious ring of statues . . .

Then there were the two brothers. She saw them clearly— one tall and dark and commanding with charismatic blue eyes, and the other more reserved with eyes that were a cool, intelligent silver . . .

And then she saw Lyon with his beautiful body and jeweled eyes and charming ways. He was in some sort of temple with . . . Her brow knit . . . *women! Women of every shape and size and demeanor. Their hands and lips were caressing him and he was smiling at them, wanting them . . .*

Quickly, she turned her gaze elsewhere and saw something else she would rather not have to dwell upon. *Animals. Large cats, ibexes, deer, foxes, wildebeests, and others she couldn't put names to.*

She shuddered, not wanting to trudge along this avenue, but knowing she must. So she continued to hover over him and to journey down this path and others and still others. Only when her head began to throb did she pull away. It would have to be enough.

Cupping his cheeks in her palms, she gazed at him, memorizing his features. Then she sighed. She'd taken from him. Now it was time to give.

"Sleep," she whispered, touching her lips to his. "Sleep and dream of fornicating with me. Of touching me in every intimate way that can never be between us."

At this point, she usually left it up to men's minds to build their own prurient fantasies around her. But something drove her differently now.

Scenes of them together—of her with him, engaged in every carnal entertainment she'd ever fantasized about in her lonely bed—flowed from her as she brushed her mouth, back and forth, back and forth, over his.

"Remember these imaginings and relish them," she murmured. "But now you must sleep, just like all the others before you have. And when you awaken . . . believe. Believe all these nocturnal fantasies of our time together were real. But let it be enough. Let me be but a fond memory. A woman you blithely plundered in every conceivable way, but whom you feel no compulsion seek out again."

She levered back a few inches and watched the false impressions seep inside him, imprinting themselves on his subconscious. Then she drew away.

At the exit from his bedchamber, she paused. The desire to turn back for one last glimpse of him nearly overwhelmed her. But she steeled herself and left the room, feeling as though she'd left a vital organ behind.

Returning the knife to the kitchen, she then tucked the ruined trousers she'd pared from his body into her basket alongside the dishes and utensils.

Behind her, the door to his hotel room swished shut and she made for the staircase. She had performed this ritual dozens of times with dozens of men. He wouldn't awaken until morning. They never did.

And when he woke, he would recall only what memories she'd given him of this night. And like all the others before him, he'd never know she'd stolen from him. For he wouldn't find himself missing money or jewels or anything tangible. No, she'd taken something far more valuable from him.

Information.

Outside his hotel, Juliette hurried along the tree-lined Quai d'Anjou at the blunt end of the Île Saint-Louis to the east. The river flowed in the direction opposite the one she went and seemed to push at her, urging her to join its rush and return to the man she'd just deserted. Above her, the moon was a round, cold eye, that reprimanded her through the sway of the trees lining the Seine. *Go back!* it seemed to say.

No! She wouldn't listen! Wouldn't look!

Her steps quickened and she began to run, fearful of nature's heady pull. Turning onto the Quai Henri IV, she spied a waiting carriage at the predesignated meeting place. Advancing toward it, she gave its horses wide berth. Though the team wore blinders, they became restive at her approach. As usual, animals were as wary of her as she was of them.

The carriage door opened and a pale masculine hand reached out to assist her inside. Once she was seated opposite Valmont, he rapped on the underside of the roof above them and the horses began to clop toward home.

After her run, Juliette's breath came in great gusts, and she pressed a hand to her breast, waiting for it to quiet. Knowing that two easily spooked equine brutes were at the head of this conveyance did nothing to slow her pulse, but she pushed the thought of them away. Better this than walking out of doors all the way home!

Meanwhile, Valmont sat with his head resting against the squabs, noting everything about her. She could imagine how she must look to him—all disheveled hair, pinkened cheeks, and crushed skirts.

From under lowered lids, his eyes skewered her. "Did you fuck him?"

Though he'd sent her to Satyr's hotel on his own errand, his tone nevertheless brimmed with outraged accusation. Like a child who'd shared a favored toy, he'd become jealous at the thought of another's enjoyment of it.

"*Non*! Of course not," she managed to get out as her breathing slowed.

She couldn't tell if he believed her or not, but he let it go for the moment. "Well, what have you brought me?" he asked.

"It's as you thought. He and his brothers are experimenting with cures for the phylloxera."

He sat forward. "And? What have they discovered?"

"So far, nothing of true merit has occurred to them, though his brothers were hard at work on the case at the time he left Tuscany. The middle brother—Raine—apparently favored hybridization, but is now taking another tack. The grafting of an American vine to an Italian one." She went on, recounting details she'd gathered from her unsuspecting prey tonight regarding the status of the curative studies recently undergone on the Satyr estate.

"And? What else did you get from him?"

That he keeps two male organs instead of one in his trousers, she thought to herself, but that was knowledge she wouldn't give him.

"He keeps pets on his land," she said instead. "Wild ones. About one hundred of them."

Valmont's eyes keened. "What breeds?"

She counted off those she could remember. "Emus, antelopes, bison, caribou, gazelles, giraffes. And cats—leopards, lynx, cheetahs, jaguars, and others. But the pair of panthers seemed more important to him than the rest. The female is set to bear offspring soon. He's worried about how the event will proceed and unhappy at being so far from home at this crucial time."

She rambled on for a moment, supplying only bits of information she hoped could not be used to Lyon's detriment.

When she finished, he sat back, rubbing his hands over his kneecaps as he considered her news. His thoughts turned inward and she let herself relax until they reached the townhouse.

"I'll say goodnight then," she told him once they were inside.

"Join me for a drink first," he said, and her heart sank as she reluctantly trailed him into the salon.

Standing beside the infamous fountain, she watched him fill the bowls of two glasses with doses of absinthe. He balanced a slotted spoon across the rim of each glass, then centered a lump of sugar upon each spoon. His hands trembled so badly that he dropped the second one and had to try again. He'd been taking the absinthe more often lately and it was affecting both his faculties and his reflexes.

"I'm tired, monsieur," she said, but he ignored her.

Setting the glasses under the fountain, he then opened two of its spigots. Ice water trickled slowly, melting the sugar and diluting the liqueur.

"Did he ask you to visit him again?"

"*Non.*" She could feel the blush steal over her face as she watched the concoction *louche*—turn cloudy—with the release of the anise, fennel, and other herbal ingredients. Within moments, the solution had achieved a beautiful opalescent green color.

Valmont's eyes studied her as he lifted his glass and took a careful sip. "You should know better than to lie to me, *ma chérie*. Now try again. Or should I invite young Fleur to entertain me instead? Naturally, I could not allow you to participate for you might bewitch us both. Still, you'd make a fine audience."

"He claimed he wants to wed me." The words burst from her lips.

Valmont's contemplated her with new satisfaction. "Ah. You *have* brought me something more after all."

Obviously pleased, he lifted the second glass and handed it to her as if it were some sort of reward. "Now, let's begin again. What did he say exactly?"

Having denied herself the drops, the thought of another panacea was welcome. She sipped at the absinthe, feeling its welcome burn, as she relayed an edited version of Lyon's proposal.

"He's not the first to offer matrimony under the effects of spirits," she cautioned. "And his offer hardly matters since I've made him forget all that transpired this evening."

She turned her head and Valmont's gaze quickened. He caught her chin and angled it so her throat caught the light. "He's marked you."

Her hand rose to cover the discoloration, which was formed in the exact shape of a man's mouth. "The color of your mood matches that of your drink."

He laughed softly and let her go. "I'm not jealous, *pauvre chérie*," he said, but she knew it to be a lie. "I know what is mine and when to share it."

"So I learned three years ago."

His face tightened. "Watch yourself. That sounds perilously close to a criticism."

"*Pardonnez moi, monsieur,*" she said. But she could see it was too late. She'd given him an excuse to turn cruel.

"You tell me he doesn't wish to see you again; then you tell me he does. Now I begin to wonder if you lie about other matters. You haven't been naughty, have you, Juliette? You didn't cuckold me tonight with Lord Satyr?"

"You know I wouldn't," she bit out.

"Under a full moon, he and his brothers are rumored to be exceptionally persuasive."

"Nevertheless, I wasn't persuaded."

"Then perhaps one of your other recent gentleman callers? Have you opened those lovely legs of yours for someone without my permission?"

"*Non.* I swear it."

He tsked skeptically. "I've taken you at your word for too many months now. Tonight, I believe I'll have a look for myself." He threw back the remainder of the absinthe and set his glass aside. Then he appropriated her drink and downed it as well. Taking her arm, he turned her toward the stairs as though escorting her to some festive social event.

Instead, he led her upstairs toward his private sanctum, a room she hated more than all the others in his opulent home. Inside, she avoided the wounded, glassy eyes staring mournfully down at her from every wall. He'd dubbed this his trophy room and he'd filled it with the heads and bodies of animals he and his father had destroyed because it pleased them to do so. Among all the possessions in his Burgundy estate, he'd chosen these sad, soulless remnants as some of the few to bring with him.

Eyes downcast, she waited as Valmont went to a basin and washed his hands. He didn't like his employees to begin until he was ready.

Once he was seated before the mammoth desk that dominated the room, he gave a brief nod. "Prepare yourself," he instructed.

"For?"

He deflected the question, nodding toward the cabinet. She knew what was inside.

"Are you punishing me?" she asked.

His hand pounded the desktop. "Did you really think I'd take you at your word he didn't fuck you tonight? A man like that?"

"Yes."

"Then you've forgotten your place in the world, *ma petite putain*. Or perhaps I should say, *ma petite* murderess."

"I'm no killer!" Juliette protested.

"So you say. Even if I could be certain of your innocence, the authorities still believe you guilty."

"On your testimony!"

"Silence! If you continue to cause me trouble, I may yet see you delivered to prison. Now see to your clothing, *s'il vous plaît.*"

Shaking with anger, she yanked off her petticoats and neatly folded them over the back of the blue and gold inlay Louis XV *chaise longue* that had once graced his family home.

He hadn't examined her in this way since they'd come to Paris. She'd thought he'd begun to trust her. That he'd somehow gotten it into his mind that she was some kind of untouchable Madonna, immune to the desires of the flesh. Little did he know how far this was from the truth. Tonight and the one prior had proven that. And perhaps he suspected her weakness for Lyon. Thus his sudden need to determine if she'd returned in the same state she'd departed. Thank God she had for she had no wish to wind up imprisoned.

The tray was there on the bottom shelf in the tall, freestanding cabinet, just as she remembered from Burgundy. She opened the glass doors and took its handles, pausing when something foreign caught her attention. The shelf above had once contained monogrammed family porcelain, but was now lined with an assortment of inexpensive bric-a-brac instead. It was an odd little collection, which didn't seem suited to Valmont's interests.

She peered at the first item in the row. A swatch of mottled brown fabric.

"Hurry up, girl!"

Her hand jerked, rattling the instruments on the tray. Lifting it, she trudged toward him, like one headed for the guillotine, and set it on the corner of his desk.

He'd already opened the two shallow, uppermost drawers on either side of the desk, which he purposely left empty for these occasions. Slipping herself between him and the desk, she perched on its lip. In one smooth movement, she lay on her back and raised her bent knees. Finding the drawers with her slippered feet, she stepped inside them so they supported the weight of her splayed legs.

Valmont stood then and raised her skirts well above her knees to bunch on her thighs. He watched her face carefully as his finger touched the tender cleft between her labia, running over it until it unfurled for him on its own.

She emptied her expression, studying the ceiling. There were twenty large wooden coffers in it. Carefully, she counted how many times the egg and dart pattern was repeated in the decoration of each coffer and where each tiny defect was. Back in the Valmont family home there had been fifty coffers above his desk, each one edged with gilt.

But she took care to keep her eyes from the trophies that lined the walls. The proud red stag with its twin six-pointed antlers was the worst, only because she'd seen his triumphant father bring it home. No one but she had cared that it had still clung to life and was in pain.

Her eyes flicked to it and away. It was important not to dwell on it too long.

"I remember that day as well," said Valmont, noting the direction of her gaze.

His hands cupped her knees, then drew them apart, exposing her. He sat again, obscured from her view by her draped skirt. She heard his chair slide forward. Felt the warmth of a candle moving closer.

"I saw how you were that day," he went on. "The stag's pain was too much for you. I held you as your stomach emptied its contents."

"Stop! For pity's sake."

"You were only sixteen that summer. Remember?"

The first metallic instrument slid inside her passage, chilling her. They were physician's tools, and he used them to periodically examine the girls in the house for disease as French law dictated. Because she'd been born without the pelt of hair most women grew to protect their private parts, she consequently felt their every cold touch all the more keenly.

"I remember perfectly," she said. "It was about the time your father's vineyard began to fail. I pitied you."

"You adored me. It was the first time I noticed you. You were already so ripe, even at your young age."

A finger brushed her clit. She squirmed away from it and closed her knees, horrified. He never did such things. The absinthe was making him brave.

"*Excusez-moi.* An accident." His hand wedged between her legs rocking them wide again. She didn't believe him.

The instrument cranked vaginal walls apart, creating a slender tunnel for that which would follow. Once the device had opened her sufficiently, a finger slid inside, inspecting with thorough diligence.

His touch was always gentle as he poked and probed, examining her privates. What she hated most was having his eyes on her there. She always felt dirty after he touched her like this with his clean hands and his clean instruments.

The finger and crank withdrew and the candle was lifted away.

"All appears to be well. You have not yet become a slut like your mother. All things in good time, I suppose."

His was a common assumption and scarcely fazed her. Everyone knew orphans were most likely the offspring of unwed women, who were deemed to possess low morals. Since moral failings were believed to be bred in the bone, she must therefore be blamed for her mother's supposed sins.

Juliette lurched to a sitting position, pushed her skirts lower to cover herself, and lifted her feet from the drawers. As soon as her slippers touched the carpet, she skittered away to pick up her petticoats, hoping it was over. Usually he let it go at that.

But tonight she was not to be so lucky.

"Before you go, remove the tray and cleanse everything."

Grimacing, she returned for the instruments and took them and the tray to the sideboard. As she washed them in the basin, her eyes were once more on a level with the cabinet. She studied the bizarre array of objects she'd noticed earlier, each one set so neatly along that particular shelf.

Leaning closer to the swatch of fabric, she realized that it actually wasn't brown as she'd first thought. It was only stained, and appeared to have originally been dyed a dusky blue.

She examined the neighboring tokens, noticing most were blatantly feminine. A copper thimble. A coiled ribbon. An abalone comb.

Valmont's eyes bored into her back as she finished the washing and drying and set the tools out to dry on linen toweling. She held her breath, heading for her petticoats. "*Bonne nuit.*"

"Hold," he told her and her pulse tripped. His voice was always at its most gentle when he was feeling sadistic.

"A physician likes to be paid at the time services are rendered, *Mademoiselle Trouvé.*"

Mademoiselle Found. A loathsome nickname that never failed to recall her humble beginnings. If the surname of an orphaned child was not supplied, hospital officials gave him or her a generic one, such as Trouvé, the French word for "found."

"Come." He interlaced his fingers over his belly and sat back in his chair, waiting.

What did he intend? Juliette eyed the door, envisioning herself continuing on her way and bursting through it to freedom.

A chiding chuckle stopped her. "If you left, where would you go? How would you go? Would you take a boat? A horse-drawn carriage? Or walk? Past forests and rivers? Don't be foolish. You are safest here. Now, come."

"My drops."

"Later."

She let go of her death grip on the petticoats and they

dropped in a heap on the chair. Reluctantly, she went closer. When she was within his reach, he pushed back from the desk, making room for her between it and him.

"Again? Why?"

He stood and she saw he'd released the buttons of his trousers! His pecker stood from him, stiff and repulsive.

She dodged away, but he was stronger than she and caught her. Lifting her onto the desk, he shoved his trousers to his ankles and moved between her legs, already fisting his cock in rough jerks.

"Oh God, I want to put it in you," he groaned.

"*Non!*" Beyond alarmed, she brought her knees up and tried to close them and scoot away.

A hand at her hip locked her to him. She tried to sit up, but he smacked her back.

"I want to," he panted. "So badly I could die."

With his other hand, he rubbed his crown along her slit, not quite daring to act on his wish.

Her time with Lyon had left her body primed for sexual release, and as Valmont bumped and flopped against her furrow, he ignited unwilling sensation. She clenched her jaw and a tear leaked down the side of her face. More than anything, she hated that she wanted human warmth so badly that her body responded to his touch.

"Go ahead then," she taunted, desperately hoping to frighten him away from his goal. "But I promise you'll never be the same if you do."

His eyes widened, then narrowed. Still working his cock against her belly, he leaned over her. "Witch! You dare threaten to use your wiles on me? Do you think I won't fuck you? Do you?"

I know you won't, she thought. *Because you're too afraid.*

He'd known of her tricks since she'd first used them on one

of his acquaintances when she was but sixteen. Though half the man's size, she'd tricked him into believing he'd succeeded at raping her. Valmont had watched the entire bewitching in secret and had burst into the room afterward, demanding to know what she'd done.

He'd tried to waken his friend, but this had proven impossible until the following morning. Then, in her presence, he'd questioned her assailant and had been astonished to learn that the man believed he'd had her when Valmont had plainly seen for himself that no consummation had occurred.

From that day forward, he'd kept her close and had used her talent for his own benefit. But fortunately, he'd feared her magic as well.

Little did he know he had no need to. She'd secretly tried her spells on him in the past, but they hadn't worked. If he ever discovered that he was the one man who wasn't vulnerable to them, she was done for. She closed her eyes against the thought, and him.

"God, I dream of burying myself in you. Of your mouth on me. Of watching you suck other men with that lovely pink mouth."

"Silence!" she begged, slapping at him. "Be done with this!"

Still pinioning her, he yanked his cock so close that the backs of his knuckles plowed her slick furrow. "You want it, too. You're wet for me, my pretty putain. Just like my *maman* ... My father invited other men to our home ... She serviced them ... on her knees ... put her mouth on them all, one after the other ... Her belly was fat with child then, like a big ripe berry ready to pop."

Juliette covered ears with both hands and shut her eyes, appalled. Absinthe had loosened his tongue, but she didn't want to hear this.

His face contorted and fevered slashes of color burned his

gaunt cheeks. He was bucking so hard now that she and the desk quaked.

"Oh, G-God!" His eyes rolled back in his head and he made a choking sound. Warm stringy ooze spat from him. Revolted, she forgot to breathe and the room went black.

When she resurfaced seconds later, his fingers were painting his sputum over her belly. "My sweet, sweet *fille*."

"Are you quite finished?" she enquired with cold anger. Disengaging herself from his hold, she swung away and stood, anxious to go to her room to bathe away all evidence of this soul-destroying encounter.

Valmont fell back in his chair and began idly fondling the limp shaft that lolled in the V of his trousers. "He'll be back you know." His voice was slurred by drink and the after-effects of a pleasurable spilling. "You're like the Green Fairy—the absinthe. Once a man has had a taste of you, he cannot help but return in hopes of more."

Though she wanted to go, she halted in the doorway and glared at him over her shoulder. It was best to know what he was plotting. "Satyr will not return. I gifted him with an instruction to stay away."

Valmont took no notice of her words. "He has taken liberties," he rambled on. "As your guardian, I will insist that he must do the right thing."

She stared at him, aghast. "Marry me, do you mean?!" she sputtered. "But, you know that's not possible."

He rolled his shoulders, stretching. "Cease your yammering! You're obviously overwrought. We'll shelve the subject until I've thought more on it and we're both better rested."

A thousand protests hovered on her lips, each begging to be spoken.

Noting her hesitation, he quirked a brow. "Unless you'd like me to pull in a guest from the quai for you to service with that pretty mouth, *maman*? I'd quite enjoy that."

"I'm not your mother." She snatched up her petticoat and left the room without a word.

Silence fell in her wake and he stared at the empty space where she'd been. Then he opened his lips and muttered, "As good as."

8

___

Lyon opened a gritty eyelid and located the fat, glowering moon through the windowpane. Its cruel light played over his nakedness, scalding him like a thousand suns.

It was a Moonful night. A time of ritual. Why wasn't he engaged in fornication with some female or another? he wondered deliriously.

Barely conscious, he managed to lift one hand from the mattress. It landed with a thud on his thigh. Twitching a forefinger, he felt the fur that always sprouted upon him with the onset of a full moon and would disappear again by morning. He dragged his hand higher, in uncoordinated jerks against the grain of his pelt, until it found the man-cock in his thatch.

This—the larger of his shafts—bobbed at his touch, desperate for a stroke he was too weak to give. Hot as a burning poker, its entire length was so heavily roped with veins that he could hardly detect any flat expanses of skin between them.

With excruciating slowness, he forced his touch to rove beyond it, higher along his belly. The heel of his palm smacked his pelvic cock, sending shock waves through him.

Gods! It hadn't yet retracted! Which meant it hadn't achieved the single ejaculation it required at the commencement of the Calling rite each Moonful. No wonder he was ill!

Satyr males sprouted this second shaft only with the initial rising of a fully waxed moon. After a single climax it would've retreated inside his body again, but his other, larger prick would demand repeated bouts of copulation from dusk to dawn. However, it was painfully obvious that neither requirement had been satisfied.

Yet he was too weak to summon a Shimmerskin to attend him. Too weak even to jerk himself off.

Wracked by need, he called out hoarsely. "Ciao!?"

No answer came. He was alone.

Alone during Moonful. His internal clock and the position of the moon told him it was not yet midnight. By dawn, he would be dead.

Libidinous recollections of the evening swamped him, denying what his hands had shown him to be true. Erotic, half-formed images swirled nonsensically through his brain, dissipating before he could fully make sense of them.

He remembered gazing into a pair of sea-green eyes. Remembered a willing feminine softness yielding to the thrusts of his cocks. Remembered lusty, playful, pornographic engagements with . . . with whom? Had someone truly been here with him? What the fuck was going on? He sought, but couldn't find a name. Had she been a stranger?

The memories rambled on, out of control, revisiting jumbled carnal scenes involving him and some unknown female. How was it possible that his mind remembered fornicating tonight, but his body did not evince the results?

He attempted to sit up, but this only caused his abdomen to roil sickeningly. Goosebumps dotted his skin and he fought the desire to retch. His scalp throbbed like six-inch vine stakes were being driven into it.

This was what dying felt like.

Once he'd reached the age of maturity, his father had made it very clear to him that the consequences of a satyr going without a female during Moonful were dire. In fact, among those of his kind in ElseWorld, the purposeful denial of fornication was used as the harshest form of punishment. Before the onset of a Calling ritual, the groin of a condemned satyr would be latched within an iron cage, so none could attend him. It was said to be a hellish death, and no one had ever lasted through the ordeal.

Was he a condemned man? Would he die here in this luxurious hotel room, far from his brothers, his animals, and the vines?

He lay there, feeling his heart's sluggish, erratic pump. Cramps hit and he panted and curled into himself. His toes and calves knotted.

He'd always been the strongest of his brothers, physically. Now, he, who had never been ill a day in his life, was deathly so. He shut off the part of his mind that linked him to Nick and Raine, not wanting them to know. Not wanting them to experience this torture with him, via the ancient blood ties that caused them to share strong emotions, even over great expanses of time and distance. There was no point in sharing this agony. They were in Tuscany and could never reach him in time to do any good.

With everything in him he sent out a silent plea for help that would permeate only the immediate vicinity, presuming it would go unanswered. For there were no creatures nearby who had the ability to hear it.

The effort drained him, and he fell unconscious.

In the shallows of the River Seine just off the Quai d'Anjou, Sibela treaded water and seethed, her eyes fixed on the door to Lyon's hotel.

He'd fucked and abandoned her to pursue another woman

last evening. This was not something to be easily forgiven. However, she'd come here tonight, knowing it was Moonful and assuming he would want her again. Assuming he would need her. She had even hoped to hear him beg.

Yet now the moon hung full and high, smirking at her while her erstwhile lover trysted somewhere inside this building with another female.

Juliette.

Her presence here in Paris was unexpected and it greatly complicated matters. Did she even know of Sibela's existence? Doubtful. Things had been chaotic that day three years ago. It had been the only time she'd ever set eyes on the girl, and she'd been careful not to draw unwanted attention to herself.

Still, it was becoming obvious they must reconnect. For they now had Lyon in common, and it was imperative that she sway Juliette into abandoning any hold she had on him. Though she herself cared nothing for this third Satyr son in particular, she needed his protection. Her experience over the past few hours had made that abundantly clear.

Enraged by his defection in the park last night, she'd foolishly stormed back into the river instead of awaiting his return. Sibela languished at the beck and call of no male!

What had happened next, she considered to be entirely his fault. After all, he was the one who'd stirred her passions and left her before she'd gotten her fill of him. Naturally, she'd been driven to search out another willing partner. Unfortunately, in her haste, she'd chosen unwisely.

The two mer-males she'd encountered downstream had been a balm to her ego, for they'd proven more than willing to take up where Lyon had left off. She'd only meant to tarry briefly with them, and then return to the park. But they'd been so gratifyingly eager. At first.

She'd realized almost too late that ElseWorld had somehow reached its tentacles into this world and had tainted the mer-creatures' intentions toward her. Meeting her twin lovers had been no accident. They'd been hunting her, intent on delivering her through the gate between the two worlds. Exactly the thing she'd feared might happen without Satyr protection.

Narrowly escaping them, she had fought her way upstream and arrived at the park just after dawn today. By then, Lyon had gone, but his scent had been fresh and told her he had in fact returned there for her as he'd promised. And that she'd just missed him.

Searching the wind, she'd caught his fragrance and discerned that he was on the move, heading eastward. As he'd wound through the labyrinth of paved streets, she'd tracked him from her position nearby in the river.

But she'd lost his trail somewhere, and terrified of imminent recapture by those ElseWorld lackeys, she'd circled the two islands in the Seine all day, searching for a fresh one. Around mid-afternoon, she'd found it.

Though she hadn't seen him arrive here, she knew he'd gone into this building. She'd surfaced at this very spot, hours before the moon was to come, thinking he'd eventually summon her to see to his physical needs.

Instead, she had watched in horror as Juliette had leaped from a carriage an hour ago and entered his hotel. Since then, the moon had risen. Lyon was almost certainly rutting with her at this exact moment. Giving her the very childseed she herself coveted.

Jealousy boiled, uncomfortably warm in Sibela's cold chest. How dare he cast her aside! She cursed and then spat, unsure how else to vent her wrath. It galled her to stay, but she needed his help and therefore could not depart.

She heard giggling and her gaze cut eastward. The other nymphs had gathered to idle there, smugly mocking her troubles from the shadows of a great log.

"Be gone," she hissed, humiliated that they were witnesses to this debacle. "Do not think to pass the night gloating."

They snickered, but dove downstream leaving her to a solitary vigil.

Various schemes to punish Lyon for cuckolding her incubated in her head as she glowered impotently at the hotel. The current was strong here at the Île Saint-Louis's eastern end where the river was forced into dividing around the island, and she had to constantly fight in order to remain stationary.

There had to be some way of righting this catastrophe. Undulating her tail, she proceeded to pace back and forth, maintaining a course that was parallel to the riverbank.

Lyon had taken Juliette to his bed in lieu of her. Why? Men never chose another when she was on offer. And why did such a thing have to happen now, when it had never been more crucial to capture a man's heart? Or his semen, at least.

She'd had him first. But her rival had won him under a full moon. Whose claim was stronger? She feared she knew the answer, and it did not favor her.

Suddenly, the hotel door swung open and Juliette appeared. Sibela's jaw dropped. The moon was still full and high! Satyr would never have allowed her to leave his bed so early.

The mademoiselle scampered down the path toward her, juggling a basket on each arm. The clank of metal and glass indicated that they contained dishware.

"Wait!" Sibela warbled, beckoning her closer. Perhaps they could reach a bargain regarding the man both wanted.

But Juliette only turned on the quai and scurried on her way, either too occupied with her own thoughts or simply too Human to hear.

Sibela's gaze swung back to the hotel. Instinct told her Lyon remained within. A low croon burbled out of her chest and she began to hail him. She held carefully still, listening for a sign he'd heard. But her calls went unanswered. Another hour or more passed, and she sang on. Why didn't he respond?

Her tail swished fluidly and her mind worked at the same clip, but her head and torso remained motionless. So much so that a turtle mistook her for a mossy rock and attempted to crawl atop her head.

Blasted creature! She smacked it away. A Human male and female strolled by and glanced over at the sound of splashing. Though they looked directly at her, neither exhibited any astonishment.

Excitement gripped her. Perhaps the hiding-spell Satyr had woven round her last night still remained in effect. If so, that would mean she could travel on land without detection.

Eager to test her disguise, she slipped from the river to sit onshore. With efficient strokes she sluiced water from her lower body and polished herself with grasses and crackling leaves to hasten her transformation.

In a gesture so familiar she didn't even notice she made it, she patted the looping strands of jewels at her throat, adjusting them along her chest to ensure they disguised the skin underneath. For beneath the gemstones faint scars were hidden— long-healed slashes where her body had been cut several years ago and had mended itself, and a burn that stayed fresh. It was only possible to see these defects in a certain light, but the sight of them led to questions she'd rather not answer. And some males were put off by them. Hence the jewelry.

Abruptly, a sharp masculine call split the air. Her head whipped around to fasten on the high hotel window from which the unearthly sound had issued. It was Lyon, calling for help! His summons was so faint, so feeble, that she could hardly believe it had come from him.

Hastily, she returned the call, but he didn't reply. Time crept past as she did all she could to urge her Human legs to form. Damned Satyr probably had no idea what she went through for him. Did he think altering bone and reconforming skin was easy? Men!

A torturous half hour later, she at last had fresh limbs. Would they carry her? And, if so, how long would they last?

Sinking her claws into the bark of a nearby tree trunk, she levered herself into a standing position, then waited agonizing minutes for her legs to steady beneath her. Her first steps were awkward and forward progress was slow. Another quarter of an hour passed before she reached the building's portal.

A noise behind her alerted her to the fact that a man and woman were coming up the walk behind her. They passed, so near that the man's cloak dusted her. She blew a clammy breath over his neck and he shuddered, wrapping his scarf closer.

They hadn't been able to see her!

The spell Lyon had woven last night still held. For now at least. Once she reached him, he could reinforce it.

The male behind the hotel desk glanced up and came to greet the couple that opened the door. She slipped inside past the threesome, moving across the foyer with an uncertain gait.

Confronted with the staircase, she grimaced. Scaling it proved to be precisely the torment she'd anticipated. The sensation of ligament, tendon, and bone working together with each step she took was unaccustomed and awful. How did Humans stand it?

She consoled herself that she would grow used to it in time. As Lyon's chosen one—his wife, as the Humans called their bonded women—she would be safe and able to travel freely between land and sea. How delicious it would be to choose legs or tail, according to her whim. All this would have been worth it.

Finding the unlocked door to his apartments, she entered uninvited. She caught his scent immediately and looked upward. *Fuck! More stairs?!* How many did these Humans need?

When she finally arrived at his bedchamber door, her mood

was foul. There was a bed inside and he lay upon it, unmoving, unspeaking. Curious. It was widely known among those of her kind that the Satyr engaged in a frenzy of carnal diversions from dusk to dawn on a Moonful night. Why then, was he lying here now, so calm?

Twin shafts angled high from his groin and belly. Eyeing them, she stepped from shadow into moonlight, waiting for him to acknowledge her.

"No greeting?" she flung the words at him from across the room, trying to provoke him.

He made no reply. Gave no sign he was even aware of her. Her heart plummeted. Surely he wasn't . . . *dead!?*

She rushed closer and cupped a hand over his lips. Relief swamped her when she felt his breath. He lived. Peering closely at his face, she gave his cheek a gentle smack. Nothing.

"Why won't you awaken?" She hitched herself onto his bed, glad to be off her new feet, and ran her thumb over his neck. He'd healed the marks she'd put on him.

"*Arruso.* Asshole," she cursed. "I swear I'll kill you if you dare to die on me."

Without his cooperation, she would be doomed to exist in constant peril. Eventually, she would be captured. And once ElseWorld snatched her, they would discover the truth of her past soon enough. They must not be allowed to take this body from her. Without it, she was nothing. Literally nothing.

"What happened here to make you like this?" She picked up a glass from the floor and dipped her tongue into its wine, then shuddered at the bitter, repulsive taste.

The air was redolent with the smells of food. She remembered the trays Juliette and her servants had brought. Understanding dawned. Apparently, the mademoiselle hadn't forgotten all of her magic.

She tsked at him. "Fool! You ate food proffered by a faerie?

Left yourself wide open to her spells? You must've known better, but I suppose you were too blinded by lust to avoid her
trap. And what was the purpose of her trap, I wonder?"

Leaning over him, she took the root of his pelvic cock in one
hand and that of his man-cock in her other, admiring them.
They were the kind of cocks she most preferred—long, thick,
and unyielding, with a slight curve. Just right for fucking.

"You've grown since we last met," she said approvingly.
"The effect of the moon, I suppose."

Releasing the lesser one, she dipped the tip of one claw inside the slit of the larger one that grew from his thatch. Cum
welled. She bent and lapped it, gasping when she tasted her rival
on him. "Damn! She took you in her mouth?"

Alarmed at what this could mean in terms of her rights to
him, she wasted no time in reasserting her own claim. Going up
on her knees, she situated herself alongside his hip, so she faced
toward his feet. Splitting her new lower limbs, she awkwardly
attempted to straddle him.

He expelled an involuntary *oof* as she drove her knee into
his midsection at one point before managing to sling herself
into position.

Giving him her back, she rose over him on all fours and
tucked her calves along his flanks, toes pointed toward his
armpits. Her feet clutched his ribs, anchoring her to him.

Reaching between her legs, she guided the shaft that grew
from his thatch to the brink of her feminine slit. Then, reaching
her other hand behind her, she awkwardly brought his pelvic
shaft to the tight, blue mouth in the cleft of her rear. Leaving
him poised thusly, she braced her hands in front of her on his
thighs.

All she had to do now was let gravity do its work.

Her leg muscles relaxed and she immediately felt the pressure of his entry. She opened easily for him at first, but her eyes

widened as he sought a deeper intrusion. She'd taken him in her female passage once before, but he was larger than most—especially tonight. And she'd not previously had him *á deux*.

Still, fucking him on the sly like this, without his knowledge or permission, acted on her like an aphrodisiac. The power and the control were hers in this moment and she reveled in them.

"I believe I prefer you like this, so docile and cooperative," she murmured, as she attempted to fill herself with him.

Minutes passed as her gelatinous passages struggled to induct all of him. She let him take her weight, forcing him deeper and farther and faster than her body could comfortably withstand and relishing the resulting pleasure-pain. Her tissues sucked at him in a sort of carnal peristalsis as she pressed on, sometimes easing up an inch or so before angling down again to achieve a better fit. At long last, her bottom rested flush with his belly and she found herself twice impaled.

She squirmed on him, seating him as deeply as possible. "Umm," she crooned. "This is almost worth all the trouble you've put me to."

Then, reminding herself of her ultimate purpose, she proceeded to rhythmically rise and fall on him. His lengths were warm, and her channels cool, and the sensation of his advance and retreat was all the more acute due to the difference. Moving inside her, he felt thrillingly huge. The rod in her vaginal passage stretched her so wide that each shove brushed her clit. Within seconds, she climaxed, but she scarcely let it break her stride for the object of this intercourse was *his* ejaculation.

So she fucked onward, twitching now and then as his thrust excited nerve endings already over-stimulated by her recent coming. Her muscles burned at the unaccustomed exercise, and they quickly began to tire and falter.

"Nooo!" she despaired, fearing her new legs might give out on her. She punched her quivering thigh with an impotent fist. She had to bring him to completion!

The touch of warm male hands startled her and she jerked upright as they firmly grasped her hips and commenced assisting her movement. She gasped and looked at Lyon over her shoulder. His eyes were still closed, his mind distant and unaware. It was only some mating instinct that had prompted him to continue her work.

His grip compelled her to swallow to him again, and the motion forced her to twist back around to face the foot of the bed. In complete control of her now, he pushed her, then pulled, harder and faster, shoving himself in and out of her. Gratefully, she indulged him.

Her lashes lowered, turning her eyes to slits. Her claws hooked his thighs. "That's it, my darling," she crooned, her voice hot and urgent. "Help me fuck you."

Inside her he grew even fatter, even hungrier for release. In the V between his legs, his scrotum tightened. Retracting her claws, she took his balls in one hand, fondling them in the way men liked.

"Yes, that's right," she crooned. "Like that. Shoot it in me . . . oh, Gods, please!"

Hard fingers dug into her hips, pushing her away one last time, then wrenching her downward, so hard that their bodies' meeting rattled her very bones. His hips strained upward, lifting them both from the bed for a suspended moment.

A single, harsh groan escaped him and she felt him spill inside her. Her groan mingled with his and her body bowed forward under the strength of another, unexpected orgasm that crashed over her in tandem with his. Her body bucked uncontrollably as a second gush of fluid heat spurted from him into her passages. And then a third, and a fourth, until she lost count. Tears of relief coursed down her cheeks and she wiped them away, embarrassed at herself for such a weak, feminine display.

Then her head went back and she laughed aloud, rejoicing at

the wash of his life-giving semen. All had been accomplished! He'd just gifted her with his childseed and she'd felt her womb swallow it! He was hers. She was safe!

A long while later, his spillage finally slowed and then ceased altogether. His hands fell away to lie on the linens.

Breath heaved in and out of her lungs, loud in the quiet aftermath. She let out a shriek as the cock in her anus abruptly recoiled, making a squishy sound as it retracted inside his body. Her hands hit the mattress between his knees and she rose, just enough to relieve herself of his single remaining shaft. Then she flopped onto the mattress beside him.

She rolled onto her back and lay there for some time, limp and exhausted, her inner tissues still squelching. Her fingers moved between her legs, glossing the slickness of their mingled juices over her clit and setting off another round of pleasurable spasms.

Her thighs came together and she moaned turning on her side, toward him. "*Merci*, Monsieur Satyr," she whispered. "Or should I say *grazie*?"

Beside her, Lyon was silent, still.

She smiled at him, enjoying the sight of his handsome sleeping face. And to think he was all hers, for surely this momentous event solidified her claim.

Levering herself up on an elbow, she ran her fingers lightly over his belly, examining it. Amazingly, there was no sign there had ever been a second cock protruding from his flesh.

He drew a long shuddering breath, and her eyes flew to his face, watching as those beautiful lips of his parted slightly and then spoke. His words, exhaled on a sigh, were so soft she almost didn't hear.

"Ahh! Juliette."

Sibela leaped away from him as though he'd burned her. "Bastard!" she fumed, moving off the bed. "You dare mistake me for *her*?"

She swiped clawed fingertips over the abdomen she'd just caressed, drawing five pinkened stripes. Foam frothed on her lips as she cursed and spewed and raised her arm to inflict more damage.

But before she could retaliate further for his betrayal, a lightening bolt of pain struck, shooting along the insides of her legs from groin to ankle. Her legs crumpled under her, and then her knees struck the carpet.

Bent on all fours, she stared in horror at her lower limbs. The skin there had begun to shimmer and had developed a scalloped appearance.

Her fists pounded the floor and a frustrated wail emerged from her lips. Her legs had decided to become a tail again!

"Fuck!" Grabbing the bedrail, she pulled herself to her feet and shot a baleful glare at the man on the mattress. "That seed of yours better have been potent."

With that, she scurried to the bedchamber door and slammed it behind her, causing it to accidentally lock. By the time she reached the top of the hotel staircase, her flesh had already begun to join high between her thighs. When her foot touched the final step in the lobby, she had fused from groin to knee. As she passed the hotelier's desk, her gait had necessarily deteriorated into a waddle.

Feeling ridiculous, she shuffled outside, down the walkway, and across the lawn. She had to reach the Seine before she ended up floundering on shore like a fish out of water.

Her ankles chose that moment to merge and she staggered. With a hard flex of feet that were rapidly becoming fins, she dove, arcing high above the remaining expanse of land. And by the time the river's splash embraced her, the transformation was already complete.

She would wait until Satyr's seed took root and grew before showing herself to him again, she decided. By then, he would be unable to do anything to thwart its gestation. Without looking back, she began to swim downstream with a powerful stroke, already planning what she would say to him when they were reunited one month from now.

Behind her in the hotel, Lyon slumbered on, blithely unaware that he'd just fathered a child.

Lyon opened his eyes and winced under the light streaming in the window. It was already mid-morning, far later than he normally slept.

A knock sounded on the door. So that was what had awakened him. Someone had entered his apartment and was now standing just outside his bedchamber. The doorknob was visible from his position on the bed, and he saw it turn. But he must've locked it for it didn't open.

"Monsieur Satyr? Monsieur Satyr?" More rapping. "Are you there?" It was the hotelier, sounding concerned and curious.

"*Si,*" Lyon managed. *Bacchus!* His voice creaked like a rusty key turning in a thousand-year-old lock. And he had a monstrous, mind-splitting headache worse than any hangover he could ever recall.

"A missive has arrived for you."

"Put it un—" he began, only to be cut off by a wrenching cramp that seized his belly. "Under the door," he rasped, curling onto his side in a fetal position.

After a brief hesitation, a square of white appeared on his side of the door, jettisoned by an unseen hand.

"Wait! What day is it?" he croaked.

"*Lundi*—Monday, monsieur," came the disembodied voice.

He'd been asleep for *four* nights?!

The last clear memory he had was of his arrival in Paris on Thursday. He remembered stepping onto the Pont Neuf. After that, it was as though he'd entered a bank of fog.

The hotelier called to him again. "Do you require anything further?"

"*Oui.* A bath. *Merci.*"

"*Certainement, monsieur.*" Brisk footsteps faded down the staircase and then he heard the door to the exterior hall whisk shut.

He forced himself to sit up. His big feet hit the floor like thunder, knocking against a crystal wine glass sitting on the carpet and sending it rolling.

His memories of the past three days and four nights were a jumble of unnamed faces, obscure conversations, and vague locations. A vision of the Pompeii ruins flashed before him, and he shook his head, wondering where that had come from. The movement set off a new round of agony sparking through his skull.

His head fell into his hands, elbows braced on his knees. "Two thousand hells," he groaned into his lap.

He remembered meeting a woman on the bridge the night he arrived in the city. A Human woman with brown eyes and a pink dress. That had been Thursday. Had they lain together?

Friday had been a Moonful night.

He clutched his cramping abdomen and found it smooth. There was no strangled knot struggling to erupt from it. His pelvic cock must've come and gone, ejaculating and retreating inside him again. Which meant he'd fornicated at least once under Friday's full moon. But with whom?

His head lifted as a pair of seawater green eyes swam into his mind. There'd been another woman since he'd come to Paris, besides the brown-eyed Human! He tried to recall her scent or her face, some memory of her. Nothing. Had she been Human as well?

Doubtful. The bodies of most Human women couldn't accommodate him during Moonful. Shimmerskins were his usual choice on such nights. In fact, on the journey to Paris, he re-membered he'd contemplated this matter. Since he'd consid-ered it unlikely he would find King Feydon's daughter in time, he'd planned to conjure Shimmerskins Friday night when the Calling overtook him. Is that what he'd done?

His palms ran over the bed linen. She'd been here, in his bed. That other woman. He recalled being with her here. Now that he thought about it, the signs of debauchery were everywhere in this room. Discarded clothing littered the floor and the bed-clothes were a wreck. There were two wine glasses—one on the table and another on the floor. That eliminated the possibility he'd bedded Shimmerskins. He wouldn't have fed them wine since they didn't take any form of sustenance.

Sustenance. A memory flashed—of china and silver dishes bearing delicious delicacies and held by feminine hands. And of the moon rising through the window to limn long strands of pale hair. He'd dined with a woman here. Just prior to Moon-ful!

Thank the Gods. It was something to go on. Another vague impression came to him, of a female voice coaxing him to taste some French-sounding pastry. Had she drugged him with it? Or with the wine?

He stood then, intending to check the state of the dining room. But he'd risen too quickly and blood drained from his head. Feeling faint, he clutched at the bedrail.

He managed a few steps, but then pitched forward. Bracing a hand on the wall to keep himself upright, he inadvertently sent a framed watercolor tumbling. He gritted his teeth and fought the desire to retch, but lost. Crouching on all fours, he proceeded to stain the rumpled pair of his trousers lying there with his own puke.

Gasping in the aftermath, he rolled onto his side. Gods! Had he ever been so miserable? Apparently, he'd had no bath, no food, and no sex for three days and four nights. Yet the latter was what he craved most.

Spying the square of white the hotelier had slid under the door, he considered fetching it. Eventually mustering the wherewithal, he crawled the few feet necessary and then lay on his back to open and read it.

Fortunately, his eldest brother had been mercifully brief:

> *Return. You are needed.*
> *—Nicholas Satyr*

The paper fluttered to his chest.

"Bad timing, Nico," he muttered. But his brother would never have called him away from his mission here unless it was for the most urgent of reasons.

With new strength born of sheer determination, he gathered himself from the floor, opened the door, and bellowed for the bath he'd ordered as well as assistance with his dressing.

If there was trouble at home, there was no time to lose. He would have to muster the energy to travel.

When his bath arrived, he would request a *petit déjeuner*—breakfast. He wasn't hungry, but maybe food would help him recover.

Food. Salivary glands twisted, moistening his mouth. Something clicked in his brain. The fact that he'd dined with the green-eyed woman was somehow significant.

Naked, he padded downstairs toward the dining room to investigate. With each descending step, his enormous cock swung between his legs like a pendulum with two gonads as its accompanying weights. Halfway down, he caught sight of the empty table below. Any dishes and aromas from their repast were long gone. So was the woman.

Reaching the dining room at last, he gingerly searched the

air for any sign of the woman who'd been there with him. No more than the barest trace of residual feminine scents remained, but it almost seemed that there were two separate fragrances, which had somehow woven themselves together. Whether Fey or Human, Raine could've tracked them to their sources even though they were days old, but he was not so facile in that way and never had been. Only the freshest of scents were easy for him to discern. And Raine wasn't here.

Whoever his companion had been, he was certain she'd dined here at some point, in this room with him. He ran a palm over the glossy surface of the table, straining to remember.

Elusive bits of memory curled into his mind like ghostly objects visible when viewed from the corner of the eye, yet gone when fully faced: Flesh pressed to flesh. Feminine whispers at his ear. Soft hands cupping his face. She'd been inside his every orifice and he inside hers. He'd taken her here on the table, against the wall, bent over the basin in the kitchen. Other partners had joined them from time to time, and she'd brought devices of pleasure with her—a flogger, oils, and dildos of various shapes and dimensions. And . . . bananas?

His cock rose expectantly at the salacious visions and he took it in his hand, stroking. His other hand flexed, its palm tingling. He stared at it, remembering the poke of nipples. Nipples that had been unusually warm. Nipples his touch had caused to luminesce!

Satisfaction settled over him. It was a sign she'd been faerie. One with intriguing carnal inclinations, apparently. And he'd let her slip away.

Ten thousand hells!

Holding onto a chair back, he sank onto its seat. With his head bent forward between his knees, he struggled to keep from retching again—a malaise brought on simply by the effort of standing for so long.

Why was he so exhausted? After a Moonful Calling, he was usually energized.

It hurt to think, but he forced himself to start again and review what he knew. Yet everything came back to one conundrum. If he'd passed the Calling with King Feydon's daughter, then why was he sick? And why wasn't he sated?

The "whys" came at him from every direction. Why couldn't he remember the precise physical details of her body's appearance beneath her clothing? Why couldn't he distinguish her from all the other generic females he had taken under him over the years?

It was both disturbing and confusing that his mind insisted he'd been carnally sated, yet his body raged that it had not. Why couldn't he recall the actual sensation of joining himself to her more clearly? It was as if someone else's sexual fantasies played out in his head, instead of a sequence of real events.

With the impact of a lightening bolt, the answer came to him. His memories of the liaison were vague because it *hadn't happened!* None of it. Or at least not all of it.

The flame of anger lit in him. The Faerie were notorious for their tricks. Feydon's daughter had come here, had used her ways to bespell him, and then she'd stolen his seed and left him to pine and sicken. The Calling ritual, which required that he engage in serial copulation for the duration of moonlight, hadn't been completed. The fact that his twin cocks had ejaculated once, but likely no more, lay at the root of his entire problem. He should be thankful he'd had that relief at least. Otherwise, he'd be dead.

Only another Calling night with the one who'd taken his first seed into her body would bring him fully back to health. But to survive the days and nights between now and then, his body needed to mate with hers, and often. He had to locate her.

His bath arrived and food. And sometime during his meal, from out of nowhere, three new clues leapt into his mind.

A gray house

A red door.

And a name.

Juliette.

9

"Have you seen Fleur this morning?" asked Juliette.

Lying in her narrow, rumpled bed in the room next to Fleur's, Gina shook her head, mussing her tangled auburn hair on her pillow. "She's not in her bedchamber?"

"*Non.* Nor anywhere upstairs."

Gina stretched, wincing. "She was with Valmont last night. I think they went out."

Juliette's hand tightened on the doorknob. "Do you know where he is?"

"You're full of questions this morning. *Non*, do you hear? If he's not in his study or the salon, ask the *majordome*. I fucked myself silly last night. So have pity and let me sleep, will you?"

She rolled over onto her stomach, displaying a backside striped with pink welts.

Juliette pulled her door shut and flew downstairs. In the past, other girls had left without a word. Theirs was a transient lifestyle. But Fleur wouldn't have gone without any explanation. Without saying goodbye.

Juliette passed a bleary-eyed Agnes on the stairway. "Did you seen Fleur last night? Or this morning?"

Agnes yawned. "She's gone."

"What do you mean 'gone'? Gone where?"

"I don't know. Ask Monsieur," she replied, referring to Valmont. "He's in the upstairs study, along with Monsieur Arlette." She raised a hand to brush a wisp of hair behind her ear. Silver flashed on her earlobe.

"Those are Fleur's earrings," said Juliette, grasping her arm.

Agnes wrested herself away and continued down the steps. "Monsieur told me I could take any of her belongings I wish. Lucky girl. Just out of the kitchens and one of her admirers must've already offered to become her protector. I suppose he was too jealous to let her keep any trinkets given to her by other men."

Juliette whirled about before Agnes had finished speaking and hurried back upstairs, almost tripping in her haste.

Was Valmont behind Fleur's disappearance? Had he been so jealous of their friendship that he'd sent her away?

Male voices reached her ears from the direction of his study. She paused outside its door, listening. From the sound of things, Monsieur Arlette was in a fine mood.

"They liked what we sent," he was enthusing. "They've requested another shipment. And we have the phylloxera to thank for that!"

"And for little else." Valmont sounded irritated.

"Why do you dwell on the past, when our future shines bright?" Arlette chided. "Our factory in Pontarlier can hardly keep up with the new demand. As more vineyards fall to the pest, wine grows scarce and its cost continues to rise. We're ahead of any competitors with the idea of pushing absinthe to fill the void. Our business cannot help but thrive."

"Who'd have thought the phylloxera would actually benefit

us in the end?" Valmont mused, sounding cheerier. "It seems my family fortunes will soon be on the mend."

Juliette heard the clink of glass as the men toasted their success. She glanced around to ensure no one had noticed her eavesdropping, then pressed her ear to the door.

"You don't look happy about it," said Arlette. "It's that blond piece, Juliette, isn't it? Just take her cherry and be done with it, why don't you? Or I will."

"I'll kill you if you dare," Valmont said mildly. "Have you forgotten that if either of us were to dip our wicks in that one, it would be an invitation for her to toy with our minds?"

"So you say."

Jars in the inkstand clanked together, informing her that Valmont had struck his desktop. "It's true! I've seen her do it, I tell you."

"Simply fill her full of those drops of hers," Arlette advised blithely. "A well-timed visit to her bed and your seed will soon be baking inside your pretty little cook's oven. That's what you're after isn't it?"

Inside the room, there was a considering pause. Horrified, Juliette put a hand to the fluttering beat at the base of her throat.

"Such an action would be risky." Valmont again. "What if she were to elicit facts about a certain matter from me, even through her laudanum haze?"

"You refer to the murder?"

"Damnation, Arlette! That tongue of yours wags far too loudly," Valmont hissed. His voice had lowered and she had to strain to hear. "Yes, it's what I refer to. All is well only as long as she continues to believe everyone thinks she was responsible. But if she sucks information to the contrary from me while I'm bewitched—well, that is quite a deterrent, wouldn't you agree?"

Out in the corridor, Juliette folded her lips between her teeth to keep from gasping. They'd as much as admitted she was *not* guilty of the murder in Burgundy three years ago! She wanted to shout for joy and to rage at them. But she did neither, and only listened on.

"I could wait outside the room while you get the deed done," Arlette suggested. "Or better yet, I could watch you diddle her. If she manages to bespell you, I can later remind you of anything you've forgotten. And help determine if she learned anything she shouldn't regarding that other delicate matter I'm not allowed to speak of in a normal tone of voice."

"What's to stop you from leaving me in the dark and taking Juliette for yourself as you did young Fleur?"

Without thinking, Juliette turned the knob and threw open the door so forcefully that it bounced off the wall. "Where's Fleur?" she demanded, striding into the room.

Both men jerked around so fast it was comical. They gawked at her for a second, then Arlette exploded into action. Moving to the door, he peered nervously along the hall in both directions before shutting it and barring it with his bulk.

Valmont favored her with a false smile and stood to beckon her nearer with a wave of his ghostly hand. "Do come in, my dear. How long were you listening?"

"Listening? To what?" She advanced on him, stiff with anger, but still smart enough to lie. "I only just arrived. I've spent the past half hour questioning the other girls about Fleur. According to them, she was with you last night, and now she has disappeared. Tell me where she is or I'll summon the gendarmes."

"Police?" Valmont chuckled as he reseated himself. That he didn't even take her threats seriously enough to come out from behind the desk galled her.

Furious, she stalked toward him. "Where is she!?"

But he only smirked, which told her he was responsible for Fleur's removal as clearly as if he'd admitted it in words.

"Careful, darling, you're becoming hysterical. I'm sure she's only taken a fancy to one of her beaux and gone off with him. You know how these girls can be with their silly notions of true love."

She knew he was lying, but if she admitted it, they would know she'd been eavesdropping. And she didn't want them to realize what else she'd overheard. Not yet.

"She wouldn't have gone without telling me," Juliette insisted. "Not without taking all of her shoes and dresses and jewels. She valued that small collection of worldly goods too dearly." She whirled around and headed for the door.

Arlette eyed her, still blocking it. But it was Valmont's voice that halted her, for it had turned silky as it did when he was at his most devious.

"What do you suppose will happen if you summon the police and tell them your preposterous tale, *ma chère*? Suppose they begin an investigation?"

She looked at him over her shoulder.

"You were particular friends with Fleur," he went on. "M. Arlette and the other girls would attest to that with no urging from me. When it comes to light that we've *unwittingly* harbored you—a fugitive who fled Burgundy while under suspicion of murder—who would the gendarmes decide to suspect in Fleur's disappearance I wonder?"

"Who indeed," Arlette seconded. "I'm sure I could arrange for a spattering of blood to appear on your rug if the inspectors need further convincing of your guilt."

Juliette glanced between them, appalled. Moments ago, Valmont had intimated that they'd trumped up the evidence implicating her in the Burgundy crime. It had been he who'd tricked her into fleeing the charges, which she saw now had only added to others' suspicions. He had then proceeded to turn her into an addict and had encouraged her phobias. She was well and truly trapped here, for he'd cut off all avenues of escape.

"Come, come. Let's speak no more on this. Forget your little friend and calm yourself for we must speak on another topic. That of Lord Satyr." He looked beyond her. "You may leave us, Monsieur Arlette."

After a moment, she heard the door behind her shut. Valmont gestured toward the chair opposite his desk. "Sit."

Leery of what he would say, but needing to hear it, she took the seat he'd indicated.

He tapped the desk blotter with the tip of a fingernail. "You know I love you, *chèrie*. You know that, don't you?"

She only stared at him, refusing for the first time to give him the reply he expected. Three years ago she'd foolishly believed him when he'd said he loved her. Since then, she'd learned he was a monster. She could not stay here to bear the child of a monster. She'd kill herself—or him—first.

He sat back in his chair and went on, not seeming to notice she hadn't responded. "Tell me. If I were to lend you to Lord Satyr, could you remain chaste? Could I trust you that much? It would be the ultimate test of your loyalty to me."

His question shook her out of her stupor. "What do you mean 'lend' me to him?"

"You proved yourself resistant to him when you went to his hotel. He's primed for marriage, and besotted with you. If you gain his trust—"

She gripped the seat of her chair on either side of her knees. "Gain his trust? How am I to do that after I just duped him in the worst way?"

He fluttered his fingers in the air, brushing off her objection. "Use your tricks. You'll find a way to manage it. My material point is to suggest that you are to lure him into another proposal. And this time, you will accept."

"Accept?" she parroted in dismay. "But you know I cannot marry him. It would be unlawful."

"And you are something of an expert on unlawful matters are you not, *ma petite* murderess?"

"You promised not to bring up that subject again."

He stood, reached across the desk, and calmly slapped her. "You're my property. I will speak to you as I wish and you will do as I tell you."

Stunned, she covered her stinging cheek and watched with swimming eyes as he reseated himself and dipped his quill into the inkwell.

"Now, I shall pen a note to Lord Satyr at his hotel in which I will offer you to him. When he responds, you will see him. You will find a way to wed him, then you will go to the heart of the demon's lair. There, you'll be in a position to find out what they get up to, which you will then report to me."

"As his wife, you'd expect me to remain chaste by 'tricking' him, as you put it? Every night he wishes to bed me? Even if I could achieve what you're asking, I don't know what long-term effect such 'tricks' might have on his mind. What if they destroy him?"

He only shrugged, continuing to write. "The price of Satyr wine is at an all-time high, did you know?" he enquired obscurely. "His family has benefited from the destruction of mine. Now I plan to benefit from the destruction of his."

As Valmont scribbled away, Juliette's gaze drifted upward to the soulful eyes of the long-dead buck above his desk. Its eyes were vacant. Dead. The way she felt.

"It will never be enough for you, will it?" she whispered dismally.

He finished the letter with a satisfied flourish and blew on it. "Stop speaking twaddle, and make yourself useful. Bring me the sealing wax from my cabinet."

Like an automaton, she rose and went to the cabinet, but what greeted her there shook her out of her daze in an instant. Beyond its glass, on the shelf positioned at eye-level, sat the odd little collection of feminine gewgaws.

Something new had been added to the very end of the row.

A bracelet. The very one Fleur had adored. The one she'd been so proud of that she hadn't removed it since it had been given to her.

Yet now, here it was, displayed upon a slip of velvet in this cabinet. Like some sort of trophy! For that's what these items were, she realized in horror. Trophies. Mementos. All taken from women.

She reached out her hand.

"Hurry, girl! What keeps you?"

Quickly she stuffed what she'd stolen into her pocket and returned to him with the wax. She held her breath when he frowned at her impatiently, but he didn't seem to notice anything amiss.

"Go now. I'll let you know when I have his reply."

Her mind and steps raced with new, terror-inspired determination as she departed his study. He would listen for the creak of the stairs to be sure she took the path to her attic room. To allay any suspicion, she did so.

Once inside, she quietly shut the door behind her. *Vite!* Hurry! Now that she'd reached a momentous decision, she must act before her courage flagged.

She fell on her knees beside the floorboard, raised it, and removed the pouch. Pulling the necklace from it, she went to the looking glass and watched herself loop it around her neck and tie it fast. She stroked down the beads once, then lifted them high to drop inside the neckline of her dress, where they wouldn't be visible.

The pouch was still heavy with coins and she jiggled it, wanting to hear the reassuring clank. Getting her handbag from the armoire, she stuffed the pouch and a few items of clothing inside it, then went to the door.

With her hand on the knob, she halted and stared blindly at the door's figured wood paneling, as an inner debate began.

Slowly, she turned her head, finding the vial of drops with her eyes.

She should leave them behind. Start anew. But the contemplation of sudden abstinence was too frightening. She went back to the table and slipped the laudanum into her bag.

Taking care to tread only on steps that did not squeak, she crept back downstairs. There, she pulled her crimson wrap from its peg and quietly left Valmont's house forever, unaware that by unleashing her emotions she had also unleashed a fey scent that only one man in Paris could detect.

10

A malevolent wind swept through the Parc Vert Galant, buffeting Lyon as he huddled in the shadows under the bridge. He glanced toward the maple trees along the riverbank. Nary a golden leaf stirred.

ElseWorld had not yet infiltrated this world, but the intentions of its inhabitants had. Leaks of its energy struck him now and then, like sparks from a smoking chimney. Having sensed he was weak, they were stirring restlessly and watching for any opportunity to take him down.

A woman passed him and slowed. She was the fifth to do so since he'd arrived here this morning. "*Non. Allez,*" he muttered and she went on. Whatever was attracting them to him in this way he didn't know. But it had long since passed the point of irritation.

Nausea and worry churned in him, making it hard to think clearly. His failure to complete the ritual three nights ago would have far-reaching consequences.

As his health declined so would his lands. Many of his grapevines wouldn't make it through the coming winter.

Liber and Ceres and the other animals in his menagerie who depended on him—on his very existence—for their continued survival would soon begin to sicken in sympathetic reaction to his plight.

And without him, his brothers could not carry on the work of safeguarding the sacred aperture, which lay shrouded in mist and secrecy, deep in the heart of their jointly owned estate. This gate between EarthWorld and ElseWorld would become vulnerable upon his death, and the results of that would be disastrous. Creatures spawned by gods of a bygone era would spill into this world and wreak havoc.

He could not die here. He would not abandon his vines or his pets or his brothers to such fates. Determination stiffened his spine and the next gust of wind barely rocked him. Wrapping his arms closer around his quaking frame, he trained his eyes on the red door along the Quai di Conti, waiting as he had all morning.

Minutes later, it opened, and a woman with a crimson cloak over her arm stepped out. She was young, with pale blond hair.

The sight of her immediately suffused him with unfamiliar emotions. Betrayal. Outrage. Longing. *Longing?!* He couldn't recall having ever longed for the company of a particular female in his entire twenty-six years. *Bacchus!* What had she done to him?

He straightened, rallying the strength to follow her. When he saw she was moving toward him, he sent up a silent word of gratitude. She headed for the bridge overhead and though she was lost from sight momentarily, he tracked her scent and knew she was making her way closer. He could scarcely credit his luck when he heard the tap of her slippers on the stone steps nearest him.

She'd started down and was coming his way almost as if she'd known he was here and wished to meet him. After the difficulty of getting himself to this park and then loitering here through the chilly morning hours, would she make it so easy for him?

Her fragrance and footsteps drew nearer, but she faltered for so long at various points along the stairs that he began to fear she'd somehow sensed he was lying in wait.

Finally, she stood on tiptoe at the base of the northwestern staircase not ten feet from him, enjoying a view of the river.

Within easy range.

The sound of her voice reached him. ". . . the broth requires a hint of cinnamon and a pinch of coriander and the *viande* may be braised within it among the coals for two hours, turning from time to time . . . "

She was reciting recipes?

Juliette paused on the bottom rung of the stairs leading from the Pont Neuf to the Parc Vert Gallant. One more step and her slippers would touch grass.

The smell of dank river clotted her nose and her every sense rebelled at it, sending dizziness tickling over her. Each of the past three mornings, she'd come here and eased a few treads farther downward than comfort allowed. But today she'd reached her limit. Try as she might, she could not convince herself to actually enter the park.

With one white-knuckled hand gripping the railing, she craned forward to search the riverbank and the grounds of the park with her eyes. It was uncrowded here this morning, for ominous clouds had gathered in the sky and the atmosphere had turned strange and forbidding.

Disappointment quickly swamped her as it had every other time she'd come here. What had she expected? she scolded herself. The fishtailed woman who'd lain here with Lyon—the one he'd called Sibela—was obviously not going to return.

This was the last time she would come here on this fool's errand. She was leaving Paris. This very minute. Going as far away as she could get. As soon as she could somehow gather sufficient funds, she'd solicit a detective in this city to search for any sign of Fleur's whereabouts.

Fleur! A sob choked her throat. Her cheek still stung with the rosy imprint made by Valmont's open hand, and angry, frustrated tears crowded her eyes. Wiping them away, she squared her shoulders and resituated the handbag and cloak in the crook of her arm, gathering her courage. She lay her fingers on the balustrade once more, preparing to turn and retrace her steps to the bridge.

As of today, she was on the run.

A surprised shriek escaped her as a masculine hand suddenly whipped from the opposite side of the railing to anchor her wrist to the narrow slope of stone. At the same time, a muscled arm snaked around her waist.

In the space of an instant, she found herself bodily hauled over the rail to its other side, where she was summarily slammed against a massive chest. The arm at her waist tightened, lifting her to dangle several inches from the ground. The hand rose to cup the back of her skull, pressing her nose into that chest and thereby muffling any protests.

Dropping her belongings, she punched and slapped at unforgiving male rib and sinew, but her captor took no notice. Crisp leaves thrashed and crackled under his boots as he dragged her away. For the moment, fear of him had superceded other terrors and she scarcely noticed she'd entered the outskirts of the park.

Wordlessly, he crowded her into the shadowy lee of the bridge and nailed her spine against a cold stone support. Then he stood a moment, with his head tucked into the notch of her shoulder, taking great heaves of breath as if kidnapping her had winded him.

"Juliette?" Held so close, she felt the question rumble in his chest.

Worming her fists high between them, she threw back her head to view her assailant.

God! It was Lyon!

"You! Let go of me." Wedging more space between them, she tried to force him away. "If you're here to do me harm, I'll scream," she warned.

He didn't respond, but instead only studied her with fascinated eyes that traveled over her countenance, seeming intent on memorizing every detail. Almost as if he'd never beheld her before.

"What do you want?"

"Answers," he muttered. Turning his lips to the side of her neck, he tasted her. "And a traveling companion."

"I'm not going anywhere with you." Her challenge hung between them as they stood there, sandwiched together for an interminable moment.

Against her stomach, she felt the muscles of his abdomen abruptly twist and contract in a violent cramp. With a strangled curse, he slipped his forearm between their bodies and clasped it tight to his gut.

When he eventually straightened, he grasped her hips, drawing back enough that she was able to see his face a second time. In a calmer frame of mind now, she realized something she hadn't before.

He was ill.

The natural flush of health had fled his cheekbones and shadows now lurked below eyes that were grim and aggressive. It was difficult to believe that these eyes had ever sparkled or that this face had ever been graced with dimples. What had once been golden and winsomely beautiful was now menacing and starkly handsome.

"W-What's wrong with you?"

"Nothing you can't put to rights," he growled. Kicking her

feet wide, he insinuated his bulk between her legs. She was pinned. Open.

"*Non*! You think to maul me?" she cried, swatting at him. "Here? Under this bridge?"

As if in answer, the hands on either side of her began ruching her skirts higher.

"Stop!" She shoved as hard as she could, thinking he might be easily dislodged, but quickly learning her mistake. Though he appeared unwell, he was not weak.

She let out a huff of outrage. "I don't know why I am surprised at such treatment from you here in the open air, for this seems to be your usual locale for liaisons."

"Ah, she admits to knowing me." Manacling both her wrists in one hand, he forced them against the stone above her head. Meanwhile, his other hand had worked its way under her skirt and was sliding up her thigh.

"Stop! What are you doing? Oh! That's cold!" she said, dancing away from his touch. When the hand only continued higher, she drew in a breath to scream. Until now, she hadn't dared risk drawing unwanted attention that might ultimately bring Valmont. But she couldn't blithely stand here and let him rape her!

The hand securing her wrists took them lower, until his forearm pressed against her mouth and effectively silenced her. However, he didn't proceed to fumble at his trousers in preparation for the carnal assault she'd expected. Instead, his chilled palm only skimmed farther upward, passing the naked V of her privates to find and cup her abdomen.

Long fingers quested, squeezing gently here and pressing there, and generally moving over her belly with the skill of an experienced physician. And all the while, his gaze bored into hers. It was distant, as though he didn't really see her, but rather was entirely intent on what his hand was doing.

Apparently reaching some conclusion that displeased him,

his brows slammed together and his eyes hardened in accusation. "Why are you not increasing?"

"What?" Suffocated by his arm, it came out as a squeak.

He dropped her skirts. "Answer me, dammit!"

She shot him a look that called him stupid and mumbled an inarticulate protest against the restraint of his forearm.

Realizing why she could not speak, he let go of her wrists and mouth and smacked his palms on the stone on either side of her shoulders.

"Well?"

Was he insane? "Because I-I eat little of my own cooking, I suppose. Though my weight is none of your concern," 'she added tartly.

His square chin jutted and he loomed nearer until he spoke to her nose to nose. Eyes she'd once thought warm now watched her with a cold, feral intensity that chilled her.

"You purposely mistake my meaning," he said. "I speak of the way a woman's body increases as a result of a man's seed taking root in her. I planted a child in your belly three nights ago. At my hotel."

So that was it! Because of her spell, he naturally believed they'd fornicated. And for some reason, he assumed she was with child and that she should already be displaying evidence of it.

"I assure you I'm not *enceinte* as a result of our encounter," she replied carefully. "But even if I were, I wouldn't be showing signs of it so soon."

His eyes lit with satisfaction and he drew slightly away. "Yet another admission! You *were* in my room that night."

"You don't remember?"

He hesitated, then—"Not exactly."

"What does that mean?"

He hesitated again, then confessed, "There are a few gaps in my memory of the last few days. I recall being in this park at some point. And knocking upon a red door. And a woman in my hotel."

Her breath hitched. "What else?"

"Today, I came here and waited. When I saw you come out of the townhouse across the quai, I remembered you. Touching you. Kissing you." His eyes fell to her lips, then returned to meet hers. "I remember virtually nothing else of substance between the time I arrived in Paris Thursday night and when I awoke in my hotel this morning."

She shot him a look of shock tinged with guilt. He'd only been supposed to forget *one* night. Her magic had never worked so thoroughly on a man that he'd lost the memory of three!

He gave her a little shake. "You did something to me when we were together. Something to make my mind faulty. What was it?"

"You're mistaken," she protested. "Not about everything. I did meet you at your hotel Friday, but we didn't . . . do what you think we did."

"Don't lie," he gritted.

He cupped the cheeks of her rear and lifted her, sighing as he aligned his monumental erection to her furrow. "It was you in my bed. My cock knows it. I know it. It was you." His lips brushed the angle of her jaw. "Unless you've got a twin."

She'd set her hands at his shoulders, preparing to argue and shove him away. But at his last words, she stilled, suddenly alert.

"Madame? Is this man bothering you?"

Their heads whipped around. The enquiry had come from an officious-looking man, who stood a few yards away on the park walk. Seeing the frustrated blaze in Lyon's eyes, he stepped back.

"It's all right," Juliette assured the interloper. "I know this gentleman."

"Such indecency!" he sputtered, obviously noticing the suggestive way she was being held. "Cease this behavior *immédi- atement!* Or else I'll return with assistance and see you both ejected from this park. There are women and children about, you know."

"Go," Lyon muttered darkly. "*Vite!*"

With a self-righteous snort, the incensed man scurried off and they resumed their conversation.

"You're certain you bedded a woman who resembles me. In your hotel room?" she asked. "Not here, under the bridge?"

"You're becoming tiresome."

"Answer me."

"Yes, I'm certain!" he blustered. Then he groaned and his eyes turned unfocused. Bracing a shoulder on the bridge sup- port, he leaned into her and put a hand to his head. "Gods! This is ridiculous," he said in a chagrined voice. "I'm actually feeling faint."

"Perhaps *you're* the one who's with child."

"My trip home is going to be precarious, while I'm in this miserable condition," he said as if he hadn't heard.

"Home!?" she scoffed. "You're not well enough to manage a trip to Tuscany on your own."

His eyes watched her lips as she spoke and his hands fell to her waist, lightly holding her. "I won't be alone. You're coming with me."

She shook her head. "I'll see you to a physician and send word to your family for you, but nothing else. I hardly know you and what I've seen of you over recent days does not inspire confidence. Besides, I've got problems of my—"

Gently, he touched his mouth to hers, cutting short her re- fusal.

"I've been called home on an urgent matter," he said, his lips dragging sensation over hers. "And I can't leave you behind. You're in danger here."

"How did you—? *Mmm . . .*" She sucked in a breath, going

up on her toes as his lips found the sensitive skin of her throat. Her hands crept up his chest and she moaned, angling her jaw to afford him better access. "I thought you were ill."

Warm fingers threaded hers, fitting their palms together. "There's ill and there's ill," he murmured, lifting their linked hands to rest against the column on either side of her head. Lips trailed along her jaw to the tendon at the side of her neck where they opened and lingered to kiss.

Her eyelids fluttered closed. *Mmm.*

A voice reached them from the bridge then, jolting her from the spell he'd woven. Tilting back her head, she saw that the man who'd threatened them moments earlier was now on Pont Neuf, conversing with another man in uniform.

"The gendarmes," she whispered. "He's summoning them."

"*Mmm-hmm.*"

She turned her head, so her chin blocked his access to her throat. When he only transferred his lips back to hers, she ducked them away.

"*Non*! I don't wish to wind up in *la Petite Force*," she said, referring to the prison for prostitutes in the Rue du Roi de Sicile.

"Come with me then," he coaxed. "Tuscany is but six days ride, and I have two mounts tethered on the quai. Escort me home . . . and . . . I'll pay you. You can serve as my nurse. Gods know I need one."

She pulled away and searched his eyes, her thoughts racing. It was as though the heavens had known of her need to flee Paris and of her need for funds, and had consequently sent him as some golden god to drive her away in his chariot. However, the heavens hadn't taken into consideration her aversion to chariots.

"*Non.*" Before he could protest, she quickly added, "I don't ride."

He gazed at her, flabbergasted. "You *don't ride?*"

"I don't get along well with animals," she felt compelled to explain.

"You *don't like animals?*"

"They make me uneasy," she admitted defensively. Looking around, she located and retrieved her bag and cloak from where she'd dropped them earlier. "At least, the larger ones do."

"Wonderful. Just wonderful." He muttered something about a king and his absurd sense of humor, then he took her arm. "We'll travel by carriage then. Come."

He tried to guide her toward the staircase, but she held back.

"A carriage pulled by horses?" she asked.

"Is there another kind?"

Her hand tightened on her bag, feeling the shape of the vial within. To survive a lengthy ride, she'd need what it contained. Traveling a few blocks in Valmont's carriage was one thing, but a multi-day jaunt would test her limits.

She stared into Lyon's face, trying to judge his trustworthiness in a mere instant of study. His expression was raw and stormy and his eyes fierce. But when she looked deeper, she saw they were the same guileless, kind eyes she remembered from Valmont's. And though he'd shown himself to be strange that night in his hotel, she was strange in her own way, too. And that didn't make her a bad person.

"Very well," she heard herself say. She, who rarely took chances, had decided to take a chance. She, who did not trust men, had decided to trust one.

He raised an arm, indicating that she should make a place for herself under his wing. "Come then, *ma petite* nurse."

She nodded and stepped closer. When her arm curved around his back, his wrapped itself over her shoulder. With his free hand on the railing, he roused himself to ascend the stairs.

When they reached the bridge, Lyon guided her southward, toward the sound of the voices. It appeared that the man who'd objected to them earlier was having difficulty persuading the local gendarme to his cause. Dalliances in the park were not un-common and the officer was occupied with his morning *café au lait*.

As they passed the pair, she ducked her head too late, for the gendarme was already squinting at her in recognition. Valmont paid him and the rest of those that policed the neighborhood to look the other way regarding any complaints against his estab-lishment. She had little doubt that her departure on the arm of a strange gentleman would be swiftly reported.

"Hurry," she told Lyon.

The mounts he'd arranged were traded in for the hire of a carriage, and soon they were ensconced inside it and leaving Paris behind. Upon seating himself, Lyon lay his head back against the leather cushion with a dull *thunk* and closed his eyes.

In the ensuing silence, Juliette watched the passing urban sights—Notre Dame, the hospital. Her hands knitted the ties of her bag as she vacillated between joy and trepidation over her departure.

But she would not have chosen to go back. She'd virtually been Valmont's captive for the past three years and the prospect of liberation was sweet. Since she'd taken care not to make friends, she would be leaving behind nothing of value. Except, of course, for Fleur.

Tears threatened again. *Poor Fleur. What had happened to her?*

Across from her, Lyon still looked to be dozing. She studied his hands where they rested on his thighs. Beeg, Fleur had called them. And they were. She shifted on her seat, nervous now that they were alone.

Her gaze roved higher to his expansive chest, the thick col-umn of his neck, and the angle of his strong jaw. And on to tan-talizing lips as sensuously carved as those she'd admired on statues of Roman gods in the Louvre.

How would they pass the time, here in this confined space? Where would they pass the nights of this journey?

Hysteria blossomed. What was she doing? Now that she'd mixed his brain, he was likely crazier than she. At his hotel, she'd made him believe they'd lain together, and he probably thought that gave him license to share a mattress with her again. If Valmont caught up to them and discovered her any less pristine than when she'd left him, he'd be furious. And dangerous.

Traffic on Rue Mouffetard slowed and her gaze went to the door, as she contemplated escape. It wasn't really necessary to flee Paris, she reasoned. She could simply assume another identity and find menial work in its outskirts, where no one she knew ever ventured. Beyond the city was *countryside*, after all. Not her favorite venue.

As soon as the carriage flagged a bit more, she might be able to leap out without sustaining an injury. Eyeing the door latch, she surreptitiously slid across the plush leather seat.

Thunk!

A booted foot came up, planting itself on the end of her seat between her and the door.

She clutched her bag to her chest and drew back against the squabs.

An amber eye opened. "Stay," he told her. "You'll come to no harm."

"You won't . . . attack me?"

His eyes burned over her. "No. I won't attack you."

For some reason, she believed him. Likely only because it was convenient to do so. And in truth, she wasn't sure her escape plan had been sound.

She swallowed her mistrust and straightened. "I'll hold you to that promise."

Apparently considering the matter closed, he shut his eyes as if the weight of the lids made them too heavy to keep open. A great sigh expanded his chest. "You are named Juliette, are you not?"

She nodded, then realizing he couldn't see, spoke her reply. "*Oui.*"

"And have you always lived in Paris, Juliette?"

"We've had this conversation before."

"Humor me."

Silence stretched between them. Outside the carriage, she heard the clop of horses on pavement and the honk and splash of geese taking flight from a public fountain. Her palms began to sweat.

"I came to reside in Paris a year ago," she told him. "Before then, I was in Burgundy."

"Go on. It's an effort for me to reply, but I'm listening."

"What shall I say?"

"Tell me . . . about yourself. Your family. About how we met. Just talk."

Doing so would help block out any random sounds of nature, so she decided to accommodate him. "I live—lived—in a sort of . . . boarding house . . . in Paris, along with other girls. I planned meals for the household, organized entertainments, and helped with the cooking."

His brow knit.

"You remember that I cook?"

"Vaguely. Continue."

"As for my family, I was orphaned in Paris as a child, sent to Burgundy, and placed in the care of foster parents. My foster mother taught me to cook and I found I had a skill for it."

"Why Burgundy?"

She shrugged. "All the orphans were sent to foster homes in the country almost immediately upon their arrival at the hospital. It was considered a better environment for us than dwelling in the city, where we might be tempted by its vices."

"And was it?"

"Since I don't know who my parents were or how I would've lived with them, how am I to know the answer to that?"

His eyes opened. "How did you come to be at my hotel last Friday night?"

184 / Elizabeth Amber

"You invited me there," she said quickly.

He made a restive movement. "A lone woman visiting a bachelor in his hotel? No, that is not all there is to be said. Begin again. From the moment we met. As if I'm a stranger to whom you are supplying all the details of a mutual encounter about which he knows nothing."

"Is that the actual case?"

A pause, then he gave her a grudging, "More or less."

"I see. Well, we met on the Pont Neuf the night you arrived in Paris. You were engaged there with another woman." She slanted him a glance. "An unusual person. Do you remember her?"

"I don't think so. Unless . . . does she have a fondness for bananas?"

"What?!" she sputtered.

His lips formed a little half smile. "Nothing. Go on."

"You followed me home and later called on me and invited me to cook for you."

"And?"

"And I did."

He frowned, clearly annoyed at her brevity. "And after you cooked, we fucked, did we not?"

She sucked in a breath at his raw language and half-rose from her seat, slapping at the leg still blocking her way. "Let me out. This was a mistake. Signal the driver to stop."

Before he could make a reply, the carriage swerved and she was sent tottering forward to the space on the seat next to him. His arm snaked out, folding around her and pulling her close until she was half-sitting on his lap.

His lips moved against her hair, sultry and seductive. "Tell me," he said. "Were you surprised to see two cocks instead of one, when my trousers came down?"

Flabbergasted, she froze, staring ahead at the gauzy curtain that swayed to one side of the carriage window. Like her heart, their vehicle began to pick up speed. Outside, the passing scenery now showed sky and pastoral landscape stretching endlessly and broken only by the occasional cottage or patch of grapevines. She very nearly hyperventilated just looking at all that oppressive nature.

"Yes," she answered at last, her voice nearly imperceptible.

"Ah." It was a sound of male satisfaction. "Then you are the one who enjoys bananas."

His arm relaxed and she sidled off him, moving back to her seat.

"You're being ridiculous—" She broke off, her mind racing as she suddenly realized to what he referred. When they had last been together, she'd embedded images of her every carnal fantasy in his mind. In view of her occupation, more than one of them had involved food. And that included fruit.

Naturally, these *would* be among the few memories he retained. Her face colored at the thought of what she'd bared to him that night, never dreaming that her most perverse imaginings would come back to haunt her. He actually believed the two of them had done those things?

"The b-bananas," she confessed reluctantly. "And the rest of it. Whatever you recall of that nature. None of it happened between us. I only made you think it did."

His steadfast gaze invited her to continue.

"It's an ability that came to me a few years ago. The first time I employed it was quite by accident, when a man tried to molest me. I tricked him, you see, in order to make him think he'd succeeded."

"As you did with me in my hotel?"

"*Oui*," she said uncomfortably.

"And since that man a few years ago?"

She shrugged in answer and her free hand crept up the front

of her dress to find the reassuring bumps of the beaded necklace she wore under it. He seemed to believe her and wasn't yet calling her a witch. It was encouraging.

"Since then, I've learned to hone my skills at deceit. To gauge the nature of what gentlemen want of me, then convince them they've obtained it."

"How many?"

"Men?" She dodged his eyes. "That's of no moment. The material point is that I implanted false memories in your mind in the way I just described. "

"I see." His eyes closed again. "Yet it's not just my mind that remembers you. My body also remembers with infallible certainty that you took my first seed that night in my hotel. You and no other."

His *first seed?*

An odd sensation prickled over her as if he'd just made a momentous pronouncement. Her eyes flicked to the front placket of his trousers, then away. Her tongue slipped out moistening her lips.

She *had* kissed him. Down *there.*

By doing so she had in fact taken his seed into her body, at least in the strictest sense of meaning. However, he had mistaken the part of her that had done the swallowing, and therefore believed she could be with child.

The truth would swiftly discredit that notion. But the thought of admitting how she'd taken advantage of him while he lay unconscious was too mortifying. She simply couldn't bring herself to do so face-to-face. Maybe later, she thought cowardly, and perhaps via written correspondence.

Though the ensuing ride rattled her teeth worse than any farm wagon might have, Lyon quickly fell back to dozing. When it seemed he'd slept for ten minutes or so, she furtively opened her bag and removed the vial.

Tilting back her head, she squeezed three drops into her throat. Undiluted, it was awful, but she managed to get it down.

The customary warmth suffused her almost immediately, lapping at her with gentle waves of serenity. As she stowed them away again, she noticed something had fallen from her bag onto the lap of her skirt. The object she'd stolen from Valmont's cabinet.

She turned it over and over in her fingers, considering it. Why, in that fraught moment as she'd stood before the shelf, had her hand reached for Fleur's bracelet, but then diverted to grasp this?

For some reason, in some way, this particular token must be significant. She crushed it in her fingers, trying to absorb its meaning through her skin. Of course, she couldn't.

Sighing, she stuffed the dingy blue swatch of fabric back into her bag.

11

A cigar dropped from Valmont's lax fingers to roll on the carpet, scorching it. Moaning, he slumped lower in the chair where he sat upstairs in his private office. His eyes began to flutter furiously, opening and closing like shutters, faster than anyone could blink. He lost control of his arm and it jerked wildly, sweeping everything off the side table, including the crystal pitcher and the absinthe glass he'd drained numerous times that evening.

He dreamed of blood. Of the blood of a woman with sea-green eyes that turned the waters of the River Loire red, then pink. Then it washed over him, licking at him like a thousand sanguine devil's tongues.

An incredible ecstasy seized him, and his hand grabbed his crotch. He was alone, yet it felt as though a hot, erotic mouth had just sheathed his erection.

"Juliette." The word was a desperate, yearning cry. In his mind, her lips were willing, sucking at him as if she couldn't get enough. He twisted on his chair, writhing under her stroke, his legs shaking and shoulders shimmying. Suddenly, every muscle in his body spasmed tight.

Cum shot from him, soiling his trousers from within, as his body bucked uncontrollably under the most violent orgasm of his life. Oh, that this heavenly sensation would never end!

Of course, it did end and he soon found himself alone again, and despairing.

Two apparitions came to him then—small, glowing creatures. They came out of the black wretchedness of his dreams as they sometimes did when he was soaked with drink.

"Are you angels?" he asked wondrously.

They only giggled in reply, their eyes mischievous. Softly nudging one another and seeming to communicate through telepathy, they began to rifle their fingers through the items on his desk. After selecting something from among them, they began backing away.

His collection! He'd taken the mementoes from his cabinet earlier, and had planned to spend the evening fondling them and reminiscing. However, he'd already been too soused to focus on them properly and had given up the attempt.

"No! What are you stealing, you spawns of Satan? Give it back!"

But they ignored him and only replaced whatever they'd taken with something else. A long slender tube. Then they faded into the fire in the grate.

"Wait! What's that you put there?" He tried to rouse himself from the chair to see what they'd left for him. But his movements were uncoordinated and he pitched forward onto the carpet and into unconsciousness.

When he woke toward dawn, he was a mess. He'd upended himself on the floor, and his chair as well, for it now lay across the back of his legs. His crotch was sticky-wet with his own spill.

Fuck! Another absinthe-induced convulsion.

And what was that disgusting smell? Apparently, cum wasn't the only thing his body had involuntarily expelled in his trousers. He'd fouled himself.

He managed to right the chair, but for the moment, standing was beyond him. With both hands, he held his pounding head. Fantastic memories of the night that had just passed came to him, making him wonder which were false and which had really transpired.

Looking toward his desk, he saw that something foreign lay atop it. The tube! Had those two glowing pygmies really come here and left it for him?

Crawling on all fours, he made it to his desk and kneeling up, discovered the gift that lay there.

It was a sheet of parchment, yellowed with age, which had been tightly rolled and tied with a ribbon. Faintly glowing fingerprints dotted it here and there, where it had been gripped. His midnight callers had not been delusions after all!

What had they left him? A treasure map?

Anxiously, he unrolled the tube, disappointed at first to see it was only a neatly recorded list of names and other information. It appeared to have been torn from some sort of large registry book. A title block in the corner caught his eye for it bore an institutional insignia. His heart stopped, then raced on when it informed him that the page had originated at the Hospice des Enfants Trouvés.

Then the name "Juliette" jumped out at him and he clutched the parchment, examining it with rapt attention. A second name leaped out almost as quickly and he groaned. Had Juliette seen this? *Non!* Even if she had, the dates would mean nothing to her. He was worrying for nothing.

But how had those imps come by this and what did it signify that they'd left it here?

Suddenly, he remembered that they had not only given him something. They'd taken from him as well. Setting the document aside, he scanned the objects of his collection that lay scattered over his desktop.

Two were missing!

The loss of little Fleur's bracelet he could've withstood, but the loss of the other—! He let out a wounded yowl and crumpled to the carpet. The blue swatch of fabric was irreplaceable—his first and most cherished memento of all!

It was too cruel to be a simple prank. The taking of his prizes and leaving of this parchment must have been intended as some sort of message to him, he decided. But what exactly had been meant?

He sat on the floor and rocked himself, mulling the riddle for an hour or more. Now and then, he struck his skull with his own fist in an effort to make it work more efficiently, but this only worsened his headache.

His faulty, drugged brain continued to ponder at a sluggish pace, forcing together puzzle pieces that should not adjoin: A dream of blood. Juliette's scrawled name. The loss of the mementoes.

How did they relate?

Eventually, he jumped to his feet, having arrived at dangerous, illogical conclusions. He'd planned to sell Juliette's virgin blood too easily! he realized. In his recent letter, he'd offered her to Satyr, full well knowing she would not be able to withstand the pressure he would bring to bear, and that he would ultimately succeed in bedding her. But now it had come to him that there were others—strange unearthly creatures—who desperately wanted his darling Juliette.

When the bright ones came again, he would go where they led and hand her over, unsullied and intact. And at that moment, he would be rewarded.

With gold. With magic. Of the kind Juliette possessed, and which he coveted.

These imagined understandings filled him with new purpose. He flew down the hall, took the steps two at a time up to the attic, and threw open the door to Juliette's room.

Her things were in place, but she wasn't there! Alarmed, he

rushed back down the stairs. Passing Gina in the hall, he grabbed her arm. "Where's Juliette?"

She recoiled at the smell of him, fanning her nose. "I don't know. Sometimes she's with Fleur in the mornings."

Gina was right. He was disgusting. Embarrassed, he scuttled to his room, threw his trousers aside, cleaned himself up, and re-dressed himself in record time.

When he found Fleur's chamber and flung the door open, relief filled him. Two girls lay there, sleeping in her bed. "Juliette? Fleur?"

"*Monsieur?*" The coverlet fell away as the girls sat up, blinking at him. Agnes and Marie.

His fingers tightened on the doorknob. "Why are you here? Where's Juliette?"

Agnes yawned. "Last night you agreed I could have Fleur's room now that she's gone. As for Juliette, I haven't seen her."

"If she's not in her chamber, perhaps she's gone marketing again at Les Halles?" Marie put in.

Fleur was gone. Of course she was. Fool! He'd taken her to Monsieur Arlette's establishment beyond the outskirts of Paris himself just two nights ago. It was a private, bucolic setting, with nothing to offer in the way of entertainment, except what he and Arlette had planned for a few special guests.

He'd lingered there for a few hours to enjoy a drink and admire Arlette's technique. To start things off, Fleur had been given to the three men who'd offered remuneration in exchange for her purchase. They were refined gentlemen of wealth and social rank, who had paid Arlette and him well to abuse her. These events were always profitable for them and the funds would tide them over until the factory reached full production.

How Fleur had fought as her customers had cornered her! Once Arlette had smacked her around some and explained things to her, she'd gotten the gist of her new place. She'd sucked off the paying clients and him and Arlette as well. All five of them, one after the other. Then the fucking had commenced.

Eventually, an expectant silence had fallen and all had looked to Arlette. He'd gone to the weary girl and kissed her and told her she was going to die. She'd wept of course, but he'd only turned her around and slapped her rear and told her to run. Told her that if she ran fast enough, she might escape her fate.

It was a lie, naturally, but it had added spice to the chase. Seeing the open door, she'd charged into the field as they always did. Her dress had been given to the hounds and once they had their fill of her scent, the hunt was on.

He looked at his hands. There'd been so much blood. Just as there had been on that day three years ago—the day of his first kill.

"Monsieur Valmont?" Agnes prompted.

"Hmmm?" He looked up at her, banishing his memories. She looked sexy with sleep. Her large, dark nipples were visible through her rumpled chemise and he knew from prior experience that her bed and her cunt would be warm.

He was worrying for nothing. Juliette had probably only gone to the market as Marie suggested. In any event, she wouldn't wander far. She was too timid to venture any great distance from his protection.

"*Allez*, Marie," he said, sending the girl scurrying from the room.

He kicked the door shut behind her with his heel and began unfastening his trousers. With stoic acceptance, Agnes rolled onto her back.

Sibela paced herself as she made her way from the Seine to the Rhône. She had just over three weeks left to conclude her aquatic journey. There was no reason to rush, for sufficient time remained.

She would soon cross into the Mediterranean, then on to the River Arno. From there, she would wend her way through smaller tributaries that fed the estate where the father of the child in her womb made his home.

Only a few moons had passed since she'd fornicated with him, but already she was growing fatter and more ungainly. And ever more anxious to be done with the birthing of the babe in her belly.

However, though she had no love for Satyr's offspring, she was careful with it. For it was a precious commodity. One that would ensure her future.

Occasionally, she copulated with other males her during her voyage, for it was her nature. Initially, she'd attempted to shun all things carnal, but had quickly failed at that endeavor. She'd been worried that the sperm of others she mated might join with Satyr's, resulting in a mixed breed that he wouldn't recognize as his own. Fortunately, the seed that had spawned this particular child had proven impervious to the influx of that from other species.

Still, she was determined that she'd refrain during the fourth and final week of gestation. She would be quite swollen by then and feared that male intrusions and excitements might do harm to Satyr's progeny.

Abstinence wouldn't be easy. By the time she was in sight of Tuscany, she would be desperate for the thorough fucking that Lyon would willingly administer to her under the next full moon.

Whether he liked it or not.

12

The carriage lurched violently, pitching Juliette forward and rudely jerking her from sleep. A pair of muscled arms was there to break her fall. Lyon. He must've been awake.

"What happened?" she asked, resituating herself upright on the seat across from him and lifting the curtain to peer outside. Seeing they'd entered a misty bosk, she recoiled. Nature. Ugh.

"There's been an accident of some kind. Wait here." Lyon shifted his bulk to exit the carriage, grimacing at the effort.

Guilt swept her. She had done this to him. Why her magic had affected this particular man so detrimentally, she was at a loss to explain. In the past, men endowed with far less physical strength and character had lost only a night's worth of memory due to its effects.

"*Non.* You're sick. I'll go." She pushed him back with her hand and he let her, sinking onto his seat with a creak of leather. She poked her head out of the window.

Fresh outdoor smells of leaves and soil and moss struck her full in the face.

"What's happened?" she called out.

The driver appeared, looking damp and chilled. It had begun drizzling. "There's trouble, Madame," he said, making the assumption she and Lyon were wed. "The carriage has been damaged and—"

Two men materialized from the haze to stand beside him, both swarthy and wearing dark fleece hats, green tunics, and trousers with red stripes.

"Come!" ordered a voice heavily accented in Russian. He gestured at her to disembark.

Wide-eyed, she ducked back inside the carriage. "Cossacks," she whispered.

Lyon nodded. "How many?"

"Two that I saw, but there's fog. There could be more. What do you think they want?"

Cossacks were favorite customers of Gina's at the salons, but she'd learned to be wary of them. Some in their ranks had become notorious for their excesses while sojourning in Paris over the last decade.

"Nothing pleasant I imagine," Lyon muttered, unlatching the door and unfolding the steps.

She put a trembling hand on his arm. "Where are you going?"

"To deal with this. They know you're in here, so you may as well come out, too. But stay behind me." Two fingers tilted her chin so their eyes met. "Keep your wits. If this turns violent—run into the woods and start moving southward. Remain out of sight, but travel parallel to the road and find your way to the next village, then on to find my family in Tuscany. I'll delay any that would chase you as best I can."

She nodded with *faux* calm as the world seemed to crumble around her. She'd never be able to make her way through the forest. Even the simple act of alighting from the carriage here amid great expanses of tree and sky was an idea too horrible to contemplate.

"I can't," she whispered, but only after he'd gone and so quietly that he wouldn't hear.

"Why have you stopped us?" Outside, Lyon's voice sounded far stronger than she knew him to feel.

Peeking through the curtain, she saw the two Cossacks step back at his intimidating stature and his tone of authority.

They began speaking to Lyon in broken French. When he responded in Russian, they switched to their native language as well and a heated argument commenced.

"There's a third one up front unhitching the horses," she heard the driver call out.

The one he spoke of chose that very moment to draw along-side her carriage and swing its door wide, motioning to her to get out.

"*Non!*" She tried to shut the door again.

He said something to her in gruff Russian and put his muddy boot on the step as though planning to join her inside.

At that, she leaped out and down the steps past him. He only laughed and followed in a smooth jump. She backed away from him, warily holding his eyes, unsure which scared her most—the natural surroundings or her pursuer!

"Run!" Lyon urged, his voice making her start. A tussle had broken out—the driver and him against the two remaining Russians.

Without allowing herself time to think, Juliette turned and lunged headlong into the mist-laden forest. Holding her hands outstretched before her, she tried to avoid any obstacles lurking in her path that might be obscured by the fog. Her flight be-came like a scene from a nightmare. On all sides, branches reached for her like giant gnarled fingers. Rocky outcroppings loomed like monsters.

The Cossack pounded behind her, quickly gaining ground. A hand snagged her skirt and she heard it rip. Then she was knocked to the ground and rolling down an incline over slick loam and rotting foliage. Unceremoniously, she slammed against something solid, sending shock waves through her hip.

Winded, she lay there gasping in the wet, with maple leaves plastered to her cheek and dress. Strong hands lifted her and bent her forward over a rounded, unyielding surface that reached waist-high. She flattened her hands on it. It was cold and coarse and smelled of lichen. A boulder.

A voice behind her muttered incomprehensible words. The Cossack. Her entire body shaking, Juliette glanced at him over her shoulder.

Keep your wits, Lyon had told her. Good advice. But her wits were muddled with fear.

A hand planted itself between her shoulder blades and she felt her skirts being lifted.

She hit at him as best she could, barely managing to hold him off. For a moment, the only sounds in the stillness were that of their harsh breathing, his unintelligible grunts, and her slaps.

Autumn air chilled her exposed legs, spiking her terror. Her skirts were now heaped high at the back of her waist and her attacker was working at the front of his pants. In seconds, he was going to rape her.

She forced herself to shut out both him and her surroundings. Pressing both hands flat on the boulder before her, she began to swirl them over it as though she were a seer and it was a giant crystal ball.

Booted feet knocked her legs apart.

"I'm stone, I'm stone, I'm stone," she chanted, hardly knowing what she said or that it had the effect of mustering her magic. Her palms heated and the wish seeped into her mind and her flesh.

Within her clothing, her blood slowed to a saunter, then a crawl. Soft, clammy skin turned dry and tough, like that of a toad.

Or of a living stone.

The Cossack let out a frightened yelp and jumped back from her. Fabric swished back into place around her ankles, but she felt nothing. As though listening from a great distance, she heard him fall, then rise again. The sounds of him crashing through the forest were loud at first, but then they lessened. He was moving away from her, in the direction of the carriage.

For some time after he'd gone, she remained fixed there against the rock, unable or perhaps unwilling to stir. Mist condensed on her gritty skin, dampening her clothes.

Then, from somewhere along the road came the unwelcome thunder of hooves. It shook the ground under her feet, making her feel. Reminding her she was alive.

The pump of blood resumed, sending life careening through her system. As one arthritic and aged, she shuddered and began to inexorably transform back to herself. Coarse skin turned smooth and malleable. Rock returned to flesh.

Aware again, she drooped over the boulder, hanging there like a limp doll. All sound had ceased, save the light patter of rain. Were the others dead?

No, please, no!

Once again, she'd fled a bad situation in a cowardly manner, leaving others to fend for themselves. She couldn't bear the idea of rousing herself to go and see what had happened to them.

"An interesting method of escape," said a voice from somewhere nearby.

She jerked around so fast she fell backwards to the ground, landing in a pile of wet leaves. "Ow!"

Lyon was sitting on a log several yards away, studying her.

Her gaze darted around warily.

"He's gone," he told her. "Your flesh-into-stone act apparently frightened the hell out of him. And he in turn scared off the others with a repetition of the tale. Care to explain that one?"

"*Non.*" Rubbing the hip she'd bruised in her tumble, she gathered herself to stand. "The driver?"

Lyon levered himself from his makeshift seat and stood as well. His face was ashen and his shirt was ripped so it hung open. "Seeing to the horses. Come. Lend me your shoulder."

In the aftermath of the Cossack's attack, she was shaking. As she slipped an arm around him, he leaned heavily on her and he couldn't help but notice.

"Are you all right?" he asked.

A drop of liquid fell on her bodice and she glanced up, noticing a cut on his chest. "You're the one who's injured."

"I'd look worse if you hadn't terrified your friend into coming back and pulling the other ones off me. For now, you'll have to excuse the blood. I'll replace your gown when we reach civilization."

When they reached the carriage, the driver was there, unhitching the two remaining horses.

"Are you unhurt, Madame?" He eyed her, obviously wondering how she'd fended off the burly Cossack and curious as to exactly what had sent him careening back in such abject terror.

"*Oui,*" she replied, stopping well away from the horses and leaving Lyon to carry on without her.

"Where are the other two mounts?" he enquired.

"Damned Cossacks took them." The driver nodded toward the forest in the direction she'd run. "Fortunately for us, whatever happened out there spooked them enough that they rode off before they could commandeer our last two." He looked at Juliette expectantly.

"I think we owe our luck in ridding ourselves of them to Russian folklore," she told him. "I barely understood my pursuer's speech, but I thought he talked of ghosts or forest spirits or something of the like. Then he went tearing from the woods."

"Thank the Gods for good old-fashioned superstition," added Lyon.

The driver nodded, looking mollified. "For that I'm grateful."

"How far is the next village?" she asked, looking dubiously at the broken carriage. Her abdomen had begun cramping. Surely her menses were not going to choose this inopportune juncture to plague her on top of everything else she'd endured today. No, the timing for that was all wrong. It must be something else.

"Two hours ahead. If we ride out now, we can be there by nightfall. You and Madame can double up on the stronger mount they left us. Tomorrow you can hire another carriage to see you onward, while I come back with what's needed to repair this one."

Falling in with this plan, Lyon tried to muster his strength.

Juliette's eyes widened. Ride? Through the countryside in the dark and rain? Were they insane?

"*Non!*" she told the driver, gesturing toward Lyon as an easy excuse. "He's ill. He can't ride so far, especially not in this foul weather. We'll have to wait here while you go for help."

"But I probably won't return before nightfall, Madame," he cautioned.

"I can travel two meager hours on horseback," protested Lyon.

She ignored him. "If that comes to pass, we'll bide the evening here in the carriage."

The driver looked doubtfully toward the sky and then back at her. "Still, if this weather worsens, you may find yourself as wet inside this thing as on horseback. And if there's wind, the whole conveyance might take a tumble with you inside."

"I can ride," Lyon argued again.

"Well, I cannot," she reminded him firmly. "And I have no interest in learning on a stormy night such as this one."

"Beg pardon, monsieur," the driver broke in. "We passed a

cabin a half mile back. I can see you that far and help you settle in for the night. Afterward, I can take one of the horses on to the village and fetch help for you tomorrow."

Juliette beamed at him. "An excellent plan."

"Then get ready for your first riding lesson," Lyon informed her.

"What?" she asked blankly.

"The carriage is beyond repair, remember?"

One miserable, wet half-mile later, Lyon sagged onto the nearest chair, soaked to the skin. Nearby, Juliette lit the candles inside the rustic cabin. She'd worn her cloak on the journey here, so she'd been spared the brunt of the weather.

"What is this place?" he heard her ask and looked over to see that she was surreptitiously rubbing her hip as if it was causing her discomfort.

Since neither mount had been deemed stout enough to take his weight and that of a second rider, she had ridden with the driver. Though theirs had only been a short journey, her horse had been unusually restive and had managed to buck her off. She'd taken a spill and landed on the hip she'd previously injured while fleeing her attacker in the forest.

"It's a way station for travelers like yourselves caught in inclement weather," the driver was saying. "You'll be safe passing the night here."

"Are you certain there's no inn close by?" Juliette asked. She stood somewhere behind him now and she sounded upset.

Though he couldn't hear the driver's response, Lyon discerned that the tone of it was in the negative.

He lost the train of their conversation then, as he fell into a light doze. And when he woke again, the driver had gone. He was still slouched on the chair and Juliette had come to sit before him on an ottoman. She was holding a bowl out to him, and whatever it contained smelled delicious.

"What's this?" he muttered, staring suspiciously at the spoon she'd stuck under his nose.

"Chicken soup."

"And that's all?"

"I mixed a dash of this and that to improve the taste, but I haven't drugged it. Nor is it an instrument of magic, if that's what you're implying."

He grunted, pushing himself straighter. His chest was bare and a blanket had been wrapped around his shoulders like a shawl. It made him feel like an invalid so he shrugged it away. Beyond her, his sodden shirt was hanging on a rope strung from the ceiling beams near the fire, but his damp trousers remained molded to him. There was a round, wet spot on Juliette's dress where his blood had dripped. She must've sponged it off while he'd been asleep.

"You need sustenance," she urged. "Eat."

He opened his mouth, allowing her to slip the spoon inside, if only so she wouldn't leave. Taste exploded on his tongue, bringing with it memories of beguiling smells from the kitchens of his childhood, where he'd often begged snacks from the cook. This was no ordinary soup. It might not be tainted with fey glamour, but it *was* magical. He swallowed and then took the rest of it, spoonful after spoonful, without complaint.

"The Cossacks took the driver's provisions," she explained as she fed him. "But we—the driver and I—found more here in the cabin. It's surprisingly well stocked. He helped me start the fire, then left almost immediately to make the next village before nightfall. Before he went, he saw to the single horse he left us in the lean-to."

All the while, she kept darting glances at something that hung somewhere above him. Having finished the soup, Lyon tilted his head back, but an overhead shelf blocked his view. "What are you looking at?"

"Hunting trophies."

With a soft curse, he closed his eyes. "A hunting cabin. That explains the provisions."

He heard the scrape of the bowl as she set it on the side table next to his chair. "You don't hunt?"

"Only when it's necessary in order to eat, and I don't take trophies."

He heard her move away and forced his eyes open, wanting to watch her. "How much food is there?"

"Enough for tonight."

"No more? The driver may not return right away."

"He assured me he would. However there are provisions enough for a week."

The rain was still pounding and had no doubt rendered the roads impassable for a day or two at least. But he was too tired to explain all that at the moment. "How long . . . have we been here?"

"Less than an hour. You look exhausted," she told him. "Now that you've eaten, you should get some rest. There's only this room, but it contains several beds."

He shifted uncomfortably on the chair, despising his weakness. In spite of it, with the coming of night, the need to bury himself in female flesh was growing critical. For as long as he could recall of his adult life, not a day had passed in which he had not done so. Until this week.

"I need to get out of these trousers."

"I'm sorry," she said, contrite. "The driver offered to help with that, but I refused him since I wasn't sure what might be, um, on display. I thought you might rather he not see any, um, *unusual* differences." She looked flustered at having made that remark and rushed on as if to prevent further discussion of it. "Can you manage getting them off on your own?"

"*Si.* Let me get to a bed first." Gritting his teeth, he levered himself onto his feet. She put an arm around him and he soon found himself ensconced on one of the narrow beds in the room. When she made to withdraw, her fingers inadvertently brushed the masculine hardness at the front of his pants.

Liquid fire shot through his veins and his hand whipped out to clamp her wrist. They remained there, frozen for a long moment. The crackle of the fire and the pound of raindrops permeated the air. Blushing, she looked everywhere except at him.

"Are you not at all tempted?" he asked, his voice low and dark. "It would help pass the time."

She shook her head and he let her go. Lying back on the mound of pillows she'd adjusted for him, he gazed at her, brooding. "Do you require payment?"

"*Non*! Why would you ask such a thing?" she demanded, looking stiff and affronted. But for some reason secretive as well.

"Because I need sex. From you. And I'm willing to do anything to achieve it."

"You said you wouldn't rape me."

"And I won't. Do I look capable of it?"

"Yes!" she sputtered incredulously, gesturing toward the voracious bulge at his crotch.

He adjusted the blanket over his shoulders again, suddenly chilled in spite of the fire. "My cock is the only part of me that doesn't seem to realize the current sorry state of my health."

"Don't put any more of your propositions to me," she scolded. "I told you in the carriage that I've never lain with a man. And that means I didn't lie with you."

A ragged laugh left him. "Yet you do lie. I may have forgotten much of our time together, but I do know we—"

"Don't you dare say it again! Even if I had done what you believe, I would be under no obligation to do so a second time."

Wearily, he covered his eyes with a forearm. "You're right. Forgive me. Circumstances have destroyed my manners."

At that, she came nearer and sat at the foot of the bed closest to his. "If you did have a woman in your hotel, can you not conceive of the possibility that she was someone other than I?"

His eyes glinted at her from the shadow of his arm. "There was no one else."

"I saw you in the park with a woman under the bridge," she countered defiantly. "Fornicating."

He lowered his arm to his chest, digesting that information. "When?"

"Thursday night," she informed him. "Once you saw that I'd noticed you, you followed me."

"To the gray house with the red door."

"I thought you didn't remember."

"Only unconnected snatches and bits," he assured her, for it was true.

"Your partner that night was the one that I mentioned to you earlier," she went on. "You told me that she was a Nereid."

"It's possible," he said, shrugging off what he considered to be an insignificant detail. "My brothers and I have lain with nymphs before."

"As long as we're on this topic, would you care to enlighten me as to how you come to keep company with mythological creatures?"

"This from someone who has the knack of implanting memories and can transform herself into stone on command?" He wasn't averse to revealing family secrets to her, but other matters took precedence at the moment.

"*Touché.*"

His voice turned serious. "I need sex from you, Juliette. By tomorrow, or the next day or at most one day beyond that, I'll be dead for the lack."

She stood and moved away to warm her hands at the fire. "Perhaps tomorrow in the village, you'll locate someone else to accommodate you."

"No one else will do."

"Oh, please," she said, scowling at him over her shoulder. "I've heard better excuses from other men seeking to bed me than to believe such nonsense."

He, lay his head back with a long-suffering sigh. "I am pathetic, am I not? You may find it difficult to credit at the moment, but I generally do not find it necessary to plead with a woman for the use of her body."

A small silence fell, then she shattered it with a quiet admission.

"I don't find it difficult."

His gaze shot to hers, but she wouldn't allow him to catch her eyes.

"I don't find it difficult to believe women want you," she repeated. "But I can't indulge you. It would be . . . unwise. For both of us."

"Why?"

"The traditional reason, among others," she said. "It's easy for a man to treat such matters lightly, but the disposition of a woman's chastity defines her expectations in this world. Whether she will be labeled maiden, wife, or whore."

A frail virgin's membrane was all that stood in the way of saving his life? "I'll wed you then! I mean to anyway."

"Don't be cruel," she said, refusing to believe him.

"Do you intend to remain celibate to your grave?"

"I don't know. I hope not." Clutching her hands, she turned to him, earnest. "You must understand that I can't give away so easily something I've guarded well for nineteen years. Simply on your whim."

"Whim? This is no whim," he said, outraged. "For those of my kind, sex is a crucial bodily function."

"Of your kind?" she echoed, wary now.

"The kind with carnal needs that must be seen to regularly, in the same way a Human's body craves sustenance in order to survive."

Her eyes widened. "But you're human. What else could you be?"

"We're both a little different from the norm, wouldn't you agree?" he asked softly.

But she wasn't ready to let it go. "That night in your hotel," Her gaze darted to his groin, then away. "I saw your body. Saw how you are shaped."

"Two cocks?"

She looked pained at his frankness, but nodded.

"And you want an explanation." He paused, deciding how much to reveal. Too much and she might run from him. And in his condition, he might not be able to stop her.

"My brothers and I sometimes . . . change. In the way you saw."

A charged silence fell.

"Are you like that now?" Her voice was barely audible.

His eyes narrowed on her, seeing the interest she couldn't hide. His hand went to the front of his trousers and popped open the uppermost of four buttons.

"Come find out."

13

Juliette watched in fascination as Lyon began to slowly unfasten the front of his trousers.

A second button fell and he toyed with the third.

"Is it only your hymen that deters you?"

"Hmm?" Her covetous eyes scalded the V that was his half-unbuttoned placket. Was that merely a shadow or could it be the sparse beginnings of his nest?

"Juliette!"

Embarrassed, she jerked her gaze to his. "What!?"

"If there is a way for me to join my body to yours, yet avoid disturbing your hymen, would you still be averse?"

Was he asking if she'd allow him to mount her from behind? At Valmont's, gentlemen paid double the usual fee for this, so she assumed it was a considerably more arduous undertaking. Though the concept of it had long appealed, she couldn't trust him. Once he was under her skirts, more could happen.

However, something must be done, for his health did appear to be declining. Already, his beautiful features were more drawn than when she'd first seen him today. Was she truly responsible for this illness in him? He'd seemed so stubbornly resistant to her spells that she had forced them on him harder than she did on most men that night in his hotel.

Non! He was attempting to play her for a fool. Gina and Agnes would laugh themselves silly if she ever told them what he was claiming in order to entice her to lift her skirts. Men didn't die because a woman refused them sex. Of course they didn't.

"I don't—I'm not sure." She shook her head. "I'm sorry."

The third button gave. "I am as well," he said softly.

Just one button left.

Her lips parted and she craned forward ever so slightly. As if he were a snake charmer and she a snake, she watched, waiting for him to release himself. Waiting to see if two cocks would unfold from him as before.

But to her supreme disappointment, that final button remained in its anchor. Instead of satisfying her curiosity, he shrugged his shoulders. This had the unfortunate effect of repositioning the blanket around him so that one end of it fell to cloak that which she most wished to see.

The muscles of his forearm bunched again and his hand moved beneath the annoying drape as, she assumed, he released the final button and himself.

Her eyes met his, and she wanted to protest. To demand. To beg. *Oh, please, please, do show me your cock. Or cocks, as the case may be.* It was absurd to even contemplate saying such words aloud to a man.

So she only watched like one starving, as his hand commenced a rhythmic, seductive stroking. Were all those bumps really knuckles she saw moving under the wool, or were two of them actually the tips of something else? Her fingers gripped the folds of her skirts. With each tug of his hand, she felt a corresponding tug in her womb. It was an agony to stand idly by and not participate. Or at least see!

Frustrated, she went to the window and gazed out at the weather, folding her arms across her waist to hug her elbows with both hands. The world outside was a maw of blackness, and she saw only her own reflection in the glass. Wind lashed, driving rain against the windowpane. Minutes passed. A void of silence yawned between them.

Behind her, a sudden groan welled up from his depths like the howl of a predator, alone and searching for his mate.

Her head whipped around, startled.

Beneath the blanket, Lyon's hand now lay motionless. His head lolled back on the pillows and his jaw was slack. Was this some kind of trick to draw her within his reach? If so, it worked. She lifted a taper and hurried closer.

When the candlelight shifted so she got a good look at his face, she gasped in shock. He seemed to have aged a year in the last few minutes. The robust energy that had seemed so much a part of him was fading. Golden skin had been cast with a dull burnish and bruised half-moons cupped his lower eyelids making him look incredibly weary. It was as if he were turning into the sculpture she'd once thought him, unearthly pale and beautiful. And still.

"Monsieur? Lord Satyr?" She shook his arm. His chest rose and fell with his anemic breathing, but he didn't stir.

Had he been telling the truth? Was this illness of his her fault? Some sort of fatal combination of her spells, her furtive tasting of his seed, and her refusal to bed him?

What if he died here and left her alone in this place? she wondered, turning selfish in her burgeoning hysteria. What if the driver never returned? What if that Cossack returned instead, or someone like him? They might not ask for her compliance as Lyon had. Men like that simply took.

"Lyon! Wake up! I don't wish to be found keeping company with a dead body. Such situations can be misconstrued. Gendarmes might take you to be my victim."

Surely she couldn't be twice unlucky in this regard. Arlette and Valmont had been right in what they'd said. With a previous stain on her record, she would be more easily thought guilty of another murder. Yet, she was innocent!

If he died, the alternative to being discovered here with him would be to walk or ride out through the countryside on her own. She could do neither.

And above all, something in her simply didn't want this beautiful man to die. Setting the candle aside, she shook his shoulders.

"I agree!" she railed at his unmoving features. "To what you asked before. Do whatever you wish to me if it will keep you among the living."

At her words, he gasped suddenly, his breath rattling in the cave of his chest. His eyes slitted open and a faint satisfaction colored them. His hand sought hers and gave it a small squeeze. Then he peered beyond her, a look of fixed concentration shading his features.

She glanced over her shoulder in the direction of his gaze. Seeing nothing unusual, she twisted back toward him in time to see his lashes flutter closed again.

"*Grazie, mademoiselle,*" he whispered, so quietly that she almost didn't hear.

Then he went unconscious.

"Lyon!" She felt his forehead and found it feverish and clammy. He was considerably more haggard than he'd been only a few moments ago. His blanket had slipped askew and she saw that in fact only one shaft lay in the slit of his trousers, rooted in his thatch. But her mood to witness carnal things had faded with his increased illness, and she only peeled the damp trousers away and then readjusted the blanket to cover him.

Why did he still suffer? She'd given him the answer he desired, yet it was having no effect. But perhaps he only needed rest. After all, no one died from a dearth of copulation, she re-assured herself again. Such a notion was preposterous. Wasn't it?

A sudden sensation of warmth came from behind her as though she had moved to stand with her back to the fire. A hand fell on her shoulder.

"Juliette." It was a man's voice.

With a curt shriek, she leaped higher on the bed fleeing the touch. Tangling in the bed linens, she took a tumble to the rug, bruising her hip yet a third time.

In her shock, she hardly noticed.

Impossibly, two men now stood not a yard away at the foot of Lyon's bed. Two *identical* men with amber eyes, tousled golden hair, and strong jaws. They were built on a massive scale, and tall, especially from her vantage point on the floor.

And perhaps most noticeably and most scandalously of all, they were both *naked*. And erect. Exact copies of Lyon in every facet and dimension, for he was their triplet.

She spidered backward until she came up against the wall behind her. "How did you get in here?"

But they didn't reply and only stared down at her with hun-gry, jeweled eyes. Eyes that catalogued her every twitch. Eyes that were the precise shape and color as those of the man lying on the bed.

Clawing her way back onto the mattress, she snuggled against Lyon, keeping a wary eye on his twins all the while.

"Lyon! Wake up!" she hissed. Patting his cheek and jiggling his jaw, she attempted to rouse him.

"He's ill," said one of the phantoms.

"Unconscious," added the other.

Their voices were so similar to Lyon's that it was as though he'd spoken. She even looked down at him to check, but saw he still slept.

"Who are you? His brothers?" She shook her head, pooh-

poohing her own suggestion, for she'd seen his siblings in his thoughts that night at the hotel. "*Non*, you resemble him, not them."

"We *are* Him," they told her in harmony.

Both took a step closer.

"Wh—what do you want?" she squeaked.

"To heal him. Through you."

She shot another glance at Lyon. His eyes remained closed, his face relaxed, and his breathing so shallow now that it barely lifted his chest. Scarcely knowing what she did, she planted a fervent kiss on his lips, thinking it could be a last farewell.

"I'm so sorry for my part in this. Please don't die," she whispered. "Please."

Then, giving the twins wide berth, she left the bed and sidled toward the fireplace where she snatched up a poker. Gripping it in both hands, she brandished it back and forth before her like a sword. Her gaze darted between the two men, threatening them with harm should they approach.

The two new Lyons had done nothing to prevent her from garnering a weapon, but they had shifted, strategically relocating themselves between her and escape.

"Who are you?" she demanded, trying to sound intimidating.

"We're what He promised," said one.

"We'll not hurt you," said the other, eyeing her makeshift saber.

"If you were to clothe yourselves and move away from the door, I might give that claim more credence. There are blankets on the other beds."

They ignored her suggestions and only stood there, silent and watchful.

"Where did you come from?" she ventured.

"He brought us," said the first one, glancing toward Lyon. "In the same way you transformed yourself into stone in the forest, He can conjure beings like us from the ether."

Her poker wobbled. "How did you know about that?"

The other one spoke this time. "Because *He* knows. We have His memories. His needs."

"We are Him," they repeated.

They couldn't have known about what happened to her in the wood earlier, unless they were telling the truth. Was it really so unlikely that Lyon, who was acquainted with Nereids and was at times possessed of a superfluous extra phallus, might also be possessed of an ability to conjure a pair of mirror-image saviors?

With the coming of that thought, she began to believe.

"We are Shimmerskins," the first of the clones continued. Since he seemed to take the lead in their conversations, she privately dubbed him One and his brother, Two. "Most of our ilk are female. The only males He can bring forth are like us. Replicas of Himself."

He nodded to his look-alike, who then went to Lyon and sat beside him. Curving a hand to his stubbled jaw, he fondly brushed a lock of hair from his cheek. "Not much longer," she thought she heard him whisper.

"He needs you to keep your promise," said One, drawing her attention back to him. He'd moved close without her noticing.

She stepped back. "What promise?" For her every backward step, he took another stride forward as if they'd begun a bizarre waltz.

Two's eyes pinned her from the bed. "To heal Him. To let us to come inside you."

"*Non*," she protested. "This—all of this—*c'est impossible*."

But when One reached for the poker, she allowed him to cover her hands with his so they both held it. His hands were warm. Strong. Alive. How could that be?

"You will be left chaste," he soothed. "As He agreed."

There was a new heat at her back as Two left the bed and

came behind her. She flinched at his touch, but his palms were gentle at her waist, then smoothed upward until they curved around her breasts, pulling her back against him. Her body recognized his as Lyon's and instinctively began to yield.

One dropped his gaze to stare fixedly at his brother's hands as they plumped and kneaded, learning the plush contours of her through her gown. His own fingers flexed over hers on the poker as if he were imagining that he caressed her instead.

"If I say you nay, will you force me?"

His eyes rose to hers again. "Don't say no," he coaxed.

It wasn't a reassuring reply, but something in his face had her slowly releasing the poker to him.

Tossing it heedlessly to clatter on the grate, he covered his brother's hands, which then eased away from her breasts to begin unfastening the back of her bodice. This new set of hands was warm as well, and as if impatient with the layer of fabric that barred them from her skin, they found the shoulders of her gown and pushed them onto her upper arms.

Discovering the necklace she wore, One paused, then lifted it from her neckline. His twin abandoned his efforts at her back, and for a moment, both scrutinized the beads with more absorption than the simple strand seemed to warrant.

"They were given to me as a child," she told them, though they hadn't asked. An odd look passed between them at that. But they said nothing and when she tugged, they let the necklace fall back into place.

Like a pair of experienced lady's maids, they proceeded to work in concert, preparing her for whatever they had planned. One unpinned her hair, combed his fingers through it, and then draped it forward over her shoulders. Two was nimble at his duties, but when her bodice slackened as a result, she caught it to her chest. Finding it still snug at the waist, she realized he'd left the hooks secured there, preventing the garment from falling.

She glanced over at Lyon.

"It doesn't seem right," she whispered. "To do this while he lies there, so unwell."

A hand lifted her chin, and One turned her back to his own visage, which was a healthier version of the man's on the bed. "Through our taking of you, He will be revived."

"How exactly will that be accomplished?" she thought to demand. "How will you begin? And why are there two of you?"

One only smiled faintly, then surprised her by moving away. At her back, Two stilled and she felt him watching his brother.

Choosing a bed adjacent to Lyon's, One seated himself on its end with his feet set wide on the floor. In profile, his shaft was almost absurdly huge and as thick as her wrist. Its cap bobbed high beyond his bellybutton, fat as an apple and as florid.

He sat back with both arms locked straight and his hands braced behind him on the mattress. Amber flashed in her direction. "Come."

Two pressed at the small of her back, and though dubious, she allowed him to urge her closer. But when they were within touching range, he released her. She tensed, assuming a complete disrobing—and more—was imminent.

However, instead of removing her garments or pushing her any farther toward his brother, Two went himself, and knelt there between his legs. Skimming his hands up the seated man's muscular thighs, he brought them to meet at his brother's groin. There, his fingers encircled the root of a cock the same length and girth as Lyon's. Sweeping his tongue over his lips, he tilted it to his mouth.

At the taking, One inhaled a sharp breath. His throat arched and his eyes drifted closed briefly before reopening to watch.

His brother's lips stretched wide to accommodate his crown, and with a back and forth motion, moistened it. A look of intense concentration shaded his face as he then moved downward onto the shaft and took it deeper, then deeper still. When he neared the root, he paused, pulled back, and then angled his throat differently as if the adjustment were necessary in order to complete his task. His arms slipped around his brother's hips to loosely embrace him, as his lips resumed their stroke ever lower until, finally, they nested in soft bristle.

Juliette's fists locked her bodice tight to her chest, and she stared as one spellbound, truly shocked at what she was witnessing. Yet she would not look away. For this was the kind of fleshly pursuit the other girls at Valmont's had often enjoyed. One of the many she'd dreamed of participating in, but had never dared.

Two began unsheathing his prize, his cheeks hollowing as he withdrew up the slickened shaft until only its knob remained hidden within his mouth. Bobbing his head, he allowed the wet O of his lips to massage the crown's pronounced plinth. Then he enveloped the entire length again, and more easily this time. And thus began a mouthing stroke that worked his cheeks like bellows, as he took and took, then surrendered, and began again.

After a moment, his elbow drew back and his hand went between his brother's thighs. He was doing something . . . taking the weight of his twin's balls and coddling them.

One looked down at the man who ministered to him and lay a hand atop his head, caressing his mussed curls. "Yesss. This is what He likes."

Then, without looking up, he spoke to her. "Watch, Juliette. And learn. For soon you will do this for my brothers."

"Oh, God!" Her eyes flew to the ruddy, corpulent rod angling high between the kneeling man's legs. The tip of her tongue slipped out and touched her lips, and she found herself imagining. How would it taste? And how would it ever fit, in her mouth or anywhere else?

At her exclamation, Two relinquished his brother with a popping sound. He swallowed visibly, licking his lips as if in imitation of her. Between One's legs, the cock he'd tended so thoroughly now rose proud and enormous, its apple polished and glistening.

Identical faces turned her way.

"He's ready for you."

"Come."

Their low, beguiling voices belonged to Lyon. As did their wicked eyes and tempting smiles and their expansive chests and muscular thighs.

Two caught a fold of her skirt and tugged her nearer. She went. In a fluid movement, he then rocked to his feet and brought her to stand facing his twin.

One sat upright and set his broad palms at the curves of her corseted waist. Closing his knees, he slipped them between hers, then widened them, drawing her closer and forcing her to open for him.

"Lift your skirts for Him," he wooed softly. "For yourself. We all stand to gain from this."

Of their own volition, the fingers at her sides slowly curled into the fabric under them. When she started to inch it higher, Two assisted, heaping the bulk of the material to tent his brother's legs and groin. Kneeling behind her then, he lightly palmed the back of her knee with one hand, and slid his other under her bunched skirts and upward along the inside of a stockinged thigh.

Gently, oh, so gently, his fingers introduced themselves high between her legs.

Her knees wobbled and her hands fell to the powerful shoulders of the man before her, who now monitored his twin's effect on her with the careful intensity of a jungle cat eyeing its prey.

At first, only a single finger pad brushed the purse of nether lips. Then, as she began to unfurl for it, two. Deliberately, they opened her and the thickest, longest finger eased inside, testing her readiness. Her passage pulsed on it, once, and she cried out softly.

"Already, your body gushes for Him," praised the man who touched her so intimately, sounding as pleased as if she'd performed some marvelous trick.

A hand left her waist and dipped under the front fall of her skirts and she knew from One's expression that he'd found himself. His thighs went wider between hers, bringing her lower. And then he was poised at her gate, his bulbous tip taking the place of his twin's fingers.

Her virgin lips bussed his crown and parted in hesitant welcome, anointing him with her body's passionate cream. A feral growl welled from him at this initial taste of her, and another's hands held her for him as he worked his crest along her furrow, back and forth, nestling higher into her slick notch with each pass and sending hot waves of sensation spiraling up her channel.

She glanced over at Lyon, lying so still.

One's other hand left her waist and caught her cheek, bringing her gaze back to his. Then, softly, he whispered, "Are you ready for Him?"

She took a quick, indrawn breath.

Then hands—she knew not whose—came under her ruched skirts, grasping her hips and thighs and guiding her in the way of accommodating him. Amber seared her as that tumid apple, still wet from his brother's mouth, commenced its invasion.

Her slit gaped and expanded, valiantly trying to hood him.

"That's good, Juliette, so good," said twin voices that were Lyon's, and yet not.

She grimaced, leaning closer to the chest before her to tilt herself away from imminent impalement, "I'm not sure I can—"

But her lover's hands adjusted her over him in some way, and then miraculously her private flesh gulped and his knob ducked inside her.

Four groans—each a blend of pleasure and pain—infused the air in ardent harmony.

At the sound from the adjacent bed, Juliette looked toward Lyon again and saw he'd changed position and was now turned on his side facing them.

"Lyon?"

But there was no reply, and his eyes remained closed.

"The rest will follow more easily," said the man before her, drawing her eyes back to his.

"I'll hold you to that," she said, then gasped as his cock recommenced its ingress.

Petting her hair and caressing her shoulders and back, Two whispered soft encouragements to her as his twin tunneled steadily deeper and deeper still, until it seemed he would never finish coming inside her.

Her body struggled to accept the fullness, and she cupped his neck so her fingertips met at his nape. "It's too much."

"Relax," soothed the other man from behind her. His hands went under her skirts again, curving over the bones of her hips to alter her position a second time on his twin in the same way he'd earlier angled his own mouth on him.

"You were made for Him," One murmured, and his thumb came between their bellies to brush the swollen bud at the front of her stretched slit.

Four male hands then began to lift and lower her in a rolling motion that slicked her up and then inched her down an unforgiving, persistent intruder. Something was different now. With each stroke, her clit dragged against the masculine pole and sparked with sensation.

And still she took more. Began to want more. Crave more.

Her legs tightened around his, helping her to move on him as he sought harbor in her throaty embrace. "Almost there," their voices coaxed.

And then, at her soft cry, he sank home and her nether lips

were planting a wet, open-mouthed kiss to his groin. Incredibly, she had taken all of him. She rested her forehead on his chin, wanting to push him away, but trying to grow accustomed to him in the hope things would later improve.

His hand curved at her neck and his lips turned to her ear, his breath fresh as he spoke. "You were not virgin."

"What?" Her head jerked back, so she could search his eyes. She'd felt no tear, no rip of her membrane.

"There was blood on your thighs," Two confirmed. "Before he came into you. Virgin's blood." He rubbed her shoulders, trying to console her. But there was no way to fix this.

She looked over at Lyon, who slept on, oblivious. Was it her imagination or did his complexion appear somewhat healthier now? "You swore this wouldn't happen!" she raged to the room at large.

Then she hit the chest before her with the flats of both hands and tried to wrest herself from the lap that supported her. Under her dress, One's grip tightened, keeping him safely lodged inside her. She winced and pushed his hand away from her right hip.

Two nudged her skirt aside and found the purpled bruise there. "You fell?" he asked. "In the woods?"

She shrugged and gave an irritated nod. "Yes, what of it? Let me go."

One's eyes met his brother's over her shoulder. "You fell in a manner that was too jarring for your delicate membrane to withstand," he told her. "It was not I who took it from you, but a prior accident."

Her struggles faltered as she remembered how her abdomen had cramped after the Cossack had assaulted her. *Mon Dieu!* How unfair! Even though he hadn't succeeded at physically raping her, she'd apparently lost her virginity to the Russian after all.

The notion that she was no long pure reverberated in her mind, panicking her. Though she certainly hadn't consciously planned to ever return to Valmont, it was somehow frightening to have that exit so firmly cut off. She could not let him find her again. Not now that her body's circumstances were so altered. He'd consider it a betrayal and would punish her—see her imprisoned or dead. No, she could no longer think of going back, but instead would only look forward. Regardless of who was at fault, she had to accept that she was changed.

Upon that thought, a great weight left her and she realized her uppermost emotion was that of simple, profound relief. No longer would she have to fret over that fragile, feminine commodity. No longer would she have to guard it so strenuously.

She was open.

She shifted her hips. Wide open.

The stoic member residing within her keep twitched in response, eager and ready. The man she straddled had been watching her, waiting, and now correctly read her willingness to continue on with him. The last moorings at the waist of her dress slipped free and her gown was taken from her and tossed away, leaving only the meager coverings of chemise and corset.

With a hand at her lower spine to keep them wed, One maneuvered himself farther onto the mattress until the backs of his knees met its edge and her calves rested fully upon the linens at either side of him. Lying back, he took her with him and her palms braced themselves in the lee of his arms.

His broad hands took her hips and began sensuously rocking her, teaching her throat to ride his impalement in a lusty stroke similar to that he had previously enjoyed from his brother. Her hair fell in waves around her shoulders, its ends dusting his torso as she studiously followed his every instruction.

Beside her, Two lay propped on an elbow, offering gentle praise and caressing the terrain of her body from breast, to corseted rib, and hip and thigh. Then his touch left her and a moment later the mattress depressed as he came to kneel on the bed before her. A hand eased under the fall of her hair to cup her nape and the tips of his fingers lifted her jaw. When her eyes found his phallus, she suddenly realized why Lyon had summoned twins.

They were not planning to take turns with her. They would enjoy her together.

An avid excitement coursed through her. And then her lips were parting and stretching around a new cock and it was sliding along her tongue and bringing with it the taste and memory of this phantom's creator.

"That's good," Two whispered. His hands held her skull and she let him come deeper, allowing his girth to widen her lips and fill her mouth. And still she took more.

Inches away from his root, she made a soft, garbled protest.

"Relax," he soothed, pulling back. "Breathe."

His brother's touch began roaming, reassuring and strong as it massaged breasts peeking from her corset, then swept down her back to reclasp her hips. The pace of his spearing had lessened and was slow and steady now—calculated to keep her poised on a razor's edge of need, but not allowing her to tumble over it to completion. She ached for a harder, faster ride, but it was impossible to speak and urge her mount on.

Under their combined tutelage, she began to breathe through her nose and relax muscles she'd been unaware she could control, and then the cock was dipping from her mouth into her throat.

Amber glinted up at her, intense and salacious, as One watched her service his twin. And then he was dragging her up his own length until she almost lost his crown, and then ramming her lower to swallow him again, over and over. Hard hands bit her thighs, pulling them apart until she was wide open to his rut. Soon his belly was oiled with her cream, and his taking had become a slick slide that rubbed her clit with each delicious stroke.

She settled into the juicy rhythm of riding and sucking, and as she began to hurtle toward orgasm, the compulsion to close her legs was strong. But One controlled her now and she could only go along on his ride.

Two's fingers flexed at her nape as he thrust himself in her mouth with increasing strength. Her cheeks ballooned with each plunge and hollowed with each retreat.

Under her, One's fucking had turned fierce. At last—just what she'd craved! Her every thought, every breath, every cell narrowed to focus only on the passionate thrill brought to her by each humid slam of their hips. A coil of sharp, desperate need twisted inside her and her fingers clawed the bed linens, her eyes squeezing shut as her body strained toward . . .

A strangled moan left her, as two cocks speared fathoms deep and held, shuddering. Readying. Her lovers' fingers and hands and arms locked her tight to them. A single breathless second later, masculine shouts split the air as their passion broke and they shot themselves in her throats in hot, intermittent, seemingly ceaseless spurts.

Inner muscles she hadn't known she possessed contracted on them like lecherous, milking fists. As she took from them, they gave until she was so filled with their taste and their scent and the wonder of it all that she tipped over a precipice and crashed on her own wave of concupiscent joy.

Even as she still pulsed for his brother, Two was already slipping from her mouth. And with a kiss to the feminine lips that had so pleasured him, and a poignant smile that felt like a farewell, he left the bed.

She and his brother continued on until her nether slit was choking and gasping and gulping with the onslaught of his spill and her coming. A frail protest soughed from her as he carefully lifted her from her perch before she was ready to go, and drew her upright from the bed. Having been held wide for him for so long, her legs were almost reluctant to once again meet. Standing behind her, he hooked his arms over and around hers, so her shoulders were thrown back and her arms were loosely secured behind her. Her eyes closed, and with a sigh of contentment, she let her head loll back on his shoulder.

And then another body stood before her, this one somewhat more human than her other lovers' had been. Her lashes fluttered open. "Oh, *Dieu*—Lyon!"

His gaze heated at the sight of her wanton appearance, roving flushed breasts that plumped high over her corset and noting the gauzy chemise that lightly veiled her belly and upper thighs. Long, pale waves of hair had tangled and tendrils of it curled damply around her face. His brothers' mouths and hands had marked her skin and she was slick with the rub of their desire and her own.

Glittering amber found emerald, and his mouth curved slightly, sensuously. The backs of his fingers rose to fan over her outthrust nipples, brushing back and forth, then lingering to scissor-pinch and roll them between his knuckles. Sensation shot straight from his touch to her private core, reawakening the fading throb of her recent coming.

She made as if to embrace him, but One's arms restrained hers. She stilled, suddenly sensing the anticipation of the man behind her and wondering what it portended.

Her eyes roamed Lyon's face, seeing the renewed flush of good health. "You're better?"

But he only nodded as his arms slowly threaded hers and his brother's, and his palms slipped low to curve over her rump. His tumescent length bumped her belly as he leaned close to nuzzle the slope of her throat.

"You've been fucking other men. I can smell them on you."

Startled by this statement, she let out a huff. "A situation *you* engineered."

"Yes. But you enjoyed it, did you not?" His lips opened on her skin and he kissed her, sucking lightly. His hands on her backside flexed over its rounds, as palms and fingers began to leisurely explore the shape of her.

"Yes," she whispered, enjoying his touch on her nakedness. "Yes."

Shifting his legs wider, he dipped so his crown caught at the hem of her chemise and nudged it and himself between slender thighs that were washed with another's spill. He groaned and started to rock her, plowing his gauze-sheathed length along a furrow that still quivered with the thrill of another's rut.

"I can taste them on you. And feel where they've been— here, between your legs."

Umm. She relaxed against the chest behind her again, and her eyes drifted half-closed at this new gently rasping pleasure.

When Lyon lifted his head, it was to look beyond her at his brother. An odd glance passed between the two men, and there was a primal gleam in his eyes when they found hers again. His massage of her rear cheeks became a more dominant, purposeful stroke that kneaded once . . . twice . . . thrice.

And then, with exquisite gentleness, he spread her cleft, in invitation.

Wary now, she straightened, but his lips dusted over hers, murmuring and quieting her. His brother released her arms, then slid a hand to her belly to lift the chemise's hem and expose her.

She exhaled deeply as Lyon's pristine, velvet knob tipped upward from its stroke between her thighs and pierced her tender feminine slit. An erotic groan rumbled from him as his fat crown pressed on, opening and stretching lips still sensitized by another's use of them. Her pink folds gasped and caressed, trying to draw him higher, eager to show him what they'd learned. But he held back, allowing her only a taste for now.

Thighs tensed around her and she felt his brother's smooth, wet apple at the puckered *oignon* Lyon held ready for him.

Green eyes flew open and clung to amber, seeking reassurance, as that other cock, still drenched from the lick of her nether throat and its own coming, prodded the resistant opening in her rear.

She set her hands on the sculpted chest before her, her eyes fixed, as she tremulously awaited what would come. Lyon kissed her then—pressed his open mouth to one that yet another of his phantom siblings had fucked, and he tasted her passion and hesitation, and her curiosity.

The pressure of this second, unfamiliar intrusion had her rising on tiptoe and sealing her mouth tighter to his. Then he swallowed her cry at the slick, sharp bite that accompanied the dilation of her ring. And as his brother's knob slipped inside, Lyon's did as well so that she held both captive within her.

Two pairs of masculine hands found her waist and hips, and a slow, dual penetration began. Another's cum eased Lyon's heat deeper, but his entry was measured, setting a pace that his twin matched. The tactile sensation of their engorged cocks, so heavily roped and knotted with veins, drilling inexorably inside her was incredible.

She felt the tension in the muscled torsos at her chest and back and knew these men went more gingerly with her than their natures urged. And she yielded to them and yielded still more, with soft gasps and whimpers, until at last, she found herself twice impaled.

"Ahh, Juliette," her lovers groaned in those voices that were so alike.

"*Dieu.*" She stilled, almost afraid to breathe lest she burst from their occupation of her.

Lyon kissed her passionately and deeply and his brother brushed her hair aside and pressed his mouth to the angle where throat met shoulder.

She returned the kiss, so full that she wanted to scream at them to leave her. Yet when they reversed their slide, she conversely wanted to rail at them to return. Lyon set the tempo of their carnal grind that gradually increased in vigor and strength. Sandwiched between them, she felt the bunching of muscles in ridged bellies as rigid cocks were shoved and retracted in precise, parallel tandem.

And soon their thrusts turned hotter, even savage. With each ram, their cockslits kissed her so hard and so deep that she was lifted to her toes. Air seemed to ebb from the room as a second orgasm bloomed within her. As if sensing she was close, they both withdrew, retreating so far and fast that they suctioned her channels and their knobs teased her gates. Then as one, they drove home, and three bodies merged in a furious, perfect ecstasy.

Syncopated jets of semen throbbed inside her, initiating the pulse of her own contractions, then increasing the tender agony until her vision dimmed and sparks of light pinged and splintered. If not for the bodies on either side of her, she would have crumpled to her knees.

The masculine arms that enfolded her shuddered as great spasms rocked her fraternal lovers. Sultry, grateful tears of their cum filled her, then wept from her, trickling down the insides of her thighs.

At length, she felt the man behind her kiss her hair, then gently pull out. "*Grazie,*" he whispered in Lyon's seductive voice. And then he was gone and only Lyon remained.

She sagged forward against him, bumping her forehead to his chest, her breath coming in pants in the aftermath of their coitus. Long moments later, he lifted her from him and carried her to the closest bed, curling her in his arms. She lay there, facing him, so splendidly replete that she felt unable to move. Now and then, her body still twitched involuntarily under the subtle pulse of an orgasm that had not yet fully ceased.

Nearby, the fire snapped and from the darkness outside came the orchestral song of raindrops and thunder. Their

230 / Elizabeth Amber

breathing eventually slowed and they lay side by side contemplating one another in companionable silence.

She ran the backs of her fingers along the golden skin of his taut belly and lower, feeling the soft tufted nest of him that was moist with the pearls of their coming. Finding the base of his shaft, she traced up its length. He was still hard.

Her eyes found his, a question in them.

"Later," he murmured, caressing her cheek. "Rest."

Then, without looking away from her, he touched the bruise at her hip as if he'd learned through his brothers that it was there and understood what it meant. "I'm sorry."

She shrugged, not wanting to speak of her loss now. That was the past. Here, lying before her, was her future. Perhaps. But did he mean to have her only for tonight or for a few nights, or for all nights to come?

"Enough uncertainties," she murmured, rolling onto her stomach and elbows to gaze at him. "Explain to me what you are that you can conjure other beings from nothing."

"Ah!" He fell onto his back, taking her with him and pulling her to lie across his chest. After a considering pause, he spoke. "You know of the mythological satyr?"

She propped her chin on a fist atop his chest to better see his face. "Followers of Dionysus? The wine god?"

He nodded. "Or Bacchus in Italy, but they are one in the same. The Satyrs have been his disciples since time immemorial." He paused, eyeing her, then continued almost reluctantly. "My brothers and I are his descendents. Even today, we protect his legacy on our estates—the vines begun by him and a gate that stands between his world and this one."

His hold on her had tightened as he'd spoken as if he'd suspected she might flee at his sharing of this news, but it relaxed again as she only calmly digested what he'd told her. She had more questions, of course, and asked them as they came to her.

And he answered, open and easy, as he had been at Valmont's before his illness. In time, they grew quiet again.

Studying her face, he stroked her hair, and finding a soft nipple peeking from among the long strands, began to idly toy with it until it firmed under his touch. Another hand smoothed down the slope of her back and his expression heated. "Can you take me again?" he asked in a voice turned dark and seductive. "Where my brothers have had you?"

She smiled slowly, willing.

And so it went on through the night—they talked, and ate, and slept, and mated. As though they were the only two people who mattered, and what they did here together was a private activity removed from social mores or censure.

The foul weather had rendered the cabin a cozy, intimate haven. Their world had grown smaller and safer, for the moment.

She'd given him the gift of life, and as dawn approached, he gave her a gift in return, explaining the facts of her origins and filling her with wonder at the startling news that her father had been a King.

The sun came and went again, and then another one like it. And still they stayed close, cuddling, fondling, and joining their bodies so often that soon neither knew where one began and the other ended. It was a time for sharing kisses. And sharing confidences—at least some of them. Oblivious to the passage of hours, they knew only each other.

Then, with the next dawn, the carriage returned.

14

EarthWorld, Tuscany, Italy, November, 1823

"Welcome to my home," Lyon said, with satisfaction in his voice.

Juliette gazed around the great hall they'd entered, trying not to gape. For the interior of his *castello* was an unexpected disaster. Though this room and the adjacent one were enormous, scarcely any furniture inhabited them and what there was had been chosen for comfort rather than style. And it all appeared so antiquated that it could not possibly have been chosen within recent history.

Various implements utilized in the cultivation of grapes or in the production of wine were haphazardly set here and there, indicating that this marble-floored, chandelier-hung mansion functioned as a workspace as readily as it did a living quarters. It was easy to see that not only had all his efforts been directed toward the out of doors, but that he'd also managed to bring the outdoors, indoors.

Nearly an hour before their carriage had reached his home,

he'd noted the boundaries of the Satyr estate for her as delin-
eated by an immense stone wall nearly six feet thick, a vestige
of ancient fortifications. Once inside it, they'd passed various
ruins, follies, statues, and gazebos on their approach here.

Though it was autumn, the air was unseasonably moderate
inside the grounds and there were expansive carpets of bloom-
ing phlox, vinca, valerian, various ivies, ferns, and grasses. Fruit
and herbs, that elsewhere only grew in spring or summer, still
seemed to be thriving here despite the season. In the distance
there were the endless hills that were patchworked and terraced
with grapevines, indicating that his holdings were far more extensive than the Valmont family's had been.

And, after viewing all of this, Juliette had been anxious to
enter his home if only to escape the profusion of nature. Traveling almost two weeks with him, she'd become somewhat in-
ured to all things bucolic, but still found them vaguely threatening.
Eventually she'd been relieved to note that the wilds of cypress,
hawthorn, and vine on his land were giving way to tamer gar-
dens, arbors, and pavements.

Then this magnificent *castello* had come into view, and she'd
seen it was comprised of a collection of five majestic towers
that somehow assembled themselves together in a pleasing
manner as viewed from a distance. Its outer walls were of granite, heavily veined with iron and even streaks of gold that
glinted in the sunlight and which gave it a splendid regal cast.
Heraldic shields displaying the ancestral Satyr coat of arms
were sculpted at intervals, alternating with medallions depicting wildlife—most notably jungle cats such as lions and panthers.

Since his property and the exterior of his home had been so
impressive, she'd expected the interior to be as well, and it was
in large part. The rooms themselves, at least what she had seen
of them, were elaborately designed with gleaming wood finishes mixed with Tuscan and Carrera marbles. A dramatic cen-

tral tower rose above them and its winding staircase, complete with a lustrous carpet and a decorative parapet, led the eye upward.

"There's a viewing room at the top," he told her seeing the direction of her gaze.

She waited for horror to sweep her with its chill, but was surprised to find that the idea of gazing out over a natural landscape was far less repugnant that she would've thought it only two weeks ago.

He put an arm around her and hugged her with almost boyish enthusiasm. "What do you think?"

"It's the handsomest estate I've ever seen. But you might have warned me," she said, only half-teasing. "You described it as comfortable and unpretentious."

"It is, isn't it?" Lyon drew away slightly to glance around them, and she saw he looked perplexed. He seemed to be genuinely unimpressed by his own luxurious holdings, as only a person who'd grown up surrounded by such grandeur could be.

"However," he went on, "it's our home, and you may change it as you wish."

Juliette ignored his pointed remark, for he'd been dropping similar, unsubtle hints for some time. He made no secret of the fact he expected to wed her. Soon, she would have to tell him that this was impossible and the reasons why, but ever the coward, she continued to put it off.

Though he assured her he would not be back to full health until the next full moon came, he looked fit to her, and well able to withstand her explanations. Except for some residual memory loss, he seemed the same as ever. Those lapses were strangely selective, for he'd recalled nothing of their time at Valmont's so far, and she'd told him only what was necessary in order that he petition an investigator in Paris to initiate a search for Fleur.

Perhaps once his report arrived, she would reveal her own unfortunate news.

They'd spent the two days until the carriage driver had rescued them, indulging in what could only be described as an orgy of amorous experimentation. It had seemed perfectly normal at the time as she'd immersed herself in it, and she was startled to realize she wished herself back there in that rustic hunting cabin amid the woods. There, reality had been suspended. This glorious man had been completely hers and she his. Here, their relationship was less certain.

Ten days of travel had passed since then, and he'd been inside her as often as not, though their engagements had of necessity been less frequent on their route than before. He'd gradually regained strength, just as he'd explained would happen through his bedding of her. Though beds were often not the locale to which his amatory inclinations had led them thus far. A carriage, a bench, a floor, a table, a wall—all were locations suitable for intimate pursuits in his estimation, and she'd found him to be right.

A servant joined them just then, and he gave the man instructions regarding their trunks, for he'd had some clothing selected for them both at a shop along their journey. Then he returned to her and cocked his head to gaze at the room once more, as if trying to see it through her eyes.

"This place is solid. Dependable. As I am. But you are free to make any alterations in the dressing of either of us, within reason. I only ask that you not turn my home into an obstacle course stuffed to the gills with fragile objects I must constantly avoid or else find myself apologizing for their inadvertent destruction."

Before she could decide how to reply, there was a skirmish at the door and a girl appeared.

"Lyon! You're home!" she shrieked, dashing to loop her

arms at his waist. He stroked her hair and returned the hug. She looked to be about thirteen, with eyes that were bright and intelligent. And it was clear Lyon was a favorite of hers.

"And you brought Juliette!" The girl hurried to stand before her, where she skidded to execute a rather lackadaisical curtsey. "Nicholas read Lyon's letter to us, and I could hardly wait for you both to come!"

"Oh," said Juliette. "You must be Emma?"

"*Oui! Bonjour*! That's French, and I learned even more from this book, so that we may have a conversation." She held up a book that bore the title: *Conversational French for Young Ladies.*

"Later, Emma, once Juliette has settled in," Lyon interrupted. "Now tell me—have you been taking care of Liber and Ceres in my absence?"

"*Oui!* They'll be so pleased to see you!" This she flung over her shoulder as she rushed away toward the back of the house. Upon her departure, a man and woman appeared in the front doorway.

"You look ghastly," the woman told Lyon, her face a picture of concern. She was pretty and petite, her arms barely reaching around his bulk as she hugged him in welcome.

"Your wife has quite the way with words," Lyon told the man who accompanied her.

"Nevertheless, she's correct," he replied.

This, she knew, from having peered into Lyon's brain, was his eldest sibling, Nicholas. At a village along their route, Lyon had posted a letter to him, informing him of the expected date of their arrival. Juliette had been worried about how she'd be received, but the woman and girl at least seemed friendly. However, Nicholas was a bit too handsome and intimidating to be as easily read.

Startling blue eyes suddenly pierced her as he directed a question her way. "What have you been doing to my brother?"

Surprised to be included in the conversation, and in such a way, Juliette foundered for a reply.

"Nursing me back to my current state of good health," Lyon supplied before she could speak. "I assure you I looked far worse before my journey home with her began."

The woman beamed at her then and came to take her hands. "Welcome, sister," she said in a cultured voice. "I'm Jane, and this is my husband Nicholas, and the hoyden who dashed through here a moment ago is my sister Emma. Lyon has told you of our ties?"

"Yes." Their eyes roved each other's faces, searching for similarities.

Jane hooked a companionable arm through hers and gazed wistfully around the great hall. "I would suggest that we have tea, but Lyon chooses to decorate rather sparsely which makes entertainments difficult. I hope you plan to make some improvements in his living situation, for sometimes I despair of him."

"I have advised her she is free to do so," Lyon put in.

Nicholas mumbled something that sounded like he was offering thanks to the heavens at this news.

"Only do not look to my eldest brother for decorative advice," Lyon warned her, having overheard his brother. "For he chooses to reside in a museum."

Nicholas' lips curved slightly at that, revealing a flash of white teeth. "At least a museum has adequate seating."

"You're English?" Juliette enquired, swinging her eyes back to Jane.

She nodded, smiling. "Yes. And you're French, Lyon said in his letter. Our father certainly traveled far and wide to bring us about. Jordan is Italian. She's our third sister and will return to the fold soon I hope. Raine has just gone to retrieve her from Venice."

These people were said to be secretive and clannish. Yet how readily they were taking her into their fold and assuming she and Lyon would wed.

"Raine has gone?" she heard Lyon ask, though it was more a statement than a question.

"*Si*. His need for a leave-taking is the reason I summoned you. He departed on his errand yesterday once we sensed you were within a day's range. Jordan is in some difficulties and left the estate on her own. He's gone after her of course, but he has left us with something to caretake in his absence."

Lyon's eyes lit. "The grafted vines?"

Nicholas glanced at Juliette as if unsure she was to be trusted. Neither of them were aware she'd already gleaned this information and far more from Lyon in his hotel as he slept.

"You may speak freely in front of her. She knows all I've had time to tell her and I intend that she learn the rest sooner rather than later."

Nicholas nodded, too easily satisfied. If she'd agreed to be an instrument of Valmont's deceit, they would have made her job easy.

"They're thriving," he replied in answer to Lyon's implied question. "So far. We've got a dozen begun in the glen."

"And how goes the auction?"

"We expect a hundred or so to congregate here for it and the unveiling of the new vines six weeks from now."

"So soon?"

Nicholas shrugged. "Raine has promised to return with Jordan by then, and I trust that he will. Still, without him we're spread thin. We've yet to hire a chef and there are dozens of details to manage. With Jane involved with my son and household, there's been little time to orchestrate it all."

"It's my responsibility," said Lyon. "I'll deal with it now that I'm home. As it happens Juliette is an excellent cook and I have observed her to be supremely talented at organization on our travels."

All eyes turned to her.

But she was shaking her head before he even finished.

"Have pity," Lyon cajoled, his considerable charm ratcheting up a notch. "My brothers and I alternate in hosting duties. This season it's my turn and I'm hopeless at designing these things."

"I assure you my brother doesn't lie," said Nicholas, drawing a good-natured glower from his brother.

"Can't you hire someone to help?" said Juliette.

"I'm attempting to," said Lyon.

Her heart began to race with excitement. To be put in charge of such an affair would be a dream come true. Even if she couldn't see it through to completion, she could set it on the right track for someone else to carry on afterward. "Who has done these things for you in the past?"

Lyon flicked a nonchalant hand in the air. "One chef or another. In all fairness, I warn you it's a large undertaking, requiring not only cooking skills but management skills as well. We hold these entertainments twice annually. Once one ends, planning for the next begins. However this is an additional, more modest function in order that we may introduce our solution to the phylloxera to other vintners and induce them to begin their own plantings come spring."

Warming to his brother's proposal, Nicholas chimed in. "Raine will introduce the plants he has grafted and prepare everyone for the coming wine we will produce with them. Normally it would take several years for the new vines to mature, but we have a way with these things . . . "

There was a charged pause.

"The question is, will the taste of the new grapes be acceptable," said Lyon. "The French are notorious snobs when it comes to wine."

"Oh?" said Juliette.

Belatedly recalling her heritage, he shot her a teasing grin. "*Pardonnez-moi.* Present company excepted."

He turned then, his face wreathed in smiles as he looked beyond her toward the empty rear doorway. "Liber! Ceres!" he called out.

Juliette spun in time to see two slinky black panthers bound toward him to stand with their paws on his chest and back, as if they were bookends and he, a book. The force of their weight would have knocked over any mere mortal, but Lyon didn't even rock under it.

"I missed you!" he informed them, beginning to roughhouse.

"Emma, darling, your dress!" said Jane, shaking her head at the mess her sister had become through her fetching of the beasts. No one seemed at all concerned that the animals Lyon petted were capable of ripping out his throat with a single swipe of a paw.

One of the jungle cats suddenly bounced Juliette's way to lick her hand.

"G-get *away* from me!" she shrieked, stumbling backward.

Everyone stopped what they were doing and looked at her, stunned.

"Down!" Chastised, the animals obeyed Lyon's command instantly, sinking to lie on the marble floor.

Badly shaken, Juliette dashed through the nearest door, so eager for an escape that she didn't realize until too late that she'd entered a large closet.

"I forgot!" Lyon called after her. Then to Jane and Nicholas in *sotto voce*, "She doesn't like animals."

"So I gathered," said Nicholas.

"I didn't know!" she heard Emma wail behind her, and then came Lyon's comforting tone, reassuring her.

Lovely. She'd just upset a child and made a fool of herself

before Lyon's relatives. Dropping her bag on a shelf, Juliette rummaged through it, and with trembling hands, prepared her drops and took them. Distraught and absorbed in her task, she didn't notice when Lyon joined her.

"They may look frightening, but they're pussycats," he assured from behind her.

She slipped the dropper back inside the vial with a *plink*. "They're animals. With an instinct to kill."

There was a small silence.

"What's this?" he asked, his gaze sharpening on the bottle.

The drops slid down her throat, and she waited for their resulting calm to wash over her. "Medicine, given to me by a physician."

He took the bottle, put the tip of his tongue to the rim, and drew back, frowning. "Opiates. How often do you take it?"

"As often as I require it." She reached for the bottle, but he held it fast.

"Are you an addict?"

"Only since our carriage ride began," she lied. For in truth, the opposite was true. Since the night in the hunting cabin, she'd required the drops only sporadically. It was as if being in his sphere of influence had somehow made them less necessary.

"Then now that it is over, you won't be needing this." Lyon slid the vial in his pocket.

She only shrugged. "It's easily had. I can no doubt get more if I want it."

He set his broad hands at her waist. "Don't," he coaxed. "For me. For us. Don't."

Her eyes searched his, and her heart twisted at his concern. Whereas Valmont wanted to cage her with her addictions and phobias, Lyon wanted to set her free of them.

"You may have noticed that I'm unusually afraid," she murmured. "Of certain things. Animals. The drops help me with that. I don't want to use them, but at times it seems I need them. And in truth I've used them far longer than the carriage ride."

He tucked her close, wrapping protective arms around her and rubbing a hand over her back. "Liber and Ceres recognize you as fey. They would rather die themselves than hurt you. They're descendents of Bacchus's familiars and for that reason if no other, I am their caretaker."

"It's not just animals, but the outdoors in general that puts me off. I—I had a difficult experience a few years ago."

He drew away to see her face, but she shrugged and shook her head, unwilling to speak of it.

"I'm here now," he said, hugging her again. "I'll help you through taking leave of this crutch. As you helped me through my illness."

"I'm not sure it requires the same cure," she said with a small smile.

"You may be surprised how quickly a cure is wrought, for your body's rhythms will be different here. You'll find many things easier now that you're on our land. It's where you were meant to be."

15

From the corner of her eye, Juliette glimpsed an ethereal glow in the woods just beyond where she stood at the edge of Lyon's garden. She turned with a feeling of foreboding and saw what appeared to be a dozen or more lanterns bobbing through the trees. They were moving swiftly and erratically, and they were coming her way. Ghostly, childish giggles and a whiff of grape-must accompanied them.

"*Non!*" she breathed, backing away.

But of course the lights only continued closer, until she saw it was exactly as she'd feared. The bright-children—those mischief-makers, whose arrival was a harbinger of momentous and often unfortunate occurrences—had come again to haunt her.

Why did this have to happen now, when things had seemed to be going so well for her? She'd been here on Lyon's estate over a week. He had almost fully recuperated from his illness and had been exceptionally amorous of late. He'd told her his attentions were in preparation for an ancient Satyr ceremony known as the Calling, after which his recovery from the effects of what had occurred—or rather, what had *not* occurred the night she'd tricked him in Paris—would be complete.

It seemed that under the full moon, which would arrive tonight, his body would alter in the way she'd seen it a month ago in his hotel. Together, they were to engage in a carnal ritual, which she'd begged him to describe and he had.

What he'd revealed had exceeded her most perverse and delicious imaginings and she was now anticipating the reality with equal amounts of trepidation and yearning. However, this rite of his normally took place in the open wood, at some designated location she'd yet to see on the grounds. And though this was the site he would prefer, he'd resigned himself to her inability to endure so long a time in a natural setting, and had assured her they would undertake the ceremony in his home tonight instead.

Yet with the lessening of her dependence on opium, she'd discovered a desire to broaden the scope of her world and had recently also discovered in herself a longing to please him where she could. And this had been the impetus for her foray into his garden this afternoon. Since he was now visiting his eldest brother in some secret fraternal endeavor that he'd claimed would prepare them both for tonight, it had seemed a good time to make such an attempt in private.

Of course, she'd only meant to venture to the boundaries marked by the tiled courtyard at the rear of the *castello*. But giddy at the success of attaining that goal without trouble, some foolish impulse had tugged her to go beyond fountains, terracotta urns, black-painted Attic vases, and jeweled mosaic flooring. And beyond potted lemon trees and statues where the landscape had given way to wilder plantings and then to the beginnings of an oak and cypress forest.

She spun around, locating the golden edifice that was Lyon's home just uphill from where she stood. It wasn't so great a distance. She lifted her skirts and scurried off, retracing her steps

on the path toward home. Perhaps she could make it there before she was caught. Perhaps she could outrun whatever disaster loomed.

So she ran, knowing all the while, it was a wasted effort, for
the imps would catch her and wreak whatever havoc they liked,
regardless of her wishes. She felt for the oatmeal she'd continued to carry with her as a talisman, thinking herself an idiot
since it had proven it didn't ward them off. They were almost
upon her now, and there were far more of them than she'd ever
seen at one time.

Then they were prancing ahead of her, where they gleefully
blocked her path. She came to a standstill so abrupt that she almost pitched forward into their midst. Her eyes searched for a
way to pass them, but they spiraled closer, forming a dancing
ring around her from which she could not escape. Small hands
brushed her skirt in passing and flitting feet made whirlwinds
in the leaves. Like some sort of luminous lasso, they held her
prisoner within their merry, undulating circle.

"*Nonononon!*" she wailed, yanking her skirts away. Unable
to stand their proximity any longer, she tried again to lunge free
and to her surprise broke through their orbit. Undismayed,
they followed her, forming a living barrier to her right. She
veered left in response, away from Lyon's home. Behind her,
they wove among the trees, all devious grins and twirls.

Now and then, a few separated from the pack and moved to
one side of her or the other and she always swerved in the opposite direction. A few minutes later, she realized they were in
control of her flight and were in fact herding her in a direction
they wished her to go!

She swung around to confront them, only to discover that
they'd disappeared. She put a hand to her chest to calm her
heart. Her breath puffed in and out, visible in the autumn air.

Why had they gone without making their usual mischief?
Had something scared them away? Turning toward the *castello*,

she looked upward to its gleaming golden towers and took a step in its direction.

But when she glanced directly ahead, she saw that a woman had materialized on the path between her and her destination. She was fragile and beautiful—and shockingly nude, at least what Juliette could see of her. Dark, lustrous hair draped her face, shoulders, and much of her body, hanging in long silken strands that fell almost to her knees. It was damp as if she'd recently come from the bath. Or the river.

"*Mon pere et ma mere m'ont abandonné*," the creature announced. Her words were musical, chanted. Almost a croon.

Juliette pressed her fingers over her mouth. *My father and my mother have abandoned me.* The phrase was well known to her. Those very words were engraved above the doorway at the Hospice des Enfants Trouvés, which had taken her in as a foundling.

"You remember, don't you?" lilted the voice.

"What do you want? Who are you?"

The woman tottered unsteadily forward until her belly bumped Juliette's and her hair dripped on her shoes. A furtive glance downward informed her of something she'd initially overlooked. The woman was heavily swollen with child. Her features were indiscernible through the curtain of her hair, but there was a strange pearlescent scallop-shaped design on the skin of her forehead where it was visible, and on her legs.

Juliette stepped back from her, wary.

From among the great swag of necklaces she wore, the creature selected one, seeming unfazed by the lack of welcome. Untangling it from the others, she pulled it over her head and held it out, attempting to encircle Juliette's neck with it. It was green with algae and Juliette recoiled from it.

"What's wrong? You act like it's a sea-snake," the woman said, sounding annoyed. She looped it back around her own throat and turned it until she located the pendant hanging from it.

This she lifted between two fingers and tugged it forward for display. Juliette glanced at it, seeing it appeared to be cast pewter or perhaps iron, rendered pitch black with corrosion.

But it was familiar.

Strangely intrigued, she took it and held it to drape her palm so the necklace stretched, momentarily tethering them. With growing excitement, she ran her thumb over the grime, trying to determine what it covered. Engraved upon it were two sets of numbers, she saw, both barely discernable.

Eagerly, she scratched with her nail and peered closer. The first set was easily revealed: 1804. A number identical to the birthdate inscribed on her own necklace!

She scratched diligently at the second. It was more stubborn, but her companion stood patiently as she worked at it, and eventually it was exposed as well. 8901! This was the number that had been assigned to Elise to indicate her place among the ranks of abandoned children at the hospice in Paris. The number on the necklace she had worn that summer they'd met three years ago. Her own ranking had been only one digit off.

She tightened her fist around the medallion. "Where did you get this?"

"Do you not know me?" Sea-green eyes identical to her own blinked at her. Then the necklace was pulled away as she bent slightly and speared her fingers through the front of her hair, pushing it back from her face.

"Do you not know me?" she asked again.

"Elise?" Juliette's asked, her voice laced with burgeoning hope.

The woman reached toward her to stroke curls the color of almonds. "Light and dark. That's what your Madame Fouche used to call us, remember?"

Juliette let out an amazed cry and enveloped her in an embrace, which she didn't notice was only half-heartedly returned. She drew back, a confused look on her face.

"But everyone believed you dead!" It came out as a choked whisper. "Even I. For a time I was almost convinced I'd killed you myself. There are those who still accuse me of it." Her tone begged for an explanation.

Sea-green eyes shifted, secretive. "It wasn't possible to return to you."

The brevity of this response was so like Elise, for she'd always been private. When she'd first come to Burgundy, she'd revealed little about the sixteen years of her life prior to their meeting. They'd been constant companions that summer, but at its end, Elise had gone.

She took the woman's pale hands in hers and determinedly sought to bring back the girl she'd known. "Elise, I saw your name in the hospice registry in Paris. Inscribed just below mine. And from this I also learned that our arrivals there were not months or days apart, or even hours. But only minutes. We were born and delivered there at the same time! On December 20th of 1804."

The woman shrugged, looking uninterested.

"But, don't you know what that means? This evidence, coupled with our similar eye color and the numbers? It's too great a coincidence. It has to mean we're sisters, just as we once pretended."

"Wonderful," came the wooden response.

What was going on here? Elise had returned, yet she was not the sister Juliette remembered. It was almost as if another inhabited her body.

Her sister's swollen belly inadvertently bumped against her own flat one—a reminder that another being did in fact currently reside within.

"I'm to be an aunt?" she asked, lowering her gaze.

"*Oui.*" Brightening at the introduction of this new subject, she lifted Juliette's hands and placed them on her abdomen.

When she felt the kick of a child, a smile curved Juliette's lips. She'd taken so much from this dear woman. Very nearly taken her life. Even if she hadn't killed her, she'd been responsible for the assault on her that day. It was a joy to see her well and to know she'd soon bear her a niece. Since she had so little family—to suddenly add two members to it was a momentous event and joyful tears burned her eyes.

"I've come here to birth it." Her sister slanted her a significant glance apparently expecting her to grasp something she did not.

"Oh. Well, I'm glad." Juliette glanced at the scallops on her arm, and saw that they seemed to be rapidly fading, rendering her ever more normal. "Oh, Elise, where have you been all this time? Did you transform into the river to escape our attackers, and then were unable to find me again?"

"But don't you remember? We did find each other again. Only a month ago. On the bridge in Paris."

In a shocking flash, Juliette realized that she'd been right in her guess that night on the Pont Neuf. Elise and the woman she'd seen with Lyon were apparently one and the same.

"Ah! You begin to comprehend our situation."

"But Lyon said his . . . partner . . . that night was a Nereid. One named Sibela."

Her companion looked a bit startled at her having this knowledge, but quickly recovered. "My sea name. However, I saw you again after that, though you didn't notice me. It was the very next night, as you were leaving his hotel." She set her hands on her distended belly. "The night he gave me this."

Juliette snatched her hands away and clasped them over her heart where a dagger of dread had just struck. Slowly her eyes rose to search identical ones. Reading the answer she'd feared there, she whispered, "It's Lyon's."

"Yes." Elise polished her hands over her belly, looking pleased with herself. "It's exactly one month since he and I lay together in his hotel. And tonight is to be a full moon," she hinted. "The child will require its father."

She paused then. Waiting.

But Juliette just stood there, staring at her, unable to speak. Then, after an agonizing interval, she resigned herself to the fact that she must act selflessly.

"Yes," she said dully. "Of course. I understand."

After all that she'd put her sister through, and in view of her fecund state, it seemed the only answer she could give.

16

Lyon slammed his front door shut, causing its frame to shudder. Then he forced himself to face three obvious facts.

It was Moonful.

The Calling had begun.

And Juliette was gone.

The knowledge reverberated in his skull, shocking his entire system.

Standing on the uppermost step of his *castello's* rear garden porch, he surveyed the courtyard and property beyond, as if expecting that by doing so she might magically reappear. When he'd returned home from Nick's a few hours ago, he'd sought her out. But she'd been nowhere to be found.

The servants had all just now departed, as they traditionally did at dusk, adjourning to their quarters just outside the estate. Before they'd gone, he'd rallied every one of them in a search of his entire home and its immediate grounds, but to no avail.

Gods! He ripped a hand through his hair in acute frustration, then took the only action left open to him. Loping down the stairs and across the bright mosaic of the courtyard, he banged the back garden gate wide.

She wasn't comfortable in the outdoors. Yet she'd run from the protection of his home. From him. Had she gone of her own free will?

Her scent was fresh in the garden. She'd been here recently, but was gone now. As she'd grown more comfortable with him and her own origins, she'd stopped holding herself so tightly leashed and her fey fragrance had slipped the reins that had once held it bound. The soft whispered tease of it was now such an integral part of his life that he couldn't imagine losing it.

"Juliette!" he called out, knowing it was useless.

He traveled on, making his way in the direction of the sacred glen. Secreted in the forest at the center of all the Satyr landholdings, it lay at a location equidistant from his and his brothers' homes. He moved surely toward it through the twilight, for he knew this path well, having trod it once a month for his whole adult life. But rarely had he done so with less enthusiasm.

Perhaps her flight was his fault. He'd tried to properly prepare her by explaining the upcoming ritual, but had he only made her afraid? If only he could find her. Calm her. He could convince her—

Arrgghh! His swiftly changing body forced him to a halt. Doubling over, he braced his hands on the bunched muscles of his thighs. His fingers bit into his flesh as he sought to endure the pain-pleasure phenomenon of his cock thickening and lengthening in preparation for the night to come.

"Down, boy. The one you seek isn't here," he muttered caustically.

After a moment, he was able to move on. His swollen prick cried out for release, straining in the now excruciatingly tight quarters it occupied in his trousers.

His state would only worsen. Soon he would be incapacitated, overtaken by an instinctive drive to fuck. Going into Human society to search for Juliette was unthinkable in his condition. Any search of his land or beyond its confines would have to wait until morning.

His legs began to sting from hip to ankle, as pores widened to sprout a familiar downy fur. The short sepia pelt tickled at his genitals and rasped his skin. Within minutes he would transform into something closer to beast than man.

The Change that occurred at each monthly Calling had always seemed to hit him more keenly than his brothers, sharpening primal instincts that lay dormant between Moonfuls. Perhaps it was why he felt such a kinship for the animals in his menagerie. They too were driven by instincts too savage to be palatable to some.

At the first of the ancient gnarled oaks, he faltered, gripping the silver bark until it scraped his palm and fingertips, as new agony engulfed him. Immobilized, he gritted his teeth against the building of a terrific cramp. A strangled curse escaped him when his second cock forced itself from the region of his pelvis, nearly ripping through his trousers in its voracious search for female flesh.

He wrenched buttons open and enveloped it with his hand, using a milking motion to momentarily soothe it before tucking it back within the fabric and moving on. Need drove him now, and he picked up his pace, cantering on furred, muscular legs toward that deepest, most secret part of Satyr Forest.

By the time he reached the edge of the sanctuary, his thought processes had begun to devolve and his utterances had deteriorated to monosyllabic grunts.

Moss. Soft. Good. Cunt.

On silent feet, he entered the lair where he and his brothers had met every month since they'd achieved manhood. Here, they gathered in supreme privacy to assuage an all-consuming lechery brought on by a moon waxed full. Humans never came here for they sensed the strangeness of this place and turned away long before reaching its perimeter.

Nicholas was already within and glanced over at him, having no doubt scented his approach. His eyes were a narrow glint of sapphire, turned almost black by lustful intentions. Jane stood with him, shadowed in his embrace. Her bodice had been loosened by his brother's hands, which were busy beneath it and her skirts.

A vaguely confused expression flitted over his face at Lyon's appearance in the glen, for he hadn't expected him. They'd met earlier in the afternoon to initiate the ritual with sacred drink, and Lyon had explained that Juliette wasn't yet ready to come here. Since Nick had eased his own wife into such matters only a few months ago, he had understood.

And yet now here Lyon stood, alone. But any explanation would have to wait. He threw off his shirt, boots, and trousers, leaving them where they fell.

Nicholas had already turned back to his wife. As Lyon's feet took him across the soft mossy floor, he felt his brother's hunger for the woman he held, and it sent his own need higher. Raine was still in Venice, and likely with Jordan. Their fraternal emotions came to him now as a feathery brush of salaciousness, and they provided a link that kept the three of them bound with the ancient Satyr, particularly during the Calling.

His physical metamorphosis from the waist down was complete now, and he moved with the mist, among pale stone shapes and the earthy smell of decay. Larger than life statues hovered in a frozen, waiting silence. Writhing figures with enormous phalluses and others with lush breasts posed together in lewd embraces, their faces wreathed with an ecstasy engendered by their couplings.

The monuments were meant to inspire lust in those who ventured within the bounds of this secret circle. He could feel them watching; knew that they were pleased by his arrival. The wild orgies of his ancestors had once taken place here for weeks on end during the Callings and Bacchanalias of long ago, but the statues witnessed less frequent bouts of debauchery these days. They were hungry to gaze upon his naked flesh, urging him to immerse himself in carnal pleasures.

At his approach, one of the statues moved, startling him. It was a female. A live one, not a statue after all. And she was nude. Nick glanced over, having noticed her as well. But her scent was fey, and obviously sensing she was no threat, he turned back to his wife.

Lyon took eager steps in her direction. He'd planned to conjure Shimmerskins for his mating, but now—

"Juliette?" His voice became a question, as he realized there was something wrong about her scent. It was familiar. It was Juliette. And yet not.

She came close and touched him with her pale hands. He stroked her hair. Why was it dark instead of the color of almonds? Some fleeting memory flitted into his mind and was as quickly gone.

"I have something of yours," she crooned, distracting him. She tugged his fingers from her hair and spread them over her swollen abdomen.

His eyes dropped. "Mine," he whispered shaping her belly with his broad hands.

Cunning sea-green watched him, and she covered his hands with her own. "Yes."

The moon chose that moment to show itself and he groaned, his throat arching as he tilted his head and felt the heady caress of its light. Nearby, Jane moaned as his brother entered her.

"Come." With a hand at the back of her neck, Lyon urged the mother of his child toward the stone slabs that dotted the glen.

"Come. Yes," she told him. "That's exactly what I hope to do. I've not had a male between my legs for a week and I'm desperate for a fucking, my love."

Love. The word resonated through his system, swirling through his mind and pricking at his skin.

The numerous horizontal slabs were as big as tables and were conveniently placed here and there at just below waist height, so a female could easily recline upon one of them while a male took his comfort between her thighs. Lyon threaded among them, leading her to a particular destination—the horseshoe-shaped birthing altar at their center.

There, he helped her to kneel in the moss so her belly was protected in the lee of its stone U. Then he moved behind her, positioning himself between cool thighs and bracing his hands on either side of her.

She splayed her legs wide and tilted her rear, clearly offering herself to him. Though he wanted Juliette, he would fuck this woman—whoever she was—for she carried his child. And with the one he preferred gone, he had little choice but to take a substitute.

In one smooth motion he slammed into her, his twin cocks spearing her anally and vaginally with all the force this ritual demanded of him.

"Yesss!" the woman shouted. Her channels were experienced at welcoming a man and she ground her plump flesh against him, angling herself as he wished, when he wished. But he felt the wrongness of her.

Love. The word was an ache, a wound on his soul.

Above them, the moon was as cold and unfeeling as a crystal ball, perfectly round and satisfied at the sacrifice it was requiring of him. He'd fucked hundreds of Shimmerskins here and as many Humans and other assorted female creatures elsewhere in every location imaginable. But now he craved only one woman. And she wasn't here.

A quarter of an hour later, he shouted his release and his creamy seed pumped into the body he embraced. His voice echoed and entwined that of his companion and that of the other two occupants of the glen, as they, too, found their pleasures. His spill was the first step in assuring a safe birthing for his offspring, and a need to bring it safely into this world would see him through the long hours of fucking that lay ahead.

Cool air wafted over his sweat-slicked back as he stilled, both of his cocks momentarily as empty as his heart. His sides heaved with the force of his breathing, yet he felt utterly unfulfilled. He had just spent seed meant for Juliette in the receptacles of a Nereid for whom he felt nothing.

Love. The word blossomed in him. Warmed him, winging his thoughts away to another.

Gods, Juliette. Where are you? She was never far from his heart as he proceeded to pass the night in a way that would satisfy ritual, duty, and a bloodlust that was innate to those of his kind.

Dawn came, and with it, a girl child was born.

Its mother screeched her way through its delivery, cursing and scratching him. Once the babe arrived, Lyon tended it, bathing it in the warmwater spring next to the birthing altar, and then patting it dry. Satyr males always took over the care of their newborns during the early hours after their birth, and joy filled him at doing so. This was his daughter. His firstborn. And he would protect and care for her for all of her days.

Wrapping her in his shirt, he carried her to her weary mother, who had curled up on the altar after bathing herself. Females were always exhausted after the Calling—particularly after a birthing—and usually slept the following day away. However this one would not sleep until he had some answers.

The baby began to fuss and its mother stirred. "Hush her, will you?" she complained. "What came before was nice enough, but that birthing business is something I don't care to repeat."

At the sound of her irritated voice, a flash of recognition lit his eyes. His brow furrowed as he tried to place her. He'd never frequented the Nereid beyond a brief time in his teens, when he'd discovered they were not to his taste.

"I know you," he said.

She opened one irritated eye. "Obviously!" she said, gesturing toward their daughter.

He shook his head, trying to clear it of the last vestiges of the Calling haze. Then suddenly, all clicked into place.

"Sibela," he snarled softly, as the memory of her came back to him. "Damn. We were together in Paris. Under the bridge." He frowned, glancing at the child in his arms. "But that wasn't Moonful. So how—"

"And who is this?" Nicholas interrupted, studying the babe Lyon cradled. The first streaks of dawn were fingering the sky and the Calling had released him from its grip as well. He'd brought a sleepy-eyed Jane along with him and was still refastening the hooks at the back of her bodice.

"My daughter apparently," said Lyon. He handed her off to Sibela. "Who needs sustenance."

Sibela looked ready to argue, but his glower had her acquiescing. With a long-suffering sigh, she put the child to her breast. "Ow! Damnation!"

"Ninety Hells," muttered Nicholas. "And you are?"

"Sibela," she said, introducing herself.

"Your wife's sister," Lyon explained. "And Juliette's. We met in Paris."

"Another sister? How wonderful!" Jane said. Sensing the undercurrents but not knowing what to make of them, she elbowed her husband. "Isn't it, Nick?"

He grunted.

Jane's expression slowly altered, indicating she was beginning to wonder how this affected Juliette's situation. Ever polite, she reached out to embrace Sibela, albeit with reluctant enthusiasm. But Nicholas forestalled her, drawing her back to his side. Placing a kiss on her forehead, he then urged her in the direction of their home.

"Go to the *castello*, Jane. Rest. We'll speak later."

She yawned. "I won't be able to sleep until we determine what's going on."

A look at his grim face had her voice dying away. "I'm fine, Nick," she said gently. "Just let me visit the spring to wash and I'll return. Wait for me."

With a weak smile in Sibela's direction, she departed. As if unable to help himself, Nicholas watched her go until she was swallowed by the forest.

This was precisely the way he felt about Juliette, Lyon realized. The desire to watch her and to have her near. Where was she?

"Ow! Stop that!" His gaze swung back to Sibela and saw that his daughter had woven her tiny fingers into the thatch of necklaces that graced her mother's neck and was tugging on them as she nursed.

Nick looked at him, raising his brows. *A Nereid?* his expression asked.

"It gets worse," Lyon warned.

Nicholas shot him an incredulous look.

"I know this must be unraveled and explained, but first I have to find Juliette," said Lyon.

"Wait," Jane called out, having returned.

He spun around, impatient, and saw she held out the trousers he'd earlier cast aside.

"Might I suggest an altered appearance before you return to her?" she said tactfully.

"My apologies," he told her, though she'd seen him this way many times before. There were few secrets among the family.

Snatching them on, he then located his boots and tugged them on as well. And by the time he was done, Jane had wrapped Sibela in her cloak.

Then they all departed for his home.

※   ※   ※

Moments later, Lyon bounded up his front steps ahead of the others, flung open the door, and found his beloved's scent. It was fresh. *Thank the Gods!*

"Juliette!" he bellowed.

"Here," came the soft reply. Following her voice, he found her calmly awaiting him in the main *salotto*.

Her gaze swept him, then she looked away. He could imagine what she made of his appearance. Having donated his shirt to his daughter, he was bare-chested and Sibela had, as usual, marked him during their lovemaking.

Reaching her, he took her in his arms and tilted her chin. "Look at me," he said. When she complied, he was relieved to see her eyes weren't clouded with opium. She hadn't used it since that first day she'd come here, but he'd worried that the stresses of last night might've driven her back to it.

Gently, she tugged away from him. "It's all right. I know what happened. I understand my altered place in things." But she didn't, for she was stiff. Distant.

He gave her a little shake, concerned at her apathy. "Your place remains the same. As my life. My love."

Someone pushed between them.

"Here. I hope you'll know how to deal with this," Sibela said to her, foisting a squalling baby into Juliette's arms. "I have no abilities in the arena of parenting, nor any desire to learn." With that, she ensconced herself on the single sofa Juliette had recently ordered for the room from a shop in Florence, and she proceeded to snuggle in for a nap.

Juliette stared down at Sibela's deposit, her expression appalled. A tiny fist waved, and she instinctively captured it in her hand. The baby quieted almost immediately, but as if it had transferred its mood, her own face crumpled.

"Yes, of course." Ducking her head, she turned to carry his offspring from the room.

Lyon bit off a curse and caught her arm. "Juliette—"

"Please. Not yet."

"Don't roam far," he told her, frustrated. "We have things to discuss here and your input is needed."

She nodded, keeping her head turned from him. She was crying. "*Un moment.*"

"Stay where I can see you," he instructed, releasing her, but not yet ready to trust her out of his sight again.

"Lyon!" Jane scolded softly, overhearing as she and Nicholas came to join them.

"Sit with her," he said, unapologetic. "Make sure she doesn't leave."

Seeing his worry, Jane did as he asked, settling Juliette and the child on the opposite end of the couch from Sibela and seating herself between them. At the disturbance, the baby began to cry again.

"Your daughter needs you," Jane murmured to Sibela.

"If Juliette wants the father, let her take his child," Sibela replied.

"Shut up," Lyon growled. He lifted the child from Juliette and deposited her at Sibela's breast.

Sibela raised her brows, but took the girl inside the cloak where she began suckling. "A fine way to speak to the mother of your firstborn."

"In spite of the child, I sense that your claim on my brother isn't as strong as you'd like," said Nicholas. He turned to Lyon. "Why is that?"

"What do you mean?" asked Sibela, straightening. "What greater claim on a man can a woman have than to bear his offspring?"

"Yet Nick's right. I still feel bonded to Juliette," said Lyon.

"But, why, when Sibela is the one you so obviously mated last Moonful?" Nicholas put in.

Lyon turned to frown at Sibela. "And how did that happen exactly?"

She smirked, studying a clawed fingertip. "Why, don't you remember, darling? You were quite ardent in your hotel that night, though a trifle lethargic."

"You mated yourself to me while I slept?" Everyone in the room stared at her with equal expressions of shock.

Unfazed, Sibela let out a huff. "You would have died had I not. If you are angry with anyone, it should be Juliette. She deserted you. *I* saved your life."

"She's right in that at least," said Juliette.

"You knew she had come here," Lyon accused, his gaze finding her. "And you purposely left me to her last night."

"She's my sister and carried your child," she replied, pleading for him to understand. "You'd told me how your children must be birthed, so I let her go to you. It seemed best that I hide away from you under the circumstances, until the necessary things were ... done."

"You left me to another woman as easily as that?" Lyon shook his head, surprised by how this wounded him.

"Elise has the greater claim on you," Juliette insisted. "And I owe her. She was nearly killed and has been lost for three years because of my folly."

"Wait!" Nicholas held up his hands. "Who the hell is Elise?"

Looking confused, Juliette gestured to where Sibela sat on the couch. "My sister."

"There's yet a fifth one?" Lyon asked in horror.

"She's dead," said Sibela at the same time. "Or as good as."

Seeing the deceit in Sibela's eyes, Juliette became suspicious. "But you said—"

"I suppose I omitted a detail or two when we last met," Sibela admitted slyly. "Actually, I'm not your sister, but am in fact only a caretaker of her body. I'm originally of the sea, but lost my own shell long ago and must make do as I can. That day you and she were attacked by hounds in Burgundy, I happened along quite by accident. My host was aging and I'd been searching for another. Your sister was injured and dying, so I took her body for my use and kept her from such a dire fate. A symbiotic relationship."

"You seem to be in the business of saving lives in unorthodox manners," murmured Nicholas.

Juliette's voice was thready as she searched Sibela's eyes. "Is there anything left of her in you?"

Sibela shrugged. "She's here, but sublimated."

Seeing that his daughter was done with nursing and Sibela looked at a loss as to what to do next, Lyon lifted the bundled newborn from her and cradled her in his arms.

The sight of him holding his tiny daughter obviously made Juliette's heart squeeze. Seeing this, Jane gave her a comforting pat. "Tell me about her—our sister." And then Juliette seemed to realize this affected not just her. Though she may have lost one sister, she'd recently gained another.

"I met our sister—Elise—the summer we were both sixteen," she began. "I'd been living with a foster family in Burgundy. She didn't like to talk about her past, so I don't know much of that. But we became friends and she taught me things. Unearthly things."

"How to transform," guessed Lyon, swaying side to side as he gently rocked his daughter.

Juliette nodded. "We had to keep it secret because my foster mother was superstitious and condemned magical practice. We used to rove the countryside experimenting with our gifts. I learned to fixate on something so thoroughly that I would become it. This didn't work with everything. Only with natural objects. A flower. A tree."

"What happened to her?" asked Lyon.

"Yes, I'd like to hear your version of that myself," said Sibela.

"There was a boy. A man really—older than I," said Juliette. "I foolishly agreed to meet him in a tryst one afternoon, but Elise intervened. We all argued, but she prevailed and we left together. On the way home we were attacked by hunting dogs. To escape, she dove into the Loire to become a nymph—what we called a mermaid back then—and I joined with the nearest oak. Though I was present when she was assaulted, I couldn't see from my vantage point. I could only hear. Everything." She shuddered and touched her hands to her ears as if to block out sounds that still tortured her.

"Which is no doubt why you're wary of animals," Lyon murmured.

"There's something I wonder at," Sibela mused. "Unlike you, I *did* see the attack that day and it seemed to me that the dogs had come hunting specifically for your sister. I pulled her deeper than they could swim, and they eventually, and very reluctantly let her go."

"You think it was murder?" asked Jane.

She shrugged.

"Many did think so at the time," said Juliette. "I was accused of it because I was found by the river, with her blood everywhere. There are still warrants out for my arrest."

"You went on your merry way and let Juliette bear the guilt and stigma of being a murderer? Knowing she was innocent?" Lyon asked Sibela.

"How was I to know what goes on in the Human system of justice?" Sibela protested.

"There's still something off here," said Lyon. "In spite of everything, I feel bonded to you, Juliette." His eyes narrowed on her. "Why is that?

"Did Lyon mate you after you bespelled him in his hotel?" Nicholas demanded, as if it were nothing out of the ordinary to ask such a question of a lady.

"No!" said Juliette. She looked daggers at Lyon. Jane and Sibela had closed their eyes again, leaving her to deal with him and his brother.

"Yes, I told him about your magic that night," he said without a trace of regret. "Of necessity, there are few secrets among the members of this family."

"Did you touch him in any way that could be construed as carnal?" Nicholas pushed.

Juliette stared at her lap.

Still in charge of his child, Lyon came to kneel beside her and nudge her with his elbow. "What happened?" he coaxed.

Her tongue crept out and she licked her lips. "I know it was wrong, but I couldn't help myself. I swear to you I've never done anything like that before."

"What?"

"She tasted you," grumbled Sibela, adjusting her position on the couch, so that Juliette and Jane were forced to stir as well. "I scented her on you that night in your hotel. But that doesn't release you from your obligation to me."

Juliette covered her face with her hands.

"Let me be clear," Lyon said to her. "You're saying that before you left my hotel, you imbibed my seed?"

"Lyon! Must you be so blatant?" mumbled Jane.

"Answer him," Nicholas said grimly.

Juliet ducked her head still lower and nodded, blushing with embarrassment at having to admit it in front of everyone.

"This changes things," Lyon said in a satisfied voice.

Sibela sat forward rubbing her eyes to stay awake. "How?"

"It means Juliette has the prior claim," said Jane. She reached over again and gave Juliette's hand a reassuring squeeze.

"But you lay with *me*," Sibela struck her chest with a fist in emphasis. "In the park—before you knew she even existed. And—and I carried your brat in my belly for four weeks. Surely my rights to you take precedence?"

"First Moonful childseed is what determines the bond," said Nicholas. He held up a hand before Sibela could start shrieking. "But you both have a claim."

"Am I to wed two then?" Lyon protested.

"You know you can't give the protection of your Will to both. Only to she who has the dominant claim."

"I won't have you abandon my sister for me," said Juliette. "If you wed anyone, you will wed her."

"There! We have her blessing." Sibela spread her hands in a gesture that indicated the matter was settled.

"She's not your sister," Lyon informed Juliette, ignoring Sibela. "She's a parasite who has taken your sister's body for her own use."

"He's right, I'm afraid. I'm not going to give your sister back to you if that's what you're hoping," Sibela told her. "Without her, I am nothing. And I can't have that."

Lyon stared at her consideringly. "What is it you want for all your devious plotting? Not our child obviously."

She shrugged. "I feel no connection to it. But it gives me a foothold—so to speak—in this world. What I want from you is protection. This body I inhabit is in danger through no fault of mine. Left to my own devices, I fear ElseWorld will eventually take me. In their clutches, I'll be powerless. I'll kill this body rather than allow that to happen."

Juliette gasped. "Don't you dare!"

"Perhaps we can arrange something less drastic," said Nicholas.

"You know, I went to considerable trouble to mate with you that night," Sibela told Lyon, aggrieved.

He raised a brow. "Yet Juliette is my choice, and the one I will wed."

"No, Lyon," Juliette murmured.

"I know you care for me," he insisted.

"*Oui.* I do."

Dimples creased his cheeks and his eyes suddenly brimmed with wry humor. "I was hoping to hear you say that before a member of the clergy."

"I'm wed to you in body and spirit. Let that be enough," she cajoled. "Ceremonies to solidify such things aren't necessary, are they?"

Lyon was already shaking his head. "Your protection requires these official ceremonies."

She leaped to her feet, looking desperate. "I won't marry you!" she shouted.

"Why the hell not?" he shouted back. His daughter began to cry.

"Because!" She looked around, wild-eyed, then back at Lyon. "Because I'm already wed!"

Every eye opened and flew to her.

"To whom?!" Lyon demanded, flabbergasted.

"To Monsieur Valmont, in Paris!" She looked shocked at what she'd said and backed away toward the door as if afraid she might be punished. "It's a closely guarded secret. I'm not supposed to tell. I didn't mean to wed him in the first place. But the day Elise was killed, he gave me opium, and then later claimed he'd seen me kill her. I was too drugged to know what I'd done."

Nicholas took the crying child from Lyon, then watched him sweep a protesting Juliette into his arms. Lyon's eyes shifted to his daughter, then to his face and Nicholas nodded, silently promising to look after the child until he returned.

His brother then carried Juliette from the room, leaving Nick to watch over the three remaining females within. With the couch taken, he wandered to sit at Lyon's new desk, which Jane had informed him Juliette had deliberated over for hours before purchasing for his sibling. Testing the leather chair and finding it a good fit, he half-reclined in it, propping his boots on the desktop and laying the child on his chest, with one arm under her legs to secure her. His other hand idly rubbed her back until she quieted and slept.

His eyes drifted over the couches and the sleeping women there, lingering on Jane. Then it wandered over the desk top and he noticed a letter, still sealed with wax. His attention was caught when he saw it was from a Monsieur Valmont in Paris. It had been sent to Lyon's hotel and forwarded here.

Without hesitation, he opened it.

17

Two nights later, Juliette was toiling alone in the *castello*'s kitchen with preparations for the meeting of the vintners that was to take place on the estate in January. This was what she enjoyed most about the process of cooking—the experimentation and creation of new and wonderful delicacies.

Night's curtain had fallen and the staff had already retired to their quarters away from the estate when she heard Lyon enter the room. She flicked a glance his way, then turned back to her work. He'd been gone today, overseeing the winterizing of the upper terraces of the vineyards with Nicholas. His hair was damp and glinted in the candlelight. He'd bathed when he'd come in and looked healthy, rugged, and far too handsome.

A pair of muscled arms wrapped around her waist from behind, and he tucked his chin in the nook of her shoulder. "I love you."

She froze with a teaspoon of cinnamon lifted halfway to a bowl of chocolate pudding. Then she dumped it in the batter and began to stir.

Sibela had been gone for two days now, having left her child in their care and even gone so far as to refuse to help name it. Lyon had stepped in and dubbed her Giselle, after his own mother. Though she'd tried not to bond with the tiny babe, Juliette feared she had done so the moment she had been placed in her arms.

For her and Lyon, Sibela's absence had been a time of healing. But the uncertainties regarding her imminent return, and of other matters, still lay between them.

"Here. Taste," she instructed. Twisting within his hold, she lifted the spoon with one hand and cupped her other beneath it for spills.

He took the pudding from her, sampling it. "It won't put me into a deep slumber, I trust?"

She smiled, shaking her head. "It's something I'm considering for your upcoming gathering. I wouldn't rob you and your brother of your audience by putting them to sleep, I promise you."

His eyebrows rose with approval as the flavors she'd carefully concocted bloomed on his taste buds. "Ambrosia," he pronounced. Taking the spoon from her, he tossed it on the counter, and then linked his hands at her spine.

"The food of the gods?" Juliette rested her forearms on his chest. "Perhaps you should invite your Bacchus to dinner. He might find it to his liking."

"Perhaps I will."

She stared at him, aghast. "He wouldn't come, would he? I mean, that's not actually something you can do?"

He grinned, looking delighted with her, and reached to tuck a curl behind her ear. "No."

"Thank the heavens. I'm already nervous at being in charge of an event for a hundred. If you dare add a God into the mix, I might swoon."

He stared at her a moment, his face slowly turning serious. "Juliette."

"Not now," she said. Unprepared for the direction in which she suspected his conversation would veer, she pulled away to return to her work.

"We have to reach an understanding," he said from behind her.

"Where's . . . Sibela?"

"How the hell should I know?!" he said, irritated. "Trolling the Arno. Fucking anything that moves. Or as we recently learned her to be capable, possibly fucking anything that doesn't."

She shot him an uncertain glance.

"Did you think she planned to linger at my side like some devoted concubine? That she cared for me? Or I for her?"

She shrugged. "*Non*, I suppose not."

"It wouldn't matter. We have arranged things so that she will receive my family's protection. And that's all she wants of me."

"And Giselle?"

"She'll stay with us." His voice softened, its concern melting her heart. "Will that hurt you?"

"Of course not. None of the fault for this tangle lies with your daughter. I love her already for she's something of Elise. And you."

"So you readily love her. But can you love her father?"

"Are you certain you want me?" she scoffed, stirring the pudding ever harder. "A woman who may as easily greet you as a block of wood upon your return from the vineyard as might greet you as a Human? Or as a fire to burn down your home. Or a—"

"Shh," he soothed, pushing the bowl aside and tilting her chin to look at him. "You can learn to guide your gift. I'll help you. Just as I would need your help if I were learning to cook. For instance, if you were to hand me a . . . " he picked up a utensil from the countertop behind her and stared at it blankly.

She glanced at it over her shoulder. "A spatula."

"Yes, well. Not being familiar with it, I would require instruction regarding how to use it, wouldn't I? If I didn't know better, I might mistake it for a tool of exploration."

Slyly, he let its edge drift down her chest so its tip lifted the neckline of her bodice just enough that he could observe what was hidden below.

She batted his hand away and replaced the spatula on the counter, smiling, as he'd meant her to.

"It's a failing of mine that the same experience dulls for me over time," he admitted. "I love that you are unexpected."

"But I'm not free for you," she objected.

The flats of his hands made circles on the back of her waist. "As we speak, my attorneys are in Paris petitioning Valmont for a divorce. You soon will be free."

She looked at him, doubtful.

"Juliette." His voice was frustrated. "I didn't want her." They both knew of whom he spoke.

An uncomfortable silence fell.

"And I won't lie with her again," he went on. "Or any other woman. It's you I wanted with me in the glen. It's you I want. You I love."

She let out a ragged sigh.

"Is it so horrible to hear?" he said, giving her a tiny shake. "I assure you that a part of me is horrified to hear me admit it, for I never expected to feel such an emotion toward any woman."

"Oh, Lyon," she said, relaxing against him. "You make everything seem so easily done but—"

"Tell me how I can make it up to you. Tell me what you need. What you like," he said against her throat. "Kiss me."

"Make me."

She gasped and put a hand over her lips as if to call back her words. But they hung in the air between them, suggestive and potent.

A knowing expression spread slowly over his face. "Ah. It comes back to me now."

"What does? *Non*, don't tell me." She waved a hand between them in emphasis. "I don't want to know."

"The memories you gave me that night in my hotel are still here with me, just jumbled. But more sort themselves daily." His eyes studied her, fascinated.

And then his voice came again in the quiet candlelight, low and velvet. "You wish to be . . . coerced."

She looked away. "*Non.*"

"I recall differently."

He lifted her onto the countertop, knocking things askance. A bowl overturned and several peaches rolled out.

He palmed one, testing its firmness, obviously caught in some memory. A memory she'd given him of a sun-warmed peach, halved and nearly overripe, coming high between her legs to stroke along her most private feminine flesh. Of hard masculine fingers pressing her furrow open with the pulpy fruit until its astringent juices mingled with her own and trickled down her thighs. Of a hot mouth kissing her there, licking, tonguing, and tasting her sticky-sweetness.

Why hadn't she kept this and other unnatural notions to herself? With other men she'd bespelled on Valmont's behalf, she'd lodged only the most perfunctory and general visions of wickedness in their brains.

His eyes cut to hers and she gave a little moan. Oh, God! That he knew her secrets!

"Don't," he said, correctly reading her expression. "There's no room for shame between us. We have no one else to please in carnal matters. They are private. For us. For pleasure. We hurt no one if we follow our desires. We hurt only ourselves if we refrain."

She moistened her lips. "Such desires have lead me into trouble in the past. Nearly lead to the death of my sister. If I hadn't accepted the attentions of Valmont in the first place—"

"Valmont?"

She nodded. "Yes, I'm ashamed of it now, but he was the man who wooed me that summer I was sixteen. Elise sensed what he was. A monster. But I was blinded by his flattery and attentions, and I believed his lies. The same day she forced us apart, she was attacked and then just . . . gone. In penance, I put away all wicked thoughts of men. Until you came. And now, I think of little else."

"My own lust has led me in many directions in twenty-six years. I can assure you I am far more wicked in such matters than you could ever be."

His hands went to the fastenings of her dress and hers rested on his shoulders.

"In here?" she whispered. "What if someone comes?"

Dimples flashed. "I assure you someone will."

Button by button and lace by lace, he proceeded to disrobe her where she sat. "Here is how it will be between us tonight," he instructed, in a voice gone almost solemn. "When I have finished undressing you, you will give yourself completely into my handling until I say otherwise. You are allowed to refuse me only if something repulses you or causes pain. Not because you are afraid. Fear has no place in this room. Not between us. Not tonight."

If she agreed, his eyes promised, he would make her fantasies reality. Her breath quickened. Did she dare? She wanted to.

"I-I don't want to be afraid or feel unsafe," she said, worried.

"It seems we are perfectly matched. It so happens I have a need to assert myself tonight, but I have no wish to hurt you."

The mantel clock clicked, indicating it was about to chime. "Eight o'clock comes. Once it sounds, so my rules begin. Now if you agree, you will count the beats aloud."

Seconds later, the first bong sounded, and she heard herself speak.

"*Un . . . deux . . . trois . . .*
Her dress was lifted away.
quatre . . . cinq . . . six . . .
Her corset and chemise were taken.
sept . . . huit."
Silence fell. He stood there fully dressed, not touching her. And she sat on the table before him, naked.

Then he took the pins from her hair and brushed it free so it veiled her. "Now, you have agreed to become an object whose only purpose is to follow my instruction. Which is this—for me, you will be three openings now, nothing more, nothing less. And all will be made available to me for whatever purpose I choose. Say yes."

He was purposely crude and in this moment it was what she wanted from him. She slanted a glance at him through her lashes. "Yes."

"Lower your eyes from mine," he scolded gently. "An infraction of this instruction will earn you a punishment. A broad hand slid around her to find and rouge her rear.

An image of Gina's backside, pink from the strokes of a lash came to her mind, and her core pulsed.

Her eyes lifted to his, hoping to read what he had planned.
Smack!

"Oh!" She gave a little jump on the counter when his hand landed on her rear. It stung, startling her and sending a tiny thrill thrumming along her feminine cleft all the way to her clit. Her gaze snapped to his again, finding it as stern as that of a displeased schoolmaster.
Smack!

Her other rear cheek received the same treatment. Shifting, she put her hand where his had struck. Her skin was warm there, like Gina's must've been after a lashing. Realizing what he expected, her gaze dropped to her lap, finding the place where pubis and thighs met to form the V of her privates. For the first time in her life, she almost wished her body grew a nest there as other women did, so she wouldn't feel quite so naked in contrast to him.

Two hands reached, moving into her vision. Golden and strong against her paler skin, they cupped her breasts and she lifted her own hands to the back of his, feeling them flex as his thumbs stroked over her nipples. The pink-tipped peaks grew turgid. And warm. Looking down, she saw that they'd become shaded with the strange luminescence only he was capable of bringing forth.

"That's better," he said softly.

She wanted to look at this face—to read what he was thinking but she didn't and found herself strangely excited by the fact that this window to his thoughts was forbidden.

Lifting her, he scooted her backward until ther thighs were partially supported by the counter. His legs stood between hers, and the fabric of his trousers rasped delicately along the insides of her knees. A hand went behind her and she saw he'd picked up the bowl she'd been stirring when he entered the kitchen. The spoon she'd been using was still there, half-drowned in the dark pudding.

"Lie back," he instructed softly. Eyeing the bowl, she hesitantly obeyed. Once she had, he set it on her midriff and bade her hold it there. Its glass was cool against her palms, but the mixture inside warmed her belly.

Transfixed, she watched his hand take the spoon and languidly begin to stir. The scent of cinnamon wafted to her, and a moment later the spoon lifted and hovered over the bowl, dark batter dripping from it in slow, viscous plops. He moved it toward himself as if planning to have a taste.

The muscles of her abdomen contracted, hard, as rivulets of creamy warmth dribbled low on it, then lower still, between her legs.

At the odd sensation, she half sat up on one elbow to look at him, and the bowl wobbled.

"That's one punishment, for later," he cautioned, without glancing up from the batter's drizzle. When she didn't look away, his brow rose and he found her eyes. "Would you care to make it two?"

Her lips curved smugly as she lay back. "It's not much of a punishment, when the recipient enjoys it."

The spoon went back to replenish its contents, then she felt the back of it come against her most private flesh, frosting her.

"We'll see how far we can take it then," he suggested.

The spoon's handle came to her, prodding slightly, drawing along her furrow like a slender plow, until her moist pink heart lay open and vulnerable to his artistry.

"We'll see if we can find where the line is drawn between punishment and pleasure," he suggested, his tone rife with a carnal knowledge he did not yet share.

With the precision of a master, he began painting her in a leisurely fashion with the sweet, chocolaty colorant she'd prepared. Now and then, he dipped the spoon into his palette—the bowl she still held for him.

And all the while, he spoke to her, telling her how he was looking forward to tasting her concoction, and how his brothers and the guests he'd invited to the upcoming assembly would likely enjoy doing the same.

Something brushed her clit, oh so lightly, and she moaned. The spoon plunked into the bowl, abandoned. His voice drifted to her through the spicy air, a dark, suggestive whisper of things to come.

"Your pudding is warm," he told her. "And I haven't yet dined tonight."

Broad hands took her thighs lifting them over strong shoulders, so her heels dangled at his back. Her fingers clutched the bowl and she took a harsh, indrawn breath, waiting. The other girls in Paris had spoken of this rare pleasure with longing, for it seemed most paying customers did not offer it.

The clock tick-tocked, far slower than her heartbeat.

Then that beautiful mouth of his settled on her mouth that could not speak for itself, and he began to feast.

And much, much later, for dessert, he fed her mouth peaches, and then bananas.

As he remembered she liked.

"*C'est magnifique!*" Juliette stepped back from the ice sculpture and smiled at its creator. It hadn't been an easy matter to communicate what she wanted to this Italian sculptor who had never before worked in ice.

A statue of the wine god Bacchus, it would be the crowning touch to the festive table that would sit in the center of the gathering to be held in Lyon's ballroom in a few weeks. Until then, it would be kept in this cave for cooling as he continued to work on it.

"*Si. È magnifico,*" the grizzled man agreed shyly, beaming in self-congratulation. He glanced beyond her, put his hat on, and ducked his head to go. "*Scusi.*"

Still smiling, Juliette turned.

"*Bonjour, Juliette.*"

She stared, blanching at the sight of Monsieur Valmont.

He stepped close and pinched her chin between his thumb and index finger, holding her face to the light to examine it.

"Tell him to go," he murmured. The Italian had hesitated

behind him in the opening to the cave, sensing undercurrents of trouble.

She yanked away from him, reminding herself she was no longer his terrified, addicted puppet. Then she felt something cold and hard at her rib. A pistol.

"Tell him, or he dies." His voice chilled her.

Looking reluctantly to the sculptor, she bid him a convincing farewell, and then watched him go.

"Lyon has gone to meet you in Florence," she told Valmont. "Why did you come here instead? Your solicitor's letter to us indicated—"

"Did you fuck him?"

"Who?" But she understood his question and knew the answer to it could be easily read in her face.

To her shock, tears formed in his eyes and he brushed them away. "It was mine, and you gave it away. I had uses for it. I meant to make a trade. But no—you couldn't keep your legs together long enough. *Putain*, just like your mother."

"But you've agreed to the divorce, your solicitor said. You were going to sign papers in Florence. Today."

"You're not the only one who can trick wealthy men," he said smugly. "Do you know what your lover agreed to in exchange for you?"

She shook her head, hoping to humor him until she could find a means of escape.

"I asked him for three things, none of which I thought he'd accept: First, an obscene amount of money. Second, that he desist in his efforts to combat the phylloxera for a period of five years—long enough for my business interests to thrive. And third, that he arrange, for my private entertainment, a hunt of his precious animals here on his land. And he agreed to *all* three conditions! Can you imagine that?"

"*Non*, you *bâtard*. I won't let you do that to him. I'll come back with you to Paris. Now."

"But I no longer want you. He has taken from you that which I valued most. Made you impure." Then in a bizarre reversal he said, "Do you want me, Juliette? Do you want your brother? It would be too bad of us. But perhaps if no one knew."

With that, he rapped her on the head with the butt of his pistol and all went black.

When Juliette woke, they were in the woods near the river. She was lying on her back on the hard ground, and he was using her belly to pillow his head, and as a rest for the butt of the pistol he was training on various random targets.

Raising a hand to her hair, she groaned. It came away with blood from where he'd hit her.

"Ah, sweet sister. I rested my head on our mother's belly just like this when you and that other one were inside it. Did you hear me singing to you?"

When he broke into a soft bout of *Frère Jacques*, she tried to sit up, but found she was too woozy.

"I've never understood why *maman* gave you and Elise the magic," he went on, abruptly ending his song. "Why not to me? I was a good boy."

She pushed at him. "You're speaking gibberish."

But he rambled on as if he didn't hear. "Papa hated poor *maman* because she cuckolded him to beget you. He punished her. Made her suck the pricks of men. Disgusting men. He told her it was her penance—that she would be made to suffer the whole time you were inside her. Nine months, it went on. And then he promised her that afterward, her babies would suffer in her place."

She began to listen more closely. "How old were you then?"

"Just a boy of eleven. Too young to lose my *maman*."

Swiftly her mind did the arithmetic. His mother had died in childbirth when Valmont was eleven. That would've made it the year—1804. The year she and Elise had been born.

"After she died, I took you there to the orphanage and

282 / Elizabeth Amber

kissed you both and put you in the basket. It was snowing. December. Almost Christmas. I knew my papa would kill you as you had killed my *maman*. I couldn't let you die. Not my sisters that I had kissed through my sweet *maman*'s belly."

To her horror, Juliette suddenly noticed he was aiming his pistol at a specific target now.

Not ten feet from them sat one of Lyon's ebony panthers. Liber or Ceres. She wasn't sure which.

Valmont's eyes narrowed as if he were about to pull the trigger.

"Don't shoot him."

But the shot rang out even as she spoke. The cat flinched under its impact, then lunged toward the stream. She felt its pain, and pushed Valmont away. He was an excellent shot. He'd aimed to wound and would do so again and again, providing a slow, cruel death for his victim.

Valmont took aim yet again.

"Don't!"

His voice hardened and he grasped her wrist in a bruising hold. "I don't take instruction from sluts. You see, I've arranged a private hunt for just the two of us this afternoon. Your lover agreed, after all. And I know how you enjoy the suffering of animals."

He took aim again.

"Wait!" She managed to twist away and gain her footing. "You say you want magic? I'll give you mine."

He stood, his face lighting with greedy interest.

Reaching a hand into her skirt pocket, she grabbed a handful of the oatmeal she carried there to ward off evil. Perhaps for once its effect would work!

"Here! Magic, just for you!"

Whipping out her hand, she flung the bits of oatmeal into his face. He staggered back, appearing afraid for a moment that she might be casting a spell. Her trick wouldn't fool him for long, but it provided a chance to escape.

Since he was blocking her way to the forest, she whirled in the opposite direction. The river. Terror shook her, worsening when she saw that Lyon's cat stood on its bank. Even from a distance, she could see its eyes were glazed with pain. Panic had left her emotions unguarded, and its pain easily became hers. In an instant, her only choice was clear. She would not allow this innocent, beautiful creature—one of Lyon's favorites—to die.

Herding the cat before her, she entered the river with it at her side. Neither wanted to go, but they went. Together. Water surrounded her as she submerged, entering the cavities of her body and filling her up.

The swift moving current became the pump of her blood, the beat of her heart. The swirls and eddies styled her hair around her, in long, serpentine waves that coiled and uncoiled. She spoke to the panther in the language of the water, calming him, holding him, healing him. Making it easier to hide him and herself. Twin opalescent dorsal fins grew at her shoulder blades, ripping from her gown and fluttering like faerie wings to keep them afloat.

How easily old habits returned. It was as though the past three years of denying herself this had never passed.

"I can wait as long as you can," Valmont informed her. He'd apparently realized her ruse, come after her, and was waiting on the bank.

A few moments later, she heard him give a girlish shriek. As she watched through the translucent, undulating current, she saw another figure move beside him.

"Our paths cross again," a voice said in greeting.

"How did you get here?" he demanded, obviously mistaking his visitor for Juliette. "You were just in the stream! Why is your hair dark? And not even wet?"

"When last you saw it, it was wet with my blood. You killed me. Remember? Until now, I knew only your face, but not your name. Now I have both."

"Elise?"

Juliette could've told him it was Sibela, returned from her wandering. But she remained hidden, watching.

His face contorted. "Elise? Why will you not stay dead? Leave me be, won't you? You're always trying to tear me apart from your sister."

Sibela went closer and gently pushed away the gun barrel he'd directed toward her. Then she stroked her hand upward and over it until she touched his wrist.

"I know you want Juliette, but take me instead. I understand you. I want you, my darling brother. All of you. Come to me. I offer forgetfulness. You long to forget, do you not?" Her hands were traveling up his arms now.

"Yes." His voice had turned mesmerized and calm.

"Your father was a monster." Her arms encircled his neck. "And you just a boy of eleven. Let me take away the hurt. The pain. With one kiss, I can take it all away."

As Juliette watched from her underwater lair, Sibela drew close to him and her lips pressed his.

He stood calmly in her embrace, an insect in the web of a spider, as she kissed him. Her long tongue entered his mouth, his throat, and then reached deep to taste the heart of him. For a moment its beat stopped and in that instant, her soul shoved his aside and entered his body.

Stealing his breath, Sibela made it hers.

The female body she'd inhabited for the past three years crumpled to the ground. Seeing this, Juliette's blood stirred and warmed. Heated with a rush of adrenaline. Legs reformed. Eventually Human again, she swam to shore, pulling the cat with her.

Finding itself rescued, the panther leaped away. As if it had never been wounded, it shook the water from its fur, then dove into the forest.

Sibela was standing there, licking her new lips as if to taste her current host. Running her hands down herself, she shifted her shoulders in what appeared to be an effort to fully assume her new mantle.

"Is she dead?" Juliette ran to her sister's body. She glared at Valmont. "Did you kill her?!"

"Don't be so dramatic." It was Sibela, speaking from inside Valmont's body and using his voice. "She only sleeps. Her body was mine for three years, and it will need time to readjust to life without me to direct it."

Juliette's eyes searched Valmont's and her brows knit in confusion. "Sibela?"

She nodded. "Your Satyr engineered the idea of my taking this body as host, so that you might have your sister and be free of your erstwhile husband. He meant to bring Valmont here for me tomorrow, but since I came upon him now, things worked out the same in the end. Now that I'm divorced from your sister, I'm safe from Elseworld. *Ah!* It's good to be male. No more corsets or breastfeeding.

"Oh, and by the way, it seems I killed your sister that day in Burgundy. Or at least Valmont did." She chuckled, delighted. "How easily I've assumed his body, that I would say 'I' in that way."

"Explain about the killing," Juliette demanded.

"He was angry at Elise for keeping you apart," Sibela told her, before digressing to say, "He is far more easily read than your sister, for I had little enough of this kind of information from her in three years, yet he is an open book. That will make it easy to transition into his life in Paris."

"Help me get Elise to the house."

Sibela readily agreed, and Juliette had a feeling it was more to test her new strength than to be kind.

"He's stronger than she was. How nice," said Sibela, as she easily lifted Elise to carry her.

"Finish your explanation," Juliette urged as she led the way.

"Yes, yes. On that summer day, he struggled with Elise when she came to thwart your tryst with him. And he ripped her dress in the process."

Sibela flexed Valmont's hand where it clasped Elise's skirt, as if she remembered seeing that hand do exactly that.

"Her blue dress," said Juliette. In a flash, she realized the blue swatch in Valmont's office had been a piece of Elise's dress. The dress she'd worn the day she'd been attacked!

"He gave a piece of it to his dogs and they tracked her scent with it. They meant to kill her, not you. You couldn't have done anything to stop them, even if you hadn't been locked in your transformation."

Entering the house, they took Elise upstairs and Sibela settled her on a bed as Juliette directed, then helped exchange Juliette's wet dress for a dry one.

"Is it true? What he said? That he was my brother. And Elise's?"

Sibela nodded.

"How appalling. That must be why our magic didn't work on him. We both tried it on him and sometimes on each other, but to no avail."

"There's nothing more you can do for her now," said Sibela once Elise had been tucked in. "She'll sleep for a day or more. Come, see me off." She headed for the stairs.

"Off?" Juliette glanced at Elise, who seemed to be resting comfortably, then reluctantly followed Sibela downstairs.

"Off to Paris and my new home."

"What about Giselle?"

Sibela waved a careless hand. "She's better off here."

Juliette dogged her outside to where Valmont's horse was tethered. Without thinking, she stroked its muzzle. Only then did she realize she seemed to have completely abandoned her fear of animals with today's revelations. Lyon had said things would be easier for her here on his land and he'd been right.

An odd look crossed Sibela's face as she swung up on horseback. "This new body yearns for liquor."

"Absinthe," said Juliette. "Valmont was addicted to it."

Sibela sighed. "I suppose I'll sicken for a while as I fight his addiction?"

"It's not easily fought."

"But I'll win. This body is too indispensable to me to rot it out."

Juliette hesitated, then said, "You may sojourn here with us while you fight it if you wish. Traveling will be difficult otherwise."

Sibela eyes sharpened. "I'm not he, you know."

"I know," said Juliette, contrite. "I'm sorry. It's hard to remember."

"I will be different than him. I am myself and I have forced his essence too deep for it to have any influence over me. Regardless, you won't have to look at me—or him—much longer."

Lifting the flogger she found on the saddle, Sibela absently stroked its knotted leather tails. "By the way, who is Gina?"

Juliette's eyes went to the whip. "She's, um, one of the women Valmont employs . . . I mean, that *you* employ in the Paris house. To entertain gentlemen."

Sibela flicked the leather, making a popping noise in the air. Her horse shifted, nervous. "She likes this," she stated. Her eyes sought Juliette's for confirmation.

Juliette nodded. "Yes."

Sibela ran the leather strips across her palm one last time, then set the whip into its holster. She might not be human, but the half smile that played on her lips was more human than any Juliette recalled seeing on Valmont's face before. "I'll look forward to meeting her."

288 / *Elizabeth Amber*

Suddenly, she began to wonder exactly what uses Sibela might have put Elise's body to while she had inhabited it. "Will Elise have memories of the past three years?"

Sibela glanced at her, understanding her underlying concern. "It was never my intention to hurt her body. On the contrary, I was grateful for the use of it. And I took care of it in my own fashion. I realize it's no longer as pristine as you or she might prefer. Alas, I have a voracious need for fucking. Not so immense as your Satyr lover's perhaps, but still large."

"You forced Elise to have carnal relations with men other than Lyon?"

"Men, women . . . and other creatures. But there was no force involved. She was entirely sublimated during my inhabitation."

"But will she remember?"

Sibela shrugged, then wheeled her mount around. "I don't know. You'll have to ask her."

Lyon paused outside the door of the chamber Juliette had arranged for her sister a week ago. It was just down the hall from their own, uncomfortably close. But he'd made no objection.

"You'll never guess, Elise, I've become an accomplished cook!" Juliette was saying. "It's nothing for me to prepare a dinner for two dozen guests or a party for even more. Lyon adores the crème brûlée Madame Fouche taught us to make that summer. Remember?"

"Yes." Elise's voice was listless, a frail echo of Juliette's patter.

"Remember how Madame used to despair of us, the way we ran wild through the countryside? And the pomegranates we pilfered from the orchards of Monsieur Ramsay? Our lips and fingers would be bright red, yet we would protest our innocence."

"Umm-hmm."

Lyon nudged the door open and saw that his daughter lay sleeping in a bassinette Juliette had placed in the room. Though she continued to bring her into Elise's sphere, like Sibela, Elise had shown no interest in his offspring as yet. Giselle had been entirely relegated to the care of Juliette and a wet nurse.

Setting aside the brush that she'd been using on her sister, Juliette smiled at him in welcome.

"She'll be bald soon if you keep tending to her." He came to stand by the bed and they both looked at the woman lying there.

Elise blinked at them, silent.

"She looks well, doesn't she?" asked Juliette.

No. She didn't. She looked like a beautiful wraith. The dress she wore did nothing to disguise the scars on her chest that had been made by the hounds that had attacked her. She seemed to purposely choose such outfits and keep them unbuttoned as if determined to make everyone she met uncomfortable.

Lyon fingered Sibela's necklaces, which lay abandoned on the bedside table, pulling one out. It was a long strand with a pendant hanging from it. He remembered Sibela wearing it, and had seen one like it gracing Juliette's throat.

"I took them off her," said Juliette. "They seemed to be irritating her skin."

"That one burned," said Elise, nodding at the beads he held and touching her chest.

Lyon studied the shape of the burn scar she'd indicated. It matched the shape of the pendant. "It's iron," he said. "Iron burns the faerie."

"But I've touched iron often enough and come to no harm," said Juliette.

"It only burns a fourth child of the fey. Not a first or a second or third. It means you're the last born of your sisters," Lyon told Elise.

"Has it always burned you?" Juliette asked her, looking concerned.

Elise shrugged. "I rarely wore it but I had it on that day we were attacked, and Sibela kept it on."

"*Scusi*," Lyon murmured, as something occurred to him. "I need a word with Nicholas, and I sense he's just arrived downstairs."

Suddenly Elise's eyes darted to his, sparking with more enthusiasm than he'd yet seen in them. "Yes," she murmured as if she'd read his thoughts. "My answer is yes."

Juliette looked between them and slowly rose to her feet. "There was no question asked."

Lyon went to the railing just outside the bedchamber and bellowed for his brother.

"He asked one." Elise frowned, fingering the bedcovers. "Didn't he?"

"Not aloud," said Lyon, returning to consider her.

"Oh."

"Nicholas meets with the ElseWorld elders today," he said. "They're demanding that you be turned over to them, Juliette. You're not yet wed and not yet a mother, so they consider you fair game. You will of course not be handed over, but this means there will be further difficulties. More attempts from them to storm the gate between their world and this one. They would bring their wars here if they could, but Elise—"

"What does that have to do with Elise?" Nicholas asked, overhearing as he entered the room.

"They demand that a daughter of King Feydon wed one of their leaders." Lyon gave his brother a significant look, and sudden comprehension crossed Nicholas' face.

"Yes," whispered Elise, rising to stand beside the bed.

"No!" Juliette gasped.

"If Elise agrees, their demands will be satisfied," said Nicholas.

"What's to stop them from using her blood to cross over to this world?" Juliette protested.

"She's a fourth child. As such, her blood is unusable to them for such purposes," said Lyon.

"Won't they be angry when they find they've been duped?"

"They'll be made aware of it beforehand, but the gift of her will mollify them."

"It seems a perfect solution," said Nicholas.

"For everyone but my sister!" shouted Juliette.

"I said I'll go." Elise's voice was still creaky with disuse.

"No!" Juliette repeated whipping around to her, then calming her tone. "There's no obligation to do so. You've been through enough!"

She turned to Lyon, expectantly. "Hasn't she?"

"I can't give you the answer you want, Juliette. It is her decision."

"Elise, please. Give yourself time to heal. Time to better consider this decision," Juliette begged. She took her sister's hands in hers, but Elise gently pulled away as if her touch had hurt.

"Time is a luxury we don't have," said Nicholas. "A decision must be made now. When I leave this room, I go to the gate."

Elise put on her slippers. "I'm ready."

"You belong with me," said Juliette. "If you leave I go with you!"

"No!" Lyon, Nicholas, and Elise all spoke at the same time.

"I'm not the same girl you knew," Elise told her, trying to explain. "I hardly remember that summer. But I remember everything of the last three years. Much of the time, I wanted to die. Imagine being a puppet, at the mercy of another's whims and actions." She shook her head, unwilling to go on.

Juliette looked to Lyon for help. "But I've just found her again."

Elise stepped toward Nicholas and the door. "Try to understand. Our lives have taken vastly different paths. I have been so long in the company of another. My heartbeat owned. I've done and seen things that make me unfit for a place here."

Lyon could see that her every word was like a poisonous stake being driven into Juliette's own heart.

"Sibela led her down paths we cannot know," he said as kindly as possible. "She has her own demons to face. Let her face them as she must."

"There's a summit in ElseWorld, which is what we'll be attending," Nicholas told Elise. "Many there will vie to wed you, but you will choose when, whom, and whether to marry."

Elise nodded, then returned to Juliette and voluntarily embraced her for the first time since Sibela had departed. It was obvious this scheme had breathed new life into her. "Don't be angry with him," she whispered. "Lyon is a good man. He loves you. I'm glad to know you have this family. This life. It's perfect."

Juliette's grip tightened. "Then why not stay?"

Elise tugged away. "It's perfect for you. Not for me. This task I undertake will give me a purpose."

"We're in your debt," said Lyon as she passed him on the way to the door. "You'll be able to return to us once a year."

Elise smiled, her eyes showing the first glimmer of humor he had yet seen in her. "Like Persephone from Hades."

Nicholas gestured her forward. And then she was gone and he after her.

A month later, a letter came, rendering Juliette free to wed and giving her a poignant glimpse into her past. It read:

Monsieur and Madame,
I have informed the courts of the mistake I made three years ago in my accusations against Juliette. Since I have documents

signed by Tuscan officials and a letter from Elise herself attesting that she is alive and well, they have given me no argument and the unfortunate matter has been closed. Juliette is absolved. There was no murder.

However, I regret to inform you that your suspicions regarding Mademoiselle Fleur's whereabouts appear to have been well founded. With my assistance, evidence implicating Monsieur Arlette in her murder has been uncovered and I am soon to testify at his trial.

Mademoiselle Fontaine (Gina) sends her love. She and I are getting on quite well. She no longer works the salons, but is proving an excellent manager of the other girls in our employ. We have closed our house on the Quai di Conti and have opened a second, larger house in an arrondissement *which is more accepting of our services.*

Enclosed is a portrait of your mother. In the process of moving, it was found among my (Valmont's) belongings. I have no use for it, but you may.

With gratitude,
M. Valmont

EPILOGUE

EarthWorld, Tuscany, Italy, January, 1824, Moonful

For the first time in ages, there were six who gathered in the sacred glen, which had been designed centuries ago by the hands of Gods. Three daughters of a Fey king and three sons of the ancient Satyr, together.

Just outside the glen, snow was falling, crisp and bloodless. But here, all was warm. It was as if they and this sanctum were encased in some glorious, giant snowglobe. But the snow fell outside of the realm where they convened rather than inside.

Under a moon that was a fat, triumphant orb of light, six became three, as couples united. To the susurrous song of swaying oak, ash, hawthorn, and cypress, they added the sounds of humid slaps, joyful shouts, and lusty moans that accompanied their lovemaking.

And with their joining, their circle was complete.

As they drove their bodies higher and higher in celebration of primordial ritual, masculine seed was spilled. Juices rich with their life blood flowed into vines, old and new. Rejuvenating.

Lending them the strength and character of those that guarded this land. And continuing their tradition of safekeeping the legacy of Bacchus, the God of Wine—most revered of the ancients.

And with their joining, vines that had been grafted to one another by man, turned fruitful.

These vines had been brought together in unlikely pairs, much like the three couples who now populated the glen. This rootstock from two continents—America and Europe—also coupled here on this night to become one. First buds formed like magic. And with the first buds came flowers, and then grapes, one after the other as if seasons were passing in an instant.

Two days from now other winegrowers would assemble elsewhere on the estate to view these very vines and would find them well developed and ready to be promulgated as new stock of their own. Through these vines, an entire industry would be saved from a destruction that had been caused by the tiniest of marauders—the phylloxera.

Nearly two months had passed since Juliette had come to this land. Tonight was her first mating with her new husband here in the glen. By this physical sharing in this particular place on this particular night, any mischief she'd made for him in Paris would be forever healed.

The sweet decay of vegetation as it returned to the soil from which it had sprung filled her lungs, but she was unafraid of nature now. Shaded by trees, the lush earth was a dappled blue-black, and she relished the wild beauty of it. Amid statues and altars, Lyon made love to her—a full love wrought of body, mind, and heart. And in this Calling she would willingly accept her husband's seed, and it would find fecund soil within her and be nurtured there.

And by their joining, two precious children would begin to grow.

Their children. A son, Marcus Lyon. And a daughter, Fleur Elise. Juliette, who'd had no one of her own only a few months ago, now had many in her life to love and to love her. And it seemed that next Moonful she would give birth, and her family would expand.

Tonight marked a new beginning.

A new life.

One filled with family and hope and love.

She looked forward to it.

Author's Note:

Grape phylloxera is a tiny aphid-like insect that feeds on the roots of grapevines, stunting their growth or killing them. The pest was accidentally imported to England and France on American vines around 1862. It reproduced with devastating speed, and by the end of the nineteenth century, phylloxera had destroyed two-thirds of Europe's vineyards.

The destruction was eventually halted by the discovery that this nearly microscopic insect does not attack the roots of American grapevines. By grafting the rootstock of European vines onto American ones and replanting vineyards with the new grafted stocks, Europe's wine grape industry was saved.

For the purposes of this story, the date of the infestation is set at approximately thirty-nine years prior to the actual date. Additionally, the account of how the phylloxera problem was solved has been fictionalized in the series and all characters involved in that process herein are products of the author's imagination.

This book is a work of fiction. Dialogue and events are the product of the author's imagination, and any resemblance to actual events, groups, or individual persons, living or dead, is entirely coincidental.

Turn the page
for a tantalizing preview of
LORD OF THE DARK,
by Dawn Thompson!

On sale now!

1

Gideon, Lord of the Dark, one of the four guardians of the Principalities of Arcus, stood upon the tallest phallic column in the stone garden at the edge of the amphitheater. He'd stood there for some time, observing the ritual mating of his friend and fellow prince appointed by the Arcan gods, Simeon, Lord of the Deep, and his human bride, Megaleen. He hadn't felt this lonely since the gods of Arcus flung him—the most revered archangel of the Arcan otherworld—out of paradise never to return.

The wind ruffled the silver-white feathers in his magnificent wings, and he was aroused, a cruel trick of the gods that made his wings sensitive to touch—even the caress of the wind that bore him aloft. But he couldn't fault the wind this time, not entirely. It had been some time since he'd satisfied those urges, and watching the ritual had made him hard.

Gideon glanced about. There wasn't a *watcher* in sight. The dubious-winged watchdogs of the gods that kept him celibate were conspicuous in their absence. Scarcely breathing, he opened the crotch of his skintight eelskin body garment that fitted him like it did the silver-black eels that had worn it before him and freed his thick, burgeoning cock for the air to soothe . . . or not. Then, springing from the phallic stone, he soared off over the satiny breast of the water into the dawn.

The sunrise that should have been golden shone over the water blood red—a sure sign there would be a storm before nightfall. Gideon could taste it in the salt-drenched air. Soon the innocent-looking ripples that lapped at the rocks would roil and churn, and great white-capped combers flinging spindrift would roll up the phallic columns, turning them black against a blacker sky. He would be home in his cave on the Dark Isle by then, safely out of the tormenting wind.

The stone garden was vast, encompassing the underwater Pavilion like a fence above the waves. In fair weather, the sirens would sun themselves upon the rocks and sing their haunting songs. In the center stood a little islet, a tiny spit of land, too small to build a shed upon, but large enough for a siren to lose herself among the greenery: Muriel's Isle. Gideon swooped low, his wing tips tinted pink in the fiery sun. Yes, she was there, Muriel, Queen of the Sirens, lying naked in a bed of lemon-grass, pleasuring herself.

Gideon touched down at her feet arms akimbo, his naked cock hot and hard and red in the fiery dawn, the mushroom tip slick with pre-come. The wind of his motion in flight had neither cooled the fever in his shaft nor relieved him this time. The tall shadow of his enormous sex, throbbing in response to the sight of her writhing below, stretched across her naked belly. Her eyes riveted to his penis, she narrowed them to the fractured sunbeams dancing about him like a misshapen halo, for the rising sun was at his back.

Muriel smiled, still working her nipples between her thumbs and forefingers, as she undulated against the clump of lemongrass she had captured between her thighs. Grinding the grass spears into her hairless sex had crushed them and released their fragrant oils, spreading their lemony scent. She always smelled of lemongrass and ambergris, come to that. Gideon wondered if she pleasured herself thus often.

"You could not bear their mating ritual either I see," she said, nodding toward his erection.

Gideon seized his cock and flaunted it. "Would this not better serve you than that clump of weeds you're straddling?" he said.

Muriel laughed. The sun shone red in her eyes, moist with the glaze of arousal. "At least these 'weeds' will let me rise up afterward," she said. She gestured toward his cock again. "The last time I let you put that weapon inside me I couldn't walk for a sennight."

"That was a long time ago," Gideon said.

"It's still as large," she observed. "Such a cock is wasted upon the likes of you, Lord of the Dark. Will you not face reprisals? You did the last time, as I recall."

Gideon dropped down to his knees and plucked the lemongrass from between her legs. He shrugged, and his massive wings made a rustling sound. Palpating like a pulse beat, their motion thrummed through his body to the core. "I am hoping that the watchers are all occupied at the amphitheater gazing upon Simeon and Megaleen as they perform their nuptial rite. You cannot have him, and I cannot have her. What harm to comfort each other, um?"

Gideon didn't wait for an answer. He was a man of few words, and he'd expended what he would allow for the moment. She was ready and willing, despite the repartee, and they both were bitten sore for wanting. He spread her nether lips and lowered his tongue to her clitoris. Muriel's hips jerked forward, and she uttered a strangled gasp as he laved the engorged bud to hardness.

"You are a master at that," she crooned, moving against his mouth.

Gideon didn't answer. The citrus tang of the crushed lemon-grass mingled with her salt sweetness, for she was of the sea, was like an aphrodisiac. He tasted her deeply, his tongue gliding on her salty wetness as she laced her fingers through his hair and arched herself against his mouth, begging him to take her deeper still.

When she reached to stroke his trembling wings, his head shot up, her juices glistening on his cleft chin. "*No*, not yet!" he panted, for, aroused as he was, if she touched his wings now he would come. Their sensitivity was his curse, his punishment for falling from grace with the Arcan gods who had cast him out, lest he ever forget. There wasn't much likelihood of that. His existence was a living hell, a constant torment of unclimaxed arousal, except for stolen moments like now, when the watchers looked away and he could cheat them and reach orgasm submerged in willing flesh. It had been thus for eons, and so it would be until the end of time. It was a moment to be savored, not to be rushed, for it happened so seldom. "I will tell you when . . ." he murmured.

There wasn't time to strip off his eel skin, though he did open the front, inviting her hands to reach inside and caress his broad chest; anything to keep them away from his wings. He groaned, as her arms encircled his naked torso beneath the silvery black eel skin, and groaned again as her hands slipped lower, gripping his taut buttocks. Gathering her close, he feasted upon her breasts, laving her tawny nipples erect, hardening them beneath his tongue until she writhed against him, begging for his cock to enter her.

Gideon's loins were on fire. Pulsating waves of riveting heat ripped through his sex, his belly, and thighs. Leaning against her skin to skin, he savored every recess, every orifice and crevice in her salt-drenched nakedness. She was as the sea itself, undulating, cresting and eddying, spilling over with pure passion. It was no wonder so many seafarers succumbed to her wiles. She was the ultimate seductress, a mistress of libidinous lust, but that is all she was. All else was shadows. There was no love in her, unless it be for Simeon, and even that was suspect. Muriel, Queen of the Sirens, was an enigma, just the one to bring him to climax with no fear of attachment. While her loins sizzled with drenching fire, her heart was as cold as the Frozen Sea that marked the northern boundaries of the Arcan archipelago. A sea not even Simeon, Lord of the Deep would venture near.

Denied his wings, her fingers gripped his cock; it leapt in her hand, the hard, thick mushroom tip ready to explode. He could bear no more. Raising her hips, he took back his shaft and thrust into her, filling her from the thick root of its anxious bulk to the hot, smooth head leaking pre-come. A deep, guttural growl spilled from his throat as the folds of her swollen labia gripped him.

Matching him thrust for shuddering thrust, she ground her body against him to take him deep inside the dark mystery of her sex, and he cried aloud, "Now! My wings . . . stroke them *now* . . . !"

Her fingers ruffling the silken feathers felt like a lightning strike. Gideon cried out. It *was* a lightning strike! Dry lightning snaking down through the red dawn sky from the outstretched hands of a watcher hovering overhead wrenched him out of her and pitched him over in the singed lemongrass unclimaxed.

Muriel scrambled out from underneath him, her shrill voice guttural and deep. She sprang to her feet, pounding her thighs with clenched fists, her fair, translucent skin normally tinged with green, the color of sea foam, now splotched with the crimson blush of unfulfilled passion.

"Damn you, Gideon!" she shrilled. She glanced aloft, where

the creature, neither male nor female, hovered like a humming-bird, its fingers crackling with more charges showing blue-white against the red sky, as the lightning passed between them. "And you!" she spat out. "You have no dominion over *me*! How dare you hurl your missiles in my direction?" Her eyes snapped back to Gideon, attempting to right himself in the smoldering grass at her feet. "You have had your last in me, dark one!" she seethed. "Get your pleasures upon someone else. I like the flesh raw on my bones, not cooked! You see me no more!"

Still dazed in pain, though his shaft was frozen in stiff readi-ness, Gideon watched the smoke ghosting from Muriel's skin, where the lighting had seared her. Screaming like a banshee, the enraged siren plowed through the lemongrass, and Gideon winced at the hissing sound her body made as she dove into the water and disappeared beneath the swirling eddy her exit had created.

Surging to his feet, Gideon raised his arm and shook his fist at the asexual creature still hovering over him, fresh lightning threatening. Where had it come from? He was so sure he'd eluded the watchers this time. It did not speak. Watchers pos-sessed no powers of speech, and Gideon spread his wings and soared off through the sky that in the space of half an hour had turned from blood red to a jaundiced yellow hue as the storm drew nearer.

Gideon didn't look behind. The watcher wasn't following. Though it wouldn't be far off, it never appeared unless, like now, he attempted to relieve himself inside a woman. His sex would not go flaccid, and he loosed a bestial howl that echoed back in his ears as he soared off over the water. The cave was his only refuge. There, he could relieve himself. The gods weren't completely without pity. But there was only emptiness in it, no warm, fragrant womanly flesh, no arms to hold him, no lips to receive the urgency of his kiss. It had been *so long*. Still, if he had it to do over again, he would do the same. If he were faced with the thing that had earned him his fate—cast him out and driven him into darkness—he would embrace it, just as he had that fateful night so long ago when he made the choice that had damned him only to lose the prize.

No, he couldn't think about that now. He wouldn't let his mind take him there again. *Damn the wind!* It was growing stronger, as was his need. Below, the black volcanic sand of the Dark Isle loomed before him. He passed it by. He was in no humor for a trek through the black marshes in his present state. He touched down before the entrance to his cave instead and glanced about. Nothing moved in the petrified forest that flanked the cave on three sides, except the gnarled and twisted trees, their naked branches clacking together in the wind, like ghostly applause mocking him. No foliage grew upon them, or upon anything on the Dark Isle. It reeked of death, as if the gods had cursed the isle as well as its keeper.

Gideon glanced skyward. There was no sign of a watcher, though that didn't comfort him. They were there, ready to swoop down at any moment if he should entertain any thoughts of finishing what he'd started with Muriel. There was no hope of that. Gideon was alone on the Dark Isle. He stormed into the cave and barred the towering double doors of ebony wood that shut the world out and everyone in it.

He was still aroused, still tasting the siren's salt-sweetness. Cursing under his breath, he stripped off his eel-skin suit and stomped along a narrow corridor that led to a pool of dark water. Above, a narrow waterfall spilled over the cave wall through a crevice in the rock. It tumbled like a ribbon to break the surface of the pool below, where a thin mist of steam was rising. The pool was heated by an underwater current from the nearby Fire Isle, one of many in the chain of islands flung like a crooked arm into the sea east of the mainland.

Gideon flexed his wings until they furled close to his body, and plunged into the water. Even folded thus, his wings were massive, their tips touching the ground. They used to disappear, all but two nubs on his shoulder blades, lightening his load, but no more, not since his fall from grace. Now, he was cursed with their weight, and the sexual crisis they brought to bear waking and sleeping, and he would be for all eternity.

Sinking down into the warm, rippling pool, Gideon groaned. How good it felt on his sore muscles. Keeping well away from the cascade, he floated on the surface, listening to the roar of the water and the ragged beat of his shuddering heart. The tightness in his groin called his hand to his hot, hard cock. If he didn't relax, it would never go flaccid. Maybe if he just shut his eyes and floated there, inhaling the soft mist rising all about him, it would be enough. It was a pleasant fiction. There was only one way to stop the achy, drenching fire that gripped his sex, and he began to stroke himself, long, spiraling tugs on his curved shaft, the heel of his hand grazing the rigid testicles beneath.

How he hated relieving himself this way. His mind reeled back to the little islet and the brief blink in time's eye that his burgeoning cock had felt the soft, silky heat of willing flesh. Another minute—maybe two—and he would have come inside the siren.

"Damn the watcher!" he seethed, pumping his cock ruthlessly.

Beneath him, his wings were like lead, pulling him down into the water. How black its satiny breast was, with only one torch lit on the rocky wall. Calling upon his extraordinary strength, Gideon surged upward, his wings raining water. His feet found bottom, for that part of the pool was shallow. His breath was coming short, not from exertion, but from the climax that was about to rock his soul, and he plowed through the water to the fall spilling down and stood beneath it.

White water poured off him, spindrift mixing with rising steam as the flow of falling water beat down upon his wings, upon his naked skin, every pore acutely charged with the palpitating rush of orgasmic fire ripping through his loins. One last spiraling tug on his pulsating shaft, and he watched the seed leave his body in long, shuddering spurts, as the water creamed over him, spraying out from his unfurled wings in crystalline droplets.

Gideon cried out as the climax took him, the bestial howl echoing back in his ears amplified by the acoustics in the cave. When had his wings, those traitorous wings, unfurled? He flapped them now, and rose hovering over the pool, beating the water from the silver-white feathers. It rolled off them with the same ease it would have done rolling off a duck's back.

Soaring higher, he wended his way to the edge of the pool and touched down on the smooth, cold marble. He groaned again. The melancholy sound drifted over the water and became part of the roar of the little waterfall across the way. How he detested the ritual. How he abhorred that he'd once again squandered his seed thus. His cock was flaccid now, but not sated. It would never be sated. That was part of the curse. He had climaxed, but there was no satisfaction in it. Tomorrow, the wind would ruffle his feathers and he would grow hard again, with no soft hand to ease his torment, no warm, sweet, welcoming womb to receive his seed. No hand but his own would service him, and no womb save the night or the pool of dark water would have him, should he prowl the archipelago until dawn swallowed the darkness again . . . and again.

He snatched the torch from its bracket and thrust it into the water, his nostrils flared at the hissing, spitting steam and noise it made, casting the pool in darkness. Then furling his wings, he stomped back to his sleeping chamber. It had been days since he'd closed his eyes, and he was exhausted.

There was no bed. He could not lie in one long enough to sleep. On his back, pressure upon his wings would bring arousal. Were he to sleep upon his belly, the weight of the wings would crush and smother him. He stepped into the sleeping alcove, a hollowed-out niche in the cave wall that fitted him utterly. There, he would sleep through the rest of the day and night standing, hopefully through the storm, until the dawn came stealing, throwing beams of morning at his feet through the narrow apertures high in the eaves, no wider than arrow slits. He closed his eyes and crossed his arms over his broad, muscled chest. Yes, there he would remain until the dawn touched his wings with silent sound that only he could hear, setting off the cruel vibrations, making him hard again.